I0768890

Book 1

A LitRPG

by

M.G. Driver

ISBN: 979-8-88993-028-0

Written by M.G. Driver
Cover Art by Vinoillust

Table of Contents

Chapter 1

Birth of a New Crime Lord

Alvin was never one for fighting. Hell, he hated the thought of getting his nose broken or even having a fingernail cracked. Even wooden splinters from wheelbarrows or sparks from arctech wagons frightened him, despite him being nearly twenty-five years old.

Why, then, was he in the midst of a brutal gang fight in a smog-filled alley lined with pulsating, green pipes?

Before he could answer that question, a straight punch cracked his nose from tip to base, causing blood to spurt and bone to fragment as he staggered backward, tumbling over broken wooden boxes filled with gooey, grimy trash. He didn't even know why the two gangs were fighting, only that he had been ordered to come here to help.

Alvin could barely register his surroundings after the first hit, stumbling about, coated in filth from the trash heap. He tried to support himself against the wall that was layered with never-ending pipes, boarded-up windows, and metal doors.

Unknowingly, he began to stagger toward the rival gang, oblivious to the shouts of his friends as he tried to swipe the goo from his face.

"Who the fuck is this blind idiot?" One of the rival gang members laughed at the stumbling Alvin. He ran his hand over an engraved metal pipe, causing the runes to glow bright yellow before he smashed it right down onto Alvin's head with a loud *thud*.

The runes seemed to imbue additional properties into the metal pipe, the additional force and strength cracking his skull through the dirty auburn hair that became stained with blood and bits of meat. His body plopped onto the ground without a word, dead on the spot. "Fucking hell! Riker killed him!"

Alvin's allies grimaced, but did not care too much about him dying. They were too preoccupied with keeping themselves alive as they struggled against their opponents. After all, he was just cannon fodder—most of them were too.

"One down, nine to go, boys!" Riker announced, boosting the morale of the rival gang.

Alvin's corpse was kicked to the side, slumping against the wall beside a decaying rat corpse and abandoned junk. Shouting and clangs of metal echoed through the alley as bright runes and blood decorated the walls amid brilliant flashes and streaks.

"Shit, they got way more arctech gear than we do! Retreat! Leave Alvin's body behind!" Alvin's crew beat a hasty retreat, leaving their rivals behind, all of them cheering and heckling the fleeing enemy.

"You two, check that idiot's pockets for anything good. Rest of you, head back with me. The Boss will be pleased to hear this. The Seven Snakes are such pushovers, pah," Riker ordered before spitting on the ground.

Two of them remained behind, putting on grim faces as they began to scavenge through Alvin's clothes. They, too, were practically cannon fodder, albeit not as weak as Alvin had been. Such was life in the underbelly of Raktor.

One of the members served as a watchman in case anyone stumbled upon the bloodied scene. He spotted two patrolling local enforcers about to pass the entrance to the alleyway, but instead of trying to flee, he smirked at them, locking eyes expectantly.

"Having a good day, sir? Hopefully, nothing to see here?" The gang member had a wide grin on his face as his palm rested on the edge of the metal pipe secured to his belt.

The law enforcers recognized the gang member by his outfit and bowed politely as though they were at a ballroom function. "Of course. Nothing to see at all." Without waiting for a reply, the enforcers continued along their route, quickening their pace.

"Good. I really didn't want to pay a visit to your wife again!" The gang member chuckled as he watched them flee. He returned to the other gang member, who was still checking the cadaver for anything valuable.

"Seems like there's nothing here..." the other mumbled audibly, sighing to himself.

"What do we do now? Just leave the body here?" the first asked.

"Better to sell him off—maybe the alchemist will have a use for it."

Suddenly, the corpse jerked violently, its limbs flailing about, scaring the two gang members. "What the hell? Did the fumes get to him or something? Is he a deviant?"

It eventually stopped thrashing, coming to a complete standstill. The two gang members glanced at each other, hesitant about what to do next. They were hardly trained for a corpse coming back to life, especially in such a violent manner. Nothing particular of the sort came to mind, but in such an environment, violence was usually the best solution.

"Fuck if I know, but best hit him a few more times!"

The two men retrieved their bent pipes, with the first taking the lead and swinging down on Alvin. In a blink, his eyes flew wide open, grabbing the first gang member's wrist with one hand while he kicked out hard against the first's shins, causing the man to yelp in pain and drop the pipe instinctively.

As the first fell to the ground, Alvin dodged another hit from the other, flipping his body in a deft martial fashion before recovering into a standing position while still gripping the wrist of the first. He twisted it far beyond human capabilities, making the first gang member scream out loud.

With a stomp, the arm of the first was cleanly broken, allowing Alvin to retrieve the dropped pipe and quickly fend off the other. Only a single parry was needed to catch the other off guard before Alvin performed a stab to the gut. The stabbing force was like a brick, smacking into the other gang member, his body toppling.

Before he could even hit the ground, Alvin lunged forward in a single fluid motion, grabbing his face and slamming it down into the hard concrete. A sickening crack of bone and a slight squishing sound could be heard as his skull cracked, the concussion knocking him out cold.

The first gang member watched in horror as Alvin began to turn around and walk back slowly toward him before kneeling down on his broken arm, pinning him. Alvin rested the tip of the pipe on the first's thigh while he whimpered and struggled to get free, pain wracking his nerves as Alvin pressed harder on the broken arm.

"Who hired you to kidnap me? Where's my exosuit?" Alvin asked the first gang member with a stern expression. "Where's Xanius? Which star system is this? Where's the nearest hyperlane?"

"Wh—What the hell are you ta—ARRRRRGH!" The tip of the enchanted metal pipe pierced his thigh, causing him to let out an agonizing scream before Alvin used the same tip to smack his cheek, ripping off a bit of skin in the process with a copious amount of blood spurting.

"Answer the questions."

The first gang member yelled back as he thrashed about, a reflex from the incredible amount of pain jolting through his body. "I—I don't know who the fuck Xanius is! What the fuck is an ex-o-suit?"

Alvin carefully examined the first gang member's face for a good twenty seconds before finally releasing him. The man let out a sigh of relief, his eyes still watching Alvin walk back to the other unconscious person.

Without another word, Alvin stomped on the neck of the other, crushing the windpipe completely.

[SYSTEM MESSAGE]
You killed Red Lions Thug, +10 EXP.
Your level has increased from level 1 to level 2!
All stats increased.
Bonus free points granted.

"What...?" The purple box that suddenly appeared in front of Alvin's face was jarring, and he tried to swipe it out of the way with his hand. What was a hologram doing here? He did not recall installing any invasive interface systems into his nerval jack.

The first gang member didn't wait for Alvin to figure out anything; he was already attempting to crawl away, hoping to get somewhere more populated so that someone could save him.

He grunted as he tried to use his good arm to drag himself away, unable to stand after his shin had been fractured by the earlier kick from Alvin. *How did he suddenly become so strong? Wasn't he cannon fodder like us?! It's like his body was enhanced!*

Before he could move further, a firm grip lifted him by his collar and tossed him back against the wall with a loud thud, causing him to gag as he slumped to the ground once again.

Alvin crouched next to the remaining member, his amber eyes staring deep into the frightened attacker's soul. "You and I are going to have a long chat about this place."

* * *

"Shit... Shouldn't have left those two idiots to it," Riker grunted as he stomped back to the alleyway where they had just fought. "Fucking fodder can't even handle such a simple task. Pah, I got better things to do than babysit some kids."

He reached the entrance of the alley, noticing there was no one there at all. He also noted that Alvin's body was missing, though there seemed to be clear signs of a second fight—a much bloodier fight.

That put him on guard, made him wary. *Enforcers? No, if it were them, they would be openly crawling all over the place, trying to claim credit for a measly promotion.*

His body tensed while he held his pipe at the ready, prepared for battle. His eyes darted about, scanning his surroundings quickly. "I don't care who the fuck you are. Don't think you can just mess around on Red Lions turf!" Riker shouted in bravado as he crept into the alleyway.

A voice wafted in from above in a taunting fashion. "Looks like there's no shortage of second-rate thugs in this 'city.'" Riker glanced upward, only to see a looming shadow dropping toward him from the never-ending pipes. A knee brutally collided into him, splintering his collarbone into fragments.

He couldn't even scream. The air was knocked out of him as he collapsed onto the ground, but his battle instincts and adrenaline kicked in, keeping him conscious while he rolled. He bore the brunt of the pain and quickly recovered into a fighting stance, creating some distance between him and the unknown assailant. *Who is it? Another gang?!*

"You? The idiot? How the—" The sight of his assailant shocked him into silence.

An eyebrow twitched on Alvin's face, but he remained expressionless, merely lunging forward with his right arm swinging his metal pipe downward in a predictable smash.

Riker smirked and blocked the incoming attack, but it was a feint, with Alvin instead punching with his left arm, nailing him in the guts. The Red Lions gangster doubled over and fell on his butt, grimacing as he tried to regain his stance, but it was far too late.

Alvin was already on top of him, attacking with the utmost precision, targeting all the major joints with the clear intent to break them. Riker screamed as he suffered a rapid barrage of strikes, unable to move any of his severely bruised and broken limbs. "You. Who the fuck are you?" He roared in an attempt to scare Alvin off. "Don't you know who I am? The Red Lions will never let you Seven Snakes off, you cocksucker!"

A swift kick to the jaw caused a snapping sound, rendering Riker unable to talk. Alvin leaned in close, glaring at Riker with bloodshot eyes. "My name is Kyle Hawthorn, Dominator of the Kablsk Spice Routes, Ruler of the Neadrsa Flow, and Crime Lord of the Melsura Star Sector. And *you* are the first step toward my new empire."

Title Obtained: Former Crime Lord
A bigshot in your previous life. So much for that, huh?
+10 INT, +10 CHA

Title Obtained: Martial Arts Expert
The best things between you and death are your fists.
+10 STR, +10 DEX

Title Obtained: Murderer
Everyone has to start somewhere.
+2 STR, +10% increased damage to humans.

Welcome to Raktor!
Kyle Hawthorn: Level 2
Max HP: 13(+0)(+0)(+0) | **Max MP:** 0(+0)(+0)(+0) | **Max STA:** 13(+0)(+0)(+0)

Status Effects
None

Stats

Race: Human | **Class:** Unassigned | **Subclass:** Unassigned
STR: 24(+12)(+0)(+0) | **DEX:** 22(+10)(+0)(+0) | **INT:** 22(+10)(+0)(+0)
VIT: 16(+0)(+0)(+0) | **CHA:** 20(+10)(+0)(+0) | **Free Points:** 5

Equipment
None

Skills
None

Titles
Former Crime Lord
Martial Arts Expert
Murderer

Chapter 2

Seven Snakes

"This was supposed to be an easy fight!" A meaty hand slammed down on the wooden table, causing the map made out of parchment on the table and empty mugs of ale to tremble. The same hand pointed menacingly at a group of young men, who flinched.

"All you had to do was defend against the Red Lions, and instead, you idiots turned it into an ugly fight that got one of the fodder killed for nothing. We lost control of that entire block!" The owner of the hand berated the group, chiding them for their incompetence.

"It wasn't our fault—Riker was too strong! We need more equipment and trai—" one of the guys complained, infuriated at the one-sided scolding.

"You're useless, Damian. I could have easily beaten him with one hand tied behind my back if I was there. Back in my heyday, I was a champion in this sector! Me, Ulon Baktar! Even the Ardent Cretins were small fries during our time." The gang leader of the Seven Snakes smacked his chest with that same meaty hand.

Then why don't you go there and fight them yourself, huh? Damian internally raged as Ulon Baktar went on a spiel about the good old days and how the Seven Snakes used to be a great gang, controlling more than five districts in the South Sector. Now they were a small-time racket, barely a factor in the criminal underbelly of Raktor. Damian was not even sure they truly controlled the district now, with the Red Lions moving in.

The only reason why most of the twenty gang members remained behind was that they were far too weak to join the other gangs, as well as being locals of the district. Their friends, family, and acquaintances were all here. Leaving the gang meant their relationships would be in jeopardy, which was a form of blackmail used by Ulon. Damian grimaced, shooting a glare at the man. *If only I had enough strength to kill him in a duel to become leader instead...*

But it was not for lack of trying; Damian had seen braver gang members get killed. Ulon had a unique necklace made out of three green crystals that continuously healed him as well, causing any duel to turn into a battle of attrition. *Until I find a way to overcome that necklace...*

"Don't you know how I became the leader? I dueled the previous one as per tradition, winning easily! It is ALL of you, the useless trash, that is dragging down the reputation we once had!" Ulon accused.

Before Ulon could continue his monologue any further, the door burst wide open, causing everyone in the room to turn their heads immediately. A shocked murmur spread through the group like wildfire, their eyes not believing what they were seeing. *What?! Alvin?!*

Alvin—or rather, Kyle Hawthorn—entered, dragging the badly beaten-up Riker behind him, who was still whimpering as the rough flooring continuously cut into his wounded limbs. Kyle had Riker's enchanted metal pipe strapped to his belt, his clothes still stained with dried blood.

Tossing Riker to the side without care, Kyle walked up to face Ulon directly, who was still sitting behind the table in shock. "You are the gang leader of the Seven Snakes?" Kyle asked stoically.

"Al-Alvin, I heard from Damian that you were badly hurt. They thought you were dead! Where did you find Riker? Was it another gang that intervened? Did we get back the block?" Ulon hardly cared about Alvin's survival. He was far happier seeing one of Red Lions' goons in terrible shape, focusing on Riker's bruised face with glee. A victory was hard to come by in the Seven Snakes, even for all of Ulon's ranting.

Kyle snapped his fingers in the air, a light but somehow extremely clear and attention-grabbing action. "Answer the question."

Ulon was taken aback by the sheer confidence and authority that Alvin now exuded out of nowhere. Instead of replying directly, Ulon was more angered by the fact that this lowly fodder had the audacity to act like he was in charge.

"Yes, I am your leader, and I order you to get back in line before I punish you again! Seems like the fight has made you forget how things are run around here!" Ulon roared as he stood up, clearly in a furious rage. Kyle, however, did not break his gaze, staring right into Ulon's eyes.

"I heard you killed the previous leader in a duel. As per tradition, I challenge you to a duel for the position of gang leader."

The entire room was stunned, with some members even rubbing their ears to make sure they weren't hearing things. Seeing Riker badly injured was one thing, but now the weak Alvin was suddenly standing up to Ulon? Damian couldn't believe what he was witnessing, attempting to step forward to intervene and save Alvin from a premature death. "Boss, please forgive him. He may be a bit muddled from the fig—"

Ulon held up a hand, motioning for Damian to shut the fuck up, before he squinted his eyes at Kyle, completely serious. "You do know it's a life-or-death duel?"

"Life or death only matters for you." The arrogant reply and the nonchalant expression on Kyle's face irked Ulon even more, pushing him over the edge.

"Good. If you want to be beaten to death so bad, I'll happily oblige. I won't be killing off my property so soon, though. I'll have you taste punishment!"

"Very well." Kyle immediately delivered a solid kick in place, smacking the entire table right into Ulon and toppling him over his chair. The impact had the flimsy wooden table splintered in the middle, catching Ulon off guard and slightly disorienting him from the shock.

Before Ulon could even make a move, Kyle grabbed the enchanted metal pipe from his waist belt, charging right in and smacking it as hard as he could on Ulon's undefended head. A loud snapping sound was heard, Ulon's forearm bone shattering in a desperate attempt to block, a solid gash of blood erupting.

Enchanted Metal Pipe (Basic)
A pipe to bend the rules.

[**Active**] **Reinforcement**: Increase damage done with blunt force attacks.

Cost: 2 MP   **Duration:** 30 seconds   **Cooldown:** 2 minutes

However, unlike Riker's activation of the engraving, Kyle's pipe did not glow at all, showing no apparent difference from a normal pipe. He couldn't feel any bonuses or special effects being applied either. It did not matter to Kyle for now; as long as the weapon existed, he could use it. It was all the same to him.

Instead of crying out, Ulon bore the pain and began to try and fight back while he still lay on the floor, throwing a few punches and kicks, engravings on the three crystals of his unique necklace glowing green. A green aura enveloped Ulon, healing the wound on his forearm like magic and mending it slowly, the healing process of the body accelerated. "Hah, you think you can—"

Another quick smack on his arm interrupted Ulon, cracking his forearm again, followed by a flurry of rapid hits. Kyle wasn't about to let Ulon heal, continuously whacking the man, keeping up the barrage. Damian and the other gang members were rooted to the spot, none of them stepping forward to intervene in the duel as they watched a masterclass in unforgiving violence play out right before their eyes.

"Wai—WAIT! STOP!" Ulon screamed, sticking his other good arm out, which was unceremoniously hit by the enchanted metal pipe too. Kyle whacked with consistency, never stopping and with a constant breath, as though he were pounding dough in a rhythm.

The beating continued for three minutes without pause, the necklace's glow beginning to fade. Ulon could barely talk now, his face a complete mess covered in blood and snot, the green aura failing to keep up with the damage inflicted. Kyle finally grabbed the metal pipe with both arms before smashing it right down on Ulon's head, a soft little spurt echoing through the office.

None of the other members dared to move even after the duel had ended, shocked by the sheer brutality revealed by Alvin. It was like a different human—no, a monster—had awoken within him.

Kyle was about to raise his metal pipe to hit Ulon again when an intrusive message in the form of purple "holograms" appeared once again in front of him. He noticed no one else reacted to the appearance. *I must be the only one who can see this.*

[SYSTEM MESSAGE]
You killed Ulon Baktar, +500 EXP.
Your level has increased from level 2 to level 9!
All stats increased.
Bonus free points granted.

Kyle rested his bloodied metal pipe on his shoulders and bent over to rip Ulon's necklace from his neck, curious about the source of the green aura.

Necklace of Healing (Basic)
For the timid of heart.
+3 INT, + 3 VIT, + 1 CHA

[**Active**] **Heal (Basic):** Restores a tiny amount of health.
Consumes internal arcia energy instead of the user's arcia energy.
Cooldown: 10 seconds

Arcia? Kyle did not focus on that right now, instead glancing around at the frightened gang members. "Anyone else want to try me?"

The gang members shook their heads rapidly, including Damian. While Ulon was a slob and a lazy leader, there was no doubt he was well-defended and had a solid constitution. The number of hits Kyle had to deliver to kill Ulon was a testament to that. Kyle didn't even look tired, his eyes still staring directly at them with rapt attention, while his pipe still had beads of blood trickling down its length.

"No, leader." Damian bowed immediately, a hint of fear showing on his face as he realized that Kyle could beat all of them up without breaking a sweat. *If I couldn't beat Ulon in a duel, I certainly can't beat Alvin now!*

"Good. From now on, the gang is under me. The name shall remain the same. Who's the oldest gang member here?" Kyle asked.

Damian and the gang members looked at one another, completely confused about Alvin's apparent memory loss. *Does he really not remember anything about the gang?* "I've been here the longest, about five years now, Alvin."

"Okay. The rest of you dump him into the nutri-recycler or the air lock and get out of this room. Throw that 'Riker' guy into the cells. You stay. Also, from now on, my name is Kyle. Got it?" Kyle motioned to the corpse of Ulon and the unconscious Riker with a dismissive tone.

The gang members were clearly confused. They began to whisper amongst themselves, wondering if Alvin had finally gone senile or had been pushed to the edge by the near-death experience, developing a completely different personality out of nowhere. *More importantly, though, what the fuck is a nutri-recycler?*

A loud and clear snap rang through the room again. "I said, 'Got it?'" Kyle stared them down with a stern expression, causing the rest of the gang members to nod their heads vigorously, exiting the room while carrying the dead Ulon and unconscious Riker, leaving Damian alone with his new leader.

Kyle kicked the broken table apart, retrieved the somehow structurally sound chair, and sat down on it before staring right at Damian. "Name?"

"Alvin, do you not remember me? What happened to you in that fight? I swear, I didn't mean to abandon you; it's just…" Damian rambled before looking up into Kyle's eyes, seeing that he was extremely serious and not in a joking mood. The blotches of blood that stained Kyle's hair, clothes, and face only made it more apparent.

"My name is Damian, Leader," the man formally replied after a few seconds, to which Kyle finally nodded.

"I'm going to be asking some questions. You will answer immediately and directly to the best of your abilities."

Damian nodded. *Did he lose all his memories, and another personality took over?*

"Good. I only need to know four things. First, economic factors. What is the current state of the economy? Average debt per person?"

"Eco-what?" Damian was already lost.

Kyle took a long, deep breath, slowly exhaling in exasperation. Damian rubbed his hands nervously as he saw a glimpse of irritation cross Kyle's face.

"Fine. What is the population of the city?"

"Yes, sir. The city of Raktor is home to approximately eight million people. We are currently in the South Sector." *He did lose all his memories.*

"What is the level of technology here?"

"Level of technology…? Well, most of the new stuff runs on arctech, machinery, and so on. I'm not sure how to explain it." Damian scratched his head, completely confused as to what Kyle was asking.

Kyle frowned visibly, causing Damian to tense up before asking another question. "How does this city make money? Do you have a currency system?"

"Make money? Alvin, now you're talking like some strang—" Damian caught himself, aware of Kyle's increasingly frustrated glare. "Ah yes, the city is a big trade hub, so most of the money comes from trading and services. We're at the edge of the empire, bordering two other nations. There are a good number of factories in the South Sector, but they are still fairly new and not scaled up yet; mostly research. The currency is rakels."

"So a nascent industrialization society…"

"Na-sce-nt?"

"Ignore that. How do the Seven Snakes make money now?"

Damian was familiar with this, having been in the gang for nearly five years. *Something Alvin should be familiar with too.* "Oh, the usual. We provide protection services to traders and stall owners in this district as well as other shops. We also trade in alcohol and own a few brothels. Or at least we used to."

"Alcohol?"

"Yes, wine; moonshine mostly. There's a city-wide ban on alcohol and many other things now, so the gangs have been fighting or negotiating for every inch of territory to cash in on potential customers. That was why we were fighting for that area, Alv… Kyl… Leader, sorry."

Kyle's eyes seemed to light up. It seemed that one of his first steps had already been accomplished. "How rich are we now relative to the rest of the city? Top five percent, I assume?"

"Pe-rc-ent? What's that? Actually, we've been in debt to the Crimson Swords in the East Sector for about three months now," Damian said with a sheepish smile.

Kyle's eyes immediately lost their light, but he was unfazed. There was still a chance.

"You mentioned arctech—What's that?"

"Arctech is equipment that relies on energy, specifically arcia energy that can be found stored in arcite ore."

Kyle recalled seeing the term "arcia energy" in the intrusive purple window that had previously appeared for Ulon's healing necklace. "Arcite?"

"A mineral that provides arcia energy, other than living beings like us and leylines. Something that powers weapons like your metal pipe."

Kyle checked his still bloodied metal pipe, noticing the runes on it. It did not activate when he was swinging it for some reason.

"How big is our gang? This can't be all the members, right? Where are the rest? I was told by a Red Lions member that we control an entire district."

Damian was ashamed, seeing Kyle ask it with such confidence. "This is our full strength. Twenty men are all we have. We used to be bigger, but we barely have any money to recruit anymore."

Damian watched Kyle grip the metal pipe even harder, causing him to tremble as Kyle's face seemed to simmer with rage or disappointment.

Kyle pondered for a moment before realizing something was missing. "Are drugs banned? Psychedelics? Hallucinatory products?" Kyle tried every term he could think of that Damian would register.

"Ps-ki-eric-ks? Drugs? What? If you're talking about hallucinations, an engraved arctech array or a potion would be able to inflict illusions. We have alchemists in the city, though such potions are ridiculously overpriced and hard to procure. Only the well-to-do use them on the regular for parties..."

A small smile appeared on Kyle's face as he heard the keywords he wanted to hear, which only frightened Damian even more. It was the smile of a businessman who knew they had found a hole in the market.

"Now we're getting somewhere."

Chapter 3

Carving Out a Market

The next day...

Kyle's entire body was aching. He had overexerted himself during the fight, and his muscles screamed for rest. He sat in an opulent red velvet chair, the bloodstains from yesterday long gone and replaced with a slightly worn formal suit appropriated from the stash of the gang. Ulon's humongous suits clearly did not fit him.

He was in Ulon's private room, now obviously his. It was filled with useless trinkets, trophies, and a gaudy stuffed head of a wildlife Kyle had never seen before. All extremely distracting and a waste of time, in his opinion.

It had been a bit more than a day since he arrived in the city of Raktor, somehow waking up in another person's body, along with a holographic interface reminiscent of VR games.

It's far too real to be a VR game... Kyle pondered as he checked his face in the mirror, looking nothing like how he had in the past. His face no longer had the perfection of designer genes cultivated over centuries, and his auburn hair was a stark contrast from his previous pristine jet-black hair. Clear blemishes, pimples, and terrible skin all made for what Kyle could only refer to as "mediocre" and hardly attractive. *Not an issue now.*

The first rule of thumb for Kyle when entering an unknown and potentially hostile environment was to ensure his safety. By instantaneously taking out Ulon, he had temporarily secured his position as a leader of a gang, albeit of a small one but easier to control and tweak to his preference. *Twenty weak members are hardly enough to serve as a buffer against enemies...*

Efficiency was the name of the game when one wanted to be a galactic crime lord. Kyle did not beat around the bush, immediately coming up with a simple step-by-step plan.

1.   Build a solid base or group of people to perform menial labor and reach a position preferably on the same level as his previous titles. Remain hidden from the big powers as much as possible.

2.   Find a niche market to sell, preferably illegal, so as to exploit profit margins. Scale up and dominate the market, then establish a monopoly and maintain it.

3.   Figure out how the hell he survived and woke up in another person's body.

There is also the issue of the gang I attacked when I arrived. No doubt, they will come knocking sooner or later. From what he learned, the Red Lions seemed to be a much larger gang, controlling four South Sector districts. He needed to potentially prepare for war.

To protect himself and his followers, he would need money—and lots of it. And he would need it extremely soon, with the Red Lions poised to pounce if the Seven Snakes showed any more weakness. Until then, he had to remain low. Kyle winced as he tried to move his arms, sore from exhaustion.

On his neck was the Necklace of Healing, which he still had no idea how to activate. *I was not able to activate the pipe as well. Does this mean my body can't use arctech?*

He also had no idea how to access the purple box properly. He tried swiping with his hands, and when that didn't work, he tried a verbal command. "Holographic Interface. Menu. System. Statistics."

As soon as he said the last word, a window appeared before him.

* * *

Kyle Hawthorn: Level 9
Max HP: 34(+0)(+0)(+0) | **Max MP:** 0(+0)(+0)(+0) | **Max STA:** 34(+0)(+0)(+0)

Status Effects
None

Stats
Race: Human | **Class:** Unassigned | **Subclass:** Unassigned
STR: 38(+12)(+0)(+0) | **DEX:** 36(+10)(+0)(+0) | **INT:** 39(+10)(+3)(+0)
VIT: 33(+0)(+3)(+0) | **CHA:** 21(+10)(+1)(+0) | **Free Points:** 40

Equipment
Necklace of Healing (Basic)

Skills
None

Titles
Former Crime Lord
Martial Arts Expert
Murderer

Kyle tried to focus on activating the necklace, which suddenly did the trick. The same green aura enveloped his body, healing him by a tiny amount. Kyle noticed that it originated directly from the necklace rather than his own body. *It seems to be using its own internal energy rather than any arcia energy within me, just like the message said.*

It, however, did not do anything to alleviate the exhaustion his muscles felt. Kyle surmised that being tired was not considered health damage and could not be healed. *This will be a problem; I will need to learn more about how this holographic statistics interface works.*

He inspected the statistics in front of him, his attention drawn to what seemed to be his body's parameters in terms of strength, dexterity, intelligence, and so on. *How do the statistics work?*

He noticed that he had a few free points, recalling a message about "Bonus Free Points" being allocated to him, thanks to the level up. To figure out how the stats worked, he decided to perform a small test.

The easiest one to test now would be strength. Kyle got up from his chair and attempted to lift the bedframe of Ulon's luxurious bed, his arms straining.

Assuming the statistics scale linearly, let's increase strength by half. I should then theoretically get a fifty percent boost in strength.

Information: Free points allocated.
+20 STR

He tried to lift the bed frame again, expecting to be able to do it with ease given the linear boost. However, he could still barely move it himself, though he could tell he was struggling less, albeit a tiny bit. *Seems like the statistics' scaling is not linear.*

It would be difficult to prove the equation on which the statistics worked without an accurate strength meter. Kyle could not begin to fathom how to even measure intelligence without a Galactic Era Council–approved diagnosis.

He also noted how simple it was to have free points allocated, with almost no implementation delay to his body. *Could be useful in a tight situation—I'll save the rest for now.*

Kyle explored other features of the holographic interface, especially interested in the description of items that he touched. He tried touching a few items around, such as the chair that he was sitting on, hoping to obtain a message. However, no intrusive purple message appeared. Kyle concluded that it did not work on mundane objects.

He did not know if other humans had the same interface, but given the fact that it displayed every single piece of information—both past and present of the individual—Kyle knew better than to reveal such detail to those around him. Especially when he'd only been the leader for a day. *I will not let myself be betrayed again, that is for sure.*

Kyle dragged himself out of the room, assuming the strong and stern posture again, before returning to the main office. A crime lord must always espouse and demonstrate strength, dominance, and competency, even when running a small-time gang.

The broken table had been replaced with another basic table. Atop was the same parchment with the map of Raktor, the bloodstains of Ulon cleaned up. Damian was already waiting for him in the office.

"Can you read and write?" Kyle asked as he walked toward the desk and sat down.

"Um, yes, but if you're looking for dictation writing or proper calculations, my younger brother can do much better than I can."

"Fetch him."

Damian soon returned with a young kid barely eighteen years old. "He's Keith."

Keith looked up at Damian in utter confusion, silently mouthing to his brother. *"Doesn't Alvin already know me?"*

In response, Damian gave him a look that boiled down to "Shut the fuck up and play along."

"Good, come here." Kyle retrieved a large, bulky book from a bookcase, which looked like an account of the gang's finances. "Read this out loud."

Kyle couldn't read the language of the book but could somehow speak the same language as Damian and the rest. *I must find a way to fix this impediment in the future.*

Keith was excited, having not been able to touch the account books under Ulon. He began to read out loud, using his finger to trace the myriad numbers. "This year, Year 369 of the Yual Reign, in the month of Autirth, 42,262 rakels were obtained as revenue. The deficit is..." He hesitated, glancing at Kyle.

"Continue." Kyle's demeanor frightened Keith, spurring him to read on.

Every month that Keith read out, Kyle's expression only got darker and darker until he was almost boiling with rage.

When he had learned about the gang's power ranking in the sector, he had chosen the smallest gang possible in the vicinity. When starting from scratch, it was wise to never aim for the big guns immediately. Kyle did not think he could directly take on the Red Lions or even the Ardent Cretins, the supposed major gang of the South Sector, alone. Kyle was also not intent on being a subordinate and "climbing the ladder." He had far better things to do than listen to someone else.

"Ulon was a great gang leader," Kyle muttered sarcastically. If he had such a subordinate back in the Melsura Star Sector, he would have instantly executed him by particle irradiance from the nearest star.

"As of this month, the month of Autirth, the total deficit we owe to the Crimson Swords is approximately 1.2 million rakels, with an expected due date of four months on the last day of Decaber. The end of the year."

"So what I'm hearing is that even if we cut all our expenses right now, it will take us around thirty months to come close to repaying the debt, assuming there is no interest. And that is assuming the accounts are accurate."

"Yes, sir, though the interest rate is a tenth year on year." Keith was still stiff.

Kyle didn't react anymore. He was already far too incensed to care. Instead of wasting emotions and energy on being outraged, he focused on Keith. "You seem like you are good with finances and accounts."

"I used to train under a scholar before we came here… sir. Leader." Keith still couldn't get used to calling Kyle sir. The change from the weak Alvin, who always cared for them, to this distant Kyle was too drastic.

"Good. From now on, you'll be my assistant with financial issues. Every night, you are to spend one hour teaching me how to read and write as well. Do this, and there will be a reward for you. Now leave us."

"But Alvin, you already know how to read and write… I mean, yes, sir! Leader!"

"Stick to sir."

Keith nodded, bowed stiffly, and took his leave. An awkward silence filled the office as Kyle thumbed through the account books while Damian shuffled his feet nervously.

A few minutes passed before Kyle suddenly spoke up. "Damian, how many alchemists do we have under us?"

"Huh? None. We never had any alchemists to begin with."

"Not a single one within our protection racket or influence?"

"Hmm…" Damian scratched his chin. "There is one member of the Alchemists' Guild in our district, but he's a bit feisty. No matter which gang tried to approach him, he always refused to pay the protection fee, even under constant threat. He lives in his shop, and it is well guarded by traps and his own private mercenaries. Ulon never managed to get him to budge."

A well-protected alchemist… "Get ready, we're going to visit him. Bring out the cash reserves." Kyle stood up, patting his pants before moving to leave. *Perhaps we can complete the second objective soon. But we'll need to do some scouting first.*

"What? Now?" Damian was caught off-guard. He had never seen their gang leader be so proactive in his five years as a goon. Ulon usually lounged around and got others to do things for him.

"If not now, then when? Once we're bankrupt?" Kyle retorted. "Lead the way."

Damian hastily retrieved rakels into a medium-sized coin pouch before the two exited the Seven Snakes' base, coming out of the basement of a five-story building into a narrow street that was fairly isolated.

"The alchemist lives near the food market. We regularly buy our meals from there as well," Damian explained as they walked through the street. Homeless squatters, rubbish heaps, and small workshops painted the landscape, with kids covered in grime laughing and running through the sparsely populated street. The same never-ending pipes and barricaded windows dominated the walls, as rickety wagons rattled up and down the cobblestone road.

He had already accepted the fact that Kyle was an amnesiac and needed to be taught from scratch. There was also something about the straightforwardness and strength of his new gang leader that drew Damian in—a far cry from the repulsive and irredeemable Ulon. He could not say the same for the rest of the gang members, however.

A few turns and corners soon had them at a dense food market. Stalls and carts with colorful banners carved with magic peddled their harvest or forage from the nearby forests and monster regions. Arctech wagons hauling goods from beyond the city came in various types. Kyle noticed that many bore different license plates and insignias, no doubt coming in from other countries.

Kyle looked around and found a few monster parts and limbs that he had never seen before. Some were even selling mealworms as a meal, but Kyle barely flinched when he saw that. *I've had worse.*

He also noticed a few people sitting at the corner cafes with smoking pipes, blue smoke puffing through the air. The aroma was intricate, the smell of blueberries floating through the air. "That's a popular hobby among the people—smoking Euria Seeds," Damian explained.

"Addictive?"

"Sorry?"

"Is it hard to quit the hobby?"

"Oh, not at all. I think the body faces a mild resistance after quitting but would return to normalcy fairly fast, within three hours at most?"

Damian and Kyle navigated through the crowd before finally reaching a standalone two-story house positioned in between two blocky six-story office buildings, making it seem anachronistic. A medium-sized sign hung on top of the entrance, reading "Haui's Alchemy and Alchemical Products."

Another sign, the emblem of the Alchemists' Guild, hung next to it. Kyle knew from experience that a highly prized industry would naturally have a consortium or cartel around it. *No doubt a strong association... He must have quite a backing, then.*

The ground around the house was carved with engravings similar to those on Kyle's metal pipe. The engravings were laid out in a circular fashion, forming a sort of defensive line that could go unnoticed as mere scribblings. Upon closer inspection, the lines of the engraving were hardened with metal to prevent accidental tampering.

"I assume those are the traps."

"Yes, sir, but he won't use it against new customers. You've never visited him before, so we should be okay."

Kyle entered the shop without hesitation. It was pretty spacious inside, with a few shelves with potions of all sorts. There were already a few other customers inside—all humans—who were calculating the total for potions they were looking to buy.

He eyed the other customers, noticing that they were keeping a close eye on him as he walked through the shop. *It seems some of them are security—about five to seven well-trained guards.*

He glanced at one of the price tags of a greenish-looking potion. "Five thousand rakels... Impressive." Holding the potion up in his hand, another purple box appeared in front of him.

Health Potion (Basic)
Restores a moderate amount of health.
Cooldown: 30 seconds

Another dark-yellow flask was on a different shelf, Kyle reached out to examine it.

Stamina Potion (Basic)
Restores a moderate amount of stamina.
Cooldown: 30 seconds.

Six hundred rakels... Kyle glanced around the shop, finding no hints that the alchemist was involved in some mass supply. *He is not as rich and powerful as I first thought—he makes money by selling the far more expensive potions on a small scale.*

"Best be careful with that, young man. Once broken, it's considered sold." A husky voice wafted in from the back of the shop. It belonged to an old man in a purple robe who rested his head on a counter, lazily fiddling with a chisel in his hand and spinning it with his fingers.

Kyle placed the potion down and walked up to the counter. "Mr. Haui, I presume." They both sized each other up for a brief moment.

"Indeed. Any particular potion you're looking for? Or just browsing? Or perhaps..." Haui's voice trailed off, a tiny hint of hostility long honed toward shoplifters apparent in his squinting eyes.

"I am looking for something of a different quality. Something more exquisite and *different,* if you know what I mean," Kyle replied with a slight emphasis, much to the confusion of Damian.

Haui's eyes showed signs of recognition, but wariness crept in as he stared at Kyle, scrutinizing him and his clothes. "Haven't seen you around here before. New in town?"

"You could say that. If your offer interests me, this could be the start of a great business relationship." Kyle nodded knowingly toward Haui.

"Hmm..." Haui seemed to be weighing the pros and cons in his head, while Damian still continuously looked back and forth between them. Every hour since Kyle became the gang leader was a complete rollercoaster of emotions for him.

A minute of silence passed before Haui finally placed the chisel down on the counter. "Follow me." Haui motioned to a side door that led to a stairwell. *An illegal operation. As expected for such a well-defended alchemist.*

The trio walked down the stairs, only to enter a basement filled with potions that were clearly not the same as what was displayed in the front. Kyle was not one for stereotypes, but the entire place looked like a stereotypical alchemist lair right out of an Ancient Earth fantasy holofilm. "Take a look. Every aphrodisiac, poison, curse, and illusionary potion I know of is here. I won't call them the best in Raktor, but I can guarantee they'll get the job done."

Kyle nodded, walking through the shelves and rows upon rows of potions. He noticed a few boxes of herbs stacked in the corner through his peripheral vision, though he continued picking up potions and examining them. Each type of potion was well-labeled and displayed in small quantities.

Assuming he performs all his production in-house, he does not seem to have enough ingredients to engage in mass production just yet. Could it be a restriction by the Alchemists' Guild? With such a high-value product, it was only natural for a guild or cartel to control the supply and pricing. Kyle had worked with other crime lords to artificially control the rate of mining, even though the exotic ore they were selling back then could be found in abundance. *All for profits.*

He ran his hand through the various flasks, using the holographic interface to inform him about their properties. Kyle still put up an act, acting as though he was oblivious to what the potions could do. As Haui explained certain potions, he continued touching as many flasks as he could, the purple message continuously updating. He only gave each message a cursory glance before moving on to the next while Haui still talked. *There is still a chance of earning more, but only if I find evidence of the right potion here. I need a proof of sorts.*

He had just touched his hundredth unique potion since he arrived when another purple box appeared in front of him.

Title Obtained: Potion Inspector (Basic)
Ah, you seem to be looking for something very specific.
+5 INT, increased accuracy of the description of potions examined.

Kyle held the same potion and noticed the description had been upgraded.

Mind-Bending Potion (Basic)
Sends the user on an illusionary trip fueled by their subconscious, rendering them incapable of normal functions. Lasts up to a day on a full dose.
Recommended Dosage: Half a bottle for an adult human male every three days.
Ingredients: Poair Leaves, four remaining ingredients unknown.
Cooldown: 30 seconds

"Perfect."

Chapter 4

Reorganization

"Sir, are those potions really worth it? Mind-bending doesn't last long, and that's a bit too many Stamina Potions. Sure, the recovery potions are relatively cheap, but they will be impossible to reverse-engineer as well. Alchemy has always had the highest failure rate in terms of industries. Too much prior knowledge is required to make even a basic potion... sir."

Damian was still coming to terms with how much Kyle had spent on the potion, twelve thousand rakels, despite the fact that they were still in debt.

Kyle did not reply. With the scientific knowledge he had from his former life, distillation would be a cinch. He did not need Damian's approval for now, either.

The food market was still just as crowded as when they first arrived, hectic and bustling with activity. The locals seemed to be on lunch break, gossiping about everything under the sun. Kyle took a slower walk, keeping his ears peeled for any rumors—a vital skill in a foreign environment.

"Did you hear? The Veiled Angels subjugated three gangs in a row in the West Sector!"

"Wow, so the Violet Demons are neck and neck for domination, aren't they?"

"Yeah, they both hold twelve districts each. I feel bad for the gangs trapped in the last six remaining. A bloodbath is going to happen over the next few months, for sure. I only hope the Sanctum of Yual will not intervene this time; it would be even worse."

Thirty districts in a sector... Kyle was listening intently when Damian tugged his shoulder to the side. "Sir, see those two? Local enforcers of the Sanctum."

He pointed to two men nearly covered in white, only the engravings of gold and red on their shirts, pants, and shoes breaking the monotony. They were simply patrolling, checking the stalls of the food market.

"Sanctum?"

"The main religion of the Yual Dominion." Damian sighed internally, now truly believing Kyle was a completely different personality from Alvin. "They enforce the law of the Yual Dominion around here, though the local enforcers usually close one eye to gang activity. They are far too understaffed to make a difference here even if they wanted to, though it would be best if we did not directly clash with them."

Another significant power to watch out for. Kyle frowned. He had long forgotten the feeling of being a small fish in a big pond. Back in his former life, he had been the most prominent crime lord for a long time, dominating entire clusters of stars. *Perhaps that was why I was so easily betrayed at the end...*

The two walked back to the gang's base through the food market.

As they neared the entrance, Kyle suddenly spun around and faced the other man directly. Damian gulped, the familiar, stern expression on Kyle's face reminding him how brutal the new gang leader had been against Ulon.

"Damian, was it? I understand none of the gang members have been formally educated or trained, with the exception of Keith."

"Huh? Yes, indeed. We never had the money for that."

The best underlings are loyal ones who are competent. As of now, they seem to be lacking in both physical and mental training...

Kyle frowned, not replying and re-entering the Seven Snakes base. He had not really paid attention to it the first time he had entered, but now he focused more on the décor, layout, and furnishing.

"How big is this base?"

"Sir, we own the entire basement floor of this building. It is only one floor, though—a downsize from our previous five-story building that was lost."

"I assume 'lost because of debt,'" Kyle remarked.

Damian nodded timidly. Why was he feeling ashamed of how far the gang had fallen? Perhaps it was because he had been singled out as the oldest gang member, making everything seem like it was his fault.

"Show me around."

"Sir, you've already seen your office and your—"

"I meant everywhere else. I want to see the rest of the base."

It was unheard of for gang leaders to actually leave the vicinity of their room or office, much less tour the quarters or common areas shared by the members. What if they poisoned him? Backstabbed him? Ulon had never gotten too close with others to avoid that very scenario.

Damian glanced at Kyle's face, who didn't seem to give a shit. He conceded, bringing him on a tour of the base.

The base layout was exceedingly simple. The entrance led into a short hallway, immediately splitting off in a T-junction. To the right were the gang leader's quarters, including the office, personal room, and shower. Left was the rest. A big, bold red sign indicated that clearly.

Upon turning left, the two entered a large open common area joined to rooms along the side. The common area was filled with junk of all sorts. Heaps of broken metal, twisted wooden frames, and half-crushed pipes were stacked on the corners.

At the center, the gang members were out in force, playing games with one another on snooker tables the size of a room or training on sandbags and weights in the middle. A stolen arctech speaker playing garbled music echoed against the carpeted floor and dusty walls. The layout was extremely haphazard.

Most just lazed about on one of the many benches or sofas lying about; some were obviously stolen from an aristocrat's setting, with the prior fluffy, pink upholstery now a diminished brown-stained disaster.

Kyle's eyebrow twitched upon seeing the rampant mess. He was not one to fret about cleanliness, considering he had been covered in blood since he could remember. However, it was the sheer disarray and lack of organization among them that really got to him.

"Damian. I would like to ask you a simple question."

Damian froze, noticing the fearsome expression on Kyle's face. "Anything, sir."

"You've been here the longest. Are you invested in making this gang better?"

It was a hard question. In hindsight, Damian knew he could have left the gang at any time. There used to be people he cared for in their group, but five years of continuous fighting and hustling was a long time. Now, he was the last of his generation, wondering if he should jump ship with his younger brother.

Damian immediately disregarded the thought. He owed it to his former friends to make the gang the best he could. This was the reason he'd even stayed on when Ulon had been the leader. He was still on the fence about whether Kyle would be a good boss, unable to shake the impression of the formerly weak Alvin.

"Yes, sir. I am." Damian resolved himself, answering truthfully.

"Good. From now on, you are in charge of discipline and training."

"Discipline? What?"

"Let me provide an example. Gather everyone here."

Damian gathered everyone while Kyle waited patiently, standing near the entrance of the common area. It took close to ten minutes for all twenty gang members to assemble, and even then, they were standing in a disorderly manner, yawning and scratching in unthinkable places. Only Damian and Keith stood tall.

"It's the second day since I took over," Kyle began, his face stern, hands clasped behind his back. "I've noticed a clear lack of discipline, organization, and training among you. You two, run to the other end of the common area, touch the wall, and come back." Kyle pointed to two random gang members.

Confused, the men looked around, trying to figure out who was being called out before they realized it was them. The request didn't click in their heads.

"Huh? Me? Why the hell would I do—"

"**RUN!**" Kyle bellowed with such force that the two gang members nearly shat themselves. Without further hesitation, they started to run, reminded of the sheer brutality Kyle had inflicted on Ulon just a day ago. The other members were shocked at the volume of Kyle's shout.

They ran as fast as they could, touching the wall before coming back, but they began to slow down upon returning, obviously tired from sprinting the distance.

"How far was that other wall?" Kyle asked Damian, who looked lost as he tried to estimate the answer in his head.

"About twenty-five meters, sir," Keith answered quickly.

"You're telling me two of our members who are involved in protecting stalls, traders, and our businesses are unable to maintain a sprint for more than twenty-five meters?"

No one replied, their heads kept low, ashamed by the performance of their comrades. Some even felt they might not have done any better themselves. The returning runners panted and heaved, looking as though they had just finished a marathon.

One of the braver gang members stood up to Kyle, incensed at the entire thing. "Hey, fuck you, Alvin! You think you're a bigshot now just because you got a lucky kill on Ulon? We ain't all pushovers nor dumb—you must have drugged that bitch to hell and back!"

"Are you crazy? Keep your head down!" his friend urged, but he shrugged it off.

"Hell no! We really gonna let this weak Alvin fucker just walk all over us like that? Ulon is one thing, but this fodder? We all know he cheated!" The brave idiot postured, pushing his way past the others to stand in front of Kyle, bravado leaking through.

Kyle smiled as though he had been expecting this, though he did not make a move.

The brave gangster grinned. "Look at this, lads. All this weak cunt can do is stand and smile! There's no way in hell he beat Ulon fairly in a—"

Before he could continue, Kyle grabbed the man by the face and swept him from under his legs, slamming him hard onto the ground with a loud crash. The man remained motionless, unconscious from the sudden attack. Kyle let out a deep sigh while slicking back his hair, returning to his original position as though nothing had happened.

The other members tried their best to avoid looking at their fallen ally, though it was clearly impressed on them that Kyle was even tougher than Ulon had been. No one dared step out against him now.

"Next, you two. Lift that sofa up and move to that position. Before placing it down, hold it for thirty seconds."

The next pair didn't hesitate this time. They lifted a heavy three-seater sofa, albeit just barely, and dropped it onto the floor within ten seconds.

Kyle sequentially gave each pair a different physical task in the common area, with the gap between tasks reducing with each passing minute, causing them to exert even more strength. Moving things, sprinting, lifting, and shuttle runs to pick up random pieces of trash. Even Damian and Keith were not spared from the physical tasks.

The goons were not dumb—they were thoroughly aware that they were being forced to clean up the place. Little by little, they saw the direct result of the work, and some even began to joke among themselves as they picked up months' old rubbish.

After thirty minutes, they were all sweating profusely, their shirts stained at their backs and armpits. Nonetheless, they were not angry at Kyle. Instead, they felt good about the place being clean.

They stood in a loose group, marveling at the common area transformation from a literal trash heap to a functional space. Even the trash and litter on the floor and the bulky heaps of broken metal were nicely swept to one corner.

"Holy shit. Have you ever seen the common area look like this before? I didn't even know it *could* look like this." They murmured among themselves, admiring the work they'd done. Ulon had never done anything like this before, and suddenly Kyle did not seem like such a bad leader after all. They knew they would have never cleaned up the place if it were not for his orders.

"Every day." Kyle suddenly said, causing the gang members to turn around and face him.

"Every day, I will come into the common area. If it does not look like this, Damian will be held responsible. You will all report to me in this manner, standing in a row every morning at the crack of dawn, understood?"

"Yes, sir!" After witnessing the fruits of their work, the gang members were much more receptive to Kyle.

"The structure of membership is now redefined. All of you are associates, except Damian, who will act as both underboss and acting captain from now on. Through the training and vetting process, you will then be inducted as 'vipers,' proper high-ranking members. Work hard."

Damian's face glowed brilliantly, knowing how big it was to be declared the underboss, the effective second-in-command. Ulon had never allowed anyone to be the underboss in his entire reign.

The gang members, now associates, were also excited about receiving training. None of them wanted to remain weak and disheveled like they had been under Ulon, nor be as dumb as the guy who was still out cold near the trash pile. The band of misfits was already making bets on who could become a viper first.

Kyle beckoned for Damian and Keith to follow him, returning to the office. "Do you understand now?"

Damian nodded vigorously. "You provided seemingly meaningless orders, but all the small tasks eventually became something great. It instills into them a simple idea: 'If I listen, good things will happen.' The membership hierarchy is great as well."

"Not as eloquent as I would put it, but yes. All tasks I give will point you toward a greater goal or objective. Moving on, the physical training program shall be done in this manner, with the objective of strengthening their overall physical capabilities first and foremost. Write down what I am about to say."

Keith nodded, sitting at Kyle's desk and scribbling down whatever the man dictated. Some of the words flew way over his head and had to be replaced with something that sounded similar. Soon, the training regimen was completed on parchment.

Damian took the paper and went over it. His eyes bulged as he continued reading each line. "This... This is madness! No human can exercise this long without assistance! How can we possibly complete this?"

"With these." Kyle retrieved a dozen Stamina Potions he had bought in from Haui's shop, placing them on the table.

Stamina Potion (Basic)

Restores a moderate amount of stamina.

Recommended Dosage: One bottle for an adult human male every eight hours.

Ingredients: Poair Leaves, Water, remaining ingredient unknown.

Cooldown: 30 seconds

Chapter 5

Supply and Demand

In the Red Lions' base...

The Red Lions were much larger than the Seven Snakes. The gang controlled four districts, with more than three hundred men in total.

Each of the three subordinate districts was controlled and managed by their respective sub-leaders. They were now eyeing the Seven Snakes district, which would be an easy kill, but they weren't the only enemy facing the Red Lions. Both larger and smaller gangs were trying to test them with small skirmishes.

No gang wanted a full-on bloodbath between them—they were there to make money, not to be mass murderers.

At this very moment, the sub-leader of the adjacent district to the Seven Snakes was training hard against a wooden dummy in a massive training yard nestled between buildings. Winding up a punch that caused the reddish armor set to elicit striking neon-blue lines reminiscent of arcite fuel, he delivered a devastating strike, cracking the wooden dummy figure into half.

Two Red Lions associates ran up to him, getting down on one knee while waiting for the sub-leader to acknowledge their presence. Panting, he grabbed a towel from a servant and wiped off the sweat on his scarred forehead. He ran his other hand through his spiky, dark-red hair before tossing the towel back and fixing his gaze on the two underlings. "Speak."

"Boss Wrent, we still can't find any trace of Riker. We suspect one of our rivals has imprisoned him."

"Who?"

The associates looked at each other before one gulped and bowed lower. "Boss, we think it's the Seven Snakes."

A bellowing laughter rumbled through the yard. "The Seven Snakes would dare to act against me? The Left Paw of the Red Lions?! Ridiculous! That fat slob Ulon and his twenty hooligans could never pull off such a feat."

"But Boss, Riker was last seen heading toward their district, where we recently took over ownersh—"

Wrent raised his hand. "Or maybe a bigger gang is impersonating them and trying to get us to fight one another. I wouldn't put it past those Ilysian Punks or the Wretches, and it wouldn't be the first time they did such a thing. Our main headquarters is still at war with them. Focus your search on the punks from Versia."

"Yes, Boss. What do we do about the Seven Snakes?"

Currently, Wrent had more than sixty men under him, three times the number of the Seven Snakes. Nevertheless, a cornered animal was just as dangerous as a wounded one. Wrent was playing the slow game. Any pyrrhic victory would leave him weak and vulnerable to the other sub-leaders and external rival gangs.

If I can subjugate the Seven Snakes while the headquarters and other sub-leaders are busy with the Ilysian Punks and the Wretches, it would be a big boost to my reputation and allow me more of the take.

"Hear my orders. Keep an eye out for any booming businesses of the Seven Snakes. The moment any of them stand out, we'll target them one by one with persistent harassment, crippling their finances. They're already in debt, which will eventually force them to capitulate without a single loss of life on our side. Ulon will come crawling for mercy soon enough."

* * *

The next day...

Kyle observed intently as he poured out a tenth of the Stamina Potion, mixing it with stored rainwater as the base, representing nine parts. He then swirled the mixture around before pouring it into an empty flask, filling it to the brim.

Diluted Stamina Potion (Basic)
Restores a tiny amount of stamina.
Recommended Dosage: One bottle for an adult human male every hour.
Ingredients: Poair Leaves, Water, remaining ingredient unknown.
Cooldown: 30 seconds

Title Obtained: Potion Crafter (Basic)
Mixing water with an existing potion might be mind-numbing but still worthy of recognition.
+5 INT, increased description of potions examined, +5% chance to craft an intermediate potion when using basic materials.

Kyle immediately put down the diluted potion and picked it back up.

Diluted Stamina Potion (Basic)
Restores a tiny amount of stamina.
Recommended Dosage: One bottle for an adult human male every hour.
Ingredients: Poair Leaves, Greis Powder, Water
Cooldown: 30 seconds

"Finally, the entire list of ingredients is visible to me. The exact recipe might be missing, but it's a start." Kyle quickly retrieved the Mind-Bending Potion.

Mind-Bending Potion (Basic)
Sends the user on an illusionary trip fueled by their subconscious, rendering them incapable of normal functions.
Recommended Dosage: Half a bottle for an adult human male every three days.
Ingredients: Poair Leaves, four remaining ingredients unknown.
Cooldown: 30 seconds

The description had barely changed, much to his frustration. "Looks like I don't have the necessary skills to see such a complicated recipe yet," Kyle mused, noting a difference in the number of ingredients between the two types of potions.

He repeated the process of diluting the Stamina Potions, but no new titles, skills, or information appeared. "I'm relying a bit too much on this holographic interface, it seems. A very addictive thing, shall I say. Perhaps when I get back to the Melsura Star Sector, I should buy out as much of the VR game industry as possible..."

With 120 diluted potions, he ordered Damian and another member to distribute them to the others who were now undergoing a hellish training regimen. Then, he called for Keith.

As soon as the man entered, Kyle asked, "How much cash reserve do we have?"

"Um, about twenty thousand rakels since you spent the other half on the potions. That was last month's revenue." Keith was much more receptive to Kyle now, as they had witnessed a relative increase in competency of their gang, especially with the increased discipline.

"What are our current expenses?"

"Hmm... Food, utilities, equipment maintenance should amount to ten thousand rakels, assuming five hundred for each gang member. This also considers that there would be no future fights with the other gangs."

That reminded Kyle that they still had Riker in their custody. *If I let him go, the Red Lions will come for us. I can't afford a fight now. Seeing as they have not approached us yet, there's no need to stir the pot. Let's keep it that way.*

"Are you familiar with Poair Leaves and Greis Powder?" Kyle asked.

"Huh? Oh, yeah. They're pretty basic ingredients. Used a lot for simple bandages and as a spice. It is quite abundant at the food market."

Kyle's eyebrows twitched. He recalled seeing a large number of crates filled with Poair Leaves in the alchemist's basement. Each crate could probably hold about a thousand kilograms based on his estimates, and judging by the size of the potion, not many needed to be used for each. *Very interesting...*

"How much are each of the ingredients?"

"Erm..." Keith tried to recall in his head. "Maybe about twelve hundred for a sack of Poair Leaves, twenty-four hundred for the Greis Powder."

"Good. Go buy a sack of each and come back. Try to remain as inconspicuous as possible."

"Yes, sir."

"Wait. While you're out, buy a sack of Euria Seeds."

"Raw or crushed, sir? Do you need a smoking pipe as well? It will cost about sixty-seven hundred."

"Raw. No, no pipe needed."

While Keith was gone, Kyle quickly calculated. *Each Stamina Potion was sold to me by Haui for six hundred rakels. Assuming I can nail down the recipe, I can potentially enter a price war with him. However, I'll have to add something more unique to the concoction...*

The sacks arrived, but they were too bulky to be placed in the office. Instead, they were stored in the common area. The associates were currently resting from their training, gulping down their diluted Stamina Potions. It was not super effective, but every little bit helped.

Some of them watched as Kyle scooped a handful of each into separate, smaller bags before heading into the kitchen. "What the hell is Alvin up to now? I'd like to say that I prefer this personality compared to the one before, but isn't this change too drastic? Is he a chef now?"

"Better than the shitty Ulon who just lazed around. I actually feel more productive now. I can somehow see the makings of a great gang."

"Man, I joined the gang to fuck around, not get drilled this hard." One of the associates was still reticent about the entire training program, lolling about on the sofa. However, he still secretly appreciated the clear growth plan set forth, already fantasizing about him becoming a bigshot in the future. He just didn't want to work that hard for it.

"Rested enough, associates?" a stern voice suddenly said from behind. "If you have time to chat, you have time to train and get stronger. We haven't completed the exercises for today. Move!" Damian ordered.

As the associates continued their training under Damian's supervision, Kyle was in the kitchen, neatly arranging the ingredients.

Poair Leaves (Basic)

A bunch of leaves of an evergreen shrub known as Poair.

A common ingredient in tea to provide relaxation and a base ingredient for many potions.

Not recommended for raw consumption.

Greis Powder (Basic)

A powdered form of an uncommon rock found in mountainous regions. It is touted to improve virility and libido.

Not for the faint of heart. Do not attempt to snort.

Euria Seeds (Basic)

Seeds with extremely mild intoxicating attributes, along with the dense flavor of sweet acidic fruits.

Extremely hard to crack with human teeth.

Kyle grabbed a seed, looking around the kitchen to find anything to crush it with. However, the kitchen was extremely barebones, only having the basic utensils. In fact, it looked like they barely cooked at all. Kyle now understood why they had been buying food from the food market.

None of the gang members knew how to cook, and the gang didn't have the money to hire a chef.

Instead of getting upset, he focused his efforts on the current task. He placed the seed in a small stone bowl and used the tip of his metal pipe to smash it, being careful not to break the bowl as well. The seed was now flattened, with the oil squeezed out.

He carefully poured the oil into a flask before holding it up to examine it.

Extracted Euria Seed Oil (Basic)
The oil of a Euria Seed.
Someone went to town on the seeds for sure.

He crushed a few more seeds before collecting enough to fill a flask. The description didn't change, prompting him to boil it over a stove.

A copious amount of blue smoke began to waft out of the kitchen, attracting the attention of the exercising crew. "That's... a lot of smoke for a Euria pipe. Should we check?"

"Maybe he runs on Euria fumes?"

"Idiot, you want to antagonize Alvin when he's in this state? No fucking way!"

Kyle waited until nothing was left to boil, with only a honey-colored residue left behind. After the flask had cooled down, he checked it.

Pure Euria Mineral
The dissolved minerals in Euria Seed Oil. Can potentially increase addictive properties.

He then used a separate flask to mix the Poair Leaves and the Greis Powder along with water, trying to get the ratio right. Too many leaves, and it was simply tea. Too much powder, and it was more of a sludge. Too much water and nothing at all. Each flask could only hold 250 milliliters, based on his estimate.

He soon had five flasks going in sequence, boiling them in tandem for different durations. He checked them all, frowning when the holographic interface did not pop up, which meant he had failed.

However, with the sheer brute force of combination over six hours of trial and error, he finally managed to figure out the recipe. "Fifteen percent of each, the rest water, boiled for three minutes."

Stamina Potion (Basic)
Restores a tiny amount of stamina.
Recommended Dosage: One bottle for an adult human male every eight hours.
Ingredients: Poair Leaves, Greis Powder, Water
Cooldown: 30 seconds

He hadn't received another title or skill, but it was good enough. He then dropped a small amount of the residue into the potion.

Addictive Stamina Potion (Basic)
Restores a moderate amount of stamina, along with a moderate temporary high.
Recommended Dosage: One bottle for an adult human male every eight hours.
Repeated consumption over a short period of time may result in addiction.
Ingredients: Poair Leaves, Greis Powder, Pure Euria Minerals, Water
Cooldown: 30 seconds

A small smile appeared on Kyle's face as he read the description. "Our first drug. And so it begins."

Chapter 6

Bring to Market

Five days later...

Six associates were lined up in a spare empty room, with only two long, wooden tables in the middle and at the side, along with chairs. They stared in awe at the equipment on the tables and the crates filled with flasks and portable arctech stoves.

Kyle had gotten Keith to use the remaining extra cash to buy them, with the one costing the most being the arctech stoves.

"You. You're number one. You'll weigh each of the ingredients before putting them into separate bowls."

Two weighing scales were on the table, the counterweight already perfectly calculated. Kyle had gotten Keith to write labels on parchment and glue them onto the weighing scales, indicating which ingredient they were for.

"Number two." Kyle motioned to another one. "You'll take each of the ingredients, put them into the same flask, and fill it up to the brim with water."

"Number three. You'll boil the flasks, for exactly three minutes each."

Kyle then moved over to the other table, where there were only Euria Seeds and a few sets of mortars and pestles.

"Four—grind as many Euria Seeds as you can. Pour the oil out into a flask."

"Five—boil the flask as long as possible until you see a dark-yellow residue like this." Kyle showed an example. "Then, for every other flask the group makes, drop in just a pinch."

"Number six. You then pack the normal flasks separately from the ones that have received the Euria Seeds residue. Everybody clear?"

They all nodded, except for number one, who had his hand raised. "Sir, sorry to ask, but what exactly are we making?"

"Stamina Potions. A stern reminder—anyone, associates or even vipers, caught drinking the Euria-infused potions will be heavily punished and imprisoned. Understood?"

"Yes, sir."

"Good. Start now."

The operation began, with the associates fumbling about as they got used to handling the equipment. However, they went slow and steady, afraid of being chided by Kyle, who watched over them like a hawk.

Soon, after ten minutes of repetitive action, the muscle memory began to be engraved into them, making the job faster and more similar to a factory line. Kyle nodded in approval before leaving the room.

The associates felt a sense of belonging and like they were part of a greater whole. They might have had more passion for the job if they didn't realize that they were basically performing menial labor, just like factory workers.

Kyle's idea of the production line wasn't exactly unique to them—there were already plenty of workshops and factories in the vicinity doing the exact same thing for other products, though they had yet to see one making potions en masse due to tight supply controls by the Alchemist's Guild.

As they continued to work, they began to mutter to themselves, "Wait a minute... didn't I join the gang so I wouldn't have to do this kind of thing?"

Kyle wasn't too worried about the recipe leaking; he didn't expect to retain a monopoly over such a simple modification to an already existing potion. He assumed there were already thousands of alchemists who could do exactly what he was doing right now; the issue was the Alchemists' Guild and its apparent laws against mass production.

He had yet to learn about the exact restrictions, but it was enough for him to try to lower the production cost while evading detection. This alone would be more than enough to cut into the market and begin making some much-needed profits to fuel his other plans.

Kyle returned to his office to check a list of all businesses owned by Seven Snakes and sort them out by revenue. It wasn't so much of a list, seeing there were only two external businesses: a pub and a brothel. The brothel was performing very well by relative standards, providing the majority of the revenue.

He had been learning to read and write from Keith every night for the past few days. As he could already speak the language, reading was fairly easy to pick up, though writing still needed a lot of work.

He called in Damian. "In three hours' time, we'll visit the highest-performing brothel that the Seven Snakes own."

"You mean the Lusty Arcian?"

"Yes. Once the potion production has filled a crate, we'll bring it with us. Got it?"

"Yes, sir."

"One more thing… I want you to give Riker three Euria-infused potions in a single day. Follow the recommended dosage of one every eight hours. After that, don't give him any more, even if he asks for it."

"What? Why are we giving him our product?"

"Just do it. Make sure to feed him and provide water. I'll check in four days later."

Damian was uncertain about Kyle's intentions, but agreed instantly, having lost all hope of trying to understand his mind.

* * *

The brothel was very well hidden, as prostitution was illegal in the city. It was nestled on the second floor above a reputable restaurant, but only accessible via a hidden side entrance.

It was narrow and cramped, the violet carpet in the hallways stained with bodily fluids from years of use. A dense fog of Euria particles constantly hovered just under the arctech bulbs overhead that flickered white against the blue hue.

Kyle entered through the main entrance, noticing the décor to be highly feminine in every sense of the word; the flowery impression permeated the entire lobby area, while a sensual tune wafted in through the perfumed air.

"Oh, my dear Damian, did you bring a new customer today? It's a bit too early for playtime, no?" A toned, muscular man was resting his head on his arm against the countertop, smiling at the two of them. He wore a pink formal shirt with black pants and sported a slick hairstyle.

Kyle was mildly impressed by how well the man carried himself. "Good afternoon. I'm here to meet Slavin Tudor."

"That's me!" the man said cheerfully before taking a closer look at Kyle. "Hmm... I think I remember seeing you before in the Seven Snakes."

"He's the new gang leader of the Seven Snakes, Kyle..." Damian glanced back at his new leader.

"Just Kyle is fine."

"Oh my... Ulon is dead? Finally! That fat pig deserved it; I never really took a liking to him. So, to what do I owe the pleasure? Perhaps you have come to sample some of our products? They aren't ready yet, but I can call in a few of them as a special gift to our new leader."

"I'm here to observe the operations if possible and discuss future plans regarding finances. You two"—Kyle motioned to the other two gang members outside who were carrying a few bags of potions—"leave them here and return."

Slavin watched intently at their reactions as Kyle ordered them around. "Glimpses of leadership qualities—something Ulon clearly didn't have. Am I about to see the rise of a new shining star, Damian?"

"I believe so. I *hope* so." Damian nodded in agreement.

"Hmm... Operations won't begin for another two hours." Slavin ran his hand over his beard, gently scratching it.

"No matter. Let's go through your finances first." Kyle pointed at the accounting book behind the counter.

"Ohh, a business-focused leader! I like you even more now. Sure, go ahead. Seven Snakes own most of this place anyway—I just run it." Slavin retrieved his account book and passed it to Kyle.

Kyle quickly glanced through the book, his eyes rapidly searching for discrepancies. "I'm seeing that most of the workers here take days off frequently?"

"Everyone in this line of work does. It is fairly exhausting, ya know? Even our customers get tired," Slavin explained. "We run out of stamina faster, so we have to rotate our workers regularly. You can see this in our expenditures."

"Indeed. Which is why I have a special proposition for you."

* * *

The nightlife was booming across the district, with hundreds of factory workers trying to relax. Many sat at the various cheap food stalls at the markets, eating voraciously to compensate for the grueling exertion of their jobs.

Construction workers, wagon drivers, and office workers alike mingled in a mess of people, patronizing every stall in the vicinity. Roadside food stall owners worked tirelessly through the night, frying up meat and vegetables in a never-ending cycle. Some grumbled as they ate at the makeshift tables and chairs propped up along the side of the road, knowing they had a long night shift ahead of them as they slurped on whatever concoctions came out of shady pots, worried about every rakel they spent.

Even kids were out and about, begging on the streets or doing menial jobs for stall owners in return for a pitiful wage. Other, far more adventurous, kids slunk through the crowds, snatching wallets and purses.

Drunkards sang and danced their stress and worries away, mingling with the bustling district's ever-growing crowd. Some stumbled home, shoving their way through the crowd. But not everyone made it out of the throng of people unscathed—some disappearing forever.

Street food was not the only thing on the menu for customers. The reputable restaurant beneath the brothel was booming as well, serving dishes to well-off families who did administrative work or ran farms, fishing trawlers, and forestry companies. Even the enforcers of the Sanctum were having a break, simply enjoying their meals and laughing heartily with one another.

At the side of the restaurant in the dark alleyway, two men were squabbling right outside an inconspicuous entrance leading to a dodgy stairwell from which a clear cloud of Euria smoke and overpowering perfume wafted.

"Come on, man. Just follow me! It's going to be okay!" An older man slapped a younger one on the back.

"I don't know… I haven't done it before, and I don't know what to do! To be honest, I'm pretty tired after today…"

"That's exactly why you gotta get it done today, Niko! Let out all that frustration from the job and have at it. Listen, I know the owner of this place, so just trust me, okay?"

Niko hesitated before nodding. The older man immediately led him up the stairs, entering the brothel.

"Oh my... Weren't you just here three days ago?" Slavin smiled at the older man. "Already back for more? Won't your wife miss you?"

"Ah, fuck her. She's probably out screwing around as well. But, err... she's still in, right?" The older man leaned on the counter, a knowing look plastered on his face.

"Madison? Of course. In fact, we've recently received some additional products, so her schedule will be changed from every three days to every two days now."

"Really? That's fucking amazing!" The older man was extremely excited, but his mood was suddenly dampened. "Don't think my aging body can keep up with it. I don't have enough grit or stamina to do it that often..."

"Ah, for that, we have a special gift for you—and for your newcomer friend as well." Slavin retrieved two potions from behind the counter.

"What's this?" Niko asked curiously, looking at the honey-colored potion. He had never ingested a potion before in his life, the cost always being far above his pay and his family's means. What kind of factory worker could afford potions on the regular? Even buying one would require approximately a month's salary for him.

"Stamina Potions, on the house."

"On the house?!" The older man nearly choked on his own tongue when he heard that. "Slavin, you must be rolling in the money now to be able to afford such expensive potions. The price of this would be almost the same as two weeks of my pay at the factory!"

Slavin laughed it off. "Haha! You are all our dear customers! Why can't I treat you guys?"

Niko's eyes bulged. A potion of this cost for free? It sounded too good to be true, but before he could question it any further, the older man grabbed the potion, popping the cork and immediately downing it.

Niko could visibly see the strength and vitality return to the old man, a far cry from his usual slack posture on the assembly lines. "Ohhh, that hit the spot! Niko, come on and try it!" the older man urged.

"Uhh... I don't know. Maybe I should save it for—"

"Don't worry, boy. I'll give you one more after you're... *satisfied* here." Slavin winked at Niko, who steeled his body. He gave one more hesitant glance at the older man, who nodded vigorously in response.

"You can trust him. Slavin's been here for ages! Come on, boy! When have I ever been wrong? Hmm?"

Niko closed his eyes tightly with trust and drank the potion straight. He could feel the cold liquid rush into his stomach before a hot, surging force raged through his muscles, relieving the aches and pains caused by factory work. Within a short period, it felt as though he had just woken up after a restful sleep, ready to start the day anew. "This is awesome!"

"Ready to go?" Slavin motioned to a book filled with portraits of their female workers. Niko gave a cursory glance at the book before shirking away sheepishly. His reaction did not go unnoticed. "No worries then; I can get you a starter girl that will go easy. Follow me."

Slavin led the two to their separate rooms, with girls already waiting inside. Niko was still hesitant, worried about what was about to happen. "Sorry, I've never done anything like this before... It's my first time," Niko confessed.

Slavin patted his shoulder with a grin on his face. "Don't worry, dear boy. You'll be a regular with us in no time."

Chapter 7

Scaling

A week later...

Slavin was gushing over how much money had been made since the introduction of the Stamina Potions. "It's working like a charm. How are you getting all of these potions?"

"A new trade secret of the Seven Snakes," Kyle replied nonchalantly as he tallied the earnings.

A tidy sum of eight thousand rakels over seven days was a significant boost to their revenue stream. Assuming nothing wrong happened, they were set to make more than forty thousand rakels from this brothel alone every month.

With the potions, the number of repeat customers had increased, along with word of the brothel spreading. Rumors of the vigorous intensity of the sex workers went viral through the district, prompting even more people to visit them.

Kyle still had plans to scale this further. "Read this." He passed a rolled-up parchment over to Slavin, who glanced through it, shock becoming more and more evident on his face as he read.

"Impressive. Loyalty programs and points will surely make even more customers come in multiple times, especially when you lock the Stamina Potion behind the program," Slavin remarked with a surprised look, wondering how the young man had so many ideas. The idea was not unique, but Slavin had never thought of applying it to a brothel, of all things.

Kyle nodded in response, moving on to the next subject. "With the stamina potions available for your workers, you could have more of them coming in."

"Yes, the size of the brothel isn't enough to accommodate all of them. Even if they were all willing to work today, I wouldn't have a room for them..." Slavin sighed.

"How much to expand to the next floor?"

"It won't cost much—about two thousand rakels a month in rent for the next floor. We'd still have to do a fair amount of work, though—the place was a complete trash pile the last time I saw it. We'll need movers to clear the floor before I get the construction crew in."

"If I get you your movers, how long will it take to construct?"

"Hmm... a week at most. The cost would be about six thousand rakels if I remember correctly. I'll have to check with Reyas again."

"Approved. Get it done as soon as possible."

Returning to the Seven Snakes' base, Kyle rallied all the associates, pausing the production of potions as well as the training that had been ongoing for two weeks now. Kyle could already see slight improvements in the physiques of nearly all of his men. Though this was only the beginning of the training, Damian was also shaping up to be much fitter than he was before.

Kyle glanced at Keith, who was standing at attention. "Have you been training as well?"

"Yes, sir, though not to such an extent due to my additional duties."

Kyle inspected Keith's body, noticing there was almost no difference between two weeks ago and now. He said nothing, but Keith could already read volumes from his disappointed gaze. Keith had always been one of the weakest in the gang, only kept around because of his prior scholar education as well as being Damian's younger brother.

Kyle expected every member to be strong—even his accountants. However, if this was the result of two weeks, Kyle was not expecting any significant improvements on Keith's part anytime soon.

"Training will be put on temporary hold. Instead, we will clean out the floor above the brothel to make space for expansion," Kyle explained.

"You mean the Lusty Arcian?" Damian's curiosity was piqued.

"Yes." Kyle still barely remembered the name of the brothel. It mattered little to him, as how much money he could make was the only relevant piece of information. Everything was about economies of scale.

The associates got ready, moving over to the new floor above the brothel with Damian in the lead. Thanks to Slavin's connection to the building owner, they immediately got access.

Damian entered the floor, almost recoiling at the stench. It was clear that a few squatters used to live here, with their refuse and junk all over the place.

"Be quick! The faster we move, the more money we'll make! Don't you want to be rich?!" Damian ordered, issuing tasks and focusing on what to clear first. The doorway was narrow, so some of the more significant trash that had somehow fused together in a burnt slag pile had to be broken apart.

Over the loud clanging of metal, Damian was overseeing the cleanup diligently, helping out wherever an extra hand was needed. Suddenly, he felt a cold shiver run down his spine as a soothing voice spoke close to his ear, its breath tickling his skin. "Damian, dear, you've grown up so fast."

Damian immediately launched his elbow at whoever was behind him, only to be stopped by Slavin, who grinned widely. "You used to be such a cute, naïve boy. Now, look at you—underboss of the Seven Snakes."

A bright-red blush began to appear on Damian's ears. "That was five years ago. Stop teasing me!"

"Do you remember when you first came to the brothel a pure soul? Oh, the screams of joy I heard from your room that night..."

Damian's face flushed, with a wave of snickering breaking out among the others who were clearly listening in. "That was only the first time, all right?"

"Sure, darling. Oh, look here. What a cutie you are!" Slavin walked up to another associate, grabbing his chin and viewing him from all angles.

The associate desperately tried to break free, pulling his head away. However, the grip was rock solid, and his struggles only elicited a smirk from Slavin.

"You seem to be a new face, and you have great looks. I think you could be the flagship worker for the Lusty Arcian! How about you come work for me? Kyle doesn't seem to appreciate your talents. You'll be treated much better here. Customers would love you! And don't worry; I won't take all the profits. You'll get a nice cut."

Fucking hell, am I getting scouted? While the associate was happy at being praised for his looks, the thought of being a sex worker did not appeal to him. "I-I-I think I'm good," the associate said with squished cheeks as Slavin let him go.

The brothel owner frowned. "A pity. Oh? How about you?" His eyes lit up again, locking onto another target to add to his employees.

The associates worked as fast as they could, spurred on by the harassment of Slavin's employment advances. Within a single day, the floor was cleared and spotless, allowing the construction crew to begin work on the expansion.

Kyle remained in his office, calculating the total profit. The bulk purchase of ingredients and flasks made the potions exceedingly cheap. It only cost about twenty-seven rakels per potion at current market rates, which meant that even if he sold them for half the price of what Haui had charged, his profit margin would be tenfold.

He could sell them for way lower at a profit margin of twofold, but that would draw unwarranted attention and bring him into direct conflict with Haui and perhaps the Alchemists' Guild. *I'm still laying the foundations for my own cartel. We'll have to play it slow for a while; moving too fast can backfire and deteriorate my standing rapidly.*

Instead of selling the potions outright, they were only provided to brothel clientele. Repeat customers could purchase them through the loyalty program, with quantity limited by the number of times they visited. This ensured that the number of possible leaks would be controlled at the start, allowing him to carefully build up his supply chain with minimal interruptions.

Kyle glanced at the office table, noting the district map with the gangs' territories marked out. *The Red Lions are our closest neighbor. Hmm…*

Kyle called Damian into his office. "It's been more than two weeks since I took over. I think it is about time."

"Time for what?"

"Expect a few small skirmishes with the Red Lions soon. With the roaring success and rumors of our brothel, it would be surprising for them to take no action. Post two associates on rotation to watch for any movements or advances. Should any issues arise, report back to me immediately. Do *not* fight without me."

* * *

Night soon came around again, and this time, the brothel's queue of customers extended all the way into the alley, with dozens of regulars willing to wait half an hour to get their fix. No one in the queue talked with one another; they were far too focused on getting to the counter.

Niko was present, having waited about fifteen minutes. His leg continuously shifted as he rubbed his hands, a slight jitter visible in his eyes, which darted around. He scratched his neck feverishly, feeling that constant numb feeling that permeated his jawline and gums as he continuously slackened his jaw.

He soon made it to the front, meeting Slavin for the second time. "Oh, Niko! Back so soon?"

Niko scratched the back of his neck and laughed nervously. "Yeah. Haha… Is Ellie around? I would like to have her again—if possible."

"Sorry, dear. She's currently occupied. If you don't mind waiting a little longer, she'll be available in… maybe an hour?"

"That's fine. I can wait…" Niko's eyes darted to the Stamina Potions on display behind the counter.

Slavin caught on, a grin appearing on his face. "The first two were on the house since you were a newcomer. You'll have to buy the potions through the loyalty program now." He proceeded to explain the loyalty program.

Niko instinctively got it—the more one visited, the more they could buy. "This is my second visit, right? So, I can only buy one, right?"

"Yes, you can. It's three hundred rakels. Want one?"

The price was high, but less extravagant than some of the other alchemist shops in nearby districts. Niko had done his research, and he knew that buying the potion right now would tank his savings tremendously. However, his first time in the brothel was nothing short of a life-changing experience. Slavin could even visibly see that Niko was beginning to radiate more confidence.

Niko was about to hand over the money when a large commotion broke out at the brothel entrance. An expression of annoyance and anger replaced Slavin's grin. "Sorry, Niko. I have some ruffians to deal with." He cracked his knuckles, grabbed a bat from behind the counter, and headed outside.

Curious about what was unfolding, Niko returned to the stairwell, only noticing that the alleyway had been blocked by more than a dozen men wearing red armbands with the crest of a roaring lion on them. They were split into two groups, covering both ends of the alley.

"Been hearing all about your good business, pimp!" The captain of the Red Lion's crew spat on the ground, fiddling with a hammer that had neon red arctech engraving along the head and handle. He was the only one wearing some kind of arctech-infused armor; the rest had basic metal pipes and sticks.

"It'd be a real shame if some hooligans were to break down and scare away your loyal customers. Perhaps you need protection from someone strong, like me. Name's Lionel." A sinister smirk erupted on his face while he performed a mocking bow.

Niko noticed the queue had thinned. Most of the customers had fled in fear of getting beaten up. Though that was a kink for some, they still preferred to be conscious when it happened. Those who remained were hoping to be compensated with free potions for the inconvenience brought about by the hooligans parading through the alley.

He contemplated leaving, but it was already too late—he and a few other customers were trapped inside, with Slavin protecting them. Niko felt useless, weak, and incompetent in the face of the Red Lions. *What the fuck have I been doing with my life? Working in a dumb factory all day, only to get caught in a fight with no real skills to defend myself with.*

"Indeed, a real shame. However, we're already protected and covered under the Seven Snakes. My apologies, *Lionel*," Slavin said eloquently with a tinge of sarcasm, crossing his arms. He was at least a head taller than most of the gang members, but he didn't intimidate them in the slightest.

"Seven Snakes? That old, fat pig, Ulon? Bah! He hasn't left his den in years! Looks like you need a lesson on who calls the shots 'round here," Lionel scoffed.

Slavin remained stoic as their staredown continued. However, deep down, he knew he could not fend off this many fighters from raiding the brothel. *The customers will need to escape through one of the other side entrances, but it'll be far too cramped.* His eyes glanced at Niko, who was already trembling as he cowered in the stairwell.

Before Lionel could order a raid on the establishment, a cry of pain erupted from the Red Lions opposite him. A chaos erupted among the six members, who were seemingly fighting something.

"Haha! Which idiot decided to interfere?!" Lionel smirked, knowing that his Red Lions members wouldn't lose to a street thug. Most likely, it was a drunk customer trying to defend the club.

Any moment now, he expected to see the beaten-up body of a no-name thrown at his feet. Instead, he saw a dismembered limb with the Red Lions armband sail through the air toward him, landing at his feet with a bloody thud. Shock rippled through the Red Lions, but Slavin remained unphased—he knew who was on the other side of the attack.

"It seems you're about to receive a lesson yourself." Slavin grinned, rolling up his sleeves.

Chapter 8

Lesson Delivered

With a confident strut, the brothel manager stepped further into the alleyway, but his grin soon turned into confusion when he saw just a single person—Kyle.

What the... Where's the rest of the Seven Snakes?

Before he could voice his question, Kyle pummeled a Red Lions thug to the ground. One by one, the members were thrown about as Kyle mowed through them. The brawl was nothing short of a theatrical performance, with groans and the cracking of bodies being broken acting as the soundtrack. It left Slavin with the urge to give a standing ovation to such a picturesque demonstration of prowess and perfection.

"Who the fuck is that? What are you numbskulls doing? Get him!" Lionel yelled, prompting the Red Lions on his side to charge forward to attack Kyle. However, one of them remained behind, clearly shaken by the brutal display.

"What are you waiting for?!" Lionel glared at him with a ferocious stare, but even his intimidation couldn't stop the member from trembling.

"L-L-Lionel, that's the guy! That's the guy!"

"The guy? What guy? Speak clearly before I smack you!"

"H-H-He was the one Riker killed before he went missing! It's a ghost!"

"What?!"

Lionel took another look at the guy who was now somehow fending off three at a time in the narrow alleyway. He was using not only his arms but his legs as well, his entire body turned into a weapon as he delivered strong kicks that cracked shins and jaws with precision. Already three members were out for the count, one of whom had his limb horribly twisted and bent out of shape by Kyle's grappling and joint locks.

Before the others could reinforce the rest, Slavin reached out and grabbed a Red Lions member's head, smashing it against the nearby wall with a loud, resounding *crack*. "Can't just stand around when the boss is in action."

The members of the Red Lions jostled about as the backline tried to urge the front forward, but the frontliners were reluctant to face Kyle and Slavin on separate sides.

"Screw all of you; I'll show you how it's done!" Lionel shouted as he shoved the members aside, coming to the front and charging at Slavin first. The neon-red hammer swung wildly at the brothel owner, forcing him to dodge or block with his arms.

His right forearm took the brunt of a downward strike, but somehow, Slavin withstood the pain, which allowed him to throw an uppercut at Lionel's chin.

Lionel backed off instinctively, dodging the incoming fist and swapping the hammer to his left hand. With a sideward swing, he nailed Slavin in the ribs, causing the man to gag and stumble backward.

Slavin winced as he resumed his fighting stance, but a sharp pain suddenly sprouted from where he'd been hit first on his right forearm, burning through his nerves. It was as if there was lava flowing in his veins at a timed interval. Before he could recover, another pain erupted from his ribs. *What?*

With a smirk, Lionel exploited the weakness, knowing his hammer's arctech engraving effect had kicked in. Three more hits landed on Slavin, with the final one crippling his knee, forcing him to the ground. "That's right! Stay down like the little dog you are. AND YOU. YOU'RE NEX—
"

Lionel was about to taunt the other attacker, but he soon noticed all six of his guys who were fighting Kyle had already been taken out. The last was dangling by the neck, Kyle nearly crushing it before throwing him to the side. The mysterious Seven Snakes fighter had not killed any of them, keeping them barely alive instead.

Lionel instinctively gulped. Even *he* didn't have the confidence or ability to fight off six of his own members at the same time. And the enemy looked like he did it with just an enchanted metal pipe.

"It's just one fucker!" Lionel laughed, the fake bravado masking the fear in his heart. "He's acting strong; he must already be tired or injured by now. GET HIM!"

The remaining five members hesitated momentarily, but then they noticed Kyle was showing slight signs of exhaustion. "RED LIONS!" one of the members yelled, spurring the rest to charge in tandem.

Good. Now I can stay at the back and make a retreat if necessary. Lionel smirked, moving toward the back.

As the members rushed forward, Kyle stretched his limbs and massaged his sore shoulders. "A good warm-up. It's been a while since I went to town."

The first attacker approached, and Kyle threw his enchanted metal pipe into the air instead of preparing to parry.

"What...?" The attacker glanced upward, distracted by the soaring metal pipe, before a palm strike from Kyle caved in his lower jaw. The world spun as Kyle wrestled him, tossing him onto the ground.

Two more attackers rushed him from both sides, with Kyle dodging the first hit with a sidestep and grabbing the wrist of the second attacker, tugging him with a skillful spin. In a blink, Kyle spun around and used his body weight to slam them into each other, sending the men toppling to the ground. Kyle followed up by stomping hard on his groin, and the man let out an otherworldly sound.

One last brave attacker charged Kyle, but the pipe had finally fallen, smacking him right in the back of his head. Disoriented, he was no match for Kyle's swift kicks and punches, forcing him to drop to one knee. The Seven Snakes gang leader delivered a spinning kick, concussing him.

"Fucking hell. He's not wearing any enchanted gear either!" Lionel was panicking now, preparing to retreat. He walked to the other exit, only to find Damian and the rest of the Seven Snakes waiting for him patiently.

"The lesson ain't over yet, Lionel." Damian grinned widely.

On the roof of the flanking building, a lone civilian intently watched the battle, jotting down notes and observing through the pulsating pipes. His eyes focused only on Kyle as the man subjugated the rest of the Red Lions, writing down the observed strength and reaction of the Seven Snakes members.

* * *

"Didn't know you were that strong." Slavin flinched as Damian treated his wounds.

This is nothing compared to what I was previously capable of, Kyle thought. "I'm far from strong. It's not about strength; it's about knowing how to use your body," he replied nonchalantly.

Slavin obviously didn't believe him after witnessing what he was capable of, but Kyle sincerely believed what he said. The two watched the Seven Snakes members tie up the Red Lions. They were now slumped against the side, Lionel's face barely recognizable.

Kyle had explicitly ordered the Seven Snakes to keep all of them alive. Kyle held Lionel's armor piece and hammer in his hands.

Breastplate of Nullification (Basic)

Calms the nerves, especially when sore.

+2 STR, +4 VIT

[**Active**] **Pain Nullification:** Reduce pain experienced by the wearer by 50%.

Cost: 5 MP

Duration: 30 seconds   **Cooldown:** 10 seconds

Enchanted Flaming Hammer (Basic)

A good ol' one-two... Except it's only one punch.

[Active] Delayed Assault: Five seconds after being hit, target will experience searing pain.

Cost: 2 MP   **Duration:** 10 seconds

I should learn how these types of equipment are made. Kyle made a mental note to ask Damian later. They seemed to be the primary way the locals of this world fought at a higher level than ordinary humans in his previous life. *Doesn't seem too prolific either; it might be another market to exploit.*

"Sir, what are we going to do with them?"

"Haul them into the holding cell and feed each of them a Euria-enhanced Stamina Potion. Give them three a day, then stop for four days."

Damian didn't understand why Kyle was giving away his product for free when it could be sold for twice its cost through the brothel. Nevertheless, he nodded and followed orders. "Does that apply to Riker as well?"

"No, don't touch him. I have a special plan for him."

An arctech wagon suddenly drove up near the brothel entrance, and four local enforcers stepped out. They saw the Red Lions members tied up and Kyle ordering the Seven Snakes associates around.

Kyle glanced over his shoulder to see an enforcer wearing a captain's cap, approaching him.

"Seems the rumor of Ulon dying was true. Been a while since I've seen the Seven Snakes this coordinated," the captain remarked as he looked at the scene with clear disinterest. Even the blood oozing and snaking toward the tip of his metal sole barely fazed him, as though gang fights were extremely common in the city.

Kyle reached into his suit pocket, retrieving a thick, pre-prepared envelope and slipping it into the enforcer's pocket. "Just a minor scuffle between friends. That's all," Kyle said softly before patting the shoulder of the captain.

"Indeed, just a minor scuffle. Nothing to see here. I suppose we'll be seeing more of this, though?" The captain didn't smile just yet, refusing to budge.

Kyle sighed, retrieved another envelope, and slid it into the enforcer's pocket as well. "Yes, there will be more of this in the future. You shouldn't waste your precious time tending to such minor incidents. Spend that time with your families. Life is more important, is it not?"

"Indeed, it is. You have a good day, sir." The enforcer captain grinned as he adjusted his pockets and tipped his cap before leaving with his squad.

Kyle soon left along with the prisoners, leaving Niko and the rest of the customers staring in awe. "Holy shit! Did you see that? Who the hell was that? I don't remember Seven Snakes having such a strong leader. Even the enforcers turned a blind eye."

"Yeah, that was amazing. I think the Red Lions might seriously be in trouble at this rate."

"That kid can't hold a candle to Red Lion, not even the Left Paw himself! I've seen him in action recently; man's a monster. If you thought this was cool, you ain't seen nothing yet."

Slavin cleared his throat, motioning for the customers to return to the brothel. The sex workers and other customers who had "finished" during the commotion had peeked their heads out of the windows to witness Kyle's spectacle.

"That man is the new head of Seven Snakes," Slavin announced proudly. "You'd better expect some big changes around here. And to those of you who were planning on stealing from us, think again."

Niko was completely amazed. The way the Seven Snakes had appeared was far too cool, as well as the performance from Kyle. Could he even join a gang like that?

Back at their base, Kyle grimaced in his room as he removed his shirt. As intimidating as he looked, he couldn't avoid a few hits, and bruises were now forming in those areas.

The Necklace of Healing provided some much-needed relief, slowly but surely restoring his HP back to full, with a ten-second cooldown. A quick swig of a Stamina Potion also relaxed his muscles. *Might be time to make some healing potions. I'll have to discover the recipe again in a similar fashion. Shouldn't be too hard.*

Before the night ended, he called all of the associates into the common area. "Great work out there. However, this is only the first of many skirmishes," Kyle warned. "Starting tomorrow, we'll be focusing on combat training on top of the existing physical training program. I will be teaching all of you directly."

Murmurs spread through the associates. The brave gang member who had been knocked unconscious smiled with expectation, hoping to prove himself against Kyle.

"Shit, he's teaching us directly? Since when do gang leaders do that?" another associate whispered to his friend.

"Fuck yeah! I want to be as strong as him. Maybe one day I'll duel him and win."

Kyle overheard that, grinning. "You can try. But before you continue dreaming, I'll provide a demonstration to mentally prepare you."

Kyle led the confused associates to a spare room, where a single Red Lions prisoner was tied up on a chair. He grabbed a nearby Euria-enhanced potion, forcing the liquid down the prisoner's throat. He then used the Necklace of Healing on him slowly, healing the prisoner to full health over a minute.

"Wha... What's going on?" The Red Lions prisoner was stunned. Was his captor saving him?

Kyle cut the ropes, allowing the man to move about. He turned to face the Seven Snakes' associates. "Since I took over, I noticed a clear lack of brutality in the way we fight, especially last night. Too hesitant. Too slow."

Before the prisoner could react, Kyle spun around and delivered a forceful elbow strike into his nose, causing blood to spurt out and him to collapse on the ground, writhing in pain. The associates were shocked at the sudden outburst of violence but were soon reminded of how Kyle had gotten into his position in the first place.

"Demonstration over. Tomorrow morning, each of you will take turns beating him up."

* * *

In another district of the South Sector, a notebook was being read by a well-dressed gentleman as he paced slowly through a large dining hall filled with people enjoying a grand feast. The candlelight and extravagant furniture were only contrasted with the lack of manners each of the diners had, eating like hooligans at a campfire. Food and liquids were tossed about.

"The Ilysian Punks and the Red Lions seem to be neck to neck, while the Wretches are still treating their wounds from the last three-way war..." the man muttered to himself as he trawled through the observer's logs.

"SEBASTIAN!" a voice bellowed from the far end of the long dining table. Everyone stopped to listen. "Why are you still working?! The Ardent Cretins don't pay for overtime, you know?" A chorus of laughter erupted from the rest of the diners as a large man stood up and walked forward.

Sebastian bowed respectfully, holding the book to his chest. "Sir, as the dominator of the South Sector, it is essential to observe and keep track of every movement within that can potentially threaten our reign."

"Yes, but currently, none of the other gangs in the South Sector can match our sheer strength. Ten districts now, with even more to come! Even if we lose every member, there's still me. I alone rule the whole damn place! ISN'T THAT RIGHT, BOYS?!"

"YES, SIR! ARES IS THE STRONGEST IN THE SOUTH!" the Ardent Cretins chanted in response, having practiced it often.

"Damn right I am." Ares nodded with satisfaction. "Now, work is important, but I order you to eat with us!"

Sebastian begrudgingly dragged his feet to an open seat, plopping down on the bench while the others feasted on the scrumptious food before them.

However, the notebook was still open on his lap, with Sebastian glancing at it occasionally. A log near the end caught his eye.

Seven Snakes has a new leader, and he beat up a dozen Red Lions alone, with no arctech equipment. Further observations will be needed. Perhaps a talk is necessary to soothe ambitions.

"This will be a problem."

Chapter 9

Red Lion

"SEVEN SNAKES! COME OUT!" a man clad in reddish armor bellowed outside the Seven Snakes' base, attracting the attention of many passersby. He was flanked by a dozen lightly armored individuals, all bearing the insignia of the Red Lions.

Many of the onlookers watched intently from a safe distance. It had been barely a day since the battle in the alleyway, but the word of Kyle's prowess had already spread through the district. It was no surprise that the Red Lions would come to harass the Seven Snakes after such a harrowing defeat.

The man continued yelling. "COME OUT! OR ARE YOU TOO SCARED TO DEFEND YOUR OWN TURF?"

Suddenly, the entrance to the base swung open, revealing a disgruntled Kyle who had just woken up, his eyes partially closed. "Who are you?" he asked.

The man was stumped for only a brief moment before cackling loudly. Every movement of his seemed to be geared toward showmanship, showing off his equipment and his dominance over the ordinarily dressed Kyle.

Kyle squinted. *He's putting on a performance for reputation and rumors. Typical.*

"Don't you know? I am the great Wrent, Left Paw of the Red Lions! It seems you've been taking good care of my boys."

"And?"

"And?" Wrent's eyebrows twitched at the defiant tone, but he resumed his haughty attitude. "I believe *you* are keeping them prisoner, and *we* would like them back. I'm sure you wouldn't want to cause an incident on this fine day, would you?"

"How much?"

"What?"

"How much would it cost in rakels to buy your members?"

Wrent's expression darkened. "Are you implying that we, the honorable Red Lions, would ever be willing to sell our—" A dark-yellow potion sailed through the air, with Wrent stumbling to catch it.

Just as he was about to berate Kyle for tossing random objects at him, he took another look at the item in question, staring intently. "This is... a Stamina Potion!" Wrent was no fool—he had already heard rumors of the Seven Snakes selling them through the brothel.

"There's more where that came from. How many would suffice?"

Wrent coughed, his eyes darting around. "Perhaps it would be best if we discussed this inside, away from prying eyes."

"Of course." Kyle gestured toward the base, and Wrent followed his lead, leaving the other Red Lions outside.

At the T-junction near the entrance, Damian glared at Wrent, knowing that the man had been responsible for the injuries and deaths of many Seven Snakes. He moved forward to disarm Wrent's sword, but Kyle stopped him.

"I can handle myself," Kyle whispered, while patting Damian on the shoulder.

It was but a short walk to the office, and the two of them entered alone as Damian stood guard.

"I didn't expect Ulon to fall so soon," Wrent remarked. He glanced around the room and saw most of the usual ornaments that Ulon had loved to flaunt were missing. "Did you come from another gang? I don't recall seeing anyone like you around."

"No, I have been in the gang for a while now. I just felt I could do better," Kyle replied, his back exposed to Wrent, who was eyeing him like a predator.

"Are you not afraid I would kill you right here? Maybe Damian was right." Wrent sneered, his right hand rubbing the pommel of an engraved, ruby-encrusted sword with a wide grin.

"You can try, if you want. I'm sure it'll do wonders for your reputation," Kyle replied apathetically, not the least afraid.

The sheer confidence exuded by Kyle frightened Wrent, causing him to be markedly more cautious. *This man isn't the same as Ulon. The slow method may not work for him. I'll have to fleece him as much as I can. There's no way the debt Ulon racked up is gone within less than two weeks. I know they still owe a million to the Crimson Swords.*

Wrent ran his hands over the arm of the guest chair before removing his sword belt and sitting down. "Perhaps your death does not affect my reputation as much as you think. No one knows you're the new leader yet."

"Enough posturing. We're both businessmen here. Let's get to the point. How many?" Kyle began.

He has an intelligent head on his shoulder, and he immediately knew from the start that I didn't care about the prisoners. A dumber gang leader would have refused based on pride. If we weren't enemies, I would have recruited him right away. Wrent was never worried about the prisoners. Kyle could kill them for all he cared, as long as he got "compensation." The Red Lions were a business, not a group based on friendship.

Wrent still had interest in how Kyle was getting so many potions. He had heard the reports of the brothel giving potions to their loyal customers, which prompted him to send a dozen members in the first place. Of course, he planned to use his weight to pressure Kyle into giving him more potions than was reasonable. The Red Lions could then easily sell them off in a heartbeat or use it in their own training.

Wrent tried to pry deeper. "You're not getting these potions from Haui, are you?"

"That's a trade secret. How many?"

Wrent remained silent for a moment, calculating in his head. *A ridiculous amount should suffice. If he rejects, it'll tank his reputation, and I'll increase the rate of harassment whether or not he releases the prisoners. If he accepts, the gang will be financially ruined, and it'll be an easy win.*

"Five hundred Stamina Potions," Wrent declared. Based on Haui's pricing scheme, it was close to three hundred thousand rakels' worth of potions. With Seven Snakes in debt, it was nearly impossible for them to even have that much in stock.

"Done. You'll have your full stock in ten days. Let me draft a contract." Kyle retrieved a placeholder contract, filling in the details before handing it over to Wrent for inspection.

He caved that easily? The potions are worth three hundred thousand! Is he stealing them from an alchemist I've never heard of?

Wrent was still stunned when he read the contract. He checked over the clauses carefully, noting that everything was in order. "A non-aggression pact over the course of the contract..." This meant the Red Lions could not attack the Seven Snakes as long as they adhered to the contract terms. *Are my members really that valuable to him? What is he using them for?*

As much as they were criminal gangs profiteering from illegal goods, contracts and agreements between gangs had to be adhered to—it was an issue of honor and reputation. Any gang that thoughtlessly broke a truce or ceasefire would immediately lose the trust of both the people and other gangs, throwing them into isolation. Even merchants wouldn't dare trade with them unless coerced by force. Going against a contract signed willingly was a surefire way to have enemies gang up against the one who broke the contract.

Three hundred thousand rakels' worth of potions was an eye-watering sum to Wrent, and he was basically getting it for free. "I accept." Wrent readily signed the agreement. *The non-aggression pact is but a façade. The real war is fought on the open market with our businesses. If he's as smart as I think he is, I'll need to expedite my plan.*

"Good. Each day at dusk, send five people to collect fifty potions at this meeting point. Pleasure doing business with you." Kyle led Wrent out.

When Wrent left, he let out a hearty laugh, attracting onlookers who were curious about the resolution. "Seems like you got a good head on your shoulders, Seven Snakes. Smart of you to appease us so readily. Let's move out!" He ordered his men to march back to their district.

A showman through and through. Kyle returned to the common room, noticing a worried Damian on the side. "Sir, what was the agreement? Did we go into more debt?"

"A ten-day truce, along with fifty potions delivered a day."

Damian was equally shocked, but not for the same reasons as Wrent was. "What? That's it? We churn out two hundred a day, even while training!"

"It's their loss. This gives us time to prepare, though we must shore up our finances. We'll begin combat training immediately—we're on a timer now. For the potions, make sure the first three deliveries are not Euria-infused. We will only infuse them randomly from the fourth day onward. Don't want their alchemist to spot too much."

* * *

Kyle acted as an instructor for the rest of the morning, teaching the associates fighting skills. He used the prisoners as dummies, sending the associates in one by one to beat them up while continuously healing them. The rest were divided into sparring pairs. Kyle focused on sparring with Damian, drilling fighting basics into him.

Title Obtained: Healer (Basic)
This doesn't seem like the right way to use healing...
+5 INT, +10% healing effectiveness.

Title Obtained: Martial Arts Instructor (Basic)
With great power comes great muscular bodies—apart from yours.
+5 STR, +3 DEX, +10% ability to break down moves.

After lunch, Damian led the training, allowing Kyle to focus on preparing for the end of the truce. There was no doubt in his mind that the Red Lions would begin to pressure them now that they were well aware of their ability to produce this many potions. *As long as we can hold on for three days after the end of the truce, it's a win for us.*

Keith was in Kyle's office, racking his brains over the gang's finances and equipment, his head resting in his hands. "Is it doable?" Kyle asked.

"To get a similar armor set like the Red Lions? I don't think so. It's far too expensive."

"Hmm..." Kyle pondered. He needed to boost the combat capability of his men before the fight broke out. If they couldn't procure enchanted armor, what other methods did he have?

"Keith, one more task for you. Set up an induction program for new members and procure a few armbands with the logo of the Seven Snakes on them. Have it done by tomorrow."

"New members?! We're so tiny. Who would even want to join us?"

Kyle glared at his underling, who immediately zipped his mouth and nodded.

More members can help bulk up our numbers, but we need a qualitative improvement across the board. Combat training could only last for ten days—not long enough to drill proper fighting skills into the associates. Sure, the physical training regimen had been running for two weeks, but that didn't directly translate into fighting potential. Kyle needed instantaneous improvements.

His mind thought about the game-like interface that he now had. Killing people would earn him free stat points and even titles occasionally. However, the points only gave him a slight marginal benefit. It wasn't worth the potential consequence of enforcers breathing down his neck for random murders happening across the sector—even *he* didn't think he could cover up every kill.

The number of people he would have to kill in ten days would be cataclysmic to reach a level where he could take on the entirety of the Red Lions. He needed something different.

The main way to solve this would be to get more potions, but as it stood, there was no chance in hell that Haui had not heard about the deal with the Red Lions or the Lusty Arcian selling cheap stamina potions for repeat customers. With the absurd number of potions being supplied for "free," the local market for potions must have been in peril by now.

Kyle decided to tackle this problem head-on, bringing a few associates to visit Haui's shop. He stood just beyond the defensive line of arcia traps that surrounded the alchemist's house, while the private guards immediately came out, brandishing their swords and maces, ready to fight.

The locals around the food market scampered away, afraid of getting caught in the ensuing fight, while a few brave souls remained to watch the outcome. Even the local enforcers didn't dare get in between, keeping a clear distance as they carefully observed, reporting the meeting to their superiors.

Haui stepped out of the store in his alchemist robes. "I was expecting you to come soon. Are you planning to raze or to negotiate?"

* * *

Kyle Hawthorn: Level 9
Max HP: 34(+0)(+0)(+0) | **Max MP:** 0(+0)(+0)(+0) | **Max STA:** 34(+0)(+0)(+0)

Status Effects
None

Stats
Race: Human | **Class:** Unassigned | **Subclass:** Unassigned
STR: 63(+17)(+0)(+0) | **DEX:** 39(+13)(+0)(+0) | **INT:** 54(+25)(+3)(+0)
VIT: 33(+0)(+3)(+0) | **CHA:** 21(+10)(+1)(+0) | **Free Points:** 20
Equipment
Necklace of Healing (Basic)

Skills
None

Titles
Former Crime Lord
Martial Arts Expert
Murderer
Potion Inspector (Basic)
Potion Crafter (Basic)
Healer (Basic)
Martial Arts Instructor (Basic)

Chapter 10

Negotiations

"To negotiate, of course." Kyle said, causing Haui to raise his eyebrows.

"I don't think one needs seven gang members to perform a rudimentary negotiation."

"Negotiations require an even playing field." Kyle nodded his head at the guards.

A smirk appeared on Haui's face, his expression confident. "I doubt your members are as prepared as my private guards. Are you sure these are the only guards I have prepared?"

"Then you would just have to account for me as well."

The two stared at each other for a brief moment before Haui finally broke into laughter. "Very good. Come in."

The two of them entered the store, with the gang members and the guards staring each other down outside.

"I must say, I did not expect you to be the leader of the Seven Snakes gang. I merely thought Damian was paid a few rakels to escort a foreign individual of note around, seeing as how he had to explain everything to you." Haui sat behind the counter, arranging his robes.

"I did not expect you to have paid for observers around the district." Kyle paced around the store slowly, looking at some of the potions he had not examined the last time he came.

"The Seven Snakes can't be the only ones patrolling around, can they? My business depends on who runs the district. But let's cut the crap." Haui's demeanor suddenly changed, his eyes glaring with ferocity. "You've been undercutting my potions through the brothel and are now flooding the market with knockoffs via the Red Lions. Even if Wrent is from another district, the fluctuations in market price would directly affect me and upset the established rule of the Alchemists' Guild."

Haui stood up and paced around, picking up a chisel and twirling it in his hands. "There were a myriad of ways I could have gone about this. The moment I heard about the brothel providing half-priced stamina potions through a... 'loyalty' program, I contemplated an assassination or a kidnapping."

"But you didn't."

"Indeed. I understand that for you to reverse-engineer my potions that fast, you must have an extremely impressive ability to decipher the closely guarded recipes of the Alchemists' Guild without external help. Maybe even a device that can do it for you," Haui replied. "And the mass-production scale is on the level of factories, something the Alchemists' Guild is clamping down hard to maintain the high price margins. As such, you are extremely valuable as long as you are able to evade detection. If I sent anyone to kill you, it would be a loss for me. I don't believe any organization I hire would be willing to kill you if they found out the true reason behind the contract." Haui sighed.

"And I can't kill you myself because you are extremely well protected. I doubt this is the full extent of your security forces as well. I would not want to anger the Alchemists' Guild either," Kyle replied. This was why he didn't just run over and kill Haui—it was far too costly, and he didn't know the full extent of Haui's backing.

Haui was surprised before a broad smile appeared on his face. "It appears that we are quite alike, you and me. Neither party can truly eliminate the other. Even if we try to, the consequences would be far too brutal. So here we are."

"What's your proposal?"

"From my observations, you can't create new potion recipes, as you don't have formal alchemist training or connections. However, your competence with reverse-engineering and mass production gives me great insight into how to target a wider audience and potentially profit off the common people, not just the upper middle class or leaders of gangs. How about this—for every potion you reverse-engineer from me, you must give me half of the profits indefinitely."

Kyle's eyebrow twitched. Asking for half was daylight robbery. "A tenth. And you must tell me the recipes."

Both of them smirked, knowing they had entered the negotiation phase.

"The recipes are strictly off-limits. I am bound by code through the Alchemists' Guild never to reveal such information to non-members. It spoils the market for other alchemists, you see. Even mass production is a no-go. However, the reason I ask for half is that I am willing to shelter you from the guild as well, by claiming you are my 'associate.' The recipes will still be off-limits, but you will not suffer repercussions. In exchange, the mass-produced potions must be of a lower quality to truly evade a deep investigation from the guild."

Quality? Is he referring to the "Basic" tag on the potions? Even if he rejected Haui now and went to another alchemist's shop to purchase potions, the Alchemists' Guild would eventually catch onto him as well, seeing how good Haui's informant network was.

"Fine. Two-tenths, but only for a year after for each potion type."

"Ridiculous. Four-tenths, for three years," Haui countered.

"Two-tenths, two years."

"Three-tenths, four years."

"Two-tenths, two years." Kyle was not budging anymore.

"Fine. Deal." Haui drafted a simple contract on parchment, passing it to Kyle to sign. A non-aggression clause was in there as well, to ensure neither party tried to backstab each other. They still could, but then it would be a breach of the contract.

Contracts between criminals were less of a legal requirement and more of a justification for retaliation. Kyle also didn't want to earn a bad reputation for breaking a contract or pact he signed—Ulon had already done enough damage. Similarly, Haui also had a reputation to uphold.

There was another clause where Haui had the right to determine what potion recipes to give Kyle. "You must understand that the more exquisite potions are heavily guarded recipes of the guild. Under no circumstances can we mass-produce this without having a strong-enough power base."

"You make it sound like we are already partners."

"Of course. Your profit is mine as well." Haui smiled. He had obtained Kyle as a future distribution network—a free money flow.

Kyle didn't lose much either. In exchange for money, he had gained a direct source of essential potion recipes and protection from the Alchemists' Guild.

"Well then, with the Red Lions now well aware of your mass production capabilities and you imprisoning their members, there's no doubt a fight will come. May I suggest this potion? Again, I cannot provide you with the recipe." Haui handed over two potions: the first being a glossy, indigo flask with a tinge of red swirling within the liquid.

Strength Potion (Basic)

Boost muscle strength for a short duration. Good for quick battles.

Recommended Usage: Drink the entire flask in one go. Active for five minutes.

Consuming another within a day will result in diminishing effects. May experience side effects after the main effect wears off.

Ingredients: Greis Powder, Water, two remaining ingredients unknown.

Cooldown: 30 seconds

The second potion was a green, infused with what seemed to be Poair Leaves that were not yet dissolved.

Health Potion (Basic)

Heals up to 50 HP.

Recommended Usage: Drink the entire flask in one go.
Consuming another within eight hours will result in diminishing effects.
Ingredients: Poair Leaves, Greis Powder, Water, remaining ingredient
unknown.

Cooldown: 30 seconds

Kyle nodded, taking a few potions. He didn't need to pay Haui, as he had already provided twenty percent of the profits.

The men walked to the store entrance before Haui stopped Kyle. "A fair warning—the Ardent Cretins already have an observer watching this district. They are always watching. Do not act too overtly if you want to remain under the radar. I'd prefer it if another gang didn't steal you away just yet. If you're going to sell potions, do not oversupply like you did for the Red Lions. That alone might already cause the Alchemists' Guild to start asking too many questions. Keep any subsequent contracts below a hundred for now."

Haui and Kyle stepped outside, only to see the gang members and the private guards about ready to come to blows. They were throwing insults with wanton abandon. Haui sighed and called the private guards back.

The gang members were astonished even as the fight broke up. Today was a day of surprises, seeing how Kyle had successfully negotiated with two separate individuals.

"Hey, I thought Alv—Kyle was all about beating people up? I was almost certain I would see Haui beaten into a pulp."

"Yeah, not sure what has gotten into him."

Kyle ordered the gang members to return with him. As he walked, he noticed a lone local enforcer of the Sanctum eyeing him carefully. *The enforcers seemed to be on to me as well.*

With so many major powers watching him, every action he took from now on had to be measured. Haui was right in that he was indeed planning to sell more potions, but he now had to limit the supply.

This also meant that prices would need to be in line with the current market. With this, Haui's profit margin for the basic potions would still be fairly secured.

He sure is crafty. I must find a way to either get rid of him or integrate him into the gang. The Alchemists' Guild must be extremely dangerous if every alchemist is like this.

Returning to the Seven Snakes' base, Kyle began his potion discovery process, attempting to master the strength potion recipe. More ingredients were involved, so he tried everything he could think of.

With a simple distillation process, he managed to separate the liquid from the dissolved Greis Powder, though another material sludge was mixed into the residue. He grabbed the flask of residue, examining it.

Residue of Strength Potion

A mixture of Greis Powder and Olio Roots.
Inflicts extreme muscle pain on consumption.

He then picked up the condensed liquid that had been distilled.

Concentrated Yul's Tears

Increases metabolism rate as well as energy transfer through the human body.
Grants explosive strength, though it should not be drunk directly in its current concentrated form.

Title Obtained: Potion Inspector (Intermediate)
It seems that you are somewhat of a scientist yourself.
+10 INT, increased accuracy of the examined potion's description.

The upgraded title allowed him to see the full ingredients of the strength and health potions.

Strength Potion (Basic)

Boost muscle strength for a short duration. Good for short battles.

Recommended Usage: Drink the entire flask in one go. Active for five minutes.

Consuming another within a day will result in diminishing effects. May experience side effects after the main effect wears off.

Ingredients: Greis Powder, Olio Roots, Yul's Tears, Water

Cooldown: 30 seconds

Health Potion (Basic)

Restores a moderate amount of health.

Recommended Usage: Drink the entire flask in one go. Heals up to 50 HP.

Consuming another within eight hours will result in diminishing effects.

Ingredients: Poair Leaves, Greis Powder, Yul's Tears, Water

Cooldown: 30 seconds

"First step completed."

Chapter 11

Addiction Symptoms

The training routine went as planned. The main reason why Kyle wanted so many prisoners was due to the mental trauma inflicted on each prisoner after combat training. No prisoner could remain sane after being beaten up by twenty gang members in a row while continuously being healed.

"JUST LET ME DIE!" One of the Red Lions prisoners shook the coarse, shoddy iron bars of his temporary jail violently. They were segregated into separate cages, ensuring they couldn't help each other break out.

"Shut up, idiot. They can't even hear you from inside this room," Lionel grumbled. It had only been a day since they had been imprisoned, but a few of the members' mental states were at an all-time low.

There was someone else in the room who clearly had it much worse, judging by the continuous groaning, the scratching of nails against rusted metal, and clattering of teeth. Lionel glanced over at Riker's cage to see him lying on the floor in a cold sweat, shivering.

He wasn't particularly surprised to see Riker here after they were captured. Kyle was that strong, after all, so he didn't expect Riker to escape either.

"Fucking hell. What did they do to you? Potion overdose?" Lionel asked, but Riker barely registered the question, only turning and tossing about on the cold metal surface.

At this moment, the main door to the room opened, revealing Kyle flanked by Damian.

Immediately, the other Red Lions members started cursing and swearing at Kyle, blasting them with everything they had ever learned in their short lives within Raktor. Kyle simply raised an eyebrow at some of the more colorful expressions they had for him while Damian was lugging a sack of Stamina Potions, giving them one each.

Lionel grabbed a potion, still astonished at how many the Seven Snakes had. This was the third one they'd received since their imprisonment. Going by Haui's price, it meant Kyle had spent more than 1,800 rakels on each prisoner. *Is this guy loaded or what?*

He noticed Damian didn't give Riker any Stamina Potions, but the moment Riker saw the potion in his hand, he turned into some sort of feral beast, lunging for it. The bars barely restrained him as Riker forced his arm through, trying to reach Lionel.

"How many days has it been?" Kyle asked Damian.

"About four full days since we stopped, sir."

"Hmm... He still seems too feisty. Open the cage."

Damian carried out the order. Riker pounced on Kyle, but the gang leader immediately parried his attacks and flipped him onto the ground, slamming him down hard.

Riker gagged, a slight froth coming from his mouth, but he was far too weak to sit up. Lionel could tell Riker had not eaten for a day or so; the food platter was still filled in the cage. Riker had barely touched it.

Kyle dragged Riker away from the room, Damian shutting the door behind them. A cold shiver ran down Lionel's spine. *What in the world are they attempting?*

Riker was tossed into an empty room and tied down to a wooden chair, Kyle being the only other person inside.

"How are you feeling?"

"F... Fuck you..." Riker was still in a cold sweat, his eyes bloodshot as he tried to keep his head up.

Kyle placed his hands on Riker's shoulder, who began to struggle but was unable to break free of the ropes and Kyle's iron grip.

"Inspect. Analyze. Identify."

Nothing appeared.

"Interesting." Kyle thought he might have been able to see a statistical table of Riker or at least a status effect of some sort, but they did not exist. He tried a few more words, but nothing happened. *Hmm...*

He examined Riker carefully, checking his eye reactions, heartbeat, pulse, and so on. *If only I had a full medical wing here. A side project for the future.*

Noted symptoms: Increased heart rate, sweating, hot and cold flashes, hallucinations, and perhaps loss of vision, not unlike dehydration.

"Riker." Kyle stood in front of him, snapping his fingers to catch the prisoner's attention.

"If you defeat me now, I'll let you go and give you this potion." Kyle pulled a Stamina Potion from his suit's inner pocket.

Riker's eyes were suddenly rejuvenated with life, and his head nodded vigorously. As soon as Kyle removed the ropes, Riker attacked without hesitation.

Kyle did not counter-attack this time, merely dodging left and right as he observed Riker's muscle movements and reaction timing. *Too slow, too weak, lack of awareness. A shadow of his former self. Perfect.*

"I've seen enough."

"N-No, wait. P-Please!" His hands tried to grab onto Kyle, missing completely as he collapsed onto the floor. Kyle tied him up again with ease and returned him to his cage.

Damian and Keith waited for him in the office.

"Continue to feed Riker, but do not give him any more Euria-infused potions." Kyle plopped down into his chair. "Moving forward, we will split the remainder of the prisoners into three groups: not infused potions, Euria-infused potions administered non-stop, and Euria-infused potions only administered on the first day.

Each gang member will rotate and defeat one of each group every day in combat. At the end of the day, I'll heal all of them. Got it?"

Damian nodded, leaving the room to pass down the modified training regimen.

"Sir, a few people have shown up at the entrance, wanting to join the Seven Snakes," Keith informed.

Faster than I expected. "Have them gather in my office as soon as possible."

Ten young men rushed in soon after. They lined up, their eyes eager as they stared at Kyle. Niko was among them, having quit his factory job after witnessing Kyle's performance first-hand, completely enamored by the prospect of gang life and strength. How could he accept languishing in mediocrity when greatness was right in front of him?

Kyle recognized most of them as onlookers from his fight with the Red Lions. He got up from his chair and inspected them for any irregularities. As he returned to the first of them, he suddenly launched a high kick toward the man's face, only stopping mere millimeters away from it. The man barely had time to react, only stumbling a step backward a few moments later.

"If you're here, you know what you're signing up for. Death is a real possibility." Kyle returned to his standing position. "I am not looking for men who simply want to take it easy or boss others around. Mutual loyalty is an integral part of how I run our group. Do right by me, and I'll do the same for you, no matter what happens."

I was right to come here! Niko's heart swelled with happiness, his fist clenching as he praised himself for making the right choice. His prior factory job was soulless, with the manager barely caring if anyone died or went missing. They were just numbers to be replaced. Kyle's words had struck a chord with Niko, causing him and a few others to nod their heads vigorously.

Kyle's modus operandi for the Seven Snakes was vastly different from the Red Lions'. His former life as a galactic crime lord had taught him an important lesson in fostering loyalty among even the lowest of members.

He did not do it because he was nice. Conversely, he had identified this method as the most secure in preventing betrayals. Something he did not do very well in his former life.

Performing a small beneficial action that is ultimately meaningless to me will mean a great deal to the recipient and will build loyalty over time. A minute cost for a great benefit. Kyle gently smiled as he noticed the expressions on their faces.

"There is a war with the Red Lions coming in about ten to thirteen days. If anyone wants to back out now, this is your last chance," Kyle said, his eyes cold and serious.

None of them backed out, standing firmly. All of them knew of the conflict. For some, it was why they had signed up in the first place. It meant a chance to get into a good position with the winning side, and everyone here knew exactly who was about to win.

"Good. Keith will now induct you. At the end, I will present each of you with an armband as associates." Kyle showed them the Seven Snakes armband bearing an elaborate crest.

A clear wave of excitement rippled through the ten men. *Formal ceremonies to make them feel important are also critical to retaining loyalty.*

The men left the office with Keith in the lead to give them a tour of the base. Kyle headed to the kitchen again, this time staring at the strength potion that now had its full description.

Strength Potion (Basic)

Boost muscle strength for a short duration. Good for short battles.
Recommended Usage: Drink the entire flask in one go. Active for five minutes.
Consuming another within a day will result in diminishing effects May experience side effects after main effect wears off.
Ingredients: Greis Powder, Olio Roots, Yul's Tears, Water
Cooldown: 30 seconds

He sent two members to collect the required materials—Olio Roots and Yul's Tears—which came separately in a sack and pot.

Kyle's face scrunched at the reported price of the Yul's Tears. A five kilogram pot was more than ten thousand rakels. *I only hope the recipe isn't too intensive on the percentage of Yul's Tears used...*

He internally cursed the Alchemists' Guild and Haui for not providing the recipe. However, Kyle was cognizant that he would have done the same. Recipes and methods of production were far too precious to be freely distributed in this kind of city.

The same brute-force method was employed as the last time, but with more than four ingredients in the mix, the number of potential combinations was a lot higher. Kyle brought in a few helpers to speed up the process, utilizing the numerous arcite stoves to iterate continually.

At one point, he had more than ten flasks going. He wrote down combinations on parchment, and crossed them out when he had failed.

Keith soon peeked his head in. "Sir, they're ready for the ceremony."

Instead of being irritated at being interrupted during the process, he put everything down and moved to the common area, where the men were already lined up.

They had already seen Kyle hard at work, so the action of him immediately stopping just for them made them feel even more valued.

The ceremony was a simple oath to the gang, and Kyle personally fastened their armbands onto their sleeves. "You are now official members of the Seven Snakes and under my protection. I will fight through Hell and back to ensure your safety, and I only ask you to do the same for your comrades—and me."

The men bowed with true respect. "Yes, sir!"

The loyalty will take a few days to truly instill, but it's a start.

Keith showed them to their bunks while Kyle continued trying to figure out the recipe.

The process proved to be difficult. There were a huge number of potential combinations, and Kyle didn't know when he would complete it—too many variables were present in the recipe. He now understood why Damian said reverse-engineering alchemy was nearly impossible without a hint or a guiding book.

As he completed his sixtieth failed potion, a new title appeared for him.

Title Obtained: Potion Crafter (Intermediate)
This title was supposed to be given on successful potions, but the failures are pretty hard to watch.

+10 INT, increased accuracy of examined potion's description, +10% chance to craft an intermediate potion when using basic materials, +5% chance of discovering basic potion recipes per attempt. This effect can be stacked and is reset on discovery.

Suddenly, it was as though three pieces of information appeared in his head, partially informing him of what the recipe consisted of. *It seems that for every twenty attempts I make, one of the variables of the recipe is revealed. Hence, with sixty crafted, I now have three variables revealed.*

Kyle quickly drew a new combination table, narrowing it down to two variables, making it simpler. With time and more failed attempts, he locked down yet another variable. Kyle could already imagine Haui's face if he knew exactly how Kyle was able to reverse-engineer recipes so quickly.

A few hours passed through dinnertime before he finally got the recipe down. "So, 15% Greis Powder, 15% Olio Roots, 35% Yul's Tears, rest water. Boiled for five minutes." Kyle nearly raged at the sheer amount of Yul's Tears he had wasted, having finished the entire pot with only one Strength Potion to show for it. *At least another product has been completed. Infusing it with Euria should be possible too.*

He didn't try to reverse-engineer the health potion just yet. It was far too costly to waste Yul's Tears on it. If the percentage were even higher, he might go bankrupt.

He sat back in his office, eating a late dinner, while Keith reported the daily finances to him.

"Sir, you can't keep burning through money like this. We don't have a lot of cash reserves left. Assuming you want to make another set of Strength Potions, it's going to wipe us out for the rest of the month unless we get steady revenue."

"It's no problem. The expansion of the brothel will be finished in a few days. We'll easily make it back, then. Who are the other rival gangs that are at odds with the Red Lions?"

"The Ilysian Punks and the Wretches are the main ones that come to mind, but they've been ignoring us for a long time."

"I want the smaller gangs in adjacent districts, anyone the same size as us and lower, to get this message." Kyle packed a few parchments into message tubes, handing them over to Keith.

"Ah, you want to ask for their help! I'll send it right away."

"No, Keith. We're going to find some customers."

Chapter 12

Arcite Technology

Wrent fiddled with a Stamina Potion in his hand, sitting at the end of a long table in a well-furnished room. "Have any of the alchemists replied? I want to know if the potions they are providing are complete knockoffs. A twenty-man team should *not* be able to produce five hundred a day."

It had been less than two days since they signed the contract, but Wrent had yet to distribute the Stamina Potions to his gang members for fear of them being poisoned. Such an outrageous production rate was banned by the Alchemists' Guild—anyone flouting this rule was either an ostracized alchemist or someone trying to pull a quick one.

"Boss, our in-house alchemists are all currently busy and will respond in two weeks' time." The Red Lions' main headquarters were still involved in violent conflict with the Ilysian Punks and the Wretches. Wrent had not yet been requested to join the conflict; his controlled district was not adjacent to any of the fighting zones.

"How about Haui? Has he replied?"

"We provided him with a few samples, and he has verified that they are legitimate, albeit with a lower efficiency than his. It could be said to be extremely diluted but still effective."

So the Seven Snakes are mass-producing it but with a much lower quality than if done by a certified alchemist... "If Haui says it's okay, then we can use it. Our priority is to distribute them to our members first for enhanced training and preparation. We need everyone ready to assault the Seven Snakes at the end of the non-aggression pact."

* * *

If everything goes to plan, the initial samples their alchemists have received won't be the Euria-infused ones, seeing as the first three crates are completely clean. Suppose it's Haui who is testing; that would be even better. Kyle tapped the table, thinking. *It's been two days since the start of the contract.*

An associate entered, passing Kyle a few replies from the other gangs. He opened them, reading the contents before calling Keith into the room.

"The new recruits won't have time to prepare for the battle. The other gangs have agreed to purchase Strength Potions from us at a fixed rate for the next month. Get the new recruits to begin production on a separate line. Follow the exact method I did for the Stamina Potions, but no Euria this time."

Kyle had sent a contract proposal, undercutting the market price of the Strength Potions with a discount of ten percent and selling them for nine hundred rakels each. *This shouldn't rock the market too much.*

"Sir, are we not planning to get the other gangs addicted?"

"Not yet. Let's not burn any bridges this early and focus on earning money first. The faster we deliver the batch of Strength Potions, the more cash we will have on hand to supply our fighters and operations."

Keith agreed and headed to the common area to set up the production lines, while Kyle considered his war plan. With the potions secured and a revenue source established, the supply contracts with the other gangs and the brothel's imminent expansion would cause his current pile of cash to skyrocket.

Nevertheless, he had to consider the method by which he defeated the Red Lions. Showing off too much would prompt the top leader of the Red Lions to intervene and most likely crush them in one fell swoop.

He knew the Red Lions at large were engaged in an open conflict with the Ilysian Punks and Wretches, which gave him more wiggle room.

However, they were not the only party involved; the local enforcers and maybe even the Ardent Cretins were watching him as well. Any actions taken would cause ripples, the consequences of which Kyle remained unsure due to his short time spent in the city.

Either way, he needed to ensure a clear combat advantage if he wanted to be able to control the flow of the fight. *Time to look for new advantages I can get.*

Kyle had Damian bring him to the nearest arctech dealer he could find. The shop was situated in the corner of the food market, with multiple types of armor and household appliances on display, all of which were powered by various forms of arcia; this was where Keith bought the arcite stoves.

The dealer wore a simple cloak, the glint of steel armor shining underneath. His demeanor and countenance hinted at a military background; the man might have been a former shock trooper for the Count of Raktor. They briefly locked eyes, their intentions exchanged without words.

Let's not pick a fight first. Kyle focused on gathering information through the holographic interface. He picked up a few items, reading their descriptions intently.

Glacial Defensive Bracelet (Basic)

Slow those who would stop you.

+2 STR, +2 VIT

[**Active**] **Glacial Defense:** Imparts a slow chilling effect onto enemies who hit any part of the engraving. Can be resisted based on vitality.

Cost: 2 MP   **Duration:** 2 seconds   **Cooldown:** 10 seconds per target

Aero Shoes (Basic)

For swift feet.

+4 AGI, +1 CHA

[Active] Sprint: Allows the wielder to move faster.
Cost: 2 MP   **Duration:** 15 seconds   **Cooldown:** 60 seconds

Breastplate of Strength (Basic)
A generic plate engraved with a strengthening mechanism.
+5 STR, +5 VIT
[Active] Strength: Allows the wielder to increase strength for as long as arcia is provided. Warning—arcite fuel is suggested.
Cost: 10 MP per minute

Kyle inspected the breastplate, noticing it was fairly intricate. Engravings similar to the metal pipe he had ran all over the surface and interior, along with what seemed like two electrical terminals meant to be connected to something else that powered the piece.

"Ah, you'll need an arcite fuel pack for that." The dealer pointed to a basic waist belt filled with canisters of a mild, cobalt-blue liquid that pulsated slowly. Kyle recognized it to be of the same arcite glow that currently powered his potion stoves, albeit more powerful and efficient. *Seems like there are different grades of arcite fuel—in solid or in liquid.*

"How much for it?"

"Well, normal civilians aren't supposed to have their own combat fuel packs without a license, but we both know we're well beyond *normal*, don't we? Sixty thousand."

Kyle's face didn't show any reaction, but he internally winced at the price. As much as the brothel was currently making, it didn't seem feasible to buy the fuel pack. Furthermore, being exposed for having a fuel pack while on a shaky gang foundation might incite the enforcers to act against him. *I've already spent enough bribing them.*

The dealer noted Kyle's reluctance. "You can run the other two items without arcite fuel, but that's all dependent on how much... *natural energy* your body has."

It seems like he's referring to the MP stat I've been seeing. I have zero right now. How do I increase it? Kyle nodded in response to the dealer before leaving. The prices of the other two items were also in the tens of thousands, representing a significant investment that he wanted to mull over first.

Kyle continued to browse the other items until he spotted something that took him by surprise. *Huh. Did not expect to find this here.*

Enchanted Flintlock Pistol (Basic)

An arcia-gorging device that shoots pellets at high speeds.

[**Active**] **Buckshot:** Accelerate muzzle-loaded pellets at high speeds, causing damage on impact.

Cost: 25 MP

The dealer scoffed at the gun as Kyle examined it. "Bah! I've been trying to get rid of that pistol for ages now. Nobody around can even use it, and it cost me far too much to acquire in the first place."

"Nobody uses guns around here?"

"There aren't any laws against wielding pistols, only laws against using military guns. The Count has much better guns being used. But seeing as you're too poor to buy a fuel pack, you might as well forget about *this*." The dealer shooed him off.

Kyle mulled as he walked back to the base. "Damian, how much is the gun and who else uses them?"

"Within the city, only the top of the enforcers, sir. But even *they* don't have the energy to arm themselves with pistols and use them; it simply draws too much arcia energy and takes time to reload. The design and manufacture of such arctech is still far too complicated for factories to produce. I've heard the military has made some headway in improving the guns, but for now, we're stuck with this."

Kyle noted the information Damian had given him. *So it's essentially a flintlock pistol that uses arcia instead of gunpowder.* Naturally, with his knowledge from the Galactic Era, it would be a cinch to dominate the market with high technology and his rudimentary understanding. But until he figured out what the current military technology was, he wouldn't attempt to manufacture any guns. Too big of a jump would open up a whole other can of worms, and he already had his hands full dealing with the Red Lions. *None of the technology here is combustion based, so showing up with gunpowder will draw too many eyes. Best not go that route.*

Returning to the base, Kyle laid out the three arctech items he had personally appropriated from Riker and Lionel: the Breastplate of Nullification, Enchanted Flaming Hammer, and Enchanted Metal Pipe.

Each item required MP to activate their skills. He had witnessed Lionel activating the hammer and Wrent wearing an armor suit that clearly had arctech capabilities. *Even with the Strength Potion, I'm at a disadvantage. When fighting, I can't use the system interface to determine their effects beforehand without touching them.*

"Statistics."

Kyle Hawthorn: Level 9

Max HP: 34(+0)(+0)(+0) | **Max MP:** 0(+0)(+0)(+0) | **Max STA:** 34(+0)(+0)(+0)

Status Effects

None

Stats

Race: Human | **Class:** Unassigned | **Subclass:** Unassigned

STR: 63(+17)(+0)(+0) | **DEX:** 39(+13)(+0)(+0) | **INT:** 64(+35)(+3)(+0)

VIT: 33(+0)(+3)(+0) | **CHA:** 21(+10)(+1)(+0) | **Free Points:** 20

Equipment

Necklace of Healing (Basic)

Skills
None

Titles
Former Crime Lord
Martial Arts Expert
Murderer
Potion Inspector (Intermediate)
Potion Crafter (Intermediate)
Healer (Basic)
Martial Arts Instructor (Basic)

He didn't have MP, nor a concrete idea how to gain it. Let's try to assign free points to MP.

[SYSTEM MESSAGE]
ERROR: Free Points cannot be used on HP, MP, or STA.

Kyle frowned, but all hope was not yet lost. Based on his understanding of how titles worked, he had a rough guess at an alternative way to proceed. *Best ask the locals.*

"Are there any items that boost the... natural energy of someone?" Kyle asked Damian and Keith.

Damian's mouth dropped while an excited expression came over Keith's face. "By Yual, Alvin! You're back!" Damian reached forward to hug Kyle in what was to be a touching reunion but instead found himself facing the ceiling of the office, his arm locked.

"I already told you to call me Kyle or sir."

Damian and Keith's enthusiasm dimmed, and Damian slowly stood up. They were a bit shaken and glanced at each other with a knowing expression. "Sir, Slavin at the brothel has a few types of... erm... artifacts of a certain nature that might boost your lifestyle," Damian replied with a hint of understanding.

"I understand if you want to let off some steam before the big fight." Keith nodded in agreement as though the two brothers were wise men instructing Kyle about his destiny, stroking a non-existent beard.

"What the hell are you two on about? I'm talking about using arctech."

"Oh, right. Sorry. It might be worth a shot to find Ulon's private stash then. It's where your current necklace came from."

"Haven't we already auctioned or trashed most of it?" Kyle recalled disliking the useless trinkets and ornaments, and when he touched them, an interface didn't pop up.

"No, those are just the public ones. I don't know too much about it, but I do know it's somewhere in the room. Though, it is just a rumor I heard from other gang members. It may not be true."

The three of them scoured the private room where Kyle was sleeping, eventually finding a wooden box in a bookcase embedded into the wall.

Keith had stars in his eyes, no doubt waiting to see what valuable items there were. "This is exciting! Maybe we can pawn some of it." He rubbed his hands together feverishly.

Damian noticed the box was neither secured nor locked. "He probably thought no one would steal anything."

They opened it to reveal a massive pile of junk, all useless trinkets. Kyle methodically went through them one by one, irked at the moldy condition of many of the statues. Soon he held a statue of a penis with stains on it, slightly used. He quickly handed it over to Keith, who had long lost the stars in his eyes and nearly gagged when he held it.

After sorting through more than a hundred objects, Kyle soon found a sapphire ring with a golden band. It appeared to be engraved, but it had somehow worn away.

Magus Ring of Theorin (Intermediate)
A ring from a former wielder of arcia.
+5 MAX MP, +25% MP recovery rate.

That's a tiny amount... Kyle immediately put the ring on his right hand, and felt a surge of what the denizens of this world called arcia energy rush through his veins like a hit of an exotic stimulant. It was minuscule in effect, but he could already tell his body had improved. He his fingers, noticing the existence of something else coursing through his muscles, though he could not pinpoint exactly what it was, where it was, and how fast it was moving. *Interesting... I don't recall any base humans having such a feature.* Kyle sorted through the rest of the stash, only finding one book of interest. It was an intricately bound tome, complete with a metal binder and leather cover riddled with engravings.

A Treatise on Arcia by Theorin
An incomplete guide on wielding internal arcia.
The theories are outdated but still provide a good baseline understanding.

"My God! I didn't know this still existed!" Damian exclaimed as he wiped the dust off the old tome. "Theorin was the first gang leader of the Seven Snakes more than twenty years ago. He was a natural-born wielder of arcia, a mage if you will. This allowed him to dominate the districts before arcite fuel became popularized. Didn't expect Ulon to have held on to it."

Kyle opened the tome, noting some of the more complicated terminology and formulas that would take time for him to understand. He would need Keith's assistance to translate it.

With this book and the new ring, he could potentially utilize more arctech in the future. Even *he* understood the limitation of his fighting skills against items that could impart special effects. *With this, it'll be an easy win.*

Chapter 13

Assault

A few days later...

"Boss, all our men are waiting for your orders."

"Good." Wrent nodded his head, wearing his reddish armor set. He strode out to the training yard where more than forty members were all lined up in formation under the evening sky. They each had a light armor set, but only four of them had arctech on them, which was the sign of the squad leaders. Each squad had ten members standing in neat rows.

"The Seven Snakes have been rapidly growing over the last two weeks. On top of that, they are still holding our men! As such, from today, we will be entering a state of war against them. Each squad is to target one of the major businesses immediately."

Wrent held up a printed piece of paper with a rough sketch of Kyle's face. "If you encounter the leader of the Seven Snakes, Kyle, retreat at once. Do not attempt to engage alone. The objective is to wear them down and split their forces. He is the only one among them who has any sort of combat training. The rest are weak idiots."

Wrent knew this war had a chance of being dragged out. If they failed the first assault, they had to wear them down slowly over time.

The Red Lions had been using the Stamina Potions, but not all of them. Wrent kept more than four hundred of them in a protected area near the armory. However, he wasn't worried about an attack on the base, seeing as he was here to defend it. This allowed him to maximize his attacking force, which he needed if he wanted to hold a numerical advantage over the Seven Snakes.

He passed a single arctech radio to each of the squad leaders. This way, Wrent would be able to monitor the situation, and the squad leaders could convey information to one another. Information was the key to winning everything—Wrent knew that well.

"These are precious pieces of equipment loaned to us by the main base. Don't you dare lose it! Even if you die, your ghost must return this to me. Understood?"

The squad leaders nodded grimly.

"A few days, a week, two weeks—we will not rest until the Seven Snakes have capitulated and returned our comrades. The Red Lions never falter in the face of adversity. BEGIN!"

"Yes, Boss!" The squads moved out, heading to their designated locations.

Wrent smiled to himself as he retreated into his office. *You may be smart, but the nail that sticks out will get hammered down first. It's just business.* He was already internally salivating at the thought of taking over their potion production process, wondering what other secrets the Seven Snakes held on to.

An hour passed, approaching dusk. The arctech streetlights flickered on, their bright, blue lights illuminating the dusty cobblestone roads. The first squad reached the brothel first, but they soon noticed that the Seven Snakes associates were already out in force, with seven guys guarding the nearby streets.

"Boss, they seemed to be onto us," a squad leader reported through the radio.

"It's expected." Wrent was calm, already having expected Kyle to be prepared in advance. *"When all squads are in position, we'll attack simultaneously."*

Another ten minutes passed before all four squads were in position. The brothel, two pubs, and a restaurant were being targeted, but the squads reported seeing associates of the Seven Snakes in the vicinity.

"Any sign of Kyle?"

"No, Boss. But there seems to be more associates than the twenty expected. Closer to thirty or even more now."

This didn't faze Wrent at all. *If I'm right, he's probably waiting at the base or somewhere in the middle where he can rapidly respond to any attacks. And the new recruits barely had a week or two for training.* "Move in now."

The squads slowly began moving into the district, positioning aggressively and standing near the targeted businesses. The customers who had initially queued up began to scatter upon seeing the threatening Red Lions members stare at them from a distance. Word spread like wildfire—it was a turf war.

One of the Seven Snakes' guards confronted them. "Hey! What are you red cunts trying here? You're fucking scaring them off!"

"I'll stand wherever the fuck I like. Why? Does your father own these streets? Didn't know this was your grandfather's road either. Mind your own business."

"You better fucking move, or—"

"Or what? Run and hide, like you always did with Ulon? Once a bitch, always a bitch."

All over the district, confrontations like this were beginning to drive the tension even higher. The Red Lions were provoking the Seven Snakes to attack first. It was all a childish back-and-forth of who attacked first and who was in the right, a game of public perception as a few brave onlookers watched the arguments grow more heated.

In a matter of minutes, it wouldn't matter who started the fight or waved the biggest stick—only who won. Wrent was about to lean back into his comfortable office chair, waiting for the inevitable victory, when he suddenly heard a loud thud in the training yard before a metal door cracked open with a repeated hammering sound.

The grating metallic sounds pierced the air, prompting Wrent to immediately exit the office to see who was attacking. A lone man was smacking away at the hinges of the armory door with a neon-red arctech hammer, and they soon gave way, sending the door to the ground with a large cloud of dust.

"KYYYYYLLE!" Wrent lunged at him, retrieving his ruby-encrusted sword from its sheath and swinging wildly. However, the arctech shoes Kyle wore glowed yellow and allowed him to move a bit faster than expected, barely dodging the ferocious attacks. Kyle quickly ran into the armory, glancing around at the numerous racks of weapons and armor before spotting the potion crates.

A tingling sensation ran down his spine as he instinctively ducked, a red energy arc slicing through the air where his head had just been. The arc crashed into the potion crates with a loud explosion, sending dark-yellow liquid spiraling into the air.

That's new.

Kyle glanced behind Wrent to see a pipe connected to a churning fuel pack at his waist and a sword glowing with arcia. "So, you've come to your death, then. Were you planning on raiding the armory to steal our equipment?" Wrent grinned, blocking the only exit.

Without a word, Kyle ran deeper inside, much to the surprise of Wrent.

"COME BACK HERE, YOU CUNT!" Wrent yelled as he charged through the armory. Kyle quickly used his hammer to smack the intersections of a few empty armor racks and tossed training weapons to stall Wrent. The well-organized armory started collapsing, the metal shelves and cupboards being overturned.

Wrent's armor prevented him from moving as fast as Kyle, rendering him unable to keep up. Kyle leapt over him with one swift motion, landing in a roll. As soon as he recovered, he ran straight out the door.

"STOP RIGHT THERE!" Wrent yelled.

Kyle didn't comply, only showing a small smirk before leaving, which infuriated Wrent even more. Wrent glanced around the room, seeing only an utter mess. No critical equipment was being kept here; all of it had already been distributed to the attacking squads. He tried to figure out Kyle's objective, since the man was clearly avoiding a fight with him.

The dark-yellow liquid oozing onto the floor suddenly made him realize he had lost the entire stash of potions. The loss of the Stamina Potions weighed on him, but his pride mattered more. How could he have failed to capture the enemies' leader when he was right there? He ran back to the office and grabbed the radio.

"Cease the attack and converge back on the base—Kyle is fleeing back through our district! Cut him off!"

"Boss, we can't. We're right in front of them. If we back off now, our reputation will take a hit!"

"Aren't they pushovers? Just attack first, knock out a few of them, and then catch the leader!"

The Red Lions squads were now torn between leaving a confrontation they started and capturing Kyle. "Fuck it. If Wrent ordered it, we'll do it!"

They quickly attacked, but none of the Seven Snakes members were surprised, knowing their plan had succeeded. "Hold as many of them here! Don't let them cut off our leader!"

Battles erupted in the street, the flickering of the arctech neon signs serving as the backdrop to dozens of men that fought in the streets in a rough melee brawl with fists, gauntlets, knuckle dusters, and pipes. Blood and the twisting of limbs became a common scene all over the cobblestone ground, with fighters wrestling and ganging up on single targets. Everything was fair game.

Much to the surprise of the Red Lions, the Seven Snakes were suddenly much better at fighting. They were able to dodge and parry effectively, to a certain extent. It was not only the effect of the homemade Strength Potions that boosted them. They had undergone training since Kyle had taken over, which was now close to a month for the original members, much like a boot camp.

Any of the Red Lions members who tried to carry out Wrent's order were instantly intercepted by the Seven Snakes. However, the Red Lions still had the edge in arctech equipment and experience, allowing them to inflict more damage as the battle continued. The fights were brutal, with both sides suffering injuries and broken limbs.

"Boss, they aren't that weak; we can't beat them instantly like we expected!"

Wrent cursed and pounded his fist on his office table, cracking it in half. "ARRRGH! SEVEN SNAKES!" He couldn't leave the base lest Kyle was performing a feint—there were still plenty of high-value resources that Kyle could quickly return to ransack.

The scale of the fights escalated, with exhaustion setting in. But the Seven Snakes were far more tenacious, gritting their teeth as they pushed back against the numerical and equipment disadvantages. "This is nothing compared to our training!"

The next hour was harrowing as the fights dragged on. Wrent impatiently tapped the table, waiting for some good news over the arctech radio. All of a sudden, one of the lights indicating an active connection to a squad dimmed. *Shit... One of the squads had their arctech radio broken?! It has to be Kyle!*

With a squad out of contact, it meant that the net he had set up around the Seven Snakes' district had fallen apart. Wrent's brow furrowed intensely as he contemplated whether or not he should enter the battle to counter Kyle's combat ability. However, he instinctively knew that he was now one step behind; entering the battle would be playing right into the enemies' hand.

"All squads, retreat now!" Wrent ordered, aiming to conserve his forces. *I must cut my losses and reorganize before it's too late!*

The Red Lions were more than happy to comply, immediately retreating and limping away.

The Seven Snakes did not chase them, instead letting them retreat slowly. They themselves did not go unscathed, having suffered a few injuries and concussions far worse than the Red Lions. The potions helped them with the grit to stay standing after the brutal clash.

Should I call for reinforcements from the main base? The brief thought flashed through Wrent's mind when he realized he was now on an even playing field with the Seven Snakes, and may have even lost. Even if half of them returned, he had no Stamina Potions left to give them.

He shuddered when he thought of how the boss of the Red Lions would react if he asked for help. The main base had problems of their own when fighting other gangs, and if Wrent admitted he couldn't handle a small-time group like the Seven Snakes, he could forget about climbing the ranks. *My position as the Left Paw would be stripped regardless of victory. I'll have to do this myself.*

Eventually, the squads returned, including the one that had lost the radio. They had to leave three of their members behind while the other squads returned intact but still wounded.

"W-What happened to our potions?!" a returning squad member exclaimed upon seeing the mess of broken crates and liquid on the floor.

Wrent didn't respond, inwardly cursing for not protecting it to the best of his ability. He took out a secret stash of Health Potions, distributing them to the squad leaders.

"One squad will keep guard and patrol the district lest the Seven Snakes try to attack while we're weak. Rotate every eight hours. All other squads are to sleep." Wrent knew they needed to rest if he wanted to have a shot at winning at all.

With the assault failing, they had now entered a protracted conflict stage.

Chapter 14

Horizontal Merger

"Sir, how did you know they weren't going to call in reinforcements? It seems stupid not to do so, seeing as they lost half a squad." Damian was confused as he oversaw the associates dragging captured Red Lions members to their holding cells.

"Wrent is a showman through and through. Any action that could potentially damage his reputation wouldn't be taken. Even then, us providing Strength Potions to many of the other smaller gangs around them has increased the number of issues their main base has to deal with, which means they can spare even fewer men to counter us," Kyle explained.

"Then why didn't we chase them down and defeat them in one single blow? Now they'll have time to recover and retaliate in a few days."

"A cornered star fleet is just as dangerous as a wounded one."

"Fleet? As in naval battles?"

"Never mind. Either way, pushing them too hard would attract more attention from the major bases. The victory over them must be complete but not too flashy."

Damian finally understood Kyle's line of thinking. It wasn't right to go all out and stomp the opposition in a domineering fashion, especially when the foundations of the gang weren't solid enough. There were too many 'big fishes' in the district watching right now. Having the Seven Snakes come to a draw or a very minor victory was less alarming.

The two of them began checking on the injured members, with Kyle healing them with his Necklace of Healing. The Red Lions were still dominant when it came to weaponry, causing some of the Seven Snakes members to fall unconscious after fighting enemy squad leaders fitted with arctech equipment. A few even had mangled or severely bruised limbs. *I should reverse-engineer a Health Potion after this.*

He soon returned to his office, tired from the intense running he had had to do. The plan had been executed perfectly, though he might have been forced to buy the Aero Shoes from the dealer to move faster. With this, the chances of the Red Lions attacking them would be much lower than expected; they were now even in numbers.

Kyle was well aware that the Red Lions still had the edge in terms of equipment, as evidenced by the damage inflicted on his gang members. Nevertheless, he wasn't worried at all. *In a few days, they will crumble, and it'll be an easy negotiation...*

* * *

Five days after the assault...

Wrent woke up groggy, his forehead sweating buckets as he struggled to get up from his bed. *Fuck. Have I been infected with a plague or something?* He could feel his heart rate increasing, and there was a general sinking feeling in his stomach.

The nerves on his jaw and spine were especially tender, as though he could feel every millimeter of his gums going numb, causing him to try to dislodge the feeling constantly.

The other Red Lions members were not faring any better either; some were puking or reporting intense nausea. "What in the world is going on?" Wrent muttered as he watched the members stumble about, lacking strength. "Hey, you. Weren't you supposed to be on patrol? What if the Seven Snakes attack?"

"H-Huh?" The Red Lions member could barely register what Wrent was saying, obviously hallucinating.

Fucking shit. What is happening?! Wrent tried to recall what had happened. *Did Kyle somehow infect the base's utilities? How is this happening to us?*

Wrent had been taking antidotes for the last two days, which had barely managed to stave off the symptoms. He had even tried a precious Health Potion, but it didn't work at all. *It isn't poison... So what is it?*

His eyes landed on the broken crates of Stamina Potions, a sense of understanding finally hitting him. *Did they drug the potions? How in the world is it so addictive?! But I tested it!*

Addiction was not a particularly new symptom, but he had not seen anything on the black market that came even remotely close to the level of addiction and mass production as this.

The strategy employed by the Seven Snakes was finally as clear as day. Before Wrent could think about doing anything, a loud bang at the base entrance was heard.

It was the Seven Snakes.

Kyle walked in, dressed in a clean, formal suit, unlike the arctech equipment he had worn previously. Damian and Keith flanked him, along with a dozen other members.

"You dare come to your own death? Red Lions, attack him!" Wrent grunted weakly. Instead of complying, the members merely staggered about, and some others suffered from mild seizures.

Kyle snapped his fingers, with the Seven Snakes moving forward to restrain the barely resisting Red Lions. The most they could muster was an infantile resistance.

"Useless!" Wrent grunted as he grabbed his sword with his right hand, about to unleash another red arc with a swing. But in a single instant, Kyle sprinted toward him with the Aero Shoes, closing the distance in merely four strides before gripping the right hand of Wrent and forcing it down.

"ARGHH!" Wrent yelled in pain as Kyle crushed his right hand with the hilt of the sword. He tried to muster the strength to fight back, but the withdrawal symptoms made it impossible. Wrent could feel that his muscles were severely weakened.

"This is no way to treat your esteemed suppliers, is it?" Kyle flashed a sinister grin.

At this point, Wrent heavily regretted not asking for help from the main base, realizing he had fully underestimated Kyle. He had become too used to the image of the Seven Snakes being useless under Ulon.

"Do it then. Kill me," Wrent said through gritted teeth as he was brought to one knee, forced to look up at Kyle. "The leader of the Red Lions will never let you off."

"Ah. Why would I ever kill my precious customers? Please, no need for such courtesy. You can stop kneeling." Kyle let go of his hand, and Damian moved forward to lift Wrent up.

They dragged him into the office, sitting him down at a table. Kyle retrieved a parchment from a message tube and slid it in front of Wrent for him to read. "I believe the samples we provided in the previous contract were much to your liking. In fact, it seems your members love it so much they're even dying for it."

"Y-You!" Wrent cursed as sweat dripped down his forehead. He could barely move his body now, and the bones in his right hand had been fractured by Kyle's grip.

"Now for our next contract, we would like to enter a mutually beneficial supply contract. If you sign this, we will immediately provide a few crates in advance for your perusal. How does that sound?" Kyle motioned outside the office window, where Wrent could see two additional Seven Snakes members carrying crates.

He could already see the hunger in his members' eyes as they watched the crates come in. They weren't dumb, knowing they were addicted to the potions now, but they didn't have the willpower to fight their bodies.

Wrent took another look at Kyle, who was patiently sitting with Damian and Keith standing behind him. While Kyle's expression was calm and serene, Wrent knew there was a cruelness hiding within. *What's more important—my loyalty to the boss or my life?*

He glanced at his members suffering outside. Wrent grimaced and finally decided to look at the contract, rationalizing that he was doing it for his subordinates. He began reading through it, noticing the clauses were roughly the same except for the fact that he now had to pay for the potions.

He read the changes to the non-aggression clause, noticing the contract had extended it to a year minimum. This was expected, but the next clause was what threw him off.

It stated that the Seven Snakes would *publicly* admit that the conflict had been their fault and their loss. They would then pay reparations in the form of potion discounts and the release of prisoners.

Wrent was utterly confused, but as he looked up into Kyle's eyes, a realization rose within him. *He's leaving me a way out—a way not to be replaced by my boss. And if I or our side in general renege on the reparation contract, our reputation will go straight into the gutter.*

With this additional clause, the Red Lions would not suffer any reputation loss, and the Seven Snakes would also have their non-aggression pact. Wrent would have a much higher chance of retaining his position and control over the district, which was precisely what Kyle wanted. In his mind, Wrent vowed to kill Kyle in any way possible. *This man is far too dangerous. At this rate, he'll take over the entire sector within two years.*

Wrent eventually relented and signed the contract with his personal stamp. "Good. I'm glad we've come to an agreement. Enjoy the potions. We look forward to your future cooperation." Kyle smirked and left immediately. While the contract was between equals, Wrent knew he had become the underling in the unspoken hierarchy, gripping his fist tightly.

As the Seven Snakes released the restrained members and left the new crates behind, the members were confused about what had just happened. Some of the members were certain they were going to be killed.

Wrent didn't know what to tell them. All they could do now was consume the potions. *I swear I'll find a way to remove this addiction and take revenge!*

* * *

Always leave a way out for a cornered corvette, lest they choose to self-destruct. It is better to milk your enemies. Kyle was happy with the result. While he would be losing the prisoners, he had run sufficient tests on the addiction properties by now. With the gang members being trained for over a month, there was no need for addiction-ridden prisoners to fight against. They could simply spar against one another.

This will also prevent the more significant gangs from clamping down on us. Anyone else that tries to attack us will risk angering the Red Lions, seeing as we are supplying them in a reparation contract...

None of the Seven Snakes were unhappy with the outcome, even though it was to be publicly declared; they all knew they had emerged as victors of the conflict. It boosted their pride and sense of accomplishment, but most of all, it caused their respect for Kyle to soar far into the clouds. All the members were comparing him to Ulon, though it was a low bar to clear. Even the new recruits who hadn't fought as much were starstruck by how easily they defeated the Red Lions.

"Holy shit! It was only a few hours of skirmishes, four days of patrols, and that's it? Is our leader some sort of monster?"

"He managed to sneak into their base alone and escape even with Wrent defending! How awesome is that? Fuck the guy who told me Wrent was a beast!" Niko excitedly whispered as they watched Kyle return to the base with the rest.

Kyle began giving out orders. "Keith, prepare the public announcement. Spread it through our businesses. Get Slavin in on it as well." The brothel expansion was going well despite the conflict, with the customers reasonably assured of the protection provided by the Seven Snakes.

"Damian, arrange for the prisoner transfer process. Return everyone, addicted or not."

"Everyone else, gather in the common area in three hours for dinner. It's time to celebrate." A loud cheer erupted among the associates. They were excited to celebrate their first victory in over five years.

Kyle returned to his office, looking at the map that showed the districts again.

The base is now secured against most smaller threats. The locals are now well aware of the resurgence of the Seven Snakes. Kyle nodded to himself, but he knew he was far from being a significant power in the city of Raktor. If he truly wanted to achieve his first original objective of building a solid power base, only when he had dominated an entire city would he consider it as some measure of success.

His eyes fell on the list of gangs in the South Sector, noting the prominent individuals and the top dominator—the Ardent Cretins. Despite the daunting challenges ahead, Kyle already had a step-by-step plan for what to do.

I used to rule nebulas, spice routes, and star systems with populations numbering in the trillions. What's a small city like this to me?

Chapter 15

Repercussions

The next day...

"Did you hear? The Seven Snakes lost to the Red Lions and have to pay reparations."

"Nah, no way. I saw them fight each other—they were at a draw! Sure, the Seven Snakes were nearly beaten shitless, but they were extremely tenacious."

"Their new leader seems to be much more competent than Ulon, but I guess a small-time gang will always be small-time."

Such were the types of rumors going around the food market and the South Sector, but they were drowned out in a sea of other conflicts. The Seven Snakes were not the only gang fighting at the time—it was the city of Raktor, so a fight was around every corner.

"Are we going to be the next dominator of the South Sector?" one of the more overtly excited gang members asked.

"Idiot, no way! How the hell are we going to overtake the Ardent Cretins? Wait, fuck that. We can't even go against the main force of the Red Lions!"

"Nah, believe in Kyle! I like him much better than his Alvin persona."

"Can't wait to have my own underlings; I'll put them through the same training routine!"

The mood in the base was festive, but Kyle was not. At least not until the waves had died down. He sat in his office, waiting patiently until Keith came in, his face clearly shaken.

"Sir, there's someone here to see you."

"Is it the enforcers? I've been expecting them." Kyle had anticipated a potential visit, seeing as they had now established their foundation in the district. He was not averse to collaborating with the enforcers—crime and law went hand in hand. Already in his mind, he was coming up with ways to entice and lure the enforcers into his pocket. *Perhaps a tax-generating scheme or even mutual assistance in reducing crime.*

He could even use the enforcers to potentially suppress some of the thug groups lurking around the district. Despite the Seven Snakes' resurgence, it was foolish to assume that they had complete control over every individual in the area—countless upstarts and small three-man gangs ran multiple smuggling rings and production lines as well.

But Keith shook his head violently. "N-N-No, sir. It-It's n-not the enforcers." Keith barely stuttered the words out, his hands trembling and with fear.

"Is he alone?" Kyle squinted his eyes, tossing out his current thoughts.

"Yes."

Kyle's expression darkened. "Have him come in. Prepare the best tea we have."

"Yes, sir."

Soon, a well-dressed gentleman in an elegant outfit walked in, his hair slicked back in jet-black lines, and his face immaculate. The suit spoke volumes of care and attention to detail—the thread count was specifically selected and the gradient of the fabric was astounding. He did not bow nor show any signs of respect toward Kyle, treating him like a decoration while he simply walked around the office and looked at the bookshelves and furniture, his luxurious walking cane tapping the ground incessantly. "How quaint. I am a bit sad to see Ulon's hallmark ornaments missing."

"They were quite a distraction, so I had them auctioned off."

"A pity. I would have hoped he kept some of my older gifts." The man finally locked eyes with Kyle before sitting in a chair meant for guests, relaxing as though he had just arrived home.

"I'm sure he appreciated the gifts, nonetheless."

"Oh, my gifts pale in comparison to the gift you gave him." The man chuckled at his own joke. Keith soon entered the room with a teapot and cup on a delicate tray, placing it down and pouring a cup for the guest. However, his hands were shaking terribly, the tea violently vibrating as the glass clinked.

The man simply smiled at Keith and turned back to Kyle. "You're doing much better than Ulon did. When I first met him, he could barely reply to me or look me in the eye. I recall him trembling continuously, unable to form a coherent sentence. Much like this poor young boy." He motioned his hand to Keith, who quickly bowed and took a step back.

"I would not use Ulon as a measure for eloquence—or a measure for anything."

"Indeed. Ulon was never able to make use of what he had on hand." The man chuckled, closely examining Keith and sizing him up. "A gait of a scholar. Sharp eyes, though bravery has to be worked on a tad more. Your abilities seemed to be far wasted here. Perhaps I can offer you another form of employ—"

"Get to the point," Kyle interjected in defiance. The man did not seem irked in the slightest, giving a mere gentle smile as he crossed his legs.

"I'm here to deliver a form of greeting from our leader, Ares UIras. He has only the best wishes for the future of the Seven Snakes and hopes to potentially forge relationships where possible. We are open to partnerships or collaborations in any future ventures."

Kyle nodded. "You may give him my thanks, Sebastian. I will surely take him up on his offer in the near future."

"Ah, a man who has done his research. Consider me surprised that even an amnesiac knows about me."

"It's hard not to know legends and myths about the vice-leader of the Ardent Cretins."

"Oh, don't flatter me. I'm simply doing my job. I'm sure that you will have your own myths in the future—if given enough time."

"Only if I am allowed to."

Sebastian's smile grew. "I knew we would understand each other. A big improvement over Ulon, as repugnant of a standard he might be. It seems like being an amnesiac is a gift of sorts; perhaps I should try it one day."

"I can have an alchemist prepare a memory-erasing potion if you so wish. Perhaps we could set an appointment?"

Sebastian laughed, while Kyle maintained a stoic expression. "Maybe when I'm retired. For now, I still have to manage a group of naughty children who only get rowdier as they age. Always aiming to become the parent, thinking they have what it takes to rule the world. Do you have any tips for handling them?"

"Some sweets or cake would make them easy to handle. A gift or a concession goes a long way to fostering trust."

"Ah, but children are quick to forget, especially when another carrot is dangled in front of them. That reminds me." He stood up, rummaging through his inner pocket.

"A token of goodwill from the Ardent Cretins." Sebastian retrieved a transparent glass bottle holding a miniature galleon suspended by wood inside. "An exquisite gift, handcrafted by one of our patrons."

He stood up and placed it on the table in front of Kyle. The boat was extremely intricate and fragile. Keith looked at it and could tell that even a slight, sudden jerk could cause the boat to collapse. For Sebastian to be able to carry it in his suit without breaking it was stupendous.

"Do be careful with it. It is extremely delicate. If one were to rock the boat too much, the pieces within would begin to crumble. Hopefully, it will still be intact the next time we meet." Sebastian took his leave, with Keith escorting him out of the base.

When Keith returned, his leader was still staring at the ship.

"Wow, I didn't know the vice leader of the Ardent Cretins was so nice! That boat looks really expensive!" Keith exclaimed.

"It wasn't a pleasant conversation, far from it. It was a threat," Kyle responded grimly. After all that he had done to make sure he remained off the radar, the big fish of the South Sector had still locked on to him. He expected someone of note from the Ardent Cretins to visit eventually, but he never expected the vice leader to come in person.

Don't rock the South Sector, lest you want your gang to crumble into pieces. Kyle knew what the warning was, clear as day. He clenched his fists tightly.

With the Ardent Cretins having their eye on him now, any sort of aggressive expansion or scaling up would be heavily scrutinized. The moment Sebastian detected a threat, Kyle knew he was the type to use everything he had to eliminate it immediately. That was the privilege of the strong, after all. Kyle used to do that in his former life.

"Keith, call Damian in. We will have to restructure the plan moving forward."

* * *

The Central Sector of the city was the most prosperous. Buildings made of arcia-infused glass towered over streets filled with automatic carriages, guided by the roads as they ferried aristocrats, nobles, and the general upper class to and fro.

An opulent and intricately detailed building reminiscent of a temple was one of the key features of the sector. While many of the locals and tourists would admire it as a work of art, it was equally feared by many of the gang leaders.

A lone girl walked up the marble steps, clearly excited as her cobalt-blue eyes darted around. She checked her pearl-white cloak, rubbing a small stain off the shiny, silver pauldrons. The golden hems of the cloak fluttered as she continued climbing, her straight dress pants and a buttoned shirt peeking from underneath.

"Inquisitor Kitana, here under orders from the archbishop." She bowed to the guards at the entrance, who respectfully bowed back. They performed a simple check on her belongings before allowing her in.

She entered the vast temple, the ceiling and pillars adorned with paintings that had been completed over generations. At the height of it, all in prime view, was a portrait of Yual, the Emperor of the Yual Dominion that ruled over the city of Raktor and others.

As she walked, she could hear whispers from enforcers and clerks who stared at her, their echoes bouncing off the concave ceiling and domes.

"The inquisitors are here? Finally, we get some much-needed help."

"Yes, the bloodbath in the West Sector between the Veiled Angels and the Violet Demons is escalating far beyond our control. If the inquisitors didn't show up, we might have had to call in the military."

"The military would never agree to intervene in civil affairs unless ordered by either the duke or the emperor."

A servant led her to a smaller audience chamber, where an old priest was kneeling in front of a statue of the emperor. There were already nine others like her standing behind rows of pews and praying. Kitana quickly took an empty spot, clasping her hands in prayer as well.

After five minutes, the priest finally stood up, turning to face them. "My fellow priests and priestesses. It is with great honor that you have come before me and the emperor today to be given a special role.

"Crime has infiltrated the streets of Raktor, defiling the empire-wide bans set forth by the archbishop. Alcoholism, prostitution, senseless violence, and the proliferation of weapons are just some of the infestations that choke Raktor by the gut. The citizens of this city do not know what true purity is and are unwilling to adhere to the law. While the archbishop has turned a blind eye to it in the past, he can no longer divert his eyes from the stray sheep that are running amok.

"You shall act as the eyes and ears of the Sanctum of Yual. You are the arbiter, the judge, and the executioner of our will and our beliefs. Those who claim to be citizens of the Yual Dominion but do not uphold the same values must be taught otherwise, by words or by fear of death. For it is only through fear that they may learn to love the encompassing embrace that is our emperor."

The priest retrieved a scroll, unrolled it, and read it. "As such, under holy appointment and orders direct from the archbishop himself, you are all now appointed as inquisitors of the Sanctum of Yual. Go forth and cleanse this city of filth and bring glory to the emperor!"

"Glory to the emperor! Glory to Yual!" The ten inquisitors bowed.

They remained bowed as a few servants brought out a series of peaked caps, with the priest bestowing each individual with one, the symbol of the inquisitors clearly visible. The inquisitors solemnly received it, with one even bearing a grim expression as though he were about to be sent to the gallows.

Contrary to the others, Kitana received the cap excitedly, a fire lighting up in her eyes as she bowed in respect. The old priest chuckled before placing his hand on Kitana's shoulder. "Keep that enthusiasm strong and steadfast. You'll need it to face down the evil lurking in the city."

"Yes, Bishop." Kitana bowed even lower.

Soon, the ceremony was over, and Kitana was already ordered to head toward another room to meet the department that she would be in charge of. Each pair of inquisitors was to oversee the assistance of a different sector so as not to clash with each other. They were not working alone—they would be reporting to the overseeing bishops of each sector and working with local enforcers.

The inquisitors talked among themselves as they walked. "I sure hope I get assigned to the Central Sector. If I get sent to the West, I'll die."

"Why did the Sanctum even assign me here? This has got to be the worst place to be stationed right after graduation!"

While the inquisitors lamented the results, they barely noticed Kitana's absence. Instead of following them, she had headed to a secluded area, grinning as she placed the cap snuggly on her head. She then glanced around, making sure no one was near. As she hunkered down, she whispered to herself, "Statistics."

Chapter 16

Corruption

The arctech enforcer wagon rumbled as it crossed rugged and poorly maintained cobblestone streets, a far cry from the pristine capital of the Yual Dominion where Kitana had lived during her training. Her inquisitor partner found amusement in her uneasiness as he puffed a Euria pipe.

The blue smoke drifted across his gray beard, with each breath relaxing his tired wrinkles that seemed to mark every inch of his face.

"First time out of Tryas?" the old inquisitor joked as he stuffed more Euria Seed Powder into his pipe.

"I'm afraid so," Kitana grumbled in reply, glancing through the back of the covered wagon. A grimy street trailed behind, with squatters half-drunk on the side of the road.

The pavement was half-covered in piss, vomit, or some other liquid. Gangs of young teenagers roamed the streets, harassing others, while dejected factory workers languished in piles of trash, blacked out from overdoses of various black market concoctions.

It was vastly different from the prim and proper feeling of the Central Sector. Here in the south, the fumes of the factories ballooned high above, while the dense streets were full of travelers, traders, mercenaries, and exiles from not just the Yual Dominion but other nations past the border as well. It was a pure melting pot of cultures, people, and the lowest of scum.

"Statistics," Kitana muttered to herself, her eyes darting around at seemingly nothing. *So, I'm still level 1. I guess Mother was right about having to kill people to level up.* She peeked back at the streets and suppressed a smirk. She could see plenty of targets just asking to be *accidentally* killed.

She caught her partner staring at her, and she calmed herself down. *Better to play a zealous, naïve girl for now to stave off any suspicion. The more naïve I make myself, the better.*

Just as the wagon passed yet another thug fight, Kitana stood up to stop the driver. The old inquisitor stood up to stop her, sitting her back down with a stern look. "Calm down, girl. Do you think you can take on all ten of them? Wait till we get to the office."

Visibly fuming, she sat back down on her seat, glaring at her partner. His face showed no signs of anger or righteous fury. "What kind of inquisitor ignores crimes occurring against the Sanctum of Yual in front of their very eyes?" Kitana kept up the act.

"The practical kind." He sighed. "I've seen plenty of people like you get killed instantly because they had no tact. Want to survive long enough to make a difference? Play it cool."

"How the hell did you become an inquisitor?"

"Because I do my job. No more, no less."

"Isn't it your job to punish crimes?"

"Oh, dear. This is what they get when they send such a fresh girl straight from Tryas. Listen, stay behind me and let me do most of the talking when we're at the office, all right?" The old man continued to puff his smoke.

Kitana internally celebrated. *Good. Saves me the scrutiny.*

The wagon soon stopped in front of a chapel.

"We're here, esteemed inquisitors. Welcome to the Magda."

The Magda was the South Sector's enforcer headquarters—a block of buildings centered around the main chapel, providing the logistics and support necessary to each of its branches situated in each district.

Thousands of cases and reports were handled here, as well as equipment procurement.

Kitana and her partner hopped out the back of the wagon, following their driver. They were led not into the chapel but into a side office building. Floors upon floors of administrative clerks handled requests for arcite ore or fuel, wagon repairs, and arctech equipment. Arctech phone lines rang non-stop at the station while stressed interns ran about with stacks of paper. The printing press shuddered violently, copies of case evidence and documentation churning out in a never-ending stream.

The two inquisitors walking through the office drew many eyes and whispers from the other enforcers, their white uniforms and decorative lapels sticking out like a sore thumb. Everyone they passed bowed to them, with the male inquisitor simply smiling and waving them off.

Soon they reached their destination—the bishop's office.

It was a grand room with a ceiling two stories high. Bookshelves lined the walls as the light from the sunset shone through the stained glass windows, filled with depictions from the Sanctum of Yual.

"Ah, Mason. Thank Yual that they posted you here instead of that oaf Fredrinn." The bishop smiled as she got out of her chair. Kitana noted her scarred hands as they approached the table, which was filled with piles of papers requesting her approval.

Mason chuckled as he came to a stop in front of the table, giving a half-hearted mock salute. "Inquisitor Mason and Inquisitor Kitana, at your service, Bishop Vernette."

"This young? Are they sure about this? I would have thought the posh ones would have all remained in Tryas, or maybe been sent to a coastal city in the north," Vernette commented as she examined Kitana from head to toe.

"Or maybe someone above has other plans for her. Who knows," Mason replied with a half-shrug. He plopped down on the sofa to their side and retrieved his Euria pipe. "So, what's the deal?"

"I think it's better if I let Baron Cain do the talking. He'll be here any minute. Would you like a drink, Kitana?" Vernette sat back in her chair, smiling gently.

"What deal are we talking about here? Are we not here to clean up the city?" Kitana ignored the offer, still playing the naïve, zealous girl. She also had to put up such an act in front of the bishop.

Vernette simply shot a fierce glare at Mason, who laughed in response. "Girl, as I said, let me do most of the talking here."

"My name isn't *girl,* it's—"

Before Kitana could finish, the doors to the office swung open, with Baron Cain walking in with two knights. The baron was decked from head to toe in luxury—a posh velvet cap, a well-pressed suit adorned with jewels and initials on the cuffs, and a handkerchief sticking out of his breast pocket, nicely folded and marked with the insignia of the Yual Dominion. The knights were equally domineering, clad in arctech armor with engravings all over the painted metal.

"Ah, my requested inquisitors have finally arrived." Cain smiled with open arms as he did not bow or salute any of them. He strutted across the room, and with a loud plop, he sat comfortably on the sofa next to Mason. The bishop and the two inquisitors immediately stood up and bowed with respect.

The nobility was far higher than those in the religious order, so even Bishop Vernette had to bow. Someone had to pay the budget.

"Hmm... You seem familiar," Cain remarked as he took a closer look at Mason.

"Yes, sir. I've worked here with your father on a different operation in this city a decade or so ago. Inquisitor Mason at your service. Though I won't claim to know the intricacy of the underground any longer," Mason said respectfully.

"Ah! Then you're the best man for the job. The nature of this operation is the same as before, and I'm sure you'll meet a lot of old faces. I have a party to attend in an hour, so let's get right to it. You two, bring out the map."

The knights walked into the center of the office, unrolling a map of the city that had already been marked with red lines and red stars indicating points of interest. "Unlike other sectors in Raktor, the south is relatively stable. However, it is this stability that is hurting my finances. I take it you understand, Mason?" Baron Cain raised his eyebrows, taking note of Mason's expression.

"Of course. You want us to rough up the current status quo. Keep them on their toes. Knock the gangs down a peg."

"Exactly. But not too much, lest they start to move their ratholes around." The baron held a wide grin on his face before his expression became even more solemn.

So, beat up the gangs a little to shake some money from their pockets. A protection racket, but run by the baron. Intriguing. Kitana listened intently.

"There's another reason I've asked you all to come here. There have been spies smuggling weapons out of our military factories and bases that are contracted to produce new types of guns and various classified arctech equipment. We lost a shipment a month ago, and I'm sure Bishop Vernette here recalls how that went."

"Poorly. We didn't find a single trace of it. Perhaps you can consider increasing the budget—twenty enforcers to a district of tens of thousands is hardly enough," Bishop Vernette shot back.

"You can't get military equipment out without having an insider," Mason remarked. "If we don't have access to the military personnel themselves, it would be difficult to clamp down on them."

"That's for the military to solve, not us. We don't have the legal authority to do so anyway. However, it is clear that another organization within the South Sector is helping the insider, and I want to know who. If it's that slimy Sebastian, I want to know immediately."

"Sebastian is still around? Interesting." Mason took a closer look at the map on the floor, counting the number of red stars marked. "That's...

That's a lot of factories. Do we even have enough enforcers to cover them?"

"You don't. I'm not planning to give you any more money until you prove your worth. Get the gangs to pay me, and maybe we can talk about increasing the budget."

"Any leads?" Mason asked.

"None as of now," Bishop Vernette replied in place of the baron. "But there are mild suspicions that it is the work of a foreign nation trying to steal our military technology. Or it could be neighboring Kregol and Perial trying to get the upper hand on us."

"Those damn backwater counties are always jealous of Raktor. I have a good mind to petition the duke for a tribunal against them," Baron Cain scoffed. "Regardless of who it is, under no circumstances can the technology be leaked any more, especially if it's being sold to the civilian population. That last shipment was the final straw. Other barons have already increased checkpoints and security at the exits and entrances of the city."

"I don't understand. We're here to protect some random factories instead of cleaning up the city?" Kitana interrupted the baron, her naïve, zealous act on full display. "From what I've seen on my way here, this entire sector is a lawless place! If you knew about it, you would have raised the budget immediately."

Cain was taken aback before an incredulous expression took over his face as he glanced between Mason and Vernette, who simply shook their heads in response.

"What? Why the fuck has everyone been hiding stuff from me ever since I got here?" Kitana challenged the three of them.

"Mason, could you please do the honors?" Cain gestured with his hands.

"Yes, sir." Mason bowed, sternly walking up to Kitana.

"Wha—" Mason's fist connected with Kitana's face, the sound of her cheekbone cracking from the blunt force resounding in the silent room.

Before she could stumble backward, Mason grabbed her by the uniform's collar and kicked the back of her knees, forcing her to kneel in front of the baron.

Kitana groaned in pain as she held her broken nose, her mind spinning as blood trickled down through the seams between her fingers, staining the carpet. "What's her name?" Cain asked Vernette.

"It's Kitana, sir. I'm afraid she's fresh from Tryas."

"Fresh from Tryas... Well then." Cain got up, patting his suit down before standing in front of her. "One rule to learn during your short, pitiful life here: don't you ever fucking talk back to me. I pay the bills around here, so I'm the law. Got it? As for the rest of you, I expect to see results." Cain spat on her head before leaving with the two knights.

The moment he left, Mason immediately took out a Health Potion and stuffed it in Kitana's mouth, forcing her to drink it. The green aura slowly mended her face, but the blood stains remained.

"Girl, I already told you to leave the talking to me. What were you thinking, shouting like that?" Mason sighed as he let Kitana rest on the floor.

"Mason," the bishop started. "If she doesn't change, she's quickly going to die here. You know someone above is counting on that."

Kitana was still conscious, but delirious. "Who? Who is going to kill me?"

"Don't you know why some fresh graduating inquisitors are sent to Raktor?" Mason asked, offering a hand to help her up. "It's usually because of three things. One, you're too talkative. Two, you're too zealous. Three, you're too naïve. And as far as I can tell, you're all three."

Might be true for the other nine, but they don't know I'm the only one who volunteered myself because it's where the most action happens... legally.

Kitana grumbled as she stood upright, slapping away the hand offered by Mason. "You're telling me they trained me to be an inquisitor so I can look the other way? I still don't understand what the fuck is the purpose of us coming here!"

Mason suddenly pulled out an arctech pistol, aiming it right at Kitana. Her training instinctively kicked in, with her trying to draw her pistol as well. However, her pistol was missing.

"Recognize this?" Mason motioned with his head to the pistol, which was clearly nicked from her.

"The truth is you're a young, naïve, half-baked inquisitor who was sent here to die. Do you know why they don't have to assassinate you? Because based on your current attitude, you would have died in less than a day on the streets of Raktor. You can't even defend yourself or keep your pistol secured—what hope do you have against the gangs?" Mason berated her. "If I kill you right now, it would be a mercy."

The sound of the arctech pistol's safety being clicked frightened Kitana; her heart pounded as she stared at the barrel aimed at her forehead. Mason's hand suddenly jerked, causing her to flinch instinctively. Opening her eyes slowly, she saw that Mason had tossed the pistol on the floor instead.

"Your safety was off," Mason remarked as he sat back down on the sofa. "Look. I will do everything in my power to keep you alive for the duration of this operation. Once this is over, you can return to your zealous, holier-than-thou solo crusade and kill yourself for all I care. At least it'll be off my record. Follow me, and I'll train you to survive. Do we have a deal?"

Kitana nodded. "What are we going to do about protecting the factories? We don't have enough bodies to cover all of them."

"I heard there are a few organizations around this sector that specialize in protection; let's knock down some doors tomorrow with a bit of lethal force, maybe talk with Sebastian. For now, get some rest."

The two of them were shown to their quarters, a luxurious studio apartment. Kitana checked the room before closing the curtains, ensuring no one was spying on her.

She nearly couldn't stop grinning as she checked her statistics again. *I was right to choose Raktor—I'm going to surpass my siblings within a year. With this much EXP running around the streets, who can stop me now?*

Chapter 17

Seductive Serpent

A few days after...

Damian settled into the chair gingerly, reveling in the soft, smooth texture of the velvet. "Look at me, Keith! I'm the king now. King of the District!"

"You'd better get out of that chair before Kyle comes back." Keith sighed as he continued poring over financial reports and inventory lists.

"What? Can't the underboss relax a little? I've been in this gang for so many years—I think my back deserves a bit of velvet."

"We're not out of the woods yet. We still owe a debt to the Crimson Swords—they are coming to collect the interest soon. If you really were the underboss, you'd get off your ass and check for opportunities!" Keith shot back, obviously stressed.

"Relax. As long as Kyle is at the helm, we'll be fine." Damian's faith in Kyle was obviously at an all-time high due to the success against the Red Lions. At the start, he was simply watching and not fully committed as of yet. Being the underboss of a small gang was significant to him, but not as much as one would expect when the gang was only thirty members strong. But being the underboss of a gang that had taken down the Left Paw of the Red Lion? That was different.

"I'm flattered by the belief placed in me. Nonetheless, I believe that is my chair."

Damian shot right out of the chair, quickly stepping out of the way as Kyle walked in. Keith also stood up, but Kyle waved at them to stand down. "No time for decorum. We have issues to discuss. We have yet to nail down exactly how to expand our operations. Let's focus on that."

Each of them took a seat, with Damian and Keith sitting opposite Kyle around the office table.

"As of now, we only have two businesses under our wing—a pub and a brothel. Which—"

"You mean the Lusty Arcian?" Keith interjected.

"Yes." Kyle could have sworn they had an obsession with saying the name but chose to ignore it. "Which is far from enough to generate the profits necessary to pay off the Crimson Swords. We have less than three months to clear the debts, and due to the Alchemists' Guild's restrictions, our potion contracts are severely limited."

Kyle didn't really see a way around the restrictions. Sure, he could ignore the ban, but only if he had enough power and connections. Defeating a subset of the Red Lions was far from becoming dominant enough to ignore such rules, so until then, he would have to play ball with Haui.

"We can look for other avenues," Damian pointed out. "Now that we have a reputation, we can begin to spread our influence throughout the district. Perhaps even begin some additional protection rackets as well."

"No protection rackets for now. Such an extortive method would only serve to turn the current populace against us. We must position the Seven Snakes as a force for good overall, something integral to the survival of the district. The moment the locals perceive that there are more cons to having us around than benefits, that is the moment we fall." Kyle elaborated. *Perhaps that is why I fell as well in my last life.*

Damian scratched his head, not sure of what else to suggest. Protection rackets had been his main job under Ulon and their primary source of income, so he was lost on what to do next.

"What we need to do is a bit of market research," Kyle continued. "The potions are one good example of us being able to enter the market, but it is limited and hampered by a strong guild. That very limitation allows the price to be far higher than its cost, so products like that are desirable."

Keith caught on quickly. "So basically anything that is prohibited under the Sanctum of Yual, correct?"

"Exactly. Any leads?" Kyle deferred to Damian and Keith, who were obviously more knowledgeable about the local area.

Keith offered another suggestion. "How about guns? We could try to break into the weapons market."

"I recently heard about two inquisitors arriving in the sector. Rumor is they're here about guns, though I don't have any details." Damian said, rejecting Keith's suggestion. He always had his ear close to the ground, having many connections with the locals due to his long years in the gang, so he was always being told all sorts of rumors.

"Then it's best not to enter the gun market until we know exactly what is happening." Kyle didn't want to poke the hornet's nest, not right after the visit from Sebastian. "We need something far more lowkey, something that everyone is doing, so that no one will bat an eye at the Seven Snakes joining in."

"Smuggling is an option. Human trafficking pays fairly well with the slave trade being ubiquitous in Raktor. Even small gangs here do it."

"Out of the question—that would also piss off the locals, and we don't have the manpower to operate in other districts either," Kyle said. "Operating there would also piss off the gangs in charge. Far too dangerous. However, you mentioned the small thug groups here. How many of them are there?"

"Well, it can be assumed that every block has about one to two. Our district has about fifty-four blocks populated, with another twenty abandoned, now occupied by squatters and others. Many small groups flock here because of the lack of enforcement, primarily from us rather than the enforcers," Keith replied.

Such a high ratio of gangs would be unheard of in the other districts. Kyle sighed at their abysmal lack of influence, contemplating his next step. He had initially improved the performance of the brothel thanks to the addictive stamina potions, so the logical next step would be to improve the performance of the pub.

"Keith, any financial report on the pub?"

"Yes, sir, but the report doesn't really make much sense. Some months, the pub reports a one-to-one ratio of revenue and operating cost."

"Down to the last rakel?"

Keith nodded, his response setting off alarm bells in Kyle's head. *Someone has falsified the accounts. Even such a business should experience seasonal changes due to events and holidays.* Kyle assumed it was Ulon, but he couldn't rule out the possibility that the pub's manager was also involved.

"Let's check the pub that we own before making our next move."

"You mean the Seductive Serpent?"

"Who the hell is coming up with these names?"

* * *

Unlike the brothel, which was run by the competent Slavin, the pub was an absolute disgrace, a place fitting of the name "watering hole." The décor was shabby, the lighting dim and flickering, and the entire place stank to high Sanctum of Yual. Empty cups were barely cleaned, with some being left on tables for weeks. Dried residue of piss and vomit lined the crevices between shoddy wooden planks, and Kyle found it hard to find a piece of wooden furniture that did not have some sort of large crack along its length.

Near the rear of the pub were three thick, long ropes hung from corner to corner in a drooping curve, upon which a few Seven Snakes members were sleeping.

"Do our members not have beds?" Kyle asked Damian as he noticed Niko dangling on the coarse rope and snoring away peacefully while a dribble of vomit seeped from his mouth, piling up in the belly button of another blackout drunk below him.

"They do, but many prefer this idea of hanging over a rope." Damian shrugged before walking up to what could be barely described as a bartender and slapping him awake.

"I... uh... Who... What?" The bartender groaned as he rubbed his cheek gently... and fell off the rope onto the floor in shambles. Seeing the man struggling to get up, Kyle's impression of him dropped significantly. *I can't have my bartenders getting drunk themselves.*

"Keith, check the finances. Where's the manager?"

"Uhh, sir? This is the manager." Damian pointed to the obviously drunk bartender, who was now staggering all over the place, banging his head on the wall and collapsing.

"That's not good." Kyle's gaze slowly turned dark, a simmering rage building within him at the sheer incompetence. Compared to the Lusty Arcian, this pub was a hellhole.

"Sir. There's no financial record kept here. Everything seems to be written in this notebook." Keith handed over a stained notebook filled to the brim with the tabs of each customer. Kyle flipped through the book quickly, noticing almost nine-tenths of the customers were Seven Snakes members, causing his heart to sink.

Furthermore, none of the Seven Snakes members had actually paid their tabs. The operational cost seemed to have been entirely fueled by the loan taken out from the Crimson Swords. *This isn't even skimming off the top in some self-interested scam—it's a complete self-scam!*

Kyle wanted to tear the entire place apart. "There's nothing seductive about this place at all! Why is it called the Seductive Serpent?!"

"It used to be quite the spot, back in its heyday," Damian replied. "Sir." He added quickly as Kyle threw him a furious glare.

"Then for our members to continue drinking here, the alcohol must be somewhat passable." Kyle took a seat on one of the creaky barstools, motioning to Damian to serve a mug. Damian immediately knew what to do, heading back into the storehouse to crack open a keg. "You seem to know your way around the bar."

"I used to bartend here before joining the Seven Snakes."

As the beer sloshed out of the keg and into the mug, a rancid smell filled the room, causing even the usually stoic Kyle to cringe in disgust.

"I think the beer is fine; been drinking it for three years, you know? Better than the swill we get at the squatters area," Damian remarked, handing the mug over to Kyle. "Don't judge a beer by its, err... smell. Or taste. And color."

Then what do I judge it by? The bubbles?! Kyle grimaced, slowly sipping a mouthful and drinking it, his eyes closed. "Any other types?"

"We got ale as well." Damian repeated the process, with Kyle taking yet another swig. The gang leader sat in silence, his eyes still closed in what seemed to be deep contemplation. Damian watched expectantly as Kyle didn't show any further disgusted reactions, buoying his hopes of validation.

Instead, the leader opened his eyes and stared at Damian before letting out a deep sigh, his anger seemingly lost. "Remind me not to trust your taste buds ever again." He didn't really blame Damian for it, seeing as Damian would have never tasted better alcohol in the first place. Kyle was simply far too used to hyper-controlled alcohol, brewed in microgravity to maximize yeast fermentation, and its replicable taste.

"Hey, come on! You might be the boss, but I won't have my taste insulted. Plenty of other folks in the district love this!" Damian took a stance. As strong as his belief in Kyle was, there were just some things he wouldn't budge on.

"Then why are these 'plenty of other folks' not filling this pub?"

"Well, we pretty much serve the same thing as other pubs."

"Really? Show me."

Without warning, an impromptu pub crawl began, with Kyle sampling various nearby pubs run by locals. The other customers gave them a wide berth, recognizing their recent victory against the Red Lions. Even though Damian was in the midst of trying to prove a point to Kyle, he relished in the influence and reputation that he had garnered for himself.

Keith, too, was amazed at the attention and respect that they were receiving. He was never one to stand in the spotlight, but for the young man craving validation, the attention soothed his ego in just the right way, his demeanor far more upright than it had been before.

On the fifth pub, Kyle knew he had lost the argument with Damian. Every pub indeed had a similar-tasting beer and ale to what the Seductive Serpent served. However, it was a good thing. *This means I have caught a potential market.*

Just as Kyle was about to conclude the pub crawl, the bartender of the fifth pub stopped him for a moment, offering a new drink on the house. "Got a new supply coming in recently. It's leagues better than the beer. Here, give it a try."

Kyle glanced at the drink, noticing it was a distilled hard liquor. "Moonshine? You made this yourself?"

"No, I've been getting it from someone else. Bunch of ragtags in the abandoned blocks."

"What's their name?"

"Oh, I wouldn't know much about it..." The bartender shrugged, his palm faced upward in an obvious gesture, prompting Kyle to retrieve a few dozen rakels, placing them on the counter. With a swift motion, the bartender grabbed the coins and slid them into his pocket before leaning over and whispering, "From what I know, they ain't a part of any gang, you know? They do their own thing. I mean everything—brewing, supply, and even scouting. Apparently, the leader is an expert in alcohol brewing. Heard he even had done proper university research on it!"

"Any ideas where they are?"

"I didn't ask, but I'm sure you'll find them around the area. Considering you haven't encountered them yet, I'll say the crew is top-notch too. Their scout is really good at observing and planning routes. I've never heard of them being accosted by an enforcer either."

Intrigued, Kyle tipped the bartender again to learn more information. As soon as he got everything he needed, he patted Damian and Keith on the back, prompting them to take their leave.

"Time to go. We got some moonshiners to catch."

Chapter 18

Moonshine

A week later...

In a derelict warehouse, a lone man was fiddling with a basic distillation apparatus, adjusting the angle of the condensation arm running into another doubler barrel. His hair was ragged, giving him a disheveled look, and his clothes were unkempt. However, his demeanor showed some semblance of noble mannerism, with a residual tinge of upper-class behavior in his actions.

A loud bang came from one of the side entrances, startling him. With a frown, he went over to see who it was. "Fucking hell, Monica, you gave me a scare. Maybe a simple knock would have sufficed."

"Shut up, idiot. I ain't got no extra hands carrying these sacks." A burly lady had kicked open a small door with her right leg, her hands occupied as she hefted two large sacks of grains and sugar, sweat dripping down her white tank top.

With a loud grunt, Monica dropped them next to a mixing container. "Where's Adrian and the rest? You the only one left in here?"

"Yeah. The rest went out to make sure there were no Seven Snakes slithering around. They've been getting real nosy with this district ever since they lost to the Red Lions."

"Sounds about right." Monica grabbed a well-worn, concrete-crusted bucket and used it as a stool. "So, is Eric still the best distiller around here?" She motioned toward him with a mocking smile.

"It's *Eric Dicar,* and yes, he should be the best in the district. Unless someone else somehow got the freshest mountain water from the Culdao Peaks nearby, we'll monopolize the market over time." Eric smirked.

"Well, cook it slow. We ain't rushing for time. If we make too much of a bang, Kyle might show up."

"Bah! It's been two weeks since he was last seen negotiating with the Red Lions. Probably cooped up and huffing away at Euria Seeds with the way he's been buying them off the market. His whole base is probably one big smoke cloud by now."

Monica chuckled and stood up. She ripped the sacks open and poured them into a container, then ground them into a mash.

Eric continued to complain on the side. "Honestly, we should have gotten a much bigger pot. Our production scale is miserable. It's barely ten gallons per batch at this rate."

"Gotta stay portable. We don't want to be pinned by the Seven Snakes or any other gang. If this district gets too hot, we shift. We agreed on this earlier," Monica warned.

Eric didn't reply, obviously unsatisfied, as he continued to tailor the temperature of the arcia stove before firing it up. Instead of asking Monica to dump the mash into the pot, they both waited, standing near the walls and peeking out of the barricaded windows of the warehouse.

"They're taking far too long. Something's up," Monica mumbled after a few more minutes passed. She was about to ask Eric to pack it up when Adrian ran into the warehouse hastily.

"Fuck. The Seven Snakes are prowling nearby. If they so much as catch a whiff of the moonshine, we'll be in trouble! I think they've been asking around for us!" Adrian gasped for air as he tried to catch his breath. "I had the other two walk in separate directions to pull off their trails, so we got maybe ten or fifteen minutes to move."

"All right, just like we practiced." Monica and Eric weren't bothered at all. They had already moved through the various districts of the South

Sector multiple times, exploiting the territorial gaps and derelict buildings in the vicinity. It wasn't the first time they were hunted by the ruling gangs who obviously would not tolerate others subverting the alcohol production and smuggling business.

They packed up the equipment nicely, placing the pots and condensation arms into neat cardboard boxes before loading them up onto separate trolleys.

"Split up. We'll meet at Point 23, got it?"

They had already premarked a series of locations in the vicinity where the operations could be performed. Even if squatters had moved in, simple intimidation or negotiations would usually suffice—a routine procedure.

Eric donned a felt cap with a flat top and put on a factory worker's garments, making it seem like he was pushing basic supplies and scrap metal around. He slowly pushed the trolley through the streets on the side of the pavement, keeping his head down.

The streets were crowded and filled with business. Construction and food supply wagons rattled by while people loitered on the sides of the streets. Schoolboys played punk and played football in the alleyways while buskers strummed a sad song for rakels no one could afford to give.

Eric blended in nicely, acting like he was pushing supplies to another factory. He saw three Seven Snakes gang members head in the opposite direction, seemingly attempting to corner off their last known location. *Hah, dumbasses.*

The relocation went off without a hitch, with Eric reaching the predetermined meeting point quickly. It was a run-down office-style building with large factory floors.

Eric pushed open the barricaded doors, hearing a loud scrambling inside and some whimpering. *I would say "fucking squatters," but I'm not any different now, am I?*

The first floor was an obvious slum, with makeshift barrel heaters blackened from the use of flammable materials. He saw five squatters in separate locations, keeping a wide berth from one another as they huddled up in as many clothes as they could, the stink unbearable from the pile of clearly unwashed linen stained with puke.

"All right, fellas, we'll be here for a few days. In exchange, we'll get you some moonshine, how about that, hmm? Maybe you guys can do a few deliveries for us too," Eric asked from outside, peeking his head through the door. His voice echoed and wafted through the empty floor, easily reaching the ears of the squatters.

The squatters nodded. It was a common occurrence in the city of Raktor, and they wouldn't say no to some free moonshine and extra cash.

"Good." Eric didn't enter with the trolley yet. Who knew if the squatters would suddenly decide to turn on him and take his equipment? *Better wait for Monica and the others.*

Soon, Monica and Adrian arrived, both safe. "Anyone follow you?" Eric looked behind them, trying to spot anything suspicious.

"No, they were all checking out the last location, so we're safe. I counted more than eight of them moving there. I really miss the days of Ulon. We could go unharmed for weeks." Adrian sighed.

"Got a few squatters in there. We've reached a temporary agreement for a bit of swill and some movement."

"Right. Let's get the stuff in before we're spotted."

The three of them shifted the equipment and set it up just like before. Adrian scoped out the area, using a crowbar to smack one of the old, rusty doors to ensure they had a secondary exit in case of a raid.

Monica huffed as she lugged the heavy equipment back into place. "Shouldn't have put the mash in first..." she said, stumbling as she shifted it across from the trolley.

"We should be good for a few days, so we can start right now. Gotta deliver some before night." Monica dumped the mash into the pot, and Eric started the fire. "Now we just have to wait."

The three of them took a rest, rotating watch duty as they sat and lay on the floor. Eric took out a logbook, noting down the specific temperature, the type of condensation arm he used, and so on. It was important to note as it helped him improve his method of manufacturing. It was his livelihood, after all.

"'Scuse me, good sir." One of the squatters found the courage to talk to Eric after a good hour, while Monica and Adrian stared at the approaching squatter warily. "If you don't mind me asking, what does this setup do?"

Eric's eyes lit up brilliantly, like never before. With a slight cough, he stood up to his full bearing, assuming the gait of a university professor of sorts. "Glad you asked! This setup distills liquor in a deceivingly simple method, using pure Cornia, malt, and sugar. Mixing them and heating them allows us to distill vapor, which is concentrated through the doubler and subsequently through the worm."

Monica rolled her eyes. "There he goes again. He just can't help explaining this shit to everybody."

"Ah, just let him have it. It's not every day that he gets to act like what he used to be." Adrian shrugged.

The other four squatters were enamored by the lecture provided. The questions asked were exceedingly childish and obviously uneducated, but Eric was more than happy to answer them.

"Sir Dicar, this is amazing!" One of the squatters stood next to Eric, staring at the setup with amazement. "With such a simple setup, we're able to be free of the Sanctum of Yual's bans. You could produce for the entire district!"

"Indeed. I strongly disagree with the alcohol prohibition. A mature man should be allowed to drink whatever he so desires. Such a ban implies a common lack of trust from the authorities, who are better than... Wait a minute... How did you know my surname?"

In a blink, the squatter next to him grappled Eric, pinning him to the ground, while the other four squatters, who had gradually gotten closer to Monica and Adrian, lunged toward them.

The two barely stood a chance against the surprise attack, having been caught completely off-guard. "What the?!" Monica struggled, but the squatter on top of her had expertly locked her limbs down in a martial art–style grapple. He took out an arctech radio, speaking fast. "Damian here, we've got them. Move in now."

Eric instantly recognized the name, dumbfounded. *The vice-leader of the Seven Snakes?! They fucking disguised themselves as squatters?!* He had never seen a gang go to such extremes to catch them in his many years of being a moonshiner. "Is this even a gang anymore? You're more like undercover enforcers!"

Damian didn't reply. Soon, the eight Seven Snakes members entered, joining the disguised squatters and capturing the moonshiners. They hauled them and the equipment back to the Seven Snakes' base, tossing them into the office.

As Eric struggled to get onto his knees with his arms bound, he already knew that there were two more captured in the office. They were the other two from his operations, having been caught long before they even relocated.

The five of them were about to start blaming one another on who snitched or was caught first, but the office door swung open with Kyle and Keith entering.

Kyle strode up to the office desk, his demeanor fierce. A domineering presence washed over the five of them, causing Eric to gulp internally. This was not his first time being caught, but it was an eye-opening experience. Somehow Kyle seemed to exude this sort of confidence and leadership that Eric had never seen before. The well-ironed formal suit Kyle wore further emphasized it as he leaned against the front desk, standing in front of the five groveling five members.

"Prepare a message to Wrent thanking him for his detailed information." Kyle motioned to Keith, who bowed and sat at a new desk prepared just for him.

"Professor Dicar, what a pleasure to finally meet you. I've heard many rumors from your customers, mostly about your incredible skills and your time at the university." Kyle looked down.

"If you truly find it a pleasure, perhaps you should consider my level of comfort being bound like this," Eric scoffed as he lay like a worm on the floor, unable to lift himself.

"My apologies. You two, untie him and have him sit in the guest chair."

Eric gingerly rubbed his wrists as the rope was undone before he sat and leaned back into the luxurious velvet chair. "Interesting that you put that much effort into capturing me and my crew. Getting bored of the potion business after a mere month and a half since becoming the leader?"

"When building an empire, it is better to diversify and hedge one's bet. Also, pubs hardly run on potions alone."

"Ah, entering the slavery business, I see."

"I don't intend to enslave you, Professor Dicar. Instead, I have an offer."

"I doubt you have anything to offer that can weigh against my freedom," Eric spat. He was well aware of how gangs wanted to use him to make their moonshine. *Brutes and grunts playing at nobility, ignorant of the true essence of brewing alcohol.*

Kyle motioned for the two guards to grab Eric off the velvet chair.

"Please, follow me. I guarantee you will be interested."

Chapter 19

New Ventures

With the other moonshiners hauled off to holding cells, Eric was manhandled to another room. "Let go of me! I can walk by myself, thank you very much." He tried to shake off the guards' grips.

Kyle nodded his head as a signal, and the two guards let go of Eric. They walked through the common area, Eric taking note of the associates training hard against dummy figures or sparring with each other. Tons of Stamina Potions were stacked in wooden crates along the side, causing Eric's mouth to fall agape in astonishment.

"I did not expect your production scale to be so huge." Eric was astonished, estimating close to a thousand potions were stacked there alone, accumulated over the weeks. "I was under the impression that you were only supplying less than fifty per day or so."

Kyle didn't reply, still walking toward an unmarked door. They entered a separate room, and this time Eric's jaw completely collapsed. Forgetting his predicament as a captured moonshiner, he ran forward, ogling at the unique distillation apparatuses that were far more advanced than anything he had ever seen, even at the university.

"I... I've never seen anything like this! Where did you get it from?" Eric was like an excited fanboy, jumping up and down as he examined the intricate details of the setup.

Kyle had implemented a factory-style distillation process, something he reverse-engineered from his memories. *Alcohol in the Galactic Era was produced much more efficiently, but at least the basic principles remained the same.*

Eric suddenly let out a loud gasp. "This condenser is extremely unique! What is the jagged surface on the exterior of the condensation arm? This enchantment on the barrel—what does it do? Is it powered by arcia to give special effects?" He ran around a series of kegs, noticing they had unique enchantments on them as well that seemed to speed up the fermentation.

Kyle motioned for one of the guards to provide three samples in small cups. Eric was hesitant, knowing there was a chance it could be poison or some sort.

"Professor Dicar, if I wanted you dead, I would have had you killed there and then, making it look like an accident."

Eric finally relented and tried the first sample. It was a high-proof moonshine whiskey, free of any impurities, and smooth on the throat. "My God! It's even better than anything I have tasted!"

Moonshine Whiskey
A high-proof whiskey distilled with precision and factory-level quality. None of that rugged taste.
Temporary Stat Effect: -5 INT, +3 STR
Duration: Depends on the imbiber's race.

He quickly drank the next sample, savoring the bubbling sensation with a sweet aromatic taste. "This is wine, but not one made from the usual ingredients... Grain wine? The sparkling sensation is not unique, but the combination is."

Cherry Sparkling Sake
A sparkling rice wine made from polished grains. Smooth taste with a posh feeling.

Temporary Stat Effect: -5 INT, +3 STR
Duration: Depends on the imbiber's race.

Eric then tried the last one. "Another grain wine, but this time with a burning sensation, highly distilled. The addition of the lemon taste gives it a secondary kick. Amazing! Where are all these recipes coming from?! I've spent my life studying alcohol, but I have never come across any of these!"

Lemon-Flavored Soju
A mixture of grains fermented. Mixed with a dash of lemon. Great with beer or yogurt.
Temporary Stat Effect: -2 INT, +1 STR
Duration: Depends on the imbiber's race.

You'd probably lose your mind in the Galactic Era, then... "Do you want to know?" Kyle asked with a knowing expression.

Eric's excitement suddenly plummeted, the circumstances of his current plight coming back to him. "Cut to the chase. What do you want?"

"Work for me, and you'll have this entire room, where those recipes came from, and a brand-new pub business to run."

"And my crew?"

"They'll be part of the gang. I'm counting on you to convince them."

"What if I say no?"

"You already know what happens."

Eric weighed the benefits in his head. For years, he had been a professor researching new methods of alcohol production. He had been expelled for no reason due to the sudden and rapid ban on alcohol, forcing him onto the streets in order to make a living.

Too many gangs had tried to recruit him, even with the threat of force, but a simple bribe and a few drops of moonshine were always enough to get the guards to go against their bosses and break away from the gang. That was how he met his current crew, anyway.

However, Kyle had shown him a new path, a chance to regain his old life. The new recipes lured him tantalizingly, and he couldn't stop thinking about all the types of alcohol he could make with the setup in front of him. *Perhaps I can learn the recipes, then slowly get away as well.*

"You have a deal. Let me talk to them."

Eric was brought to the holding cell, where the other four moonshiners were still restrained. "Eric, you all right? Just agree to whatever they say; we'll break out soon enough." Adrian said, worried.

"Yes, I've accepted their deal. We will all be Seven Snakes members for now."

"Great, I'm starving." Monica's stomach rumbled loudly. This wasn't their first rodeo, having escaped a few gangs before. "We'll be out of here in no time."

* * *

The pub restoration was now underway, with Kyle estimating that it may take two weeks to get it up and running. He had already fired the former bartender, and any existing Seven Snakes members who had a tab running were forced to work extra hard to clean up the messes. It was not any fun cleaning up a place where their own vomit and piss had caked into the seams, but no one dared to go against Kyle any longer, not after his showing of force in multiple fights.

It would still take some time for the new gang members to be accommodated, but Kyle already saw an opportunity for expansion. However, he did not rush anything, instead building a solid, loyal power base and providing enough time for the integration of new members into the fold. It would be foolish to make any major moves or large recruitment campaigns where potential spies from both the enforcers and the Ardent Cretins would enter.

Damian soon returned from the induction of Eric Dicar's crew. "Sir, the induction is complete, though I get this feeling that they may look for every opportunity to break free."

"Keep a close eye on them. They are competent in their jobs, especially Adrian." Kyle had managed to outwit them, not through prediction but by covering all possible hideout locations. Damian, being planted among the squatters, was just one of many members—Kyle had mobilized twenty members, split up to attempt to form a net around them. *If I can entice Adrian to remain with us, it will be of great benefit to my gang.*

Kyle was also aware of the seemingly close ties that the crew had with one another, something unusual in criminal groups. Holding one of them in the Seven Snakes would then serve as an additional guarantee against a potential backstab or departure.

"We should begin to appoint vipers to provide a sense of responsibility in order to tie them down."

Damian nodded in agreement. "Just like the Red Lions' squad leaders. It would be good to have an inner circle of trusted, competent members." Kyle had already previously announced the position of viper, but no one had yet to fill that role. All the associates were still gunning for it.

"Only after vetting them for a month or so. Choose the most hardworking ones or those who are competent. For example, Eric Dicar, who will be the new bartender for the pub once it has been relaunched, assuming he sticks with us. And by the way, I'm thinking about changing the name."

"What?! How can you change a name like Seductive Serpent? It's a well-known name in the district!" Damian was shocked, his nostalgia for the pub screaming out.

"Well-known for being a hellhole," Kyle shot back, but he had to admit internally that he currently did not have a better name for it. He was never the best at naming things; his daughter in his former life used to always complain about it.

"What should we do about that woman?"

"Monica? She can handle logistics for the brothel and the pub for now. But do have her and Adrian help out in the free soup kitchen and at public cleanup events as well."

"Got it. Are we planning on selling the alcohol? I got a few contacts who might be willing to buy from us," Damian offered, knowing the alcohol recipes by Kyle were bound to be a hit with the locals, especially if sold at an affordable price.

"Not for now. We'll make it exclusive to the Seductive Serpent to draw in customers and turn them into loyal regulars," Kyle replied before stopping as he saw a wide, shit-eating grin on Damian's face. "What?"

"Nothing. Just glad you kept the name."

"Get out."

Kyle was soon left alone in the office, pondering over the next steps. There was no doubt the performance of the pub would be greatly improved now, but it remained to be seen whether it would be enough to pay off the Crimson Swords' debt.

The main two income streams were the potions contracts with other minor gangs and the Red Lions, as well as the Lusty Arcian. Kyle performed a quick calculation, noticing that they were still off target, unable to clear the debt within the time limit provided. *I can't just sit around and wait for the pub to be completed—I have to look for other options.*

It was already abundantly clear that the weapons and human trafficking markets were currently off-limits. Kyle had plans for a public soup kitchen and a regular cleanup event to integrate Seven Snakes into the local social fabric. By showcasing their worth and benefit, they could stave off any lingering hate accumulated by Ulon, as well as garner goodwill and potentially information from the homeless and squatters who would frequent the soup kitchen the most. *It will serve as a good recruitment zone as well.*

Suddenly landing on another idea, Kyle quickly called for Keith to come. "Keith, I need you to find potential casino locations, preferably ones we can strongarm or buy over in good condition to reduce the amount of construction work needed."

Keith nodded. Casinos were par for the norm among gangs in Raktor. "I'll work with Damian on it. He knows much better than I do how to properly cover up a casino."

"Good. Try to get it done at the same time as the pub."

Kyle felt restricted; his movements were watched from every corner. It seemed as though he had been locked into his own sandbox by Sebastian and the other slightly larger gangs. He currently did not have the power to break through the implicit blockade, so he needed to find more advantages if he wanted to avoid succumbing to the debt.

Forgoing payment of the debt would also leave a big target on his back. Kyle was sure he was not the strongest person in the city, so enticing hitmen and assassins to target him was not an ideal scenario. *Best case, we pay off the Crimson Swords, and it's a done deal.* The completion of the loan repayment would also further boost their reputation, improving their influence in the black market and allowing them to take out bigger loans.

Kyle's eyes wandered to the map of the city beyond its borders, where the forests and monster regions lay. *If I can't expand in the city, perhaps I can obtain benefits from beyond its walls. Out there, I would be less observed and tracked.*

He still had to determine what benefits he could obtain outside the city. *Come to think of it, I have never left the city since I came here. I should ask Damian and Keith.*

However, for today, he would need to make some personal preparations before leaving, such as boosting his knowledge of arcia and its uses. Kyle was well aware that arctech would be the key focal point of many battles to come—it would be wise to learn as much as he could over the next few weeks.

The technological level of the world he was in was haphazard, and unlike historical advancements, thanks to the existence of arcia. The past few days had him setting up the in-house brewery. In the night, he studied the tome left behind by Theorin in order to understand arctech better.

The book taught the basic engravings and how to combine them and overlay their effects. Kyle had already done a preliminary implementation of the fermentation of mash in the kegs, allowing him to implement a simple decay engraving, accelerating the fermentation process and subsequently the production of alcohol.

If he had his way, he could implement microgravity brewing fermentation processes from the Galactic Era here. However, such engravings that could manipulate the very laws of physics were naturally extremely rare.

Arcia is far too amazing. If discovered, such an exotic material would have the entire human quadrant scrambling for it. Kyle had yet to find evidence that he was even in the same universe or timeline as his original one, though he still did not believe that arcia was magic or fantasy.

It was more like electricity—radiation and oil—which the locals might also consider magical. *Anti-gravity, plasma weapons, and faster-than-light travel would be considered "magic" by the people here...*

The study of enchantments had yet to yield a title or a bonus of sorts from the reading. Kyle surmised that it was a lack of implementation—he had always been rewarded for repetitive action rather than learning.

He returned to his room, where there were more than two dozen ordinary metal pipes on a table, along with Riker's next to it. A single needle-like etcher hooked up to a portable arcia generator was placed as well, Kyle having bought it to practice.

Repetition is the key to success, after all. Kyle sat down and began etching away at the metal pipes, copying the engravings on Riker's. Right now, he only had a few pieces of arctech equipment, most of which were stolen from the Red Lions' members.

It would be good if he could customize his own armor set and weapons. He dearly missed his exosuit from his former life, which made him wonder if he could replicate it in the future. The overlaying of enchantments and engravings reminded him of how nanocircuit boards were made. An arcia-printed circuit board did not seem too far out of the question. *Something to keep in mind.*

The title was not as easy to reach as previous titles were, requiring multiple days of non-stop practice. As he reached his hundredth copied metal pipe, a title was finally awarded to him.

Title Obtained: Arcia Engraver (Basic)
Those scribbles look like they might blow up soon.
+5 INT, +3 DEX, +10% chance at improving quality of final arctech equipment.

Chapter 20

Beyond Raktor

A week later...

Damian ladled fresh soup into a bowl before handing it over to a disheveled young man. "There's bread to go with it. Go over to that man there." He pointed to Niko, who was busy serving an endless queue of homeless people desperate for free food.

"Thank you so much!" The man bowed respectfully and joined the queue. Damian gave a kind smile before serving the next person in line. The Seven Snakes had booked an area near the food market and spread word through the locals that they were offering free meals to those in need, no questions asked. There were obviously a few who feigned poverty just to save a few rakels, but it didn't matter. The cost of the soup kitchen was barely a dent in their finances, and its benefits far outweighed its cost.

Some of the nearby food stall owners complained about the surge in homeless people who smelled like rotten eggs, but the local people in general looked favorably on the initiative. Neither the enforcers nor the Sanctum of Yual hardly did anything like this; if they did, it would always lead to a conversion. Many of the homeless didn't want to be exploited or tangled up in some religious mess despite being citizens of the Yual Dominion, so they were more than appreciative of what the Seven Snakes were doing.

Monica and Adrian entered the soup kitchen with a few others, all of them panting as they held brooms and large buckets filled with trash picked up from the side of the street.

Damian nodded at their buckets approvingly. "Good work. Take a breather and head out to the next street when you're ready. We got to clean up the next three streets before nightfall."

"THREE?!" Monica was about to lose her mind, but Adrian hastily tried to calm her down. "We've been sweeping the entire day!"

"Better than wasting your life away making swill in random buildings, no?" Damian smirked. "You'll get used to it."

Monica seriously contemplated running away with her crew, but Eric was trapped inside the base, spending almost all his time in the new brewery. She had an inkling Eric didn't actually want to leave and began to weigh whether her freedom was worth ditching Eric.

"Psst, Adrian. You wanna try to escape later?"

"Escape?" Adrian pondered for a moment, the hesitation clear on his face.

"What? Don't tell me you like taking orders from these cunts."

"I don't, but to be honest, they are doing something good here." Adrian motioned toward the soup kitchen. "I used to be a squatter myself before you recruited me; you know that. What they have now is nothing short of amazing to me. And I really feel much better and at ease doing something upright here."

Monica scoffed. "They are doing this so they can collect information across the district through the squatters and scout potential recruits. You know this!"

"Doesn't change the fact that they are getting free meals. It don't matter to me what they do—at least they are alive and full."

While the two of them bickered, a Seven Snakes associate ran up to Damian. "Sir, Boss Kyle wants to meet you in his office right away."

Damian quickly handed everything off to another before returning to the base. As he entered Kyle's office, he saw that Keith and Kyle were already deep in discussion. As for the topic of their discussion...

"You want to venture out beyond the city?" Damian exclaimed in surprise. "But why now? We just secured our ownership of the district, and the pub is about to be finished!"

"What we have right now isn't enough. Even with the in-house brewery, potion contracts, and the new casino and pub on the way, it would be impossible to clear our massive debt on time. If we default on that debt, everything we own right now would be up for grabs by the Crimson Swords," Keith explained.

Damian sighed, crossing his arms as he looked at the map of the nearby regions around the city of Raktor. "So what can you possibly get outside the city that can benefit you? Everyone from the villages and towns came to the city to make money—moving back doesn't make any financial sense."

"That's not true." Kyle pointed to a few regions nearby. "Every resource and commodity within the city is harvested or collected from the outlying villages or monster regions. For example, Keith and I have been tracking the production of Yul's Tears, which we use for our Strength Potion. It's extremely inefficient and requires adventurers to forage for it in the mountains."

"If you manage to get a stable supply, undercutting the market will bring eyes to us again. Aren't we limiting ourselves to this district for now because of Sebastian's warning and the inquisitors?"

"Indeed, which is why we need to establish a shell company that will begin to supply the other sectors. We need a front to deflect attention while collecting the money. In short, raw material production should be industrialized, allowing us to reap the profit from economies of scale."

"But what material should we be targeting?" Damian tried to rack his head. There were so many materials that they could focus on, but which one would provide the most profit?

"Keith?" Kyle motioned with his hand.

"Yes, sir. The report you asked for on individual consumption that has a good potential for future restrictions is ready. While the sample size is limited to this district alone, consumption of Euria seeds for personal enjoyment is quite high. Nearly fifteen percent of the population smokes it right now. Food tops the chart, but the ingredients used are far too diverse to compete against Euria seeds."

Damian quickly raised an objection. "Wait, wait, wait. Shouldn't we be targeting prohibited stuff like we discussed previously? Maybe like the raw ingredients for alcohol or arcia itself? What about Yul's Tears? That's expensive."

"The objective of this expedition is not to spook any gang or enforcers. We don't have a clear picture of how the other gangs are getting their supply, so doing anything related is dangerous, especially since we're aiming to enter other sectors and districts." Kyle had clearly learned his lesson from moving too fast. He had assumed this world was a simple pushover, but it was far more intricate than he thought. It was not going to be that easy to climb the ranks.

"Yul's Tears directly affect the Alchemists' Guild, so doing anything related to that would make Haui's partnership and protection meaningless. I am now willing to consider legal ventures as a way to make money."

It was not rare for criminal gangs to operate legitimate businesses. It helped to both obfuscate and complicate investigations into how far the criminal network spread. Kyle also considered it a diversification of revenue beyond just illegal stuff.

"Okay, so Euria Seeds. There are a few plantations of the stuff nearby, but nothing of a large scale yet, which is why it is relatively expensive. Probably impossible to buy them over with our current cash reserves," Damian pondered out loud. "Euria Trees are native to the Culdao Peaks, which are infested with monsters, mostly goblins."

"Goblins?" Kyle was confused by the fantasy-like term.

"Yeah. Small, little deformed things. Extremely primitive. There are a couple of dens around the area. Some adventurers have them estimated at two hundred per den. Very territorial. There's a small town nearby where you can gather some information. Most of the adventurers have a base there." Damian pointed to a mark on the map.

Kyle remained quiet for a while, contemplating. "Can the goblins understand human language?"

"Only fundamental words, but yes, communication is possible. But they generally kill on sight, so it's preferred to avoid them whenever possible. Hold on, you're not planning anything funny, are you?"

Kyle let out a slight grin, the same whenever he had a plan in play. "Have the pub and casino ready by the time I come back. It's time for a small excursion."

A slight shudder went down Damian's spine. *Why do I feel bad for the goblins now?*

* * *

At the edge of the South Sector bordering the West Sector was a towering gate embedded in the ancient walls of the city. It was one of the major entrances into Raktor. Thousands of caravans dragged by horses and donkeys went to and fro each day, many from the neighboring county of Kregol, passing by the immigration checkpoints.

A timetable lit up in dull blue arcia lines showed all the private transportation services to nearby villages, towns, and even other cities. Passengers wearing thick coats ran down the crowded cobblestone street, trying to find their assigned caravan while dragging their bulky luggage along, some sighing as they missed their ride.

Adventurers, mercenaries, and local gang members from the Veiled Angels and the Ardent Cretins were hanging around as well, as were local enforcers who performed random inspections on passing cargo. There seemed to be a sort of tacit agreement between the Veiled Angels, the Ardent Cretins, and the local enforcers—any wagon marked by the gangs was not inspected at all, or at least the enforcers closed one eye when they saw what was inside. Such was business at the overlap between major sectors.

A lone cloaked man held onto a thin ticket detailing the time and destination. He squinted at the timetable, trying to decipher the myriad of lines that changed rapidly.

"LAST CALL! LAST CALL FOR CULDAO PEAKS TOWN!" A young boy yelled with a loudspeaker as he stood on top of a stack of boxes. "AT BERTH 19-C, RIGHT NOW!"

The cloaked man shifted the backpack on his back and moved, buffered by the sheer number of travelers and peddlers shouting at the top of their lungs, selling goods and potions of all sorts.

"Traveling alone? Need some companionship? Buy this crazy lizard off me right now— it's sure to keep you company with its incessant laughter! If you feed it right, it can grow to human size and laugh even louder! No, seriously, buy it off me. I can't shake the damn thing off! One rakel!"

"Sleeping Potions! Don't get woken up by snores or even a bandit attack! It ain't worth your time! Just let them rob the others! Hell, just let them rob you! Sleep is way more important!"

"A headband engraved with a silence skill! Why even tolerate the dumb idiots in your wagon wagging their tongues? Get one now for five hundred rakels!"

"Afraid of your wagon and cargo being overturned? Hostile monsters got you surrounded? Don't worry; our emergency response mercenary team got you and your merchant business covered. Simply activate the device in trouble, and our nearest patrol will respond immediately, no matter the threat. Only for the low, low cost of two hundred thousand rakels!"

"Arctech wagons too slow for your liking? We got the fastest likrids on hand, race-winning steeds that can haul you a thousand yards in a jiffy! Comes with an attached handler too for an additional cost!"

The cloaked man shoved his way through the dense crowd, pushing past weary travelers and dumb tourists from the towns and villages gaping at the sight of the city. He soon made it to Berth 19, where a gruff man in dirty overalls was impatiently tapping his foot as he leaned against the metal-spoked wheels of a covered wagon dragged by two obviously jittery horses. His eyes glanced at the cloaked man, eventually landing on the flimsy ticket he was holding.

"You the guy I've been waiting for?"

"Only if this is the transport to Culdao Peaks."

"Finally! Get on. I'm already ten minutes behind schedule. My boss is going to whip my ass if I run any later." The gruff man motioned to the back of the wagon, where there were already five others sitting in place.

The cloaked man gingerly entered the wagon and placed his backpack on the floor, nodding with respect to the other passengers before sitting down quietly. The other five were already engaged in a seemingly heated debate as the wagon moved out from the berth, the cobblestones causing the seats to rumble violently as it jerked back and forth.

"Look, I don't know what kind of Euria you've been sniffing, but there's no chance in hell the inquisitors are going to allow any sort of gang or secret society to exist in Raktor again. Mark my words; it'll be a short few years till Raktor will finally be cleansed!" One of the more wealthy passengers, who seemed to be a merchant, scoffed. "I'd rather have a healthy business environment than a dangerous one when I have to succumb to the gangs."

"You really believe that? First time in Raktor? Hundreds of inquisitors have come and gone, half of them even dying. We got the highest enforcer death rate in the damn Yual Dominion. This time ain't any different. They only come in when the nobles' pockets are being threatened or they are looking to expand. To me, the bans are ridiculous and just a façade for the enforcers to take in anyone—no one outside of the major city even adheres to it," another merchant rebutted angrily.

"I agree. The bans are far too ridiculous and should be lifted." A third merchant chimed in.

"Prostitution is a sin! Drunkenness is a sin as well!" The first merchant angrily wagged his finger at the other two. "This world is sorely lacking in morals, and I, for one, am glad the inquisitors are here to purge them!"

The wagon suddenly came to a halt, with two Sanctum enforcers checking for their identity. Each of the passengers handed over their identity card as well as a city permit.

"Kris Grayborn..." The enforcer looked at the face of the cloaked man, comparing it to the identity card. He was a bit suspicious, but the enforcer couldn't be bothered to pursue the matter, signaling to the front to let the wagon pass. The cloaked man let out a sigh of relief internally. *Guess I haven't been marked yet by the enforcers.*

Kyle stared out of the back of the wagon, looking at the towering stone walls engraved with various glyphs, boosting its defense. It wasn't until they had moved far away enough up a hilly slope that he truly saw the scale of the city, sprawling across a large area with a massive river flowing through it. The South Sector looked tiny in comparison with the horizon, but it didn't surprise a galactic crime lord, who always had his sights further.

Finally, I'm out of the city.

Chapter 21

Forest Ambush

"We're camping here for the night; one more day to the Culdao Peaks." The gruff man, who doubled as the driver, motioned to a rest area that other travelers had used countless times. It was a clearing in a forest a bit further away from the main road but still big enough to have ten people sleeping in comfort.

Kyle did not set up any equipment like the rest of them, simply sitting on the ground and leaning against his backpack, observing the surroundings.

Some stars were clearly visible, though the constellations were all far different from what Kyle could recognize. *Is the orientation different, or am I truly in a different world?* Kyle still couldn't believe he had reincarnated in a different world, having grown up in the Galactic Era, where science dominated.

In any case, he could not read the stars—space travel in his former life was all done by A.I. star trackers that automatically did the calculations. He was not trained as a navigator either. However, he could see that the Milky Way Galaxy was not visible at all, a faint pinkish hue enveloping the background instead. It's as if there was a veil past a certain limit, the true distance of further stars unmeasurable due to the masking of color.

I'll figure it out when I gain more resources and power. Kyle turned his attention back to the passengers. The three merchants were still bickering over the arrival of the inquisitors, making Kyle regret not having bought the headband that supposedly silenced the environment.

"They are a feisty bunch, aren't they?" one of the other passengers remarked as he sat down next to Kyle. He flicked his hood off, revealing glossy black hair slicked back and a small scar across his nose bridge. He held out a hand, offering a handshake. "Name's Orthon, mercenary heading back to Culdao Peak. You?"

"Kris. I'm an herbalist, looking for new potential medicine there." Kyle shook Orthon's hand briefly, noticing the calluses on his palm and the unmistakable mark of a sword wielder.

"Oh, without an escort? Could get pretty dangerous." Orthon sized up Kyle, looking at his cloak and equipment, his eyes landing on the Aero Shoes for a while.

"Those three merchants seemed to be doing fine without any help." Kyle noticed Orthon's gaze but did not react. He eyed a repeating crossbow slung across Orthon's back, loaded with bolts. It was extremely luxurious and ornamental—almost as if it were meant for nobility. An interesting violet mark was painted across its body, shaped like a demon.

"Of course, they got escorts! Me and my buddy, Troy." Orthon motioned back toward the last passenger, who simply nodded as he re-tied his bow, checking the tension of the string. "It looked like a simple job; both of us were already heading that way, so we just grabbed some easy money along the way."

"How much was it?"

"Oh, not much. Just three hundred rakels per person. Barely enough in total to buy a Strength Potion, but enough to survive if you know where to buy your food in Raktor. Why? Interested in hiring us?"

"Perhaps. I'm looking for native Euria Seeds."

"Hmmm." Orthon scratched his chin. "I know they are in the Culdao Peaks, but I don't know where the largest concentration is. You might want to ask around in town."

"Thanks. I'll give it a shot."

"No worries, mate. If you ever need help, just head down to the tavern and ask for me or Troy. We'll be around for a month or two. Gonna go for a quick wee." Orthon patted Kyle's shoulder before leaving into the bushes, causing Kyle's eyebrow to twitch at being touched.

Kyle watched Orthon leave, shifted his backpack a bit further away from the campfire that was just set up and laid down to try and get some rest.

"Mr. Grayborn? Want any soup before resting?" the gruff man called out, but Kyle acted like he was sleeping soundly.

"Hey, I'll gladly take his portion if he doesn't want it." One of the merchants scooped a bowl quickly and gulped it down, burping with satisfaction. The gruff man also drank the soup, with Troy watching them intently.

Soon, they fell fast asleep, the rumbling of snores echoing through the rest area. Troy pretended to sleep as well, waiting for the merchants to be in a deep slumber. As soon as they did, his eyes slowly opened. *Time to make a move.*

He slowly got up and turned his head, looking into the forest, before signaling with a soft whistle three times. Slowly realizing something was wrong, he glanced around the area. *Where is Kris Grayborn? His backpack is still here. Did Orthon make a move first?*

Wary, he retrieved his bow and was about to walk out into the treeline when someone suddenly dropped onto him from above, slamming him onto the ground with both knees pinning his shoulder blades.

"ARGH—" Troy screamed, but a ragged piece of cloth was stuffed into his mouth, muffling the sound. Unable to turn around, he felt five hammer strikes hit his body at different positions of his limbs, causing him to yelp in pain.

Kyle walked off to grab a rope from his backpack, while Troy immediately spat out the cloth and tried to stand up, pulling out a knife sheathed in his belt and aiming it at Kyle. Kyle did not react, simply walking toward Troy with the rope.

Before Troy could move a single inch, the delayed pain from the neon red arctech hammer kicked in, causing him to scream again. Kyle immediately lunged forward and grabbed his cheeks, toppling Troy's head into the ground with a loud thud and knocking him out.

Despite the screams, the merchants and driver did not wake up, barely budging. *Drugged by the soup...* Kyle tied Troy up and dragged him into the treeline, hiding his body in the bushes. Kyle waited at another position, planning to ambush anyone coming.

After a few minutes, two men and Orthon walked out of the treeline toward the campfire with large grins on their faces. "We're getting rich today, boys! Check the merchants for any emergency response devices. Can't have them calling them on us."

The two men complied, moving forward, when suddenly Orthon grabbed them by the shoulder. "Wait! Something isn't right! Troy and the new guy are missing!"

Just as the two men began to glance around, a shadow lunged out from the sides, accelerated by his shoes. The shadow swung a neon red hammer, delivering a direct uppercut to the first man, immediately knocking him out cold.

"Shit!" Orthon cursed, pulling out his own sword. The other man began to panic as Kris leapt and weaved around him before delivering a sweeping kick and swinging the hammer in a downward strike as the man fell.

The hammer strike cracked the man's ribs, causing bone splinters to jut out from under the skin from the sheer force. Another swift kick to the head knocked out the man for good as well.

A sudden swing of the sword forced Kyle to back off, the sound of air rippling as Orthon grunted. "Who the fuck are you? An enforcer? Or the Veiled Angels? I doubt you're a Cretin—Sebastian would have you flogged for this." Orthon didn't chase after Kyle, instead retrieving the ornate repeating crossbow with his free hand, the cocking mechanism engraved with arcia.

Kyle assumed the force of each shot would be light due to the size, but the arcia enchantments along the length improved the force, accelerating the bolts faster than he expected. Two bolts whizzed past his head, while a third hit him in the left shoulder, causing him to stumble back. Blood trickled out as Kyle staggered, pain jolting through his nerves like a sharp lightning bolt.

"Never expected this, huh?" Orthon grinned, gripping the sword with the other hand and approaching carefully, assuming the stance of a well-trained sword duelist. With a powerful step forward, Orthon unleashed a three-move combo, swinging with all his might.

He nearly nailed Kyle with the second swing, but on the third swing, Kyle suddenly parried with the handle of his hammer before closing in the gap in a daring forward step, catching Orthon off guard. Capitalizing on the surprise, Kyle threw a strong left hook right into Orthon's jaw, knocking him back into a daze.

Orthon was no slouch, quickly using his sword to force Kyle to back off, though the latter was already well prepared, dancing around Orthon despite the bolt in his left shoulder. With another exchange, another knee to the stomach from Kyle caused Orthon to collapse to the floor. Kyle swung the hammer down on the back of his opponent's head three times, knocking him out cold as blood trickled through the man's hair.

Kyle panted, moved to a tree stump, and slumped against it. Luckily for him, the crossbow bolt was fairly shallow and not fully embedded in the bone. Kyle used his fingers with grit, digging into the exposed flesh as he winced. He located the arrowhead and slowly eased it out, bearing the pain.

Soon, he managed to pull out the entire shaft and arrowhead and used the Necklace of Healing to heal himself lightly as a temporary measure.

The wound sealed up as a green aura surged around it, boosted by his Healer title.

Nifty for post-battles, but that's assuming I win the battle in the first place. Kyle stood up, testing his shoulder's articulation. The healing had yet to be complete—Kyle would have to channel it a few times later. Picking up Orthon's crossbow, he examined it.

Ornate Repeater Crossbow (Intermediate)
Perfect for multiple targets.
[Active] **Force Increase:** Bolts shoot faster and harder.
Cost: 1 MP

Kyle had yet to acquire a ranged weapon, so he held on to it, slinging it behind him. He walked up to one of the unconscious attackers, wondering what to do with him.

He'd noticed that had yet to gain any EXP so far. The last time he had gotten any EXP was only when he killed Ulon Baktar, the former Seven Snakes gang leader. Even beating up a dozen Red Lions hadn't netted him anything. *Is the System forcing me to kill? That's fine, but surely I can get more benefits out of it?*

He retrieved Troy's dropped knife, using it to quickly slit the throat of one of the unconscious men, killing him on the spot.

[SYSTEM MESSAGE]
You killed Forest Bandit, +50 EXP.

Kyle waited for a while, noticing there were no new titles. *Perhaps I have to do it differently.* He walked up to the second unconscious man, slitting his wrists and allowing the blood to seep out slowly. He then stabbed the man a few times, causing him to wake up from the sheer pain and scream out. It ended with a quick jab to the nose, knocking the man back out.

Soon, the blood formed a sizable puddle, prompting another System Message to appear in front of him.

[SYSTEM MESSAGE]
You killed Forest Bandit, +50 EXP.

Huh, let's focus on getting information, then. Kyle moved on to the next. This time, he grabbed Troy's body and slapped him awake.

"Burh..." Troy groaned as he was abruptly woken up before his eyes narrowed in shock. He tried to break free of the rope that tied his arms and legs.

"Who are you affiliated with? Why did you guys assume I was the Veiled Angels?"

"W-What? I—" Troy was still lightheaded from the previous concussion but soon shrieked in pain as Kyle used the knife to dig into the ribs.

"Answer."

"I... We're affiliated with the Violet Demons! We hijack caravans for them! Please let me go!" Troy struggled against the knife while he began bleeding profusely.

"How many of you are there?"

"Twenty, no... forty! Sixty! Let me go now, or they'll hunt you down! Orthon is a big shot among us. If you kill him or me, you're dead meat!" Troy tried to intimidate Kyle, but the galactic crime lord was not having any of it.

"So I'm questioning the wrong person then," Kyle summarized before pulling out the knife and stabbing Troy in the heart. Troy's body convulsed violently for a few seconds, his limbs twitching until he finally slumped over and died.

[SYSTEM MESSAGE]
You killed Forest Bandit Troy, +100 EXP.

Last try, then. Kyle walked up to the unconscious Orthon, tying him up with a rope and slapping him awake.

"Uhh... wha... WHAT?!" Orthon stared in shock, unable to come to terms with the sheer amount of blood and gore around him. His comrades' bodies were stacked next to him, dripping slowly in a dark-red snaking river that oozed toward him. "You... Who the fuck are you!? What kind of enforcer does this?"

"Who says I'm an enforcer?" Kyle suddenly stabbed a knife deep into Orthon's thigh, gouging the bone. "I'm the one asking the questions here. Answer correctly, or else you'll end up like them."

"I'm not going to give you any—GRRRNNH!" Orthon winced as the knife was buried deeper with a twist, the pain nearly causing him to scream.

Kyle didn't stop, continuing to twist. "STOP! STOP, OKAY?! PLEASE!" Orthon relented after three more twists, his thigh already a bloodied mess through his pants.

"Where is the forest bandit's base?"

"South of here, seven kilometers. Wooden fortress, you can't miss it."

"How many of them are there?"

"There's... about twenty-five of us."

So Troy really was useless. Or Orthon is lying. "All as equipped as you?"

"No... ARRRGGH! YES, YES! WE HAVE BOWS AND CROSSBOWS!"

Kyle stopped twisting the knife for a moment, thinking deeply. Orthon noticed the hesitation in Kyle's eyes. "T-That's right! If you kill me off as well, my comrades are going to be hunting you down! No one escapes us in this forest. This is our home ground!"

"That sounds bad."

"Yes, it is. So if you wanna live, you'll—" Orthon couldn't speak any more, his eyes bulging as he choked on his blood, his windpipe sliced open cleanly by the knife. He stared at Kyle, who did not even continue to look at him, walking off. Kyle couldn't care less about the gurgling forest bandits—he was more occupied with the new system messages in front of his eyes.

[SYSTEM MESSAGE]
You killed Forest Bandit Orthon, +200 EXP.

Title Obtained: Torturer
Pain is sometimes the best language.
+5 INT, +2 STR, +2 DEX, + 10% torture effectiveness.

Your level has increased from level 9 to level 10!
All stats increased.
Bonus free points granted.
Congratulations! Classes will now be unlocked.
Class Announcement: Class upgrade (Level 10).

Please wait...

Chapter 22

Perfect Underlings

Kyle arrived at Culdao Peaks Town by foot, walking all night along the main road while chugging Stamina Potions whenever he was exhausted.

It was the crack of dawn by the time he arrived, but he did not enter the town immediately, instead tossing the bloodied clothes into a ditch nearby before changing to a clean set from his backpack.

He entered the town casually, acting like a traveler who had walked from the city due to missing the caravan. No one cared about him appearing, with Culdao Peaks being a regular stop point for travelers on foot or by wagon.

Culdao Peaks Town was a small place of close to eight hundred people, primarily hamlets, a few high streets of shopping stalls, and a central market. Already, Kyle could see the stall owners working hard, dragging out items unsold since yesterday and hoping to make a quick buck.

Looking around for an inn, he found the best one he could get, paying with rakels on the spot no matter the quoted price. Why should a crime lord live in squalor or stinge, after all? A few hundred rakels would barely make a dent in the debt either way. However, Kyle could already imagine Keith nagging him for spending two hundred rakels for a single night.

The inn was quiet in the morning, and the sleepy attendant, who had barely woken up, led him to his room, which was furnished with a queen-sized bed and a private bathroom. While not much in the Galactic Era, this was a luxury, especially when this was not the city.

As he walked through the inn, Kyle had been keeping an eye out for anything suspicious. His vigilance grew even bigger when he was finally left in the room, where he checked every nook and cranny for any engravings, enchantments, or devices. A habit from his former life.

Kyle finally loosened up after an hour of searching, lying on the comfortable bed. His mind recalled the system message about him receiving a class upon reaching Level 10. *Classes... What are they?*

Frequently Asked Questions: Classes

Classes are the main way to obtain skills, apart from equipment.
Skills are not lost upon changing classes. In order to perform a class change, hit the set milestones or approach a terminal with the requisite materials.

Terminal? Class Change? Kyle had no clue what the system was referring to. He tried asking more, but no other system messages appeared. It seemed like that was the only question that had triggered an active response from his interface so far.

Information: Classes have been generated based on your performance and inclinations thus far.
Please choose carefully.

Class Unlocked: Politician

Words are a man's strongest weapon—even better when paired with fists.
Active skills revolve around persuasion, leadership, and self-preservation.

Class Unlocked: Biochemist

Give a man a potion a day, and he'll be rich in a month.
Active skills revolve around potion enhancement, quality increments, and gathering.

Class Unlocked: Hammer Dancer

For one who uses the hammer religiously.
Active skills revolve around slamming, hitting, and breaking things.

Kyle glanced through the classes, none of them even being mildly interesting. The Biochemist class seemed interesting, but there was more to running a criminal empire than just drugs alone. *Nothing short of Crime Lord or its equivalent is good enough to satisfy me.* Kyle thought, which suddenly prompted the system message to disappear and a new one to appear.

Information: Generating unique class.

Please wait...

A few minutes passed before a new system message popped up.

Limited Class Unlocked: Crime Lord
Those who stand on top of the underworld and rule with strength.
Active skills revolve around intimidation, leadership, violence, and self-preservation. This class has a fixed upgrade path.

Kyle's face twitched at the mention of self-preservation. *Is this interface mocking me for what happened in my former life?* He begrudgingly accepted the class, causing the message to disappear and a new one to take its place.

WARNING: Class integration initiated.

Please find a safe location.

Huh? Safe location? Kyle barely had time to worry about it when a sudden jabbing pain erupted at the nape of his neck.

The fiery pain shot through the nerves, spine, and bones like lava coursing through in a rush, causing him to double over terribly. He gritted his teeth, trying to bear the pain, but it was unlike anything he had ever experienced. Not even the Dynasty's training nor the imprisonment in his former life could inflict this much punishment on his body.

His arms felt the prick of a thousand needles inside every vein, capillary, and pore while his abdomen cramped up. He bent over as he rolled on the bed, his back beginning to sweat profusely and his head thumping with the sound of his accelerating heartbeat in his ear, overwhelming his senses.

It was painful just to breathe, forcing him to take short, measured breaths to withstand whatever was happening to his body. "GRRRRHHH!" Kyle grabbed a rolled-up piece of the blanket and clamped down hard on it, his hands gripping anything he could reach in sheer tension.

His body swelled and contract in a grotesque fashion, as though something alien within was remodeling his body from within. It felt like a hot iron branding him from within, causing him to nearly cry out in pain.

As the pain continued, Kyle became more and more aware of something that felt foreign in his body, somehow integrated into the very fabric of his body. Too many effects and processes were happening internally, making it hard for him to focus on what was exactly happening, not to mention the mind-numbing pain.

Kyle had no idea how much time had passed until the pain finally subsided, allowing him to finally take a breather. His body felt exhausted, as though it had burned all his energy in a single instant. Kyle quickly activated the Necklace of Healing and drank the Stamina Potion without checking his stats. *Better be safe than sorry.*

Class Obtained: Crime Lord
Those who stand on top of the underworld and rule with strength.
+10 STR, +10 CHA, +10 INT, +10 VIT, +10% chance to persuade underlings.

Skill Obtained: Intimidation Aura (Basic)

Control those who oppose you with fear.

+50% intimidation success chance.

Duration: 5 minutes   **Cooldown:** 1 day

Skill Obtained: Penchant for Violence (Basic)

A good crime lord must be fluent in the language of the underworld.

All combat stats temporarily increase by 100% for a short duration.

Duration: 15 seconds   **Cooldown:** 10 minutes

Skill Obtained: This is My Turf (Basic)

No one gets close to you without your word.

Creates a selective domain where enemies are unable to approach.

Duration: 30 seconds   **Cooldown:** 3 hours

Skill Obtained: Designate Follower (Basic)

Can't be a crime lord without underlings.

Marks any sapient being as a follower, enabling telepathic communication.

Current Limit: 1 Follower   **Range:** Limited

Kyle didn't bother checking the skills in-depth, immediately checking the time. It was almost nighttime now—the class integration had taken the entire day. His body was covered in sweat and blood, prompting him to take yet another shower.

He glanced at his face in the mirror, realizing his facial structure had improved, with the former face being boosted with a charismatic effect closer to what he remembered he looked like in his past life. His auburn hair had become darker, matching his former black hair color. *What the hell is this interface?*

The bed was soaking wet with sweat and bloodstains from his hands, so he got the room service to change it out. Keeping his belongings with him, he left the room while they cleaned up the place, heading down to the inn's lobby for dinner.

This time, the inn was crowded, filled with many of the townsfolk. Kyle noticed the three merchants and the gruff driver were already in the same inn, telling stories about a monster attacking the forest bandits.

One of the merchant's eyes landed on Kyle's face for a brief moment before looking away and continuing to tell the story to enthralled listeners. *Is my face really that different, or did they just not pay much attention? Well, that saves me some trouble, at least.*

Kyle found an empty table and sat down, peering at the menu that had been carved into a board above the bar. Ordering his meal, he glanced around the inn, listening in on some of the conversations happening around.

"Got shaken down again by Fred. Fuck man, he used to be an all right enforcer until the Sanctum of Yual sent one of their priests into town. Now he's all righteous and holy, unwilling even to look the other way for even a moment. We used to drink in this town all day and night. Now? Not even a single drop!"

"Mate, my hands are already shaking from the lack of card games here. It's only been a week, but I'm dying right now. Maybe I should just head and join the forest bandits."

"You serious? After hearing about the monster that attacked them? What would Mary say? You can't just leave her and the kids."

"Bah! The three merchants are off their rockers. Fuck it, I'll bring them all along. Maybe I'll join the slave traders too when they make their next pass-through."

"Don't count on it. The next time they come around, Fred and his cronies will probably be all over it. A bust like that would be big on their record."

"HAH! Fred won't stand a chance against them guards. He barely swung a sword in his life!"

Looks like the prohibitions are being enforced in the neighboring towns too... Kyle took note of the conversations in town, marking them in his head for future reference. If he wanted to establish a proper supply line of Euria Seeds, this town might have a big part to play in it.

Euria Seeds had yet to be deemed prohibited, so Kyle did not have to worry too much. However, seeing how the Sanctum of Yual was willing to ban many things outright, he was certain they would soon start banning Euria Seeds, especially with the way he was about to develop the business.

There was not much else going on, mostly just other people complaining about the enforcers moving into town. Kyle did not see any idea of a local mob or mafia existing yet. There was a chance for business here, but he could only do something once he got a better picture of the town and made some more connections. *Perhaps I could set up a few shell companies here to handle the trade of Euria Seeds.*

He was also on a strict time limit, with the repayment of the debt coming up. For now, he decided to focus on finding the habitat of the Euria Seeds and the goblins who supposedly lived in the same area.

The next day, Kyle immediately left the inn as early as he could, continuously checking behind him for any tails or people watching. He was unsure if any of the city gangs had posted someone to watch over him, but he already knew that if the Violet Demons learned of him killing their forest bandits, he would have a problem.

Using a replica map bought from the town, he navigated his way through the dense forest, trudging through the foliage and dead leaves. He spotted a few animals, noticing that most of them were similar to those of Ancient Earth. Squirrels, deer, wild pigs, and rabbits were seemingly common here. He expected a bit more of a fantasy twist, seeing as goblins were already around.

As he walked through the forest, a bloody stench soon wafted through the air, becoming stronger over time. It put him on guard, forcing him to keep his hammer at the ready, his eyes darting all over the tree branches to check for ambushes.

Pushing his way through a few dense bushes, he soon got a glimpse of the source of the smell. It seemed to be a mass grave of sorts, except the bodies were all fully decomposing and rotting, clear signs that they had died quite some time ago.

Three goblins were crouched over in the mass grave, sorting through the rotten human meat and limbs. They used their little green grubby hands to scoop something out of the meat, stuffing it into dirty pouches made of leather and skin patches, grunting at one another.

Kyle decided to hide and watch, seeing as the goblins did not notice him. The three goblins worked their way through the pit, scooping continuously. Soon, Kyle finally understood what they were doing. *They are harvesting the maggots from the decomposing meat as food. Interesting...*

Suddenly, a loud, rickety sound could be heard, with the three goblins immediately scampering away toward the mountains. Kyle hid even more, lying low in the bushes as he spotted a wheelbarrow coming through a small path. It was two forest bandits, one escorting and one pushing two dead girls on the wheelbarrow.

They dumped the bodies into the mass grave pit, with one of the forest bandits peering over the edge. "Hey, look. Your former girl is doing pretty good."

"Cheh. Thought she would have been reduced to bones by now. I guess the maggots and goblins don't even like her. What a waste of rakels that one was."

They didn't converse anymore, simply heading back the same way. Kyle did not move at all, continuously observing his surroundings. He soon saw the three goblins reappear, obviously not having collected enough.

He paid more attention to their loadout this time. Each one was barely armored, with only a flint or stone knife hanging from a loose cloth belt. Only one of them had a decent metal knife, which seemed to serve as the only weapon they had.

When entering a new environment, observing how the locals worked was the best way to get the lay of the land the fastest. Kyle decided to follow the goblins back to the den before deciding on a course of action. *Maybe they can be the perfect underlings...*

Chapter 23

Mental Fatigue

Three days later...

Kyle had the place mapped out for now. There was indeed a vast amount of Euria Seeds in the region. If he somehow managed to pick everything up, he could supply the city of Raktor with up to fifty times its current consumption each year, and that was just his estimate. Not even the plantations he had learned about from Damian could produce that much in a controlled environment.

The reason no one harvested much here was due to the constant threat of goblins. While the weaker ones were sent out to forage for food, the stronger ones remained in their dens and protected the nearby areas, which somehow corresponded with a dense concentration of Euria Trees. Kyle had already watched another human harvester get chased out of some of the denser Euria Tree habitats, which seemed to be considered sacred or protected by the goblins.

The stronger goblins had much better gear from former fallen adventurers and failed expeditions. Some goblins were even stronger than Kyle, although that was rare.

Kyle had located one goblin den nested in an abandoned mining shaft from decades ago, the tunnels leading into the mountain's base. It was well defended, with nearly twenty to thirty goblins patrolling the main entrance at all times.

Working his way around the mountain, he found a secondary entrance to the same mining tunnels, though it was much smaller and subsequently less defended as well. He only saw five goblins on guard duty at any given time, and they were significantly less defended.

Kyle knew they were not the only group or tribe of goblins in the area. There might be a dozen tribes or more, but the area was big, spanning hundreds of kilometers. Even if he attacked a den and the other tribes reacted, they would take too long to respond.

However, he had found no sign that the tribes were working together on good terms. On one occasion, he had seen five goblin guards immediately kill a stray goblin who seemed to have lost his way.

This consistent observation also triggered a couple title gains over the next three days.

Title Obtained: Tracker (Basic)
Helps when those keys are always misplaced.
+5 DEX, +25% increased vision and hearing range.

Title Obtained: Goblin Observer (Basic)
Hopefully, not a green skin fetish.
+5 DEX, +25% success at learning goblin language.

Kyle had also found a small alcove nearby, a short walk away from the secondary entrance to the goblin's den. He rested there, planning how he was going to tackle this issue. There was no way of starting a Euria Seeds harvesting business without clearing the goblin tribes.

Theoretically, he should have brought two dozen Seven Snakes members and had them sequentially wipe each tribe. However, that will draw far too many eyes, especially with the enforcers in the town watching his gang's movements. *No doubt Sebastian and Wrent are also eyeing my members closely now for any anomalies.*

Hiring adventurers to fight the goblins would create unnecessary attention. Other businessmen and merchants were also interested in harvesting the bountiful Euria Seeds but were currently blocked by the high cost of eliminating the goblins. Kyle would prefer if that natural barrier remained so as to enable him to quickly develop a monopoly.

However, there was one additional benefit Kyle had over the other merchants and businessmen—it wasn't the first time he colonized a planet with local natives. If he was right, all the tactics he learned in the Galactic Era would work here easily as well. *If only I had my exosuit, I could have them revere me as a god. But let's start with the basics first.*

* * *

The same three goblins headed out to another part of the forest this time. They always sent out two groups to collect more food for the growing tribe. The tribe was always growing. This was how life was in Culdao Peaks.

They harvested fruits, dug up tubers, and sometimes pinched a few fungi, stuffing all of them into the same dirty pouches they had been using for generations. Some boasted a few newer pieces of equipment, seemingly homemade and of adequate quality.

Suddenly, one of the goblins spotted a rare sight that would make anyone in the den go crazy—a loaf of bread dropped on the ground.

Fresh.

The goblin pounced on it immediately, quickly eating half of it.

The other two saw it before immediately tussling and grappling the first goblin, trying to get a bite of the rare bread as well. Loud grunts and squeals echoed through the treeline as the three goblins fought over it.

A silent shadow loomed over them, perched on the tree branches. The moment the three goblins began to tire out from their fight, the shadow dropped, swinging a neon-red arctech hammer and caving a goblin's skull inward with a single downward swing. A follow up strike finished the goblin for good.

The remaining two goblins yelped, but before they could wield their knives, they were immediately kicked in quick succession, the wind knocked out of their chests. They did not stand a chance.

As night soon fell, a lone goblin guard in the den ran in to report to the shaman, who was the leader of the goblin tribe. Both groups sent out to forage for food did not return home.

The shaman frowned but did not think much of it. The forest was not exactly a safe place, and six goblins were hardly a dent in their numbers. The tribe had more than three hundred goblins. Goblins could already start working after two years of childhood, so the shaman was not bothered, simply sending the guard away.

The next day came and went, but the exact same thing happened. All three groups disappeared as well, never to return. Even the search parties sent to find their bodies were unsuccessful. The shaman was now worried.

On the third day, the killings stopped. The forage groups were afraid to venture out but somehow did not encounter anything. The shaman was extremely confused now but decided to put the past two days behind him. He simply doubled the number of guards at the entrance as well as at the secondary entrance.

On the fourth day, the killing resumed. Search parties still failed to find the bodies, with one of the search parties never returning as well. The shaman ordered the forage groups to be beefed up, attaching two goblin warriors to each of them.

The killing didn't stop on the fifth day, with the addition of the goblin warriors not doing anything. Now, the shaman was in full panic mode, unable to determine what was going on. The guards were still doubled, and the entire tribe was in a high-tension mode. By now, it had already lost more than two dozen goblins, along with a few trained warriors. Scouts were ordered everywhere in the forest, but they could not find anything.

On the sixth day, nothing happened. No killings, no sightings.

The pattern repeated, with the shaman unable to fix or remedy it. He could send out more troops, but that would leave the base more vulnerable. As the ninth day approached, the shaman immediately sent as many foraging groups as he could, following the pattern of no killing.

The doubled-up guards, who had been in high tension the entire week and doing continuous patrols, finally took a break, knowing that there would be no killing on this day. It was at this very moment of mental fatigue that Kyle began his attack.

The guards at the secondary entrance did not even see it coming, with Kyle activating his Aero Shoes and smashing their heads with terrifying precision. He quickly entered the mining tunnels, collapsing the structure and closing the entrance before leaving.

He then headed to the main entrance, where the number of guards had dropped significantly. The trained warriors were all taking a rest in the den itself, leaving only rookie goblins to defend the main entrance. It was a simple wooden barricade, with a few abandoned houses that used to store mining equipment or serve as dorms, along with a watch post.

Kyle noted there were a few goblin archers, but he had the crossbow from Orthon, along with twenty bolts loaded into the cartridge.

He sniped the archer at the top of the watch post with pinpoint precision, who could barely scream with a bolt stuck in its windpipe.

Moving quickly, he attacked the main entrance head-on, causing an alarm to be raised. The rookie goblins valiantly fended off Kyle, but he leapt and danced around their amateur swings, simply kicking them or using his hammer to parry their hits before cracking their limbs or bones.

After dealing with the guards, he could already hear the stronger warriors coming out from inside the den. Kyle immediately ran up to the mine shaft, collapsing only one of the beams in a controlled fashion. The initially large tunnel that could fit seven humans from end to end started to crumble, the rubble now allowing only one goblin to squeeze through at a time.

Kyle did not plan to fight all three hundred goblins simultaneously but rather reduce the number of opponents he had to face as much as possible.

The goblin warriors did not think too much, simply charging through the tunnel and running right at Kyle. The skill of the trained warriors was far better than expected, having fought adventurers and other tribes. Kyle had to focus more, practicing his combat skills in a continuous series of life-and-death duels.

The Necklace of Healing could not heal a wound fast enough during the battle itself, so Kyle placed more emphasis on avoiding wounds, parrying hits, and putting the full range of his former martial arts knowledge to the test.

He fought close to a dozen goblin warriors in a short ten minutes, killing all of them. The system messages for each kill were temporarily ignored by Kyle as he chugged a Stamina Potion and a Strength Potion to keep himself going.

An hour passed, the bodies of goblin warriors piling up next to him. Even the goblin warriors were starting to lose their original fervor, the previous mental fatigue catching up to them. They also realized that this human was the main culprit behind the killings, adding even more fear and intimidation.

Suddenly, a loud roar burst out from the tunnel, with the goblin warriors being shoved out of the way by a much larger goblin. Wielding a rusted battleax that was obviously stolen from an adventurer, the goblin was two heads taller than Kyle. Its green skin was adorned with tribal tattoos, and runes were carved into its face.

The rest of its body was covered in full metal plate armor like a knight, potentially the only complete heavy armor set that the goblin den had. The arm had a vambrace that was noticeably arctech equipment, built completely differently from the rest of the armor set. It had green arcing lines along the length, making Kyle wary about its effects.

The two stared at one another as the goblin warriors, still cramped in the tunnels, watched on in fear. Even some of the forage groups who heard the fighting did not dare to try and backstab Kyle.

"Human!" the goblin champion suddenly yelled, shocking Kyle. "You, die, here!" It spat on the ground and gripped its battleaxe with both hands, ready to duel.

Kyle didn't respond, immediately wielding his crossbow pistol and firing three bolts at the champion's head. Instead of being afraid, the vambrace began to glow brighter, before three energy bolts suddenly shot out, hitting the crossbow bolts and deflecting them away.

Point Defense?! Kyle was surprised at the appearance of the engraving and caught off-guard as the champion charged with the battleaxe, performing a deadly horizontal swing that almost nicked Kyle as he leapt backward.

With the Aero Shoes, Kyle sprinted forward faster, using his hammer to bash the armor plate of the goblin as he was still swinging. The hammer instead bounced off, unable to do any damage. *I need more power! Penchant for Violence!*

The skill activated, giving him a boost in combat stats. His body suddenly roared with a surging force from deep within, as though he had unlocked some small hidden potential in his body. The strength increase was significant enough for Kyle to feel as though the hammer was close to a tenth lighter.

He flanked the goblin as the momentum carried him around, just as the goblin was about to swing downward in a counterattack. With speed as his advantage, he delivered a kick against the goblin's shin, causing it to kneel. Kyle winced in pain from kicking a full metal plate, but he gritted his teeth and continued fighting, narrowly dodging a right hook from the goblin.

Kyle was about to lift his hammer to strike, but the champion's vambrace activated again, sending a bolt toward the hammer and sending Kyle slightly off balance. The unexpected use of the vambrace caught him off guard, allowing the goblin to recover and swing the battleaxe again, forcing Kyle to duck and avoid it.

With a decisive blow, Kyle delivered a straight right uppercut into the groin of the champion, causing its eyes to bulge. Kyle took advantage and punched the goblin's face three times in rapid succession, toppling it over.

Suddenly, the tribal tattoo on the goblin's face glowed green, a healing aura working through the body. *What?!* Kyle was not about to let him heal right in front of him, grabbing his hammer again and pummeling the goblin in the face with as many strikes as he could manage.

Despite the green aura, the goblin's face soon became a bloodied mess of meat and flesh. The rune was disfigured now, breaking the healing aura and killing the champion.

Kyle heaved as he stood up, his face and arms bloodied from the splatter. He glanced at the remaining goblin warriors, all of whom were now shivering in fear. Their champion had been killed in less than a few minutes, so what hope was there against this human?

Title Obtained: Goblin Killer (Basic)
Greenskin bad, humanskin better.
+10 STR, +5 DEX, +2 VIT, +10% damage to goblin-type enemies.

Your level has increased from level 10 to level 15!
All stats increased.
Bonus free points granted.

* * *

Kyle Hawthorn: Level 15
Max HP: 52(+0)(+0)(+0) | **Max MP:** 23(+0)(+5)(+0) | **Max STA:** 52(+0)(+0)(+0)

Status Effects
None

Stats

Race: Human | **Class:** Crime Lord | **Subclass:** Unassigned
STR: 87(+29)(+0)(+0) | **DEX:** 71(+33)(+0)(+0) | **INT:** 86(+45)(+3)(+0)
VIT: 47(+2)(+3)(+0) | **CHA:** 21(+10)(+1)(+0) | **Free Points:** 50

Equipment

Necklace of Healing (Basic)
Magus Ring of Theorin (Intermediate)

Skills

Intimidation Aura (Basic)
Penchant for Violence (Basic)
This is My Turf (Basic)
Designate Follower (Basic)

Titles

Former Crime Lord
Martial Arts Expert
Murderer
Potion Inspector (Intermediate)
Potion Crafter (Intermediate)
Healer (Basic)
Martial Arts Instructor (Basic)
Arcia Engraver (Basic)
Torturer
Tracker (Basic)
Goblin Observer (Basic)
Goblin Killer (Basic)

Chapter 24

Uplift Procedure

Kyle had to kill off a few more brave goblin warriors before they finally relented, recognizing Kyle's domineering strength. He knew he would not be able to win against all three hundred, so the method of skimming their forces slowly and funneling them through a single cramped entrance worked perfectly. It was like shooting fish in a barrel.

The goblin warriors and the forage groups all dropped their weapons in surrender, hoping to appeal to the human's morality, if any. Some tried to get a sneak attack as Kyle approached to collect their weapons, but were always immediately killed by Kyle, further driving fear into their hearts.

He picked up the vambrace of the goblin, patting away some of the meat and flesh and putting it on.

Projectile Defense Vambrace (Basic)
Blocks a certain number of projectiles when activated.
+3 DEX, +2 VIT
[Active] **Point Defense:** Fires energy bolts to block up to ten projectiles.
Cost: 3 MP   **Duration:** 1 minute or 10 successfully blocked projectiles
Cooldown: 15 minutes

Kyle rounded up the surrendering goblins at the mine entrance, tying some of them up with rope left in the storage huts. Soon, a goblin shaman appeared, escorted by warriors. The shaman was small, frail, and sickly, but Kyle could see the same runes that were on the champion carved everywhere on the shaman's visible parts.

"Human! For what purpose do you slaughter us?" The goblin shaman said with surprising clarity and some mastery of the human language, though it was accompanied by a low, guttural accent and obviously broken grammar.

"I'd like to negotiate the purchase of the tribe."

"Pur-chase? Money? The tribe is worth far more than your trinkets," the goblin shaman scoffed.

"You're in no position to take such a stance."

"The tribe is three hundred goblins strong!"

"And also must have the elderly, sick, and young still hiding in the den. You do not have three hundred *warriors*. I estimate close to fifty of your best warriors have died at my hands over the last week."

"Means human should pay reparations! For grievances! You have yet to defeat our champion!" The shaman was not budging.

"You mean this guy?" Kyle motioned to the body of the champion he had pummeled to death, causing the shaman to yelp in surprise and calm itself down.

The shaman did not immediately reply, opting for a quick chat with the warriors around it instead. Kyle could somehow pick out a few words thanks to his title, allowing him to understand a bit of what was being said.

<...strong... ambush? ...too strong...want.>

The goblins finally finished their discussion. Clearing its throat it reassumed its position. However, before it could speak, Kyle aimed his crossbow and fired bolts at two of the warriors next to the shaman, the bolts piercing their eyes and killing them instantly.

"This is taking too long, and I decided you're not worth the price. You will now all answer to me." Kyle spoke with a domineering attitude, triggering his new skill, Intimidation Aura, as well.

The sudden switch from negotiation to violence shocked the shaman, curtailing its defiant stance and forcing it to submit lest more of its kind be slaughtered. It was how self-preservation worked in the forest—the law of the jungle. The remaining goblin warriors immediately bowed along with the shaman, groveling on the floor.

Kyle did not even flinch nor hesitate when killing the warriors. For him, violence was a given, something he could do at a drop of a hat if there were no repercussions. Based on his former experience, violence and show of strength was the best way to initially pacify a native population. The rebellions would come later, but Kyle had that all sorted out as well.

"You, name." Kyle pointed his crossbow at the goblin shaman.

"Gulak, at your service!" the goblin shaman replied quickly.

"Gulak. Show me around the goblin den."

"Y-Yes!" Gulak immediately got up, clearing a path for Kyle to walk through the still-groveling goblin warriors. They escorted him down the mining tunnels, winding paths of forks and dead ends.

The goblin warriors whispered to each other as they walked, with Gulak continuously giving hand signs as though it was fidgeting with its hands. Kyle pretended not to see it, instead focusing on the abandoned mining equipment as he listened in on the whispers of the goblins behind him.

Title Obtained: Goblin Observer (Intermediate)
Entering the den of a goblin tribe alone is quite a feat.
+10 DEX, +50% success at learning goblin language.

The improved title allowed him to pick up a few words from the whispers. <...ambush...dead end...plunder...>

The tunnels were barely illuminated, save for the glow of some mushrooms and unknown jewels embedded in the walls, with former mining lanterns lit up intermittently between passages. Gulak kept making turns and leading Kyle down, all the while the number of goblin warriors and archers behind Kyle increased.

They soon reached a dead end, with Gulak turning around with a wide grin. The runes on its body glowed white, a sort of hazy optical illusion slowly masking the shaman from view from the legs up.

Gulak smirked. "Human, today you—" A swift hammer uppercut knocked its chin upward, stopping the optical illusion and sending him flying into the air before crashing into the side of the tunnel's wall. Kyle was already more than prepared but was surprised at the effect. *Optical Illusion technology? It's not as advanced as it should be, but arcia is really amazing.*

The archers launched a few arrows at Kyle, prompting him to activate the armguard he had taken from the champion, allowing him to block them with green energy bolts lancing out and deflecting them. Activating Penchant for Violence again, he rushed at the throng of goblin warriors, swinging wildly with his full strength.

He bashed through the warriors in the tunnel, sometimes even using their bodies as shields and ramming them against the warriors themselves, causing them to tumble over. Kyle methodically killed each and every goblin warrior involved in the ambush. The battle lasted for nearly five minutes.

Gulak finally came to its senses, only seeing the bloodied Kyle standing in front of it and the bodies of its brethren behind him. "Looks like you don't understand yet." Kyle grabbed the goblin shaman's neck and lifted it up, causing its legs to dangle as it tried to scratch Kyle's arms off. "I am the master of this tribe now. Your warriors are all dead. Do you still wish to resist?"

"N-N-No! I will submit!" Gulak relented, struggling against the iron grip of Kyle. It now realized that Kyle could understand goblin language to a certain degree, which was the only reason it could think of as to why Kyle knew about the ambush.

"Good." Kyle dropped Gulak to the floor. It gasped for air as it massaged its almost crushed neck. "Gather all remaining goblins in your largest common area. You will be the translator."

Half an hour later, close to two hundred goblins were all gathered in a large cavernous area, their common dining area. Gulak stood on a makeshift stage from turned-over mining carts and crates, clearing his throat.

The goblins were all murmuring with each other, staring at Kyle with curiosity and wariness. Many of them have not left the den before but have heard stories of evil humans who killed goblins for fun.

Kyle's mouth began to move, speaking to Gulak while he translated to the goblins. "Fellow tribesmen, today is a good day! A human hero has arrived and has quelled the monster who had been killing our warriors over the last week. While we have lost many of them in the fight, this human here has saved us in our time of need. With our tribe left vulnerable, this human will help defend our den from rival tribes and other creatures of the forest."

The goblins were all stunned. A human helping goblins?

"The human has offered to provide us with food, technology, and equipment as well. I have agreed to this deal in my capacity as a shaman."

The crowd of goblins didn't cheer, but they didn't react adversely either. They weren't too smart, unable to understand the implications of such a favor. Kyle estimated the intelligence of most of them to be that of an eight to twelve-year-old kid, which was just right for the next part of his plan.

Gulak dismissed the crowd, gathering the smartest goblins in a group to meet Kyle. There were only three of them: Gulak, Gringer, and Gobalt. All of these three knew the truth about what Kyle had done and were now completely subservient to him until they found a way to beat or eradicate him. *We just have to wait until the goblin king sends their regular envoy to collect tribute, and then we shall receive their assistance!*

Kyle observed the crowd of goblins dispersing. After he eliminated most of the warriors, only the elderly and the young were left behind. *The elderly are of no issue, but for the longevity of this operation, subverting the young is necessary.*

"This tribe now falls under me. I will have all goblins work to harvest Euria Seeds." Kyle showed them an example of the seed.

"This... This is a sacred fruit that only the shamans can touch when performing the rituals. Having the uneducated goblins touch them is sacrilege." Gulak couldn't help speaking out. Decades of tribal traditions were ingrained into their brains.

Kyle simply had to rest his hand on the hilt of his hammer and Gulak zipped its own mouth, no longer speaking back. "How many able-bodied goblins do we have left?"

You killed our warriors, and you're asking us this? "Fifty able-bodied goblins remain, though they are not trained to fight. It would have been much more before." Gringer was in charge of the warriors, bowing respectfully with a tinge of hatred in his voice.

Kyle ignored the veiled jab, looking toward Gobalt, who was in charge of the logistics of the tribe. "Food supplies?"

"Dwindling. Only enough to last two weeks." *Because of your filthy actions, human.*

"That's good enough. From today on, I will train all fifty warriors in a different fighting style. Gather all the weapons from the main entrance and bring them here." Kyle ordered.

The fifty warriors soon lined up in front of him, trembling as he walked through and inspected their bodies. While Gulak had claimed that the human hero was here to protect them, they couldn't help feeling like they were being sold as a product. Some of them were well aware that this human was the *monster* that had been killing them, instilling even more fear in them.

Gringer translated as Kyle talked. "All of you will be trained as archers from now on. The training routine will be tree climbing, marksmanship with bows, and knife combat."

The goblins all immediately went into a frenzy, with Gringer turning to glare at Kyle. "Tree climbing is for shitty elves, not us! We are better!" Gringer spat with derision, as did many of the newly trained warriors.

Kyle suddenly stood up, speaking in the goblin language. <Who can defeat me? Come forward.>

The warriors all froze. They did not know the truth about Kyle killing their warriors, but they had heard the story from Gulak that Kyle killed a monster that one hundred of their warriors could not.

Gringer did not dare fight Kyle. If the champion could not defend him, who could?

"Then the training routine is settled." Kyle began to order the dilution of the highly concentrated stamina potions he had brought along in his backpack. "Do not drink until I tell you to. Anyone who does not follow the order will not receive another."

The next day, the training began in earnest. The goblins were much more physically inclined than the humans, but their shorter stature limited the range of combat styles Kyle could teach them. Kyle instructed them on how to use the trees for cover, leaping from branch to branch and taking advantage of their low weight and small figure to avoid retaliation.

He had them run mock battles against each other through the forest, honing their marksmanship and combat skills. The warriors soon saw how effective the fighting style was, which was much different from their usual blunt and head-on battles with other tribes.

A week passed under Kyle's intensive training. They trained day and night, not requiring muscle rest due to the stamina recovery options provided. Kyle had brought highly concentrated potions before diluting them with water and passing them out. This meant they managed to clock in close to eight to twelve hours of training each day.

They weren't expert fighters by the end of the week, but they were competent enough that three of them could give any normal human a run for their money. Kyle was satisfied with the result but was soon confronted by Gobalt. "Human! We only have enough food for a week!"

Kyle took out his map of the forest, where a big red circle marked the location that Orthon, the forest bandit, had told him previously. "Don't worry, our food supply is right here."

Chapter 25

Raiding a Fort

Paulie roared as he drove a cleaver into the wooden table, causing the cutlery to jump. The two forest bandits standing in front of him shivered as the large man leaned back, the veins of fury clearly visible on his face.

The slaves to his left and right were not bothered at all, remaining completely still and silent as Paulie cursed and swore with every phrase he could find in his limited vocabulary.

"You're telling me that after three whole weeks of searching far and wide, you can't find a single hair or tail of the guy that killed Orthon and Troy?! ARE YOU EVEN A FOREST BANDIT?!" Paulie bellowed, chucking a glass against the wall, which shattered brilliantly. A few of the glass pieces rebounded and cut into a slave's skin, but she did not move a single inch, remaining passive.

"Boss, we really tried! The closest we could get to was Kris Grayborn, but the only thing we found was his bloodied cloak. No one in town seems to have heard of the guy before!"

"What about the three merchants who were with them? The driver?"

"They are all dead. They swore they did not know anything even under torture. I'm telling you, I think the rumors of it being a monster are—"

"SHUT UP! You know there is no such monster in the forest. WE are the monsters of the forest. The goblins, including their 'king', tremble at the sight of us!" Paulie slammed the table. He fumed for a while, before dismissing the two guys and pondering quietly.

Paulie wasn't an independent boss—most of his work and hijacking happened because of information given by the Violet Demons in the West Sector of Raktor. He would receive a cargo list, and his boys would be posted on it as guards. The stick-up was supposed to be plain and simple: money or their lives, and usually, the former was chosen.

Sometimes the drivers would be more than happy to "give up" the cargo: they got a cut from the Violet Demons directly, and their employer wouldn't be able to blame the drivers for the loss. It was an easy business, but having four of his men killed in what was supposed to be a simple nab and grab left a sour taste in Paulie's mouth.

Is it the Veiled Angels pulling a fast one on us? Or are the new inquisitors in town trying to get the two of us to clash harder? "You, bring me another glass," Paulie ordered one of the slaves. He frowned and tried to consolidate the evidence he had now. Was the heat finally catching up to him?

Frustrated, he grabbed the new glass of mead served by the slave, drinking it down in one swift motion. The glass was already jagged, cutting his lips slightly. "FUCK!" Paulie raged and slammed the glass onto the slave's head, knocking her out onto the ground with a loud crack. Blood pooled on the floor, but the remaining slaves didn't react.

"You three, grab the body, clean, and dump."

The slaves complied, hauling the dead body out of the room while another slave desperately tried to mop up the dripping blood stains. "Fucking useless idiots, why did I even agree to buy you all from Vin? I should rough him up the next time his slave caravans come around."

Suddenly, a loud bell could be heard ringing through the base. "What?! What's going on?" Paulie demanded, with the slaves all shaking their heads in response. The bell was meant for an enemy attack, but it had not been rung in the five years they had been in operation.

Scrambling outside, Paulie could only see the dead bodies of watchtower scouts falling to the ground, three arrows lodged in their necks while their faces were frozen in shock. "Wh-Who is attacking us?!"

"I don't know, but they are hitting us from the treeline!" One of the bandits at the top of the wooden walls that surrounded the forest bandit's base reported down to Paulie before an arrow went straight through the bandit's head, killing him instantly.

"GET TO COVER!" Paulie roared, running back into the room as a barrage of arrows flew over the walls, hitting indiscriminately. It was random, but the arrows lodged themselves everywhere—the storage sheds, the walls of houses. One even made it through the windows of Paulie's house. He observed the arrow, noticing it was shoddily made, but its arrowhead was extremely sharp. *Goblins? But why?*

He quickly grabbed his armor set, crossbow, and sword. The remaining forest bandits were no slouches either, quickly responding to the deaths of their comrades and firing back into the treelines.

A few goblins were hit, their bodies now visible to the forest bandits. "What? Why are the goblins attacking us, and since when were they so good at using a bow?"

"Doesn't matter. They are all stinking rats anyway. Gear up the point defense engravings. Let's show them who's the boss of the forest!" Paulie galvanized his men with a rousing shout, leading the counterattack as he climbed up the walls, firing back with precision, killing a goblin with each bolt.

The bandits' point defense engravings proved useful, but were easily overwhelmed by the sheer number of arrows that the goblins shot at them, as though they were prepared for it.

Another loud bang drew Paulie out of his momentum, causing him to turn and see a lone human at the wooden gate, which had been smashed apart by a series of hammer strikes. The man wore a cloak, but his back clearly had the ornate crossbow that Orthon used to have. *It's him!*

Paulie slapped the shoulders of the two closest guys. "Get that man! He's the one inciting the goblin attack!" Five forest bandits were already aiming at him, an indiscriminate barrage of arrows following shortly after.

The man lifted his vambrace, green energy bolts flying out and deflecting the incoming arrows. The glowing engraving began to fizzle out the moment it fired ten bolts, forcing the man to use it to block other arrows. As a sharp arrow chipped against the vambrace and damaged the engraving, the man tossed it away, leading the charge. Behind him, more than two dozen goblins wielding bows and swords rushed into the fort, climbing the walls and engaging the forest bandits in close combat.

With the goblin archers shooting from the top of the trees and the goblin warriors attacking from within, the forest bandits were pincered, forced to defend from the side and from the front as well. Paulie immediately recognized he was about to lose this fight, quickly grabbing one of the forest bandits and using him as a shield, as his body soon became a pincushion for arrows.

He ran back into his house, scrambling for his secret stash. *I need to get out of here. If the Veiled Angels catch me, it will be all over!* "You four, go block that door for me!"

The slaves followed the order, quickly carrying the furniture over to the door and barricading the door. Screams and shouts echoed in from outside as the remaining forest bandits began to waver, trying to flee.

Paulie soon managed to dig out his secret stash from under the floorboards, grabbing everything valuable, when a cloaked man jumped in through the windows all of a sudden. Paulie grimaced before waving wildly at the slaves. "What are all of you doing?! Kill that man!" *If he's here to rescue the slaves, he will never hurt them. This is my chance!*

The four female slaves grabbed anything that could act as a weapon nearby, charging at the cloaked man. Without a single breath of hesitation, the cloaked man wielded his hammer and immediately hit the front two slaves right on the head, killing them instantly, while using his free arm to punch the third in the face and sending her sprawling.

[SYSTEM MESSAGE]
You killed Female Slave, +10 EXP.

[SYSTEM MESSAGE]
You killed Female Slave, +10 EXP.

The last one did not even move an inch, already dead from a crossbow bolt buried in her heart.

[SYSTEM MESSAGE]
You killed Female Slave, +10 EXP.

Paulie now knew he was done for—a true killer had arrived.

"Wait, wait, wait! We can talk this out! What do you want? Are you an overseer of the Violet Demons? I've been following up on every payment! I've paid all my dues on time!" Paulie desperately waved with one hand, while his other hand reached for a sword on his waist.

"We can talk this out, right? Look, I'm open to switching sides. Veiled Angels? Ardent Cretins? Um... Ilysian Punks? No problem, I'll even take a lower cut!" Paulie tried to buy time as he inched closer to the back of the house, trying to feel the floor with his foot.

The cloaked man continued walking briskly toward him, his hammer on his right and crossbow pistol on the left. As he walked into attacking range, Paulie grinned and lunged forward with his sword drawn, charging with a forward stab.

This is My Turf.

Skill: This Is My Turf (Basic)
No one gets close to you without your word.
Creates a selective domain that enemies can't approach.
Duration: 30 seconds   **Cooldown:** 3 hours

Paulie continued charging when he was suddenly forced back by an unknown force field that appeared around the cloaked man, seemingly out of nowhere.

Paulie got up and tried to swing at the man, his sword bouncing off the invisible force field that seemed to extend three meters in a radius around the cloaked man. "What the fuck?!" Paulie swung desperately, his sword continuously being deflected off as the cloaked man walked closer and closer to him.

"Who the fuck are you?! What do you want?! Money?!" Paulie backpedaled, his back against the wall now as he held the sword in front with both hands. The cloaked man never stopped walking, continuously moving toward Paulie.

The force field touched the sword, the sheer resistance forcing Paulie to drop the sword as the skin on his palm was nearly shredded from the resulting friction. The invisible wall began to push up against Paulie, making him unable to move as he was pinned against the wall. The armor on his body creaked as the cloaked man inched ever closer, as though he were trying to crush Paulie with all his might by simply stepping forward.

"Please, stop! I'll give you everything you want! Jus—ARRRGHHH." The cloaked man walked even closer, the force field squashing Paulie into the wall. The cloaked man also felt resistance from the force field, like he was pushing a steel block. He pushed forward, his feet cracking against the wooden planks in the ground and causing splinters to fly in all directions.

As he took the second and third steps, the flesh was compacted, and the skeletal structure of Paulie snapped, twisted, and deformed beyond its stress limit.

The skill effect ended, causing Paulie's body to drop to the ground, blood oozing out of every orifice.

[SYSTEM MESSAGE]
You killed Forest Bandit Leader Paulie, +400 EXP.

Kyle smiled as he picked up the secret stash, wiping the blood off its wooden surface. *The skill would be pretty good if it did not have a three-hour cooldown.*

The sounds of screaming and fighting soon came to a halt outside. Kyle left Paulie's body in the house, returning outside where Gringer waited for him. "Sir, we have secured the fort!"

"Good. Call the others to transport all the food, equipment, and all the human slaves back to the den. Use the wheelbarrows the forest bandits have. If there isn't enough, make new ones."

"Yes, sir! Shall the human slaves be thrown into a mass grave too?" Gringer asked excitedly, obviously expecting some more juicy maggots.

"No, I have other plans for them. Have them all shifted to the underground caverns."

The disappointed Gringer moved as ordered, getting the remaining thirty-eight goblin warriors and archers to haul the food back. It took a few hours, but soon the entire fort had been picked clean, with Kyle nodding in satisfaction. *Given the right training and command structure, goblins can be quite an effective workforce.*

Returning to the goblin den, Kyle suddenly asked Gulak for a one-on-one meeting. "Human! What is the meaning of all these human slaves? How can we feed more than fifty of them!?"

"Not important. And we have all the food stolen from the forest bandit." Kyle dismissed his concerns, his eyes drawn toward the goblin's runic tattoos on its body instead. He recalled how Gulak had attempted to disguise himself. *Weird. Now that I think about it, these are arcia engravings, are they not?*

Gulak instinctively shuddered. "No, I am not female! No breeding!"

Kyle's face twitched before he calmed down. "I'm interested in your tattoos. You can activate them like arcia engravings?" He recalled the goblin champion healing himself.

"You are human; this is a goblin's secret. Not allowed to tell!" Gulak crossed its arms, to which Kyle suddenly grabbed his hammer, about to smack its head in. "Wait! I'll tell!"

Gulak led him to a ritualistic chamber only approved for shamans and shamans-in-training. The ceiling was riddled with twine, from which hung countless pig skins someone had carved on. Kyle noted that each of them was a specific skill engraving, which he assumed was what the shamans learned from.

A unique smell suddenly assaulted Kyle's nose, reminding him of the arcia fuel packs he had seen in action around Raktor.

The chamber was filled with arcite embedded into the walls, and some of it had already been sapped of all its liquid arcia fuel. Kyle never expected the goblins to have access to such a vein of arcite. It was small, but still something valuable.

He was still weighing whether to monetize it or not when Gulak pointed to a ritual knife engraved with enchantments, too. Picking it up, the knife was extremely heavy, but obviously not made by goblins.

Taboo Knife (Intermediate)

A goblin heirloom from the past, designed for tattooing enchantments onto the skin.

Age undetermined.

"Only goblins with achievements can receive the sacred symbols." Gulak motioned to his hands, which were adorned with tattoos. "Any lesser goblin would faint or die from the pain."

I was under the impression that engravings only worked on objects. Kyle's eyes lit up. He had a previous plan for the human slaves, but that was no longer necessary. The sinister expression on Kyle's face frightened Gulak once more, reminding it of its previous experience.

"Does this work on humans?"

Chapter 26

Secret Agents

Sasha's stomach rumbled as she tried to recall where she was. She did not see any of the same bars and cages that held her for what seemed like ages. Instead, all she saw was a small cavern with a simple stool and nothing else.

She lay in a small, comfortable bed made out of fur before a dull, aching pain seared through her, stemming from her hand. She raised her right hand to reveal a bandage, soaked in blood and another type of liquid, slowly oozing onto the forearm. *Another type of punishment?*

Sasha was used to the beatings from the forest bandits. She had been in slavery for more than twelve years now, her entire town enslaved by greedy slave traders. She could recall Vin's face full of greed when they stuffed her in a sack and gassed her to sleep for days.

Paulie's face was still vivid in her memory, as he raped her time and time again, even when she was underage. Now, at the age of twenty, her face no longer bore the joy she once had.

Her days were filled with combat, as she was continuously used as target practice by the forest bandits, forced to dodge arrows or withstand sword blows. In the hope of getting stronger, she would sneak into the weapon storage or training yard, fiddling with the weapons and learning how to handle them. She managed to do it undetected for a year before she was caught.

Strong emotions had faded into nothingness over the years, and despair and hopelessness soon filled the void. Even the other slaves were of no comfort to her, fighting with her for survival and favoritism from the forest bandits. Every day was a struggle—no one was her friend or willing to help her. With a lack of proper food and no weapons, she was unable to defend herself nor support the muscle mass needed to fight effectively.

Strangely, my stomach no longer feels hungry. And my stamina seems to have recovered…

As Sasha moved, her right hand throbbed with pain, causing her to scream. However, only a weird guttural sound came out, which helped her quickly remember why she was one of the forest bandit's favorites: she was mute. Her vocal cords were damaged, rendering her unable to talk back or scream.

However, no one responded to the weird sound as she was alone in the cavern. Loud footsteps could soon be heard coming down the hallway, with Sasha instinctively curling up into a defensive ball and hiding from view as far away in a corner as possible.

Soon, the owner of the footsteps was visible—it was a goblin. It sighed as it walked through the main corridor connecting the hundreds of small cavern rooms, poking its head inside and glancing at Sasha.

The girl immediately tensed up, but the goblin did not do anything, instead walking back briskly to wherever he came from. *Oh no! It's going back to call the others! I have to escape.*

The only thing she knew about goblins was that they thrived off the dead bodies of humans, having had former slave friends sent to the mass pits to die.

She peeked around the corner of the cavern, noticing that the patrolling goblin had long left. The room opposite was empty, leaving Sasha curious as to why there were so many rooms as she continued checking them. Some of them seemed to be inhabited by goblins before, with clear signs of their habitation lying around in the form of goblin clothing and even some rudimentary toys.

I'm staying in a goblin room? But why? Sasha began to worry even more about what was happening to her, checking each room. Somehow every room was devoid of people or even goblins, frightening her even more.

As she passed a room, an arm suddenly reached out and grabbed her, causing her to flinch and react violently, nearly punching the person. However, she stopped, realizing that it was one of the other slaves she knew—Ciel.

They weren't particularly close—no one was to Sasha. The man had, on a few occasions, joined other slaves in beating her up, stealing her food, and even raping her. Sasha had always borne a grudge for that.

However, Ciel did not take note of Sasha's angry expression, instead putting a finger on his hand and hushing her. "Stay quiet and don't make a sound! The goblins are hunting us. I know where the exit is, so follow me!"

Before Sasha could protest, Ciel ran off, motioning for Sasha to follow him. The two of them ran down a long hallway, subsequently turning a corner, expecting to see an exit. Instead, a handsome man with a dominating presence was standing in front of them, smiling.

"Where do you think you're going?"

Sasha and Ciel were startled, but they immediately ran in the opposite direction. Surprisingly, the man did not give chase, simply standing there and watching them run off. Sasha found the man's behavior odd until she saw a dozen goblins holding nets moving past the man, obviously aiming to capture them.

With the man blocking off what seemed like the exit, they had no choice but to run deeper into the corridor of rooms. They soon hit a fork, with both of them instinctively splitting up, forcing the chasing goblins to divide their forces too.

Sasha kept running, her head glancing into each of the rooms until she found what she was looking for and dashed in. The six goblins chasing her immediately surrounded the room, only to peek inside and see nothing.

The goblins chattered among themselves, preparing to give chase. But just as they were about to move off, a figure dropped from the ceiling of the room, her fingertips covered in blood from clinging onto random nocks in the cavern. She quickly tackled one of the goblins, grappling it to the ground and twisting its neck in one swift motion.

She then grabbed the knife from the dead goblin's belt, pointing it toward the five net-holding goblins, who were slowly inching toward her. The net was soon thrown, but Sasha quickly dodged it by leaping backward. Leaping off the wall around the net, she lunged with the knife in front of her, plunging it into the chest of a goblin.

Not even trying to retrieve it, she quickly punched and kicked her way through the goblins, nailing all of them in a single hit. Soon, the five remaining goblins were either dead or squirming on the floor. But to her surprise, instead of more footsteps, she could see the sound of clapping from behind.

The girl spun and threw a knife at the source of the clapping, only to see the man catch it by the handle with his bare hands. "Impressive. Much better than the young man."

Sasha turned and ran again when the man suddenly lunged and grabbed her by the shoulder, twisting her into an arm lock and dragging her with him. The man brought her out of the corridor into a wider area, where there were already six of her former colleagues waiting for her, including Ciel, who was sitting there quietly eating a piece of bread. Each of them had a similar bandage on their hand.

Instead of a joyous reunion, they all stared at Sasha awkwardly, their gazes avoiding her as they continued to talk among themselves. "Ciel, you told me she died to the goblins!" one of them whispered angrily.

"I didn't!" Ciel desperately tried to deny that, but his eyes told a different story. Sasha had long been used to such gossip behind her back, with her being the black sheep among the slaves. The main reason was that she was hard to talk to, and no one knew how to communicate with her. Sasha did not know how to read or write either, making things even worse.

However, her condition only emboldened other slaves to bully her even more, sure that she would never be able to speak the truth. She had been the target for venting anger countless times, a dummy to beat up so the slaves could feel better about themselves. Even after learning how to fight, there was no way she could fend off an entire group of slaves unarmed.

Weak, I'm too weak! From one slave master to another, only to be bullied by others! Sasha raged inwardly, but her face remained calm, heading to a corner and sitting down far away from the other slaves.

"How could she die to the goblins? The goblins were not intended to kill you, but to test you. Sasha is the only one who managed to kill a goblin. Well done." The man praised the girl, observing the reaction of the surprised slaves and Sasha, who was in pure shock. It was the first words of praise she had heard since she was enslaved.

"All six of you are what remains of the forest fort. All the other slaves are dead, either used as shields and bait, or due to collateral damage."

Ciel's heart clenched, knowing that the friends he had made over the years were mostly dead. The six slaves silently wept for a brief moment, but swiftly recovered their bearings. Death was always a moment's notice away in the life of a slave, but they never expected them to die just inches away from freedom. Some cried for their parents, who were enslaved with them, and others cried for their friends.

Sasha did not cry or weep. All of the slaves had been dead to her for a long time. Instead, she felt some sort of satisfaction, knowing that those who had hurt her, indirectly or directly, had finally gotten their due. *Except the six of them.*

The furious gaze from Sasha's eyes did not escape the man's notice. "Follow me." He beckoned to the seven slaves including Sasha, who complied on reflex and immediately got to their feet. They had spent far too long in slavery.

The man led them to what seemed to be the main exit of the mine, showing them the patrolling goblins and a few of the green monsters training with bows and swords within a barricaded wooden fort. Most of the armor they were wearing was clearly from the forest fort.

"I am the one who saved you all, and you now have a choice. Walk out the gates, and you will be free. There will be no more debts to settle between us."

Ciel and the six slaves' faces lit up at the sound of freedom, but Sasha's face remained downtrodden. She knew perfectly well that she was a long way from home—if her village even existed. Being mute and weak would only have her captured by other bandits or slavers within a week.

"Second option: Work with me, and I will train you to be strong. Everything you need to live will be provided, but the training will not be easy. You will follow my every command, but I promise no one will ever look down on you again. You will be trained to overpower everyone you meet."

Sasha's face brightened tremendously, but she quickly noticed the souring faces of the other six.

"You're offering us enslavement? Right after you freed us? Are you crazy?" Ciel spat angrily, with the others nodding in agreement.

"It's your choice. No one is forcing you either way, but you have two minutes to make that choice."

Ciel quickly grabbed the rest into a huddle, including Sasha. "I think we can make it out. The town isn't that far from here. I've been on a grocery run before. I can get us there, but we will need to make sure we can fend other goblins. Even if this man has them under control here, there are more tribes nearby."

The man interrupted. "I will provide you a basic weapon to defend yourself with."

Ciel bowed in thanks before continuing to explain. "If we work together as a team, we can fight off anything. We just need to fight for a day or so, and then we'll be in town. Then we can go our separate ways. Maybe even stick together to make something for ourselves. What do you say?"

His optimism influenced the other five, who excitedly agreed, already having dreams of freedom beyond the forest. Some wanted to return to their homeland; others were hoping to strike it rich on their own. None of them wanted to follow the command of the man, which only reminded them of their slave life.

However, Sasha broke free of the huddle, walking over to the man and standing next to him. To her, freedom without strength would only end up in slavery again. She had personally witnessed the man's strength and wanted to be as strong as him—no, even stronger. Anything that could help her take this next step, she would grab.

Furthermore, why would she want to escape with those who had been tormenting her for the last few years?

Ciel's face turned from a bright expression to a nasty scowl. He had hoped that Sasha would join them on the escape, seeing as she was the only one among them who had killed a goblin barehanded.

"One minute left."

Ciel and the other five made up their minds, collecting a simple dagger each from a goblin before walking out of the fort. They made a simple bow of gratitude to the man and left for a better future. Ciel gave a final glance at Sasha, one of pity as though she had chosen wrong. This irked Sasha even more, causing her to clench her fist. *I'll get stronger than all of you idiots, and one day, I'll have my revenge.*

The man turned to Sasha, who was the only one left. "How good are you with a crossbow? Nod for good to great, shake for not good."

Sasha nodded her head. The forest fort had crossbows, and while she had never received any formal training, her time sneaking around the weapon storage and testing them gave her a basic understanding.

The man handed her a crossbow, one she recognized to be Orthon's personalized one. "Show me."

Sasha glanced around the mine entrance, noticing a dummy strawman used for target practice. She aimed the crossbow carefully, firing a single bolt and nailing the target on the head. She then handed the crossbow back to the man respectfully.

"Good enough. Are you ready for your first mission?" The man handed her a Strength Potion and a Stamina Potion, telling her to drink them.

Sasha felt a satisfying rush of strength, as though she had somehow grown more muscles out of nowhere, while her body felt like it had eaten well for weeks. She had never felt better before, nodding vigorously in response to the man's question.

The man tossed her the crossbow and a simple knife. "There are six liabilities running toward the town through the forest now. Kill them all before they spread the word that we are here."

Chapter 27

Racketeering

"Gulak, send three goblins to observe her. Once she has killed all six, drag the bodies here. If she tries to run, kill her as well. No one leaves the forest alive." Kyle motioned as he watched Sasha leave the main entrance.

"To feed the pit?" Gulak excitedly asked. "What about the failed slaves?"

"Those who died during the surgery, throw them in the pit too. The rest who are still alive, keep them in their rooms and cage them."

"Ah, for future food, I see." Gulak bowed, leaving Kyle alone.

He did not trust any of the slaves, not even Sasha. However, based on his observation, the woman had all the right inclinations to be molded into the perfect weapon. *Hatred, revenge, anger—all of this can be easily manipulated.*

Kyle walked down to a different set of rooms, where the failed slaves were being held. Most of them had devolved into rabid primal humans, growling and snapping at Kyle. He had lied to Ciel and the other five, saying that all the other slaves had died.

In truth, Kyle had managed to save almost all the slaves except for the ones he had killed in Paulie's house. He looked into a room, noticing a failed slave that looked like Ciel's father, twisting and groaning on the floor. *At least your family will be useful for Sasha's training.*

Thanks to the number of human subjects, he had managed to figure out an approximate success rate of the Taboo Knife. It was abysmal—a measly seven out of fifty. His sample size and type of bodies were not exactly in the ideal state or range, but it was a telling sign that he shouldn't try it on himself without further assurances.

It would be impossible to do it without someone's help. The pain of engraving the arcite under the skin seemed immeasurable, and he would not be able to grip the knife effectively. Just one wrong move, and the engraving would not be as effective or create a completely different effect.

Kyle would not say he did not trust anyone. He trusted Damian and Keith to handle affairs while he was gone due to mutual benefits, but he would not trust them to do such complicated surgery. *I will have to find an extremely competent arctech engraver to do this, and I must establish trust or threat.*

He had performed a simple operation on all the human slaves, engraving the exact same enchantment he had been practicing—the force-increasing enchantment from Riker's metal pipe. Engraving an enchantment did not mean it was the end, as Kyle could simply cut off the skin where it was engraved and re-healing it, generating new skin to try again. However, with no anesthesia, it would prove to be a huge problem.

There was another huge problem he encountered: he had verified who was backing the forest bandits. When Troy had told him the truth, he was hesitant to truly accept it, but after hearing Paulie's final words, he was certain. *The Violet Demons, the second major gang of the West Sector... If they found out I pillaged their business, this could be a big problem. I have to hide my tracks as much as possible. It would be best if I remained here for a while longer to stave off the heat.*

Kyle had already been away from Raktor for close to a month. For all he knew, the Seven Snakes might have been taken over by another gang leader, but this was a necessary expedition to clear the debt owed to the Crimson Snakes.

He also knew that if he left the goblins alone right now, they would not work for him any longer, immediately rebelling. *Someone has to stay behind and supervise them with force. That's the only way.*

This meant that he would need to stay for a month longer until everything was nicely set up and could operate independently. *Once the Euria Seeds hit the streets of Raktor, the prices will plummet, but at the scale I'm selling them, the profits will be immense. One million rakels will be done in a single week if everything goes right.*

Just as he was thinking deeply, the gates of the wooden barricade around the main entrance opened to reveal Sasha dragging one of the six who had left back alive, while three goblins behind her dragged the dead slaves back to the fort. All of them wore faces of shock or anger and their foreheads had a crossbow bolt lodged in them.

Kyle's eyes squinted as Sasha dragged the remaining slave in front of him before kneeling. "The mission was to kill all of them. Why have you kept this one alive?"

Instead of Sasha talking, the slave immediately groveled on all fours, begging with tears streaming down her face. "Please, let me live! I made the wrong choice! I used to be a clerk! I can read and write and do whatever you need! I'll be your slave!" She was clearly shaken by the slaves being killed by Sasha.

Kyle pondered for a moment, glancing at Sasha's expression. *While she did not follow the orders to the letter, it seems that she has brought me back an underling. Adaptability on the fly is great as well. This will be interesting.*

"Good. Sasha, since you kept her alive, you will be in charge of her discipline. If she tries to go against me, you have every right to punish her. Name?"

"Merissa, sir!"

"Get up and follow me, both of you."

Kyle led them to another room that was now designed like an office. Kyle intended to handle the logistics of shipping the Euria Seeds out into Raktor here, but with Merissa and Sasha here, they could assist him with the entire operation.

"Merissa. You will now tally the number of Euria Seeds collected and delivered every single day without fail. You are also in charge of ensuring the well-being of the goblins. In the event they try to rebel, you immediately tell me or Sasha. Understood?"

Sasha tugged at Kyle's clothes, pointing to the office table and doing a cross with her arms, shaking her head vigorously. "You can't read and write? Not an issue. You will learn in a week." Kyle dismissed her.

Kyle quickly showed Merissa the basics, the woman trembling all the while. She was acutely aware that Sasha had been ordered by Kyle to kill them all, so she remained docile and compliant, following Kyle's orders.

Kyle then brought Sasha out back to the single rooms where the failed slaves were held. "Over the next month, I will teach you how to read, write, and fight. We will also learn how you can activate the engraving on your body to your benefit. At the end of the training, you will be strong enough to kill everyone in this den. You will then be in charge of overall operations here, ensuring Euria Seeds are being delivered consistently. Anyone who steps out of line will be yours to punish. Understood?"

Sasha nodded vigorously. She already planned to make the most of her time here—to make herself stronger and independent. This was the best training arc she could have hoped for.

"Good, let's begin."

* * *

Sebastian entered the grand office of Bishop Vernette alone, smiling at the two inquisitors and bishop who were waiting for him.

"You're a hard man to meet, Mr. Sebastian." Mason stood up to shake his hand. "Took a month of beating up your associates to even get you to respond."

"My apologies. I was busy with some other personal matters." Sebastian sat down quietly in a nice velvet chair, crossing his legs. He glanced at the serene face of Mason, contrasted by the obviously hostile expression on Kitana's face. "I assume she's the mad dog being let loose on us. Since when were the inquisitors this violent?"

"Want to find out how much more we can get?" Kitana grinned, grabbing the pistol at her waist.

Sebastian did not flinch. "Not interested. I'm more interested in how such a young inquisitor could turn out to be the most bloodthirsty in history."

"Let's just say your men were very adamant in resisting arrest. Nothing else we could do." Mason smoked his pipe before tapping it on the edge of the table. "Let's get straight to the point. Baron Cain wants more money."

"How much more?" Sebastian didn't care about his associates getting killed. They had thousands of them—a few dozen or so dying was just a statistic to him.

"I'm not privy to how much he specifically wants, but you should know how angry Baron Cain gets."

"So, you're killing my members, trashing my businesses, and then asking me to pay you?"

"Sounds about right. Shouldn't be new to a gang that runs a protection racket." Mason chuckled, while Kitana still glared at Sebastian.

"Mason. I came here to save my business, not take another loss." Sebastian sighed, tapping the holster of the chair.

"I'm sure the losses of your front businesses are more than enough to warrant an increase in payment to Baron Cain."

"I know the two of you have been investigating quite a fair bit into the factories. The entire sector is talking about it. Perhaps instead of payment, I can be of some assistance?"

Mason grinned as though he had already been expecting the conversation to twist this way, huffing out a plume of blue smoke. "What assistance?" He played dumb.

"I can provide protection to the factories you need. I'm sure the factory workers are compromised beyond belief and will never talk to an enforcer. I already have my men inside. I know everything."

"How do we know you're not going to nick the goods themselves?" Kitana scoffed.

"For one who likes to kill so much, you're surprisingly naïve." Sebastian let out a small laugh, slightly infuriating Kitana. "I'm business-focused first and foremost. Stability is the best for business. We're on the same team here, you and I."

"I think my definition of stability is not the same as yours."

Mason held up his hand to stop Kitana. "What about the districts outside of your jurisdiction?"

"Well, again. Stability is my main concern. I do not step into other gangs' districts without permission, and I highly doubt any of the other gangs would be willing to allow me to establish a permanent presence there in their factories. But I can assure you that the factories in my district will not be touched. That reduces the number of factories that you need to protect."

"Who said anything about your help—" Kitana started, but Mason held up his hand again.

"When can you start?"

"Don't be so impatient. We have yet to discuss what you will offer me."

"It's obvious; no payment required to the Baron."

"I want a deal that my businesses and members will not be touched for the next two years," Sebastian stated.

"Two years?!" Mason was taken aback. "You're out of your mind! A free pass for two years?"

"I was not talking to you, seeing as you don't have the power to make such a deal yourself. Isn't that right, Bishop Vernette?"

The bishop, who had been staying out of the conversation, sighed, finally putting down her pen. "Only if your men will protect the factories for that same duration."

"Of course."

"Then we do have a deal. So long as the protection lasts."

"Good. I will be moving my men into the factories tomorrow. Tell your enforcers to get out of our way from now on. And stop killing my men. Do not think you're invincible." Sebastian bowed to the bishop before leaving the office.

Mason and Kitana sat back down on the sofa, the angry expression on the young woman's face dissipating quickly. "Well, that went rather well." Kitana smiled as she leaned back onto the sofa, her zealous, haughty attitude long gone.

It was a ploy by Mason and Kitana: have Kitana act as an enthusiastic inquisitor and beat up gang members, forcing the gang members to come to the table to parley.

"Like I said, carrot and stick. Now we only have to cover the remainder of the factories." Mason eyed the map pinned on the wall, checking the remaining twenty districts.

"So I get to beat up another gang?"

"Maybe, maybe not. We do have enough manpower to watch over the remaining factories, though just barely. Too many different gangs watching the factories might incite them to backstab each other. Besides, with the rumors we've been putting out, no one should be stupid enough to hijack our factories."

Chapter 28

Attempted Takeover

Two weeks later...

The Culdao Peaks Town had become even more of a bustling hub of trade, the market packed to the brim. Dozens of wagons and caravans shuttled crates of Euria Seeds to and fro from the town toward the city of Raktor, prompting new businesses to sprout up along the way.

The inn that Kyle stayed at had the best businesses, with the number of merchants and travelers trying to cash in on the amount of traffic going through as well as profit from the price difference of Euria Seeds between the town and Raktor.

"Did you hear the news? I heard one of the companies is under attack by the other five!"

"Really? Didn't the six of them agree to share the habitat? Why would they renege on the agreement now?"

"I don't know, but it seems to me that eventually only one company will remain standing. As profitable as it is, I don't think it's large enough for six companies to share."

The rumors floated around the town like wildfire. It was to be expected, as it gave the town a new breath of life. Strangers from the city of Raktor that they had never seen before were now entering frequently, using the town as a base station hub for transportation. The companies' workers would bring large baskets on their backs into the forest, harvesting the seeds and selling them off en masse in the town.

Other independent adventurers and townsfolk tried to get in on the action but were somehow deterred by goblin archers and warriors defending the habitat. The biggest rumor was that the six companies had somehow managed to broker a deal with the goblins. Some townsfolk had even heard rumors of metalware and forging equipment being delivered to the goblin den.

"Trading human weaponry for Euria Seeds. This might be dangerous in the future! What if the goblins decide to turn around and attack us?"

"Bah! They're numerous but weak! Without anybody training them, they are no better than a kid with a sword. Our Yual Dominion's knights can easily flatten them. If they don't come on time, then the gangs from the city of Raktor would take care of them easily."

It was no secret that the gangs of Raktor were beginning to take notice of this massive venture, hoping to cash in on some of the profits. They had eyes everywhere, disguising themselves as travelers, escorts, adventurers, and merchants.

One such traveler, draped in a cloak, sat near the market, observing the crowded area as some of the Euria Seeds harvested by the companies were sold right here, while the rest were shipped at wholesale prices to various parts of Raktor. Merchants jostled with each other to choose the best basket, throwing hands.

The traveler was sipping on his water flask just as a young boy ran up to him. He whispered into the boy's ear, "Good, here's your rakels." He placed a hundred rakels into the boy's hands, who grinned widely and ran off. He got up from his chair, moving slowly but with purpose through the crowd, targeting a well-dressed gentleman in a suit.

He revealed a concealed knife from his wrist, jabbing the tip into the back of the gentleman, who froze. "Don't make a sound. I'm sure you don't want your wife to see your dead body on the ground here. You're not the only company executive I can use, Feldon." The traveler whispered to the gentleman.

Feldon instinctively gulped and nodded vigorously. The traveler nudged him with an elbow, the two of them moving to a more secluded area between buildings. "Who are you? What do you want?" Feldon asked, his voice shaking.

"Which gang is behind this operation?"

"What...?" Feldon's face was filled with confusion. The traveler pressed the same knife as before against Feldon's neck.

"I swear, I really don't know what you're talking about! As far as I know, we're a legitimate company! I only joined a week ago!"

The traveler carefully examined Feldon's eyes before finally letting him go. "Who's growing the Euria Seeds? There must be a hidden plantation nearby, right?"

"Huh? Our workers collect them from the forest. The area is filled with ripe Euria Trees!"

"Yet only the six companies can collect from that particular area? Do you think I'm stupid?" The traveler scowled, pointing the knife at him.

"Look, it's my first time here as well! I was just supposed to oversee the transfer and sale of Euria Seeds here. That's all!" Feldon pleaded with a fearful expression.

"Bring me to the habitat."

"W-What?! No, you'll be killed. I don't even know if I am allowed in!"

"You're a company overseer. I'm sure you'll be fine. MOVE!" the traveler growled and continued aiming the knife at Feldon, forcing him to move under coercion.

They re-entered the market area, with the traveler nodding to two other random strangers. They each had a different outfit to blend in, but they all came from the same gang. They hefted large backpacks, no doubt filled with weapons.

The four of them moved into the forest from a different approach, with Feldon forced to be in the lead. The other two opened their backpacks, passing a crossbow to the traveler.

"Keep your eyes peeled. Have your crossbows at the ready. If it's the Veiled Angels running this operation, we kill on sight. Too many, and we run," the traveler ordered the other two.

"Yes, sir."

Feldon's mind was racing as he stumbled through the foliage, continuously peeking behind him, only to see three crossbows ready to shoot him if he tried to run. *Veiled Angels? If they've got beef, it means that the three of them must be from the Violet Demons!*

The two gangs were currently at war with each other in the West Sector, with bloodbaths appearing whenever and wherever they clashed. This applied outside the city as well—money was money after all. The Violet Demons were not about to let the Veiled Angels be the only ones to profit from such a scheme.

Taking down our forest bandits and setting up their own operation? If these guys think they can get away with it, they are dead wrong... The traveler smirked as they trudged through the forest. They passed a few Euria Trees, but they could no longer spot any seeds on the branches or leaves, no doubt being harvested by the companies already.

Suddenly, a warning arrow swooped in, landing right at their feet. It was a crudely made goblin arrow, short and stubby. The group looked up to see three goblin archers perched on the branches of trees, aiming down at them with their short bows. Feldon screamed in reflex, trying to run away, before the traveler grabbed him by the throat and slapped his cheek.

"Idiot, your company already has a deal with them! Just show your company emblem!"

"Right, right." Feldon fumbled as he searched through his suit's pockets, his breath still erratic. He quickly retrieved a metallic emblem engraved with a simple logo of the company.

The goblins did not aim at Feldon any longer but aimed their bows at the remaining three. "Looks like we're not getting a free pass after all." The traveler sighed and lifted Feldon as a shield and hostage. They walked forward, the other two aiming at the two goblins with bulky crossbows.

"Keep moving!" the traveler growled at Feldon, who quickly moved. However, a single arrow grazed Feldon's cheek before a gurgling sound was heard behind him. He turned to see the traveler's neck pierced from the front by the arrow as he collapsed to the ground.

"Fuck!" The remaining two lifted their crossbows, firing bolt after bolt at the goblins. The two goblins did not stand a chance, their bodies riddled with bolts and dropping to the ground. However, another zipping sound could be heard, with one of the remaining two screaming out in pain as the arrow pierced his chest, embedding itself in his heart.

"Who's there!? Veiled Angels? Stop shooting if you don't want him to die!" The last man immediately grabbed Feldon as a hostage, a knife aimed at the neck while his other free hand hefted the crossbow in the direction where the arrow came in from.

No one replied, and no more arrows came in. A bead of sweat trickled and snaked its way down the man's face as the tension began to build within. He glanced everywhere, trying to spot any movement. All he could hear was the rustling of the leaves and the sounds of animal cries from the distance.

Out of the blue, a searing pain erupted from his back, stemming from a dagger plunged deep by a young lady. Her face was apathetic as the man yelled out in shock, immediately using his crossbow as a blunt weapon to try and hit her.

Her short white hair floated as she ducked before retrieving another dagger from her belt, jabbing both ankles of the man in rapid succession, causing him to fall on both legs. Both his crossbow and Feldon fell to the ground as well.

"Wait! I have money! Just let me go!" the man shouted in a final attempt to sway the young lady, but she showed no reaction. She did not even grace him with a response. "Fine! I won't go down without a fig—"

The man tried to say more, but his cheeks were already pierced by a crossbow bolt from his own crossbow, now wielded by the young lady. A few more bolts ended his life, with Feldon still shivering as he stared at the three dead bodies. *I signed up to be a manager, not a fighter!*

The young lady grabbed Feldon by the waist, lifting him up and walking deeper into the forest toward the mountain. "W-Where are you bringing me? The town is the other way!"

Feldon tried to convince her to change directions, but she did not reply anymore, almost as though she were mute. They soon reached an abandoned mine, where the wooden palisade walls were crawling with goblins, which freaked Feldon out even more.

They entered the fort, with the young lady unceremoniously dumping Feldon onto the ground.

"Good work, Sasha. Gulak, send out the goblins to collect the bodies," Kyle ordered with a satisfied expression on his face. "Ah, you must be one of the new employees. Feldon, was it? Welcome to the source of the Euria Seeds." He helped Feldon up, who patted his already bloodstained suit in vain.

Feldon was surprised they knew about him when it was his first time visiting. He knew the goblins were at peace with the companies, but not to the extent where company members could stay at the den itself. "I—I demand an explanation! What in the world is going on here?"

"Sasha, head back and take a rest." Kyle motioned toward the entrance. "As for your explanation, it is very simple. I am the one running this entire operation. My name is Kyle, gang leader of the Seven Snakes."

"What?! How?! I thought..."

"We have a problem now, Feldon. It seems you've been marked by the Violet Demons, and they are trying to use you as a way to sneak their way into this operation. Releasing you back into the town will only raise even more suspicion, placing you under an even bigger threat."

Feldon pondered for a moment before suddenly realizing what Kyle was implying. "You're... You're suggesting I stay here permanently! No! No way in hell! My wife and kids are still out there in the town!"

"Oh, Celine, Mick, and Daphne? Of course, I will bring them here as well for their protection." The accuracy with which Kyle knew about Feldon frightened him even more. "Sasha will handle it."

"I'm a prisoner now! My relatives are all in Raktor, my kids' school is there too, you can't just—"

Kyle suddenly grabbed Feldon by the neck, lifting him up. "You seem to be misunderstanding something here. You don't have a choice. Your life is now in my hands. Make the wrong move, and I can't say what'll happen to dear Celine."

Feldon immediately clamped up, nodding vigorously as his hands desperately tried to loosen Kyle's grip. Kyle dropped him on the ground, ordering the goblins to show him to his new room. Feldon soon noticed that he wasn't the only one here—plenty of other company workers who were compromised by the gangs were now sheltered here.

Gringer ran up to Kyle, bowing respectfully. "Sir, one of the companies seemed to have turned over to another gang. The Euria Seeds are being passed for free to their wagons just outside the town."

"Looks like the attack from the other five companies was not enough to keep them in line. Kill every worker from that company who comes to pick up the baskets."

The workers did not directly interact with the goblins, instead exchanging baskets at known locations agreed upon throughout the forest. The workers only knew this was part of the deal to not interact with the goblins, but it was a ploy by Kyle to ensure that no one knew the real nature of the operation.

Keith was the one who set up the companies in Raktor but had used frontmen to serve as the fall guys in case anything went wrong. The money invested was through yet another shell company, so even if the company's head told the controlling gang who funded him, it would end up in a dead end.

With this, Kyle had established a safe trading network of Euria Seeds, where he was the only direct profiteer. At the same time, he was training Sasha and a few of the compromised company workers, forming a secret force of his own. It had only been two weeks since he had started, but good progress was already being made.

Kyle already had plans for this force to serve as a hidden dagger that he could use to strike at other gangs' operations in the region or even enter Raktor undetected to fight in the South Sector.

With this, even if the other gangs were watching his movements, they would be unaware of this new hidden force. Sasha was also designated as a follower with Kyle's Designate Follower skill, a new arcia engraving appearing on her neck that allowed them to telepathically communicate over a long distance. The range was limited, only working up within five kilometers.

Kyle could not stay here forever—he would have to show his face in the South Sector as well as ensure everything was going on track. With only two months left to repay the debt, he could only hope there would be no major disruptions.

Looks like I've done everything I could here. It's time to return to check on the progress in the South Sector.

Chapter 29

Hijacking

The return of Kyle to the Seven Snakes was hushed and kept on the down low, with no fanfare. Kyle did not want to tip off any of the observers, be it the enforcers or other gangs like the Ardent Cretins.

He had left Sasha and the company workers behind in the goblin den to serve as the logistics and defenders, while the five remaining loyal companies continued to work as planned. Some of the workers definitely skimmed some of the Euria Seeds, but Kyle did not care as long as they did not eat too much into their profits. Kyle wasn't leaving the Culdao Peaks entirely, planning to rotate his time between the two locations by using the company's transport network to sneak in and out.

Kyle had returned three days after the reopening of the Seductive Serpent, and it was indeed a roaring success. Both old and new customers poured in like a never-ending tide, making the pub busy even during the day. In terms of financials, it was doing much better than the Lusty Arcian just due to its scale and business model.

The pub had been remodeled to a swanky new renovation layout, with a small, quaint restaurant serving as the front, while behind the kitchen was the main area filled with private rooms as well as multiple secondary sections that featured different types of music. It also had various stages for musicians to perform on, providing yet another avenue for aspiring players to make their name well-known. This was yet another small facet of Kyle's plan to integrate the Seven Snakes into the local ecosystem, ensuring their influence over multiple industries.

Kyle noted a few of the customers were smoking Euria Seeds as well. The combination of the relaxing smoke and the chill atmosphere ensured that they stayed there nearly the entire day, only leaving to buy more Euria Seeds or matchsticks. *It is good that we have acquired a source of cheap Euria Seeds—this place could be half-turned into a full smoking den.*

He met with Eric Dicar, who was now running the pub full-time while the inhouse brewery was just right behind. A wide, beaming smile could be seen plastered on his face. "This is far better than I dreamed of. I always wanted to run my own pub with my own creations."

Hook, line, and sinker. Which alcoholic would refuse the offer to run a pub, and for free at that? Kyle talked at length with Eric about his objectives for the pubs before leaving for the Seven Snakes' base again.

"Sir, here's the updated member list, along with the new recruits gathered in the time you were missing," Damian presented. "Keith and I have decided on the list of vipers now. While Monica and Adrian are fairly new compared to other members, their skills in their respective roles cannot be understated. As far as we can tell, they have no misgivings toward the Seven Snakes apart from their initial capture and the underlying threat of blackmail."

Kyle glanced through the list, focused on the vipers who acted as squad leaders. "Monica, Adrian, Niko..." He recalled Niko being one of the young men that he had seen at the Lusty Arcian while fighting off Lionel. The Seven Snakes had more than fifty associates now, but Kyle had not met all of them yet.

The new vipers had climbed the ranks due to their hard working ethic and their ability to hustle, allowing the Seven Snakes to slowly spread across the district. This, combined with the effects of the soup kitchen and the weekly public clean-up events, had skyrocketed Seven Snakes' reputation in the community. *All according to plan.*

"I trust your decision and choice." Kyle nodded his head, but deep down, he still did not trust all of them. The betrayal in his former life still ran deep in his veins, and his plans were centered around himself for now. It wasn't an issue of competency but a deep sense of insecurity hidden within, though Kyle did not openly acknowledge it yet.

"We seem to be on track to pay off the debt in the next two months, assuming no further hiccups. I think we've done it." Keith grinned.

None of the Euria Seeds were bought by the Seven Snakes gang; instead, they were routed to the other sectors to reduce their trail. Kyle complimented Keith on the complicated paper trail, ensuring no one would be able to find out. Money was collected in cold, hard cash in person rather than through bank accounts, preventing traces by the local authorities, while the money would be cleaned and layered through the various Seven Snakes businesses.

The new supply of Euria Seeds did drop the prices in the market area, allowing Kyle to make even more profits on his addictive potions, which had been selling like hotcakes in the expanded Lusty Arcian as well as the new pub.

With this, he could generate enough money to pay off the debt to the Crimson Swords, which meant his gang was in the clear for now. Kyle heaved a sigh of relief, as did Damian and Keith, knowing that one burden was finally off their shoulders.

"We also have the casino nearly ready to go. A few more days, and it will be up and running," Keith explained. "The extra time was due to there being no existing locations that had casinos—the enforcers had shut down most of them, and with the current level of heat we're facing, we're going to need to put in extra effort to hide it as much as possible."

Kyle nodded in understanding. Running a gang was an eternal battle against the law and other gangs. Every expanding gang would have to contend with the local enforcers, who usually turned a blind eye until something grew too big. Right now, they were nearing that threshold. Damian had gotten a few corrupt enforcers on the gang's payroll, reducing the heat, but there seemed to be trouble looming on the horizon.

It was due to a piece of news that shocked Kyle when he returned—the raids by the enforcers on the Ardent Cretins. It was reported to be extremely brutal, with many low-level grunts killed by what seemed to be an overzealous inquisitor.

"Isn't it a good thing that they got raided? That reduces their financial advantage over us, allowing us to expand outward even more. Right now, we're stuck in this district because of them. If the enforcers keep this up, we might have a chance to claw away some of the less defended areas." Damian reasoned.

"No. It hints that the new inquisitors who recently took office are finding evidence and warrants or going all out. They are targeting the big fish for now as they generate the most heat, but soon, the increased surveillance will trickle down to us." Kyle knew the Ardent Cretins must have had local enforcers on their payroll, so for them to get raided meant that there had been a sweeping change in law enforcement, or at least the purpose of law enforcement.

"Indeed, they are clearing the low-hanging fruit first of the big gangs, trying to weaken them. Did you see the West Sector? It's almost in full-blown conflict now—a three-way fight between the Veiled Angels, Violet Demons, and the enforcers." Keith handed a newspaper over to Kyle.

Kyle read the article, frowning. *The Ardent Cretins limiting us now is the least of our worries—the inquisitors seem to be on a warpath for some reason.*

"When was the last time inquisitors came to the city?"

"Erm... I don't think it was when any of us were around..." Damian shook his head. He had only been in the gang for five years and had never heard of inquisitors coming. However, it was obvious that the Seven Snakes could come under greater scrutiny from now on. Every step had to be measured.

One problem after another. Just when Kyle thought he was in the clear, here was another obstacle.

"We will now come up with contingency plans to deflect as much heat from the enforcers as possible. We might be on track to pay off the debt, but the enforcers can restrict our operations, which would hurt us financially." Kyle began to pace the room, thinking hard and recalling all the methods he used to evade the Galactic Council in the past.

"It's not enough to entice the corrupt enforcers. We need to blackmail them. Set them up with sex workers from the brothel if possible, or have them gamble at the new casino. Use our connections with the locals. Bribe them to do it if they must." Kyle's tone was urgent, and he spoke quickly.

"Damian, increase the number of informants we have in the local enforcers through this method."

"Keith, we will need to begin shifting the Seven Snakes base as well into a more decentralized version. And the fronts that we currently have in place for the pub and casino should be replicated for the brothel too."

"Already on it, sir." Keith nodded. "I already have the Lusty Arcian remodeled to be a beauty school at the front. As for the Seven Snakes' base, we're in the process of acquiring a total of seven different locations that our members can rotate through. The brewery will be shifted as well, along with Professor Dicar."

"How soon can we get the relocation done?"

"About a week. Not a lot of setups are needed, just the part on acquiring a lot of safehouses."

"Good, I want us cleared out of here by then before we get hit. Get Monica, Niko, and Adrian in. I want the vipers to report what they've been doing in the past few weeks since I left."

The three of them soon entered, lining up in front of Kyle. Kyle did not trust them fully yet, but seeing that they had been promoted out of the recruits meant that Damian and Keith did.

"Monica, you're in charge of smuggling the alcohol brewed by Professor Dicar to our ventures. Any updates?"

"Yes, sir. The enforcers have been doing more regular wagon checks, trying to catch anyone flouting the prohibition bans. We've been disguising the wagons as food supplies or potions, but we did have a few wagons caught over the last two months."

This wasn't good. Alcohol was the lifeblood of the brothels, pubs, and casinos. "Damian, fix this issue. Make sure the patrolling enforcers don't bother us any longer. Next, Adrian."

Adrian was in charge of observing the district, trying to pick out other gangs' spies or newly formed thug rackets. He used to be one of them, so he had experience spotting the same signs. "Yes, sir. My squad has rooted out five thug outfits so far. We've successfully converted three of them into our own affiliate rackets in exchange for protection from other thug gangs. Two thug gangs were imprisoned and are currently used by Eric in alcohol testing."

Kyle nodded, unfazed. Alcohol brewing wasn't exactly lethal, but a bad batch would be insufferable as well. It's better to try it on a few humans before serving it to their loyal customers. His eyes landed on Niko.

"Yes, sir! Security at our ventures has been stable. So far, no incursions or raids by enforcers."

"That's it?"

"Yes, sir..." Niko was obviously flustered by his lack of activity compared to the other two. The lackluster reaction from Kyle pained him. *I need to do something big if I want Kyle to recognize me.*

"Good. Keep it that way. Enforcer activity is increasing, so please keep your men under control. Do not do anything to give us away to the enforcers," Kyle lectured before dismissing all of them from his office.

Law enforcement never changes, no matter which universe, huh? Kyle smiled to himself. While there was definitely a threat from the enforcers now rising, Kyle had dealt with this for his entire former life. *As long as I play my cards right, we can make something out of this.*

* * *

The restaurant was packed to the brim. Weary factory managers just clocking off the shift, stall owners who just had a good run at the food market, or administrative clerks complaining about their day. A hundred tables and booths were filled up, with two dozen waiters going back and forth.

An old factory worker entered the restaurant, his attire shabby and grimy, stained with the grease from working the machines. He rubbed his hands anxiously, walking up to a waiter.

"Excuse me, sir. Do you need something?" The waiter was confused, wondering why the older factory worker was standing in front of him.

"Hi, I'm looking for a toilet. Really urgent. Preferably one with a golden snake."

"Ah, just right down the double doors, turn left and you'll find it." The waiter nonchalantly motioned behind him.

The old factory worker weaseled his way through the tables, trying to ignore the weird stares he was getting from the restaurant customers. He reached the double doors, opening to reveal a crowded kitchen with the smell of oil and spices filling the air.

He walked through them with trepidation, stealing a quick glance at the chefs. None of them seemed to be particularly bothered that he was there, despite not being a chef or a staff member. Navigating through the tight space, he soon reached a discreet black door, knocking on it with a specific pattern.

A small sliding notch slid open, revealing a pair of piercing eyes. "Who?" A gruff voice wafted from behind the door.

"I know Niko! Let me in!" the older factory worker said desperately.

The sliding notch closed, and the door opened. "One wrong move and you're dead, old man." The guard grinned, motioning for him to enter.

The sight beyond the door was a completely different view from the rest of the posh restaurant. Card games, dice games—every gambling game you could think of was right here. High-rollers surrounded by escorts laughed their heads on as they watched their opponents squirm on their velvet chairs. Bartenders served alcohol non-stop, with some of the customers already clearly drunk but still paying right out of their weekly pay.

The old factory worker tried his best to avoid the others, finding his way through the casino. Unfortunately, he bumped into a large Seven Snakes associate, who glared at him in anger. "Old man, you lost? Or a snitch? Whatchu doing here? Who let you in?!"

"I—I—"

"He's with me. Back off, Bosso." A young man wrapped in bling and a formal suit shoved the large guard away, who immediately lost his anger and scurried away, as though afraid of the young man.

"Niko!" The old factory worker patted him on the shoulders before examining him. He was the one who had introduced Niko to the Lusty Arcian in the first place. "You're all grown up now! Look at you!"

"Haha, thanks Karl. How's the factory been treating you?" Niko motioned to an empty booth on the side, already pre-arranged with drinks and snacks.

"Oh, you know, same old, same old. Manager got pissy as usual..." Karl sat down in the booth gingerly, feeling the velvet. This level of comfort was far beyond anything he was used to, having grown up poor. He glanced at Niko, who seemed to be comfortable in this area.

"HAHA! They always get pissy, even if you do everything right. Anyway, the drinks are for you; have a go. We got our own in-house thing going now, so our alcohol is top of the line now, or at least that's what I think." Niko poured a glass of wine, handing it to Karl.

"I don't have any money left. I spent it all on the potions from the brothel... I just can't kick the habit, you know? I tried borrowing money from the bankers and moneylenders, but they are all complaining about my low income…” Karl's face was downtrodden as he swirled the glass of wine, wondering if he needed to pay for it.

“Karl.” Niko suddenly grabbed the old man's shoulder, staring at him. “This? All of this? Free. On the house. For old times' sake.”

“Really?”

“Of course! We're friends!” Niko grabbed his own glass of wine. “Cheers!”

They drank happily, talking about their past time in the factory together and reminiscing over shared memories.

“So… why the sudden visit?” Niko finally got to the point. “Don't say for old times' sake.”

Karl's happy expression was frozen in place as he slowly put down the glass. “I need some extra cash, and seeing as the banks aren't helping, I was hoping…”

“To borrow from me? Sure, Karl, but I need more assurance that you're going to pay me back. I know exactly how much the factory pays you and how much you spend on the brothel.”

“Look, I swear I'll pay you back. I'll cut down on my brothel visits, and even if I don't pay back, you can take my assets or—”

“Don't fuck with me, Karl. I'm not the same naïve boy. You don't have any assets left; you already pawned all of it off,” Niko snarled before suddenly slamming his glass on the table with force, frightening Karl with the sudden swap in attitude. “Be real. If you want money, you'd better come up with something valuable.”

Karl gulped internally as he saw how far Niko had changed, thoroughly intimidated. “I really don't have anything left. I'm at my wit's end here!”

“Are you sure? I'm confident a senior factory worker must have access to some information…” Niko grinned.

Karl's face was confused for a moment until realization dawned on his face. “You… Nononono. There's no way. I… I'll be fired if I help you!”

"You want the money? Or nah? You'll even get a cut on top of that. Imagine spending every single day working on the floor, watching all those goods roll past right under your nose, knowing that you'll never earn more than half a rakel for any of them."

The words cut deep into Karl's heart, but his morals still lingered. "You don't know what you're suggesting—the manager would call the guards and the enforcers at a moment's notice!" Karl shook his head vigorously.

"Oh, I know *exactly* what I'm suggesting." Just at this moment, the door to the casino opened to reveal two local enforcers still in uniform. Their piercing eyes scanned the room, eventually locking eyes with Niko. They made a beeline for the young man, but to the surprise of Karl, none of the other guards or customers even bothered, simply continuing on.

Niko stood up and shook hands with both of them, though one of them had a clearly sour expression. "You'd better have a good reason for bringing us in here." The two enforcers sat down next to Karl, frightening him.

Niko sat down and leaned back on the booth, a wide smirk on his face. "How about a nice big cut of a factory hijacking?"

Chapter 30

Unexpected Windfall

The word on the street was all about how the enforcers were protecting the factories quite frequently. Even the Ardent Cretins seemed to be protecting their factories for some unknown reason. Rumor was that the enforcers finally had enough of the hijackings and were actually doing something serious about it.

Niko was not planning on hitting those factories, but rather the factory that he used to work at. He knew it inside out with Karl—all they made was some processed metal, minerals, and maybe a few basic household appliances. Nothing special, but still worth money when sold to the fences.

As far as Niko knew, the enforcers were not protecting the shipments of this particular factory, so Niko felt that it was a clean hit. With the insider information provided by his two corrupt enforcer buddies, Niko had high confidence in the success rate of this hijacking.

With Karl providing the delivery timing of the shipments in and out of Niko's former factory, it was a cinch to simply set up a roadblock in the factory blocks to stop the factory wagon. The corrupt enforcers had slowly cleared out the rest of the area while claiming that they were patrolling the area to prevent the clean enforcers from spotting the hijacking.

However, the factory wagon was nearly an hour late, slightly scaring Niko that he had been betrayed by Karl. "Fuck, where is the wagon?! Have we been set up?" Niko whispered angrily to his crew.

"Not possible, sir. I don't see any enforcers coming to arrest us. This whole block is empty!"

Niko got his crew to check around and found nothing suspicious, except for the late timing of the wagon. Just as Niko was about to call off the operation and pull back, the sound of an arctech wagon could be heard rumbling through the factory blocks. "Finally!" Niko exclaimed, preparing for a quick and fast hit.

The wagon's driver noticed the impending roadblock in front, the wheels screeching to a halt.

Niko and his crew attacked the wagon immediately, smashing the windows and dragging the occupants out. To their surprise, there were two additional factory workers inside who tried to fight back. The melee brawl was fast and brutal. "Private guards? I'm surprised the factory has enough money to hire you guys to guard shipments now!"

The crew killed the private guards and the driver without hesitation. Dumping their bodies into the back, they quickly drove to an intermediate point, splitting up the bolted wooden crates into five different wagons. They drove out in unpredictable routes and finally arrived at the Seven Snakes base through multiple transfers to shake off any enforcers. The bodies were unceremoniously chopped up, never to be seen again.

It was a simple plan and a routine hijacking—except for the fact that now Niko and his crew were on their knees the next day, kneeling in front of Kyle, who glared at him, while Damian and Keith were speechless, staring at the interior of the crates.

One of the crates was opened to reveal a full military arsenal unlike anything they had ever seen. Repeater arctech carbines, explosives, portable cannons, reactive armor, and defensive barrier deployables. There was enough equipment inside to outfit an entire squad of shock troopers armed to the teeth. The technology in the crates was obviously far beyond what the regular guy could get in Raktor and was most definitely not from Niko's former factory.

What made it even worse was that the private guards' bodies were found to have marks indicating they belonged to the Ilysian Punks. Niko gulped internally as he realized what he had just done. This meant that the Seven Snakes had effectively hijacked another gang's truck, while said gang had stolen it from a separate source.

"Did you not even stop for a moment to realize this truck was not from the same factory?! Alarm bells should have gone off in your head the moment the planned truck was an HOUR late!" Damian roared as he berated Niko.

Niko couldn't say anything, knowing he got too caught up in executing the hijacking in order to prove himself to Kyle. He glanced up at the gang leader, whose face was surprisingly not as angry as Damian and Keith's. Instead, Kyle's eyes were locked on the repeater carbines in the crates, not interested in punishing the new viper.

The carbine did not work anything like the automatic energy and particle rifles he had in his former life, but he recognized that the speed at which one could shoot with this was close to two times faster than the regular flintlock pistol. His head was racing with ideas on how he could create marginally better guns and enter the market.

Keith finished counting up the equipment. "Sir, the amount of equipment in this crate, you could outfit fifty men up to military grade. And based on what I found, it seems that the Ilysian Punks were planning on smuggling these out of the Yual Dominion back to their home country of Versia."

Keith handed over a handwritten note found on the crates. "It also seems to be authorized by one of the top dogs of the Ilysian Punks."

Not every gang was local—with Raktor being a trade hub near the border of the Yual Dominion, it had a lot of foreign immigrants or travelers who established their own gangs, especially from Versia.

"They had an insider in the military," Damian concluded. "There's no other way for them to get these many guns out other than sheer luck or a long ass stakeout at the factories."

"If so, we're going to be caught in a crossfire of hell. The enforcers will definitely be looking for the missing shipment; the Ilysian Punks will be after us for stealing them." Keith sighed. "We should put this equipment back where the enforcers can easily find it or hand it back to the Ilysian Punks."

"No," Kyle suddenly stated. "We're keeping them."

"WHAT?!" Damian and Keith were shocked.

"Kyle, we'll be trapped in an all-out war! You're talking about robbing the military here!" Damian shook his head vigorously, extremely against the idea. "You might be able to fight off the Red Lions, but the full force of the Ilysian Punks AND the enforcers is a whole other ball game!"

"Only if they find out. Were you spotted on your way back?" Kyle asked Niko.

Niko shook his head. "No, I checked the roadblock area to ensure no observers were around. We swapped wagons five times and split up, so it's impossible for them to have locked onto us."

"So this means we have some time to work with this..." Kyle glanced at the repeater guns, pulling them out.

Smoothbore Arctech Repeater
A military rifle designed by the Yual Dominion.
[**Active**] **Volley (Basic):** Fires multiple projectiles as long as one holds down the trigger and has enough in the magazine.
Cost: 25 MP

Twenty-five MP? That's a ridiculous consumption rate. Kyle inspected the exterior of the repeater, noticing that human technology had jumped faster due to the existence of arcite. It was radically different from how kinetic guns worked in his life, with the rifle's inbuilt engraving providing explosive energy to the projectile rather than contained within a bullet casing.

Kyle's mind raced as he thought of all the potential scenarios that could happen. The only reason they were stuck in their district now was that they lacked the strength and firepower. If he could reverse-engineer the guns and military-grade equipment, he could easily take over the entire district.

Furthermore, he had learned various engravings from his time at the Culdao Peaks, thanks to the records of the goblin shamans who marked them on pig skin.

"Kyle, whatever you're thinking, it's too crazy!" Damian tried to convince Kyle. "If you so much as use those guns outright to kill anyone else, the enforcers will immediately come swarming. Even our own enforcers won't be able to protect us anymore!"

"We won't be killing anyone with these guns. Keith, get every associate that is good with their hands to gather here. I need about ten of them. Don't let them see each other. I want to meet each of them individually in separate rooms. Got it?"

Keith was mildly confused before his eyes finally lit up, understanding what Kyle was planning to do.

"Damian, go to the enforcers and check up on their activity. Drop a hint that the Ilysian Punks have insider knowledge of the military. Tell Adrian to keep an eye on the movement of the Ilysian Punks. They must be suspecting the Red Lions for now. Get Monica to shift half a crate over to the Red Lion district and place it in one of their pubs."

Damian finally caught on, quickly issuing orders and leaving the base. *There is a chance the Ilysian Punks will try to probe us first, seeing as the hijacking happened in our district.*

The Ilysian Punks were known to be vicious and had never done a sit-down before. Not even Sebastian of the Ardent Cretins could get them to stop their violent streaks, which is why the war between the Red Lions and the Wretches was still ongoing.

Kyle finally understood it was because the Ilysian Punks were receiving the support of a rival country beyond the border—Versia. *This is going to get complicated fast, but the biggest rewards always carry the biggest risk.*

"Niko, from now on, you're in charge of making sure no one other than us and the ten associates get near these crates, got it? We'll slowly shift them over to a new location, where you will permanently guard."

Niko nodded vigorously, willing to do anything now to make up for his mistake. However, there was something about the grin on Kyle's face that made him feel like it wasn't a mistake.

Kyle grabbed one of the repeater guns and took it back to his office to inspect the engraving. *The basis of a gun is simple: accelerate the projectile. As such, the engravings should be basic as well.*

He dismantled the gun, revealing the interior of the barrel. It was layered four times, with the innermost layer being smoothbore. The three layers all had similar types of engraving aimed at accelerating the projectile through the barrel.

The magazine did not have bullets, but rather lots of tiny pellets. It seemed as though the gun was designed to fire multiple pellets at the same time when the user pulled the trigger. *Interesting, a mildly similar concept to a particle gun... or maybe a lethal paintball gun?*

All he had to do now was copy the engraving multiple times. But first, Kyle was worried about the system message claiming that it was unstable.

Reassembling the gun, he loaded the magazine in before getting Niko to set up a dummy in an old room where they used to hold the prisoners. Kyle quickly made a makeshift firing range with crates and scrap metal, making sure the pellets didn't ricochet all over the place onto him.

Aiming down the barrel, he squeezed the trigger, feeling the arcia energy within him drain outward into the rifle. The engraving lit up, accelerating the group of pellets in the barrel forward in a burst shot that blasted the dummy into pieces.

However, instead of Kyle firing another shot, he was forced to drop the gun. The barrel had become unbearably hot from the acceleration, while the MP drained from him was more than half of his max. The recoil from the shot was also too strong, reducing accuracy.

Did Niko pick up the defects? Kyle wondered. There was a good chance that it was simply just the technology of the era as well. He had not seen the military in action yet, so he was not privy to what their technology level was.

In some sense, the technological progression path in the world was warped by arcia. Arctech wagons moved on engravings rather than on the concept of combustion, and energy was generated directly from arcite ore without the need for boiling water either. Even wireless radio technology was done via engravings.

Kyle fired the rifles a few more times, testing out different angles and firing speeds before jotting down what he needed to modify.

The idea was simple: with the military guns now in place, he could now "create" guns of a believable technological level. There was, of course, a nationwide ban on guns, but that was not going to stop Kyle.

Kyle could have made "guns" much earlier based on his former life's knowledge, but he needed to get an idea of what the current era's type of gun was. Making one that was far too advanced would be a disaster for his plan of lying low in the meantime.

Kyle quickly drew out the engravings he needed to implement into the new gun that he was planning to sell. He was not going to sell exactly the same type of gun, as that would be a dead giveaway. It needed to seem as though it was a natural occurrence rather than them hijacking the factory. *Instead of a rifle, let's make handguns instead.*

"Sir, I have your ten members," Keith reported, bringing them to each room.

For the ten members, Kyle handed out the engravings he drew, giving a different one to each of them separately without them knowing who the other nine members were.

Each member of the assembly line was to engrave a specific part of the new handgun without knowing how to assemble the entire thing. Kyle didn't trust any of the associates, so he compartmentalized the process for them.

At the end of the day, each of the members would then ship their completed batch to Kyle, where he and Niko would assemble it into its final form. *And, of course, I'll add my own little touch at the end. A present for those who try to reverse-engineer my guns.*

"Keith. The new locations, are they ready? We will need separate ones for each of the members."

"Not yet, sir, but they have already been cleared out."

"Good. We'll start in two days."

Chapter 31

Secret War

"The Red Lions took our shipment?" A burly, tanned man covered in black swirling tattoos grunted, staring down from his chair at the man kneeling in front of him, who was bruised and bleeding. "Captain, this is not an easy conclusion to make. Are you absolutely sure?"

"I... I... Uhh, no, but all of the enforcers on our payroll are talking about us smuggling guns. I think the Red Lions leaked the information out to them so as to draw more heat to us."

"It's impossible for anyone to know about that shipment outside of us. Captain, you are one of the rare few who planned the route."

"I told you it's not me! I don't think it's any of us. I think it was a lucky hit—" The captain shook his head vigorously as the burly man stood up to his full height, towering over him.

"So you're saying the Red Lions got it out of *sheer luck?* Am I hearing things right? Our proud Versia men were stumped by SHEER LUCK?!" The burly man grabbed the captain by the head with one hand, a machete in the other, as he pressed the cold blade against the man's neck.

"We fix underground matches, casinos, and races. We DON'T do luck here, Captain. Now, speak slowly about every FACT you have gathered." The burly man let go of the captain, who coughed and nodded vigorously.

"Yes, sir. Our shipment was ambushed in the Seven Snakes district, but nobody around knows about it except for the attackers and us."

"And...?"

"Sir, that's all we have..." the captain replied sheepishly with a bowed head.

"Then the course of action is clear. A visit to the Seven Snakes is due."

"For a talk, sir?"

The burly man chuckled, swirling a glass of wine as he leaned back into his chair. "Captain, you never negotiate when you're on the losing end. If the Seven Snakes have our guns, they'll instinctively know that they have the upper hand on us. Let's show a bit of force first."

"Sir, this would be a declaration of war, and we're still fighting the Red Lions—" The captain tried to continue speaking, but a machete's blade was already lodged in the side of his neck, causing him to choke on his own blood. The burly man stood up again, squatting next to the squirming captain, who struggled to remove the machete from his neck in vain.

"The Ilysian Punks have no need for cowards, Captain," the burly man whispered to the dying captain before snapping his fingers. Two punks came into the office, staring at the captain bleeding out. "Dispose of the body. Throw it into the incinerator or feed it to the arena monsters."

The two punks nodded immediately, getting to work and hauling the body away. A cleaner servant also quickly entered, mopping up the blood. Nobody defied Makoa, who was a sub-leader in the Ilysian Punks.

"Oh, and set an appointment with my tattooist. I have another one to add now."

* * *

A week later...

The Seven Snakes bases were now fully relocated, spread out into ten different areas, with the old place being abandoned. Kyle was still teaching how to engrave, moving between safehouses, and fixing irregularities in the etching.

Just as he was done teaching a member how to engrave a cooling enchantment onto the handle, Adrian burst into the room, panting. "Sir, the scouts have spotted the Ilysian Punks heading right for us."

"How many?"

"About a dozen of them, all armed with melee weapons."

"Earlier than I expected. Gather a dozen rookie associates and meet me at the food market. Time for some training." Kyle smirked. *So the Ilysian Punks have decided to start a war instead of negotiating.*

At the food market, screams and shouts filled the air instead of the usual hustle and bustle. "Get this shit out of here!" An Ilysian Punk flipped the food stall, smashing the kitchen and scaring the customers around. "This district is soon going to be run by us! Not the Seven Snakes!"

The Ilysian Punks were already at large, sending their lowest rung to mess up the area. They targeted the food market, going through and messing up each of the stalls.

"That's right, boys, break everything in here! Those snakes ain't got no balls to defend their own turf!" The leader of the punks laughed as they trashed the place. Some of the punks grabbed food and stuffed it into their mouths, while others set fire to crates.

Just as the leader was about to order some more, a group of men appeared at the end of the street, numbering a dozen. At the head of them was a man dressed in a formal suit, his right arm protected by a weird green vambrace. On his right hand, he held an ornate crossbow, loaded with bolts. As he strutted toward them, the members behind him struck a domineering picture.

"Oh? The boss comes out to play? Acting all strong because you won against a measly Left Paw? You ain't fought the real deal yet. That Wrent is a bitch! SHOW THEM WHAT WE'RE MADE OF!" the leader ordered.

The punks cheered and charged them with pipes and crowbars, running in from all directions. Kyle simply snapped the fingers on his left hand, prompting the members behind to chug a quick Strength Potion before meeting the charge head-on.

The residents ducked for cover as a massive melee brawl broke out right in the food market. Even the local enforcers did not dare get involved in the brawl, knowing they very well might be killed by the crossfire. "Just let the Seven Snakes handle this; let's get out of here!"

The Seven Snakes fighters tried to fend off the punks, but it was clear that they were far outmatched. Despite the punks' attitude, it was clear they were all battle-hardened through multiple wars with nearby gangs, unlike the rookie associates from the Seven Snakes.

Outmatched in every way, the Seven Snakes fighters began to lose ground, slowly getting injured. The punks had no qualms about killing them, but just as one of them was about to deal the final blow, Kyle intervened, shooting three bolts into the chest of the punk. "Get up!"

The Seven Snakes member quickly scrambled to his feet, retrieving a health potion from his belt and drinking it, recovering his wounds. The leader of the punks was irked when he saw this. He knew that the Seven Snakes were well-equipped with potions, but he did not expect even their rookie fighters to be that well-treated.

"Take down the boss first!" he yelled to the punks, prompting three of them to shoot at Kyle, who activated his vambrace and blocked the incoming projectiles.

The fight continued on, with the leader continuously trying to kill Kyle and his fighters, but they were like cockroaches, healing just when they were in danger. It was as though Kyle was keeping them on edge and using the punks as training. Already, a few of his men were injured despite being stronger, a sign that their stamina was running out.

"Fuck! Retreat! Don't think you've seen the last of us!" The punks fell back, beating a hasty retreat. The food market was left in ruins, all the stalls beaten back.

"Get every other free member out here to fix up the market. Tell Keith to pay all the stall owners back," Kyle ordered, much to the gratitude of the locals. It felt as though the Seven Snakes had everything under control with Kyle in the reins, so the trust among the locals was not shaken.

However, Kyle was not happy. He knew that the Ilysian Punks were simply probing for the guns. Their shipment had been attacked here, after all. It was no surprise that the Ilysian Punks would try to test and see if they were dumb enough to show the guns off. Kyle wasn't about to let his associates use the guns so blatantly.

As dangerous as it was, Kyle believed he had found a way where he could finally come out on top and overtake the Ardent Cretins using the military shipment. However, it was a long plan and required him to buy time. Kyle knew his plan would be feasible in the Galactic Era, but whether it could work here was something else.

Back at a new office, Damian was visibly jittery, immediately jumping up to meet Kyle the moment he returned. "Kyle, I've been listening in on the enforcers so far. It's even worse than we expected. Nearly every enforcer is up and about, searching the original factory. For now, they don't know that the guns were hijacked a second time, so they are swarming that district."

"And that district is owned by?"

"The Wretches, sir. Not on good terms with the Ilysian Punks. They probably think that it was either the Red Lions or the Ilysian Punks who turned the heat up on them, seeing as they are still in a state of war," Damian frantically explained.

"You seem to have something to say."

"Sir, I truly believe that keeping all the guns on us is a death sentence. All it takes is for one rumor to spread and trigger an enforcer raid on us. We should back off now. It's far too risky."

Kyle pondered, considering Damian's opinion. *To be honest, I don't need to hold onto every military crate, seeing as I can just reverse-engineer them...*

"I understand, Damian." Kyle tapped the map of the sector, smiling to himself as he figured out a plan. "Dump all military equipment, except for two sets, into the districts I point out here. Make sure they are in a fairly visible location, but don't get spotted. Mask it with food or other items first. I want the gangs to discover them."

"You want to frame all of them and spark some chaos with the guns." Damian nodded.

"Exactly. We'll have one set in a crate here in our district as well, just to avoid suspicion. We'll turn the crate into the enforcers as soon as word gets out to buy some goodwill. We keep the remaining set for our own purposes." Kyle pointed to the Ilysian Punks–controlled districts, aiming at the closest adjacent district.

After explaining the plan further to Damian, he soon focused back on figuring out how to push forward his new plan to manufacture the handguns. It was clear that he had to present some improvements over the current flintlock or muzzle-loaded pistols, but he needed to tailor the expectation lower.

The five engravings that he had added to his upgraded version of the pistol were to make it far more efficient, so much so that even the average human with a bit of arcia energy could fire it up to three times. That wasn't as good even by Ancient Earth's standard, but it could be improved over time.

Kyle was not particularly proficient in arctech engravings, but he could immediately see issues in the flow of energy and wasteful conversion using his former life's knowledge. The engravings he had chosen would help reduce the heat generated, improve accuracy, and control the recoil. *It'll be a revolution in guns, and I'll be at the head of it.*

He already had a few prototype parts collected from the associates. He ensured that none of the associates knew more than one engraving each, preventing his recipe from spilling out. However, if he truly wanted to mass-produce it, he needed to enlist the help of a factory or two. He began to plan for a few ways in which he could start to dig his hooks into the factory workers. *Niko should probably have an idea.*

Kyle did not begrudge Niko too much—the hijacking was obviously ill-conceived in a time where they were meant to be lying low, but the potential rewards were too good to be true. He only wished he had more time to work with the equipment in the crate. It had only been a week, but he had only been working on a pistol and barely understood the engraving layout necessary for a repeater.

He assembled a prototype pistol, the glossy raw metal surface glistening under the arctech light of the office. Just as he finished putting the different parts together, a new system message popped up.

Enchanted Handgun (Basic)
An efficient gun with marks of foreign technology.
[**Active**] **Shoot:** Fire a group of pellets at high speeds The magazine holds up to eight rounds.
Cost: 3 MP

Title Obtained: Arctech Gunsmith (Basic)
Death handcrafted and delivered at high speeds.
+5 INT, +3 DEX, +10% chance to craft an intermediate pistol when assembling.

Chapter 32

Failsafe

The factory churned with a never-ending rumbling sound. Soot and fumes blanketed the entire factory floor, with large arctech furnaces melting metal and slag drifting on molten rivers. Assembly lines formed as dirt-covered workers moved their hands through the same mundane motions, twisting and screwing appliances before them.

On an upper floor, there were offices filled with arctech designers, working hard on improving engravings incrementally through every iteration. The owner of the factory at the head of the office made a simple modification to the engraving, passing it down to the next guy, who calculated a very specific parameter before handing it over to the next person. It was like a human calculator, with each designer focusing on one parameter.

In the middle of this chain was a young man, his eyes clearly glazed with boredom as he barely gave a glance at each of the prototypes in front of him. They were basic household appliances—a simple heated kettle that didn't require an arctech stove. He sighed as he scribbled down a few numbers on a piece of paper and checked another variation of the same kettle.

The hours passed slowly, his mind numb from the monotonous work. As he slowly walked out of the factory, he wondered why he had even decided to become an arctech designer. Whatever happened to all the cool equipment that he could have been making? Instead, he was some glorified single equation calculator for a fucking kettle.

However, tonight was going to be different. As soon as he turned the corner, Karl was already waiting for him with a wide grin, along with three other workers from the factory floor. "Ready to party it up, Gordon?" Karl patted his shoulder.

Gordon was stunned but nodded resolutely. He had been enticed by the raving stories Karl had told about the glamorous casinos or brothels and pubs he had never been to before. They agreed to head over to one of the casinos Karl knew.

"Don't you worry, I know a guy in there. He's the boss. I already got word from him that they set up everything for us. The full VIP treatment."

"I... I don't have that much money," Gordon stammered.

"HAHA! Don't worry, that guy used to be one of our factory workers! Can you believe it? He's one of the top dogs right now. Here they come." Karl laughed it off, while Gordon was shocked. A luxurious arctech wagon drove up to the factory, turning heads and eyes toward them as the wagon stopped right in front of them.

Niko was already in the back of the wagon, beckoning for them to enter. The five of them entered the wagon, which was coated in the most luxurious surface Gordon had ever seen. He had never imagined a simple word from Karl was able to acquire all of this.

Karl noticed the surprise on Gordon's face, nudging him as the wagon sailed off to the casino. "Surprised? It's easy to get into the good life, just like that." Karl handed him a bottle of unlabeled beer still in its glass bottle. "Homebrewed by the Seven Snakes themselves. We even have our own brewery!"

"Isn't drinking alcohol illegal under the ban?" Gordon asked worriedly, having never flouted the law before.

Karl laughed, slapping Gordon on the back. "Hey, Niko, tell him how many times you've been caught drinking over the last two months."

"Zero," Niko replied with a smirk on his face. Just at that very moment, the wagon stopped near an enforcer patrol, causing Gordon to clamp up, trying to hide the bottle of beer in his hands.

The enforcer patrol spotted Niko in the wagon, and they walked over to the back of the wagon. "Having a good night out, eh?"

"Of course. Looking forward to seeing you at the dice games." Niko tossed a bottle of beer each to the enforcers, who simply smiled and slipped the bottles under their uniforms before walking off.

Gordon's eyes shone like diamonds at how easily Niko handled the enforcers. He had no idea it was this simple to live the high life. What the hell had he been doing all his life, aiming to be some no-name arctech designer trapped in a dumb office?

Niko grinned as he caught the look on the factory workers he was tasked with inviting. *Hook, line, and sinker.*

The wagon soon arrived at the casino, showing them a whole new high life, unlike anything they had seen before. The VIP treatment was real. They had escorts and free-flow drinks tended to them like they were the kings of the world.

The factory workers naturally got carried away, having what essentially amounted to a free pass on luxury. Gordon laughed and drank with Karl and Niko non-stop, enjoying the nightlife as the sounds of coins and gambling echoed all around them.

"You see now, Gordon? What's the point in slogging away in a grimy old factory making fucking kettles with those idiots out there? You're leagues ahead of them. Don't you think it's about time you made your money's worth?"

Gordon recalled the faces of his parents, who were adamant that he got a nice, stable job, just like his dad, who worked as a construction worker. But after he had a taste of luxury? How could he ever go back to his boring old life?

Karl spotted Gordon's expression and gave a knowing look to Niko, who draped his arm around Gordon with a smile. "If you want, you can have this every night for the rest of your life. All you gotta do is just one simple job."

* * *

Two days later...

Gordon was in the office, checking his pocket watch carefully. It was about time for the workday to end, but instead of packing up like everyone else was, his eyes were locked on the owner of the factory while he was pretending to work on something.

The office began to clear out, soon leaving the owner and Gordon alone in the office. "Gordon, what are you still doing? We don't pay for overtime, you know."

"Boss, I wanted to talk to you about a potential improvement in one of the engravings. Here..." Gordon beckoned for the owner to come over and see, while his hand reached for a handgun under the table, hidden from the manager's view.

"Sorry, Gordon, but I got dinner with my family. I'll check it first thing in the morning. Just leave it at my desk." The owner waved his hand dismissively, grabbing his things and preparing to leave the office.

Just as he tried to open the door, the door swung wide open to reveal Karl and the other three factory workers, all holding knives, rope, and a crowbar. "Don't worry about your family, Boss Staten. We got them covered. You'll be speaking to us for now." Karl motioned for the other factory workers to restrain the manager down to the ground.

Staten struggled to fight back against the factory workers, but he was never going to win three-on-one. "What the fuck is this, a strike? You're never going to get aw—" A solid punch from a factory worker landed right on his face, smashing his jaw and causing his gum to bleed profusely.

His eyes wandered to Gordon, who only stared impassively at him, showing no signs of helping him. The factory workers hauled Staten onto a chair, tying him down with the rope. "All right, Boss. We would like you to nominate Gordon as the new representative of the factory with full powers. And you're going to stay out of it. This is a union request. A nice one," Karl began, taking out a Euria Pipe and smoking it.

Karl had been paid handsomely for his role in hijacking the guns, though it was a fluke. Kyle was not one to underpay those who helped him, so Karl was now a de facto associate of the Seven Snakes, though still integrated into the factory.

"Resign?! Are you crazy? I own this fucking factory! You'd better let me go or I call the enforcers on your ass—"

"Not so fast, Boss. Weren't you supposed to go have dinner with your wife and your daughter... what's her name again... Rachel? Cute little girl, nice red hair. Had to shut her up because she wouldn't stop screaming." Karl smirked.

Staten's face went blank before slowly turning into anger. "Fuckers, what did you do to her?! I'LL FUCKING KILL YOU!"

"Ah, he's too loud. Shut him up," Karl ordered the three factory workers, who began to force open Staten's mouth. One worker held it open while another took out a crowbar and positioned it against Staten's bleeding lower gum. "Every time you shout, this is going to happen."

The scream was horrendous as the crowbar ripped out a tooth from the gum, causing Staten to spasm in the chair. "Stuff this in his mouth. Don't want the blood to get all over here." Karl threw a cloth over. "Now, nod your head for yes, shake your head for no. Remember, dear little Rachel is waiting for you. She's still alive and perfectly well. Assuming you comply, it will remain so. This doesn't need to get any bloodier."

Staten nodded his head vigorously, completely powerless to stop any of them. "Good. You will hand over full authority effectively tomorrow and name Gordon as your new representative. If by any chance the enforcers hear about this or Gordon does not become the representative, you can forget about seeing Rachel, got it? And also forget about your nice home down at Wheaten Road."

Karl smiled as Staten nodded his head in acknowledgement while another factory worker took out a Healing Potion and stuffed it down Staten's mouth, forcing him to drink it. The wounds were immediately cleared up, though his teeth were still missing.

The next day, Staten held a general meeting, announcing his stepping down due to health issues and appointing Gordon as the factory's new representative. There was a mixture of shock, surprise, and anger, but Gordon felt a rush as he took up his new position at the head of the office. Just like that, he became the top dog with full power, in charge of designing the products for the factory.

He immediately fired all the existing foremen on the factory floor and instituted Karl and the three workers as their replacements, ensuring they had total control over what the factory could produce. The Seven Snakes were now fully integrated into the system while keeping a tight blackmail grip on the owner to make sure he wouldn't snitch.

Near the end of the workday, a man accompanied by five Seven Snakes members, including Niko, marched in. He had a meeting with Gordon, so he immediately walked to the office without hesitation, glancing around the room upon entering. "Manager Gordon, how do you like your new office?"

"It's brilliant, sir." Gordon got up and bowed immediately, knowing from Niko that this man was Kyle, leader of the Seven Snakes.

"Let's get straight to business. I need you to produce these parts for the Seven Snakes. We'll handle the cost, along with an added benefit." Kyle handed over a few of the requested prototype parts that he had made. Gordon eyed the parts, noticing they were mostly defensive armor pieces with basic arctech engravings. *Is he trying to outfit an army or something?*

The armor pieces were all designed to be concealed under normal clothes, while Gordon noticed that there were three sets ordered that had a much different engraving style with a note that requested him to personally produce these parts. "Sir, these engravings are..."

"Proprietary. I will work together with you to make these specific parts." Kyle wasn't about to let Gordon learn too much about the new optical illusion engraving that he had modified from Gulak.

Gordon nodded, still checking over the entire order. However, there was a snag. "Sir, the factory owners are still unaware of this takeover and will still have quotas on the production of other products to fulfill. It would be hard to switch production lines out of the blue, especially when our workers are trained to—" Gordon tried to explain before he glanced at Kyle's piercing eyes.

"I've been told you are a brilliant arctech designer. The money is there for the taking. It is up to you how much you want to make," Kyle replied nonchalantly. "Do this well, and there will be better contracts in the future. I look forward to our cooperation."

The group of the Seven Snakes left, with Niko patting Gordon on the back with a big thumbs-up.

Back in the office, Keith was already about to burst his top at Kyle spending money to fund the factory production. "I know what you're planning, but we don't have enough money to pull it off! That armor production is going to cost millions at this rate—arctech gear isn't cheap. Our associates won't have enough arcia energy to fuel the use of the equipment, which means they might need fuel packs. That's going to be another money sink... We were just about to clear the Crimson Swords debt!"

The Euria Seeds cash revenue was enough to offset the debt, but it wasn't in the tens of millions yet. However, Kyle was unfazed, simply smiling at the frustrated Keith.

"Circumstances change plans, Keith. And don't worry, money won't be a problem very soon."

Chapter 33

Auction

The Central Sector was not free of crime, though its crime was of a higher class. Rather than petty protection rackets and inane extortion, it was here where most of the money laundering, trafficking, and high-value deals were made between corrupt nobles, enforcers, and entrepreneurial gangs.

In a hidden alleyway away from the grand open streets, two bouncers dressed in suits were dutifully scanning the individuals in line, all of whom wore masks to hide their identities. In the middle of the line was a single man, holding a mundane briefcase that could barely be seen under the night sky.

As he walked up to the two bouncers, he was searched from head to toe for any concealed weapons. "Open the briefcase," the bouncer ordered.

"Sorry, but I'm planning on selling what's within. I'd prefer not to show it out here."

The bouncer grunted in response, motioning with his head to someone else inside. A well-mannered receptionist came out to greet the man. "Intending to sell something for the upcoming auction? Please follow me."

The man was led to an intermediate section, where an ornate archway that seemed to be something of a body scanner awaited him. "Sorry, sir. Just a precaution to make sure you have no active arctech equipment," the receptionist explained.

"I understand." The man eyed the scanner but was unable to spot any engravings externally.

He hardly felt a thing as he passed through the scanner, and the receptionist immediately brought him through the next door.

The man entered to reveal a red carpeted floor, dazzling with bright chandeliers glistening with oscillating arctech lights. The entrance was crowded as people lined up for the cloakroom, while others simply hung around near a bar drinking cocktails. None of them paid attention to the man with the briefcase.

The receptionist led the man to a separate section of the place, where it was much quieter. "Please wait here while our head artificer prepares to inspect your item." She motioned to a small, private room with a table and chair.

He sat quietly in the private room without making a fuss, waiting patiently while the sole arctech lantern mounted on the ceiling flickered gently. Soon, an old artificer equipped with what seemed to be a magnifying glass in one eye entered the room along with a private guard. The old artificer sighed, sitting down on the opposite chair with a plop.

"All right, let's get this over with. Whatever you think it's worth, it's going to be at least half of it, so don't get your hopes up," the old artificer said with a dismissive tone, his face clearly bored by the dozens of fake or cheap items he had to check each auction.

The briefcase was opened to reveal an exquisite handgun, somehow carved with an oriental design unlike anything the old artificer had seen before. The design was out of this world. His words stuck in his throat. "This... What even is this?"

"An arctech handgun."

"I know that much!" the old artificer snapped. "Where the hell did you get it from? This is..."

"I was under the impression that this auction house doesn't ask questions."

The old artificer coughed in a calm manner, though his hands were obviously fidgety, wanting to touch the handgun. "Yes, but it is also under our terms and conditions that there should be no ill-gotten gains that may have been obtained from our... bigger patrons."

"Rest assured, this was not stolen from the city of Raktor."

"Great! May I examine it properly?"

The man nodded, with the old artificer excitedly grabbing the handgun and inspecting the engraving on its exterior. The old artificer ran his hands over the surface, finding the grooves and the bolts used to hold the frame in place. Just as he was about to remove the bolt, the man suddenly spoke. "I wouldn't open it if I were you. I'm told it will not end well."

"An explosive failsafe—work of a master arctech designer to prevent others from reverse-engineering their inventions. As expected." The old artificer sighed. "But seeing as we can't open its interior, we cannot verify the exact operation of the gun."

"Well, it's quite simple. Point and pull the trigger."

"But does the gun not require an arcite fuel pack?" the old artificer asked. Guns were normally extremely hard to use because of their arcia energy requirements. Naturally, he felt such an exquisite pistol would have an obscenely high arcia energy cost.

"You can have your guard give it a test run. Go for it."

The old artificer nodded at the guard, who wore a metal protective glove, before picking up the handgun in case it blew up in his face. Aiming at a wall farther away, the guard pulled the trigger once, firing a blast of pellets that embedded right into the thick wall.

"Try firing again." The man motioned, to the confusion of the old artificer.

"Fire again? Guns like these can't be fired agai—" The sound of the trigger being pulled and another blast of pellets coming out shocked the old artificer, who stared intently at the private guard. "You're not a hidden mage, are you?"

"No, I can barely keep a breastplate active for more than two minutes." The guard shook his head, somewhat proud of himself. The old artificer was in pure shock, his mouth agape. *This... is revolutionary!*

"Do you understand the gun's value now?" The man smirked.

The old artificer finally calmed down, sitting back down with the handgun placed in front of him. What came next was the hardest part of the entire thing. He steeled his face.

"Seventy percent of the final auction price." The old artificer held up a finger.

"Ridiculous. You already know in your heart that this gun is an advancement in technology. Ninety percent."

The old artificer's heart clenched. This exquisite gun was bound to be a hit among the nobility. Maybe even Baron Cain might go all out for it, or merchants from other nations might grab it. "Seventy-five percent, that's as high as I can go."

"Then there's no deal." The man reached out to grab the handgun, but the old artificer stopped him.

"Wait, wait, wait, I'm sure we can talk this out."

"Ninety or nothing."

The old artificer took a deep breath before glancing at the open briefcase. "Those are the pellets, I assume?"

"Yes. Loaded into cartridges like this." The man demonstrated the reloading of the pistol, shocking the old artificer once more. *Loaded into the grip of the pistol... Simply ingenious. This man is definitely not simple—if I don't treat him well, this may be the last we see of him. We must keep him around!*

"Ninety percent, deal!" The old artificer quickly shook his hand and hastily ordered the guard, "Get this man a VIP seat immediately. He's an esteemed patron of the auction house now!"

"Keep the briefcase. Also, a change of clothes would be nice."

"Of course, anything for you!" The old artificer was nearly swooning over the handgun, knowing it could sell for way over a million rakels, maybe even reach ten million. *This is it—the key item of the auction!*

The man was given a VIP seat, overlooking the entire auction hall in his own private booth. A waiter served wine and snacks, though the man hardly ate or drank any of it, his eyes simply scanning the auction hall.

The auction had yet to start, but there were many members of high society already mingling around with each other, forming business deals and partnerships. The man noticed even a few bishops in the midst, negotiating with strangers in hushed tones in the corners.

[Good evening, fellow patrons. The end-of-the-year Decaber Auction is finally ready to commence! Please take your seats. This month's auction has many interesting things in store. Please collect a list from one of our employees.]

The door of the private booth opened, revealing a smiling, old artificer sitting down next to the man and handing him a list of items. "Good sir, perhaps you might be interested in buying a few things? Also, it would be good to know your name..."

"You may call me Hawthorn."

"Ah, Sir Hawthorn, I will commit that name to memory." The old artificer nodded, racking his brains to try to recall if there were any nobility in Raktor with that name. He prided himself on knowing almost every one of worth in the city, but no "Hawthorn" came to mind. *Perhaps it is a moniker.*

"And to whom do I owe the pleasure?" Sir Hawthorn looked at the old artificer.

"I am known as Master Xen, but you may simply call me Xen." The old artificer nodded his head before pointing at the list. "Perhaps you might see something that might interest you?"

"Perhaps..." Hawthorn glanced through the list, noting the huge variation in types of items of all curiosity. Artifacts, historical art pieces, potions, and even slaves were traded at this auction. However, Hawthorn did not spot anything that would help him until he reached the end of the list, his eyes widening in recognition.

Master Xen spotted the obvious change on Hawthorn's face, knowing he had found a potential hook to foster a closer relationship. "Ah, seems like there's something you've taken a fancy to."

"How much can I borrow?"

The old artificer stroked his beard. "I personally value the handgun to be a million rakels, so ninety percent would be nine hundred thousand."

"You're joking. The gun will go for ten million at the minimum. I guess I can't borrow any then." Hawthorn put the list aside, sighing.

Master Xen's eyebrow twitched at being called out like that, though both of them knew ten million rakels was to be expected. "Fine, you can borrow nine million rakels. However, if your handgun sells less than ten million, you will have to make up the difference. Do note that our loan interest rates are 'competitive.'"

"Not a problem. Nine million rakels it is."

The audience finally settled down, with the auction finally presenting the items in sequence.

[First up, for Item #1, we have a cyclops slave! Be the envy of your peers when you show off this magnificent specimen, one of the last of its kind.]

The host of the auction snapped his fingers, with workers wheeling in a slave cage nearly three meters tall. Inside was a bound cyclops, naked and skin shredded from the numerous whippings to keep it docile.

[Bidding begins at 120,000 rakels.]

Hawthorn didn't show any interest at all in the slave, with Master Xen noting all of this down and trying to put his finger on what Hawthorn liked. *If I can get closer to him, I might find the source of the gun. If HE is the source of the gun, I must suck up to him even more than ever.*

The auction proceeded as normal, with the items alternating between categories. Hawthorn curiously stared at the stage, as though he were watching an ancient holo-drama from Ancient Earth, where totems, broken-off stones of ancient ruins, and forgotten weapons were auctioned for millions.

[Next up, Item #33. An explorer team has dug up ancient ruins in Versia, only to find carved human-sized statues or idols of what seem to be spines. The statues are rumored to be unbreakable, and of course, the auction house did not dare to test that theory.]

The statues were displayed on the stage, made of rock and what seemed to be dried mud. It looked extremely unpleasant and more like centipedes, and many of the audience members were already thinking of what the next item was, checking his list.

[Bidding begins at 100,000 rakels.]

The auction hall was silent, leading the host to feel slightly embarrassed at displaying such an item with no interest to be found.

[Well then... If no one bids, then it will simply be kept by the auction house. Going once...]

"A hundred thousand rakels," Hawthorn suddenly said, raising his auction sign to indicate his bid. Master Xen raised his eyebrows in surprise, adjusting the magnifying glass on his eye to see the items on stage better. *I don't understand... It's just rock and stone.*

A noticeable wave of murmuring began to spread across the audience, with some of the more curious people wondering why a person from the VIP booth would want to buy such an item. Perhaps it was actually of some value?

Three more members bid in sequence, raising the price to two hundred thousand.

"Three hundred thousand." Hawthorn re-bid. Now the audience was far more intrigued, wondering whether the statues had inherent value.

Baron Cain sat with his entourage in an opposing VIP booth, wondering who the bidder was. None of his peers within his social circle would ever buy something as gaudy as those statues. How in the world would you display them?

[Three hundred thousand going once... Going twice... Sold to the VIP patron in booth six!]

"Master Xen, could I trouble your employees to bring the items up to this booth immediately?" Hawthorn asked.

"Ah! Of course, of course!" Master Xen quickly spread the order down, with the centipede statues being brought up into the large booth, mounted on trolleys.

Hawthorn stood up and walked over, placing his hands on the 'centipede' looking statues.

Ancient Exosuit Spine

Lost technology created in the Galactic Era, unusable without thorough refurbishment.

[**Active**] **Nerval Jack:** Enables a pilot to wield the exosuit through a nerval distribution network. Requires an operational exosuit.

Chapter 34

Bidding

What the fuck is an exosuit spine doing here? Kyle Hawthorn was stunned, but he quickly controlled his expression, aware that Master Xen was watching him. He twisted his facial expression to one of disappointment, sighing audibly.

"Sir Hawthorn, is there a problem with the items?" Master Xen asked gently.

"No, there's no problem. It just was not what I expected at all." Kyle took a deep breath, calmed himself, and sat back down.

The rest of the auction flew past him as his mind raced through all the possible implications of what the exosuit spine represented. *The system mentioned that it was an ancient exosuit spine... Does this mean I've traveled into the future in some way?*

Kyle ran through plenty of possible scenarios, but each one of them did not seem to solve the issue of there being Galactic Era technology on the planet. Some scenarios did have merit in them, but until he gained more power and was able to truly explore the planet's surroundings, he would have to withhold making assumptions and snap judgements. *Ancient ruins in Versia... I must see it for myself one day.*

Either way, with the exosuit spine, he now had a good reference to potentially make his own exosuit. Just because he came from the Galactic Era as a crime lord did not mean that he knew immediately how to make an exosuit from scratch. Many humans in the Galactic Era relied on cranial implants to store such detailed information, so it was expected for him to forget while he was here.

Master Xen tried to make small talk with Sir Hawthorn a few times, but Kyle was so engrossed in his thinking that his eyes were simply glazed over, as though Master Xen did not exist any longer. It wasn't until Master Xen reached out with a hand that Kyle suddenly violently reacted and entered a defensive posture, assuming it was an attack.

Master Xen quickly pulled his hand back, worried. "Sir Hawthorn, it's almost near the end of the auction. The handgun is going up now."

"Good," Kyle replied stoically, resuming his calm demeanor. Master Xen continued observing Sir Hawthorn, aware that the statues must have affected him in some way. *A curse? Or perhaps Sir Hawthorn is a non-human in disguise?*

[The final piece of the auction is a true rarity, a clear-cut innovation in the methods of gunsmithing, arctech designing, and firearms. Behold, the world's first repeater handgun!]

A luxurious cloth was pulled off a pedestal, revealing the exquisite handgun in all its glory.

[The name of this handgun is Oriental Bloom. Notice the intricate carvings on the surface of its barrel. A master arctech designer has made this handgun, so naturally, failsafes are in place if the owner attempts to disassemble it. However, the handgun is still the first the auction house has seen that can fire more than one burst at a time!]

"That's bullshit; everyone knows arctech guns can only shoot once every thirty seconds. Any faster would be a clear waste of arcite fuel or extremely exhaustive on the user. Many guns don't even have the material required to withstand the force!" one of the audience members scoffed in response.

The host did not say anything, instead grabbing the handgun from the pedestal and taking aim at a straw dummy target that was rolled out by the workers. In quick succession, the host fired the handgun three times, its recoil extremely high.

The projectiles blasted the straw dummy into chunks, with a few impacting the auction hall's wall due to the high recoil and poor marksmanship of the host. Many of the audience members instinctively cowered from the loud bangs before gaping in awe at what had just happened.

"Impossible..." The same audience member sat down with a defeated expression. However, the other audience members' faces glowed up, knowing that they had a chance to own this gun for themselves. The prestige of wielding such a gun for oneself would be enormous.

[Bidding begins at half a million—]

"One million!"

"Two and a half million!"

Baron Cain was already upright in his chair, shouting at his entourage to double-check his accounts and to call the inquisitors. "That gun, it's too coincidental!"

He leaned over the railing, trying to get a better look at the surface of the handgun. The carvings were unlike anything he had seen in his life, making it look as though it was from a completely different nation. However, it was too much of a coincidence. Losing a military shipment, and then a repeater handgun appears in the same week? If he did not hold onto that gun, it could be a disaster; mostly for him and subsequently, the military as well.

He quickly scribbled a message on the napkin, sending it to all the barons of the other sectors that were in the auction as well. *I need the other barons to stay out of the way!*

In another VIP booth, Sebastian sat with the leader of the Ardent Cretins, Ares. "Sebastian, we need to get that gun! Having that gun will boost our firepower and enable us to have better negotiating rights with the enforcers." Ares was already grinning widely, thinking about what would happen if everyone in his gang had this gun.

Sebastian frowned, thinking deeply before shaking his head. "No. Baron Cain is most likely going to go all out for this. I will send a message to him saying that we will not contest it. Acquiring that gun is a death sentence for our gang."

Ares was about to protest, but Sebastian shot him a death glare. "We agreed to let me handle the auction. Are you already not satisfied with the proceeds from the slaves?"

"Fine, have it your way."

As all of this was happening, the audience became even rowdier, with the bid reaching fifteen million.

"Seventeen million!" A loud voice echoed from an adjacent VIP booth, coming from a wealthy gentleman flanked by three guards. Waves of murmuring rippled through the crowd, with those in the know recognizing his voice through the mask.

"Shit, it's the leader of the Veiled Angels!"

"Eighteen million." Another gentleman was sitting on the opposite side of the hall in a VIP booth as well, smirking at the other. The men standing behind his seat were clearly the Violet Demons, their mouths twisted in a sinister smile against the leader of the Veiled Angels.

Despite them being in such close proximity to each other, neither of them made any moves to try and kill the opponent. Even though they were at war in the West Sector, the auction house in the Central Sector was a neutral zone. The gangs were not about to flout the unspoken rules established by the ruler of the auction house—offending him meant offending the city of Raktor itself.

Before the leader of the Veiled Angels could raise the bid any further, a clear voice from one of the VIP booths stunned the entire audience.

"Twenty-five million rakels."

Master Xen's eyeballs nearly popped out of their sockets. He was already shocked when the Violet Demons bid eighteen million, but now the handgun was worth twenty-five million rakels. Xen glanced at Sir Hawthorn's face, who had no reaction at all, simply leaning back in his chair, relaxing.

[Twenty-five million rakels! Do I hear any other bids?!] The host was naturally celebratory, having reached a personal milestone.

The floor was silent, each of the previously rowdy members becoming quiet. Twenty-five million rakels was a sum big enough to buy an entire mansion in the Central Sector.

Only those of nobility, the barons, could have that much money to spend on an exquisite handgun. As much of a technological improvement as it was, twenty-five million rakels were just too much.

Sebastian was already thinking of ways he could send men to infiltrate Baron Cain's lodging to try and snatch the pistol. The same idea was running through all of the major gang leaders' heads, only to be disrupted by a foreign voice wafting in from booth six.

"Thirty million rakels," a new man said.

Baron Cain was temporarily stunned until the realization of what just happened caused him to crush his glass in anger. "Who's that fucking peasant in booth six? Is he a foreign baron? You!" He pointed at one of the employees of the auction house. "I want to verify that booth six has enough to pay for this, or if he is just jacking up the price!"

The host was equally stunned, completely lost for words now, until an employee ran up onto the stage, whispering into his ear.

[Ahem, thirty million is an unexpected bid. Please hold while our employees confirm that the individual in question does have enough.]

Master Xen was flabbergasted before pinching himself to assure that it wasn't a dream. Kyle was surprised at the bid so far. "Who is that in booth six?"

Xen's back shot straight up, seeing a chance to ingratiate himself with Sir Hawthorn and potentially get into his good graces. "I'm not meant to tell you, and this goes against direct orders, but I know it's Harrison!"

"Harrison?"

"He's the leader of an industrialist movement in Versia—an acclaimed genius who rose to fame solely on his groundbreaking inventions. And he's only thirty-five years old!"

Sounds like someone who got his hands on a few Galactic Era relics or ruins. Now that he knew about the Ancient Exosuit Spine, Galactic Era technology having been excavated by locals was a reasonable thought. He would not consider it impossible that someone else on the planet would have the knowledge to operate or at least gleam some inspiration from the relics. "Maybe I will have to pay Versia a visit soon."

"If you do plan to, I will be more than happy to assist you in any way you may need."

On the other side of the auction hall, Baron Cain was outraged. As rich as he was, outbidding thirty million was not a small purchase in any shape or form. However, he could not risk losing the gun as well. He needed it to trace the culprit, who may or may not have reverse-engineered the technology. "You! Tell me the name of the individual in booth six!" he ordered the guard in his private booth.

"Sir, under the direct orders of Count Leon, the auction house will not divulge the personal information of any individual without their express permission, including you, sir." The guard repeated the words like clockwork, but his hands gave a different sign, the baron recognizing it immediately. *Not one of Raktor?!*

Baron Cain glanced at the other booths, recognizing the other barons who had clearly not bid on the product. *If it isn't a local competitor, then it's a foreign buyer! I cannot let them have it!*

"Fine! Thirty-five million rakels!" Baron Cain placed a bid in desperation.

[Thirty-five million rakels! Do I hear a counteroffer from booth six?]

All eyes turned to booth six, staring at the other man, who did not seem intent on bidding again. Baron Cain was even more incensed by the apparent ploy, cursing under his breath. *Was it a sham bid? Is it the seller?*

[Thirty-five million rakels going once... Going twice... Sold to the individual from booth one!]

"GET THAT HANDGUN HERE AND CALL THE INQUISITORS NOW!" Baron Cain roared with ferocity. "Tell them I want all available enforcers under me to track that fucking cunt from booth six! Send the inquisitors to trace the origin of the sale if it's a different person!"

* * *

The auction house cleared out an hour later, and the events of the night spread through the city.

Mason and Kitana were waiting in their own enforcer wagon, with Mason puffing his Euria pipe as per usual. Kitana tapped the leather seat under her, impatient, as she stared daggers into the opening of the street.

[Sir, he's on the move. One wagon is coming out of the auction house right now,] the arctech radio blurted out.

"You sure it's him?" Mason asked.

[Yes, I personally saw him enter the car.]

"All right. Kitana, get ready. We'll pull the car over the moment it enters the South Sector." Mason grabbed the wheel of the enforcer wagon, turning on the arctech engine. The arcite fuel tank churned as the engravings along the base shaft lit up, slowly rolling the wagon forward.

Just as they started moving, a wagon came out of the auction house's warehouse and onto the streets. Mason did not give chase immediately, simply moving along slowly as the target wagon sped off.

Only when the target wagon turned the corner did Mason begin to pick up speed, staying at a comfortable distance. A few minutes passed without much incident as they drove through the safe streets of the Central Sector, but soon Mason had a frown on his face.

"This path… It seems he's heading for the Ilysian Punks territory."

"So it really is the Ilysian Punks who stole our guns?" Kitana assumed. "Looks like the tipoff wasn't wrong after all."

"Or it could be a ploy by the Ardent Cretins to incriminate their rivals. Wouldn't hurt them to have one less competitor in the sector while we're wasting time," Mason warned.

They stalked the target wagon for a good two hours before the target wagon finally came to a stop at a residential building opposite a known Ilysian Punks hangout. Three individuals got out of the wagon, shifting the statues into the building. Mason stopped the wagon just around the corner, the two of them exiting the wagon and checking the surroundings.

Already, people on the street were eyeing them, with a few Ilysian Punks spotting the newcomers and running off to inform their superiors. "Fuck, this is going to get dicey. Look, find out where those three individuals went. I'm going to their hangout to negotiate safe passage. Don't want too much attention here," Mason ordered.

Kitana nodded, gripping her arctech pistol while she observed the wagon and the building entrances. She slowly moved over without too much hassle, acting calm as she walked past the wagon, checking the inside of the wagon.

The wagon was completely empty and unmarked, making it hard for Kitana to determine where the wagon came from. She found a handwritten note on the driver's seat and picked it up. *Looks like an Ilysian Punks shipment order.*

She decided to patrol around the outskirts of the residential building, entering the alleyway.

As she cautiously stepped through the grime and trash that littered the floor, a cracking sound prompted her to raise her pistol, aiming at an obviously disheveled squatter who was equally alarmed.

"W-What did I do? I'm not part of the punks! I'm not!" The squatter waved his hands wildly.

Kitana sighed, lowering her pistol and prompting the squatter to move along. The squatter bowed respectfully, timidly moving past her while taking great care to avoid touching her. As the squatter ran past her, Kitana turned to look at his back. *Eyes of Truth.*

Skill Activated: Eyes of Truth
Ignore any illusions or disguises, allowing one to see through everything.
Dependent on the Intelligence stat.
Cost: 5 MP   **Duration:** 10 seconds

As the words repeated in her brain, her pupils turned golden, and the world around her became a matrix of golden lines, breaking down things into their basic components. The disheveled features of the squatter broke down to reveal a handsome young man, notorious as a gang leader. Kitana could see all the engravings present on the man.

Kitana immediately saw the true identity of the squatter but did not give chase. *Optical illusion engraving on the suit—that's new.*

Kitana did not check the building any longer, instead heading out back onto the street to where the enforcer wagon was. *It's clear that they are the ones who made the handgun and probably used the military shipment as inspiration. It seems like they are the ones who have final possession of it. Who knew that a small gang like theirs would have such capabilities?* Kitana began to think carefully, weighing out all the possible future scenarios that would bring her the most benefit.

[Kitana, did you get them? At least tell me you found out who it was,] Mason barked over the radio.

"I did. It's the Ilysian Punks. They are the ones who robbed the military factory."

Chapter 35

Preparation

Kyle did not expect to be treated this well by the enforcers when he came in to report finding a crate of military equipment. He also did not expect to have an impromptu meeting with the inquisitors, who wanted to talk with him right after.

The three of them were now sitting in a lobby area, with Mason and Kitana both smiling at Kyle. "Only a good citizen of Yual such as you would have the heart to return such an important good. The enforcer department will confer upon you a medal of public service." Mason nodded his head.

Kyle smiled genially in response. All three of them knew that he was the gang leader of the Seven Snakes—it was an open secret. "I would prefer if I traded the medal for a more concrete benefit."

Mason nodded, getting the gist. "Before we come to that, we just wanted to check if you had seen any crates around this district as well. Wouldn't want to go door to door, banging up people just to find any."

"Rest assured, inquisitor, you have my word that this is the only crate you'll find in my territory."

"Is that so..." Mason's voice trailed off as he glanced at Kitana, who nodded. "Well then, speak."

"Word is already on the street that the Ilysian Punks have the rest of the guns. You've probably heard about it."

Mason and Kitana's faces remained calm, showing no reaction, while internally they knew that they were about to be caught in some ploy.

"The Ilysian Punks have recently been launching attacks into my district, and I'm planning some retribution. We're on the same side here with a common enemy, so I'll say a temporary alliance is in order. Perhaps we can be of some help."

Mason finally chuckled. "You mean you want the enforcers to look the other way while you attack the Ilysian Punks with everything you've got?"

"And as soon as I find even a single trail of any guns, I will let you know immediately," Kyle concluded.

"Or we could simply round them up all by ourselves."

"Inquisitor, I'm not too sure your men are as willing and motivated as mine to fight against a gang who most likely have full possession of military equipment enough to decimate a battalion. Life is precious, after all. Every death is a stain on your record." Kyle smirked.

Mason leaned back into the chair, smoking his pipe again. "A tempting offer, Alvin. Perhaps we are on the same side after all." As soon as he said the name, he tried to examine Kyle's face for any reaction but found none.

"Do we have a deal then?"

"You have my word. Any issues with enforcement, you may talk to Kitana directly." Mason motioned to her.

"Good. Then I shall take my leave now. Pleasure doing business with you." Kyle patted his suit down and buttoned it before walking out of the enforcer's office.

Mason glanced at the figure of Kyle leaving, then looked directly at Kitana. "Are you confident that the target was not him? It seems he knew that this was going to happen, as though he was setting up everything."

"We have the handwritten Ilysian Punks shipment order as proof, with a direct mark that can only be placed by the higher-ups in the gang. No way the Seven Snakes were the ones who robbed the factory." Kitana shook her head, but deep down she knew that Kyle was the one who had made the handgun and was framing the Ilysian Punks.

"Fine then. One more gang in our pocket is always a good thing. He's right; it'll take less manpower now to attack the Ilysian Punks, seeing we have his gang as cannon fodder. We'll let the dogs eat each other, then swoop in for the kill. After all, the alliance is *temporary*."

* * *

Kyle returned to one of his offices, where Damian and Keith were already waiting for him. "So, did they accept the deal?" Damian asked.

"They did. We are clear to attack the Ilysian Punks head-on right now without worrying about getting caught. Where did we plant the guns?"

"We planted them in the three districts closest to us as previously agreed, while the others are still being slowly planted."

"Good, we strike in two weeks. Gather the associates; it's time to do some preparations."

The three returned back to the old Seven Snakes base, which was still in use by most of the associates. With the enforcers in a temporary alliance now, the only thing they had to worry about now was probing attacks from the Ilysian Punks.

"Have we vetted all of the new associates?" Kyle asked Damian. He was well aware that many new members had joined during his trip to the Culdao Peaks, so he was unsure whether any snitches or spies had made it through the crack. It was especially critical now to make sure.

"We've tried our best to filter those we found shady. Many of the guys we took were desperate, mostly through the soup kitchen recruitment effort."

Kyle glanced at the assembled associates now. Those involved in the production were not here. However, there were close to seventy associates here. Their gang's growth was tremendous, with many joining due to rumors of Kyle's strength and business prowess. Others joined simply for survival or for a place to belong.

The three vipers were in attendance as well—Monica, Adrian, and Niko. They stood proudly in front of their crew, knowing something big was about to happen.

Many of the new associates were muttering to each other, this being the first time Kyle had gathered all of them together. "Associates, both old and new. My apologies to the newer ones for not personally welcoming you to the Seven Snakes." Kyle stood up on an elevated stage, speaking to the assembly.

Keith and Damian rolled out a map behind Kyle, a detailed version of just the South Sector, with the gangs' territory clearly highlighted in colors. "In just three short months since I've assumed leadership, we have achieved many things."

"We have fended off aggression from the Red Lions, fixed our finances, and trained ourselves to be a competent fighting force, able to stand up for ourselves. And this is all thanks to your hard work and dedication."

"Look at how much we have accomplished. Can you not feel it? This is true power. Who among you wants to go back to the factories, to the streets, to the thug rackets you used to be?" Kyle inquired.

The associates and vipers all shook their heads. Now that they had a taste of power, wealth, and authority, who would be sane enough to give that up to pursue a meaningless job in a factory line or to wander homeless?

"But are you satisfied with what we have today? Even now, bigger gangs look down on us from above. The Ardent Cretins watch our every move. The Red Lions gang wants to keep us in check. And even now, the Ilysian Punks dare to attack our district. If it's a fight they want, they'll get it!"

"YEAH!" Niko cheered as the rest of the associates roared in response.

"Over the next few months, everyone will undergo the same training course. Keith, bring it in." Kyle snapped his fingers, leading Keith and Damian to haul trolleys full of crates, equipment produced by the factory now run by Gordon.

"Thanks to your hard work, the Seven Snakes can now afford proper arctech equipment for all of you. The vipers and Damian have been tailoring the equipment to each of your needs. Keep proper care of this equipment; each of you gets only one set. Use every available time to familiarize yourself with the weapons and armor," Kyle concluded, dismissing them afterward.

The associates happily ran over to grab their new arctech equipment.

"My god, we're loaded! Not even the Red Lions have such equipment. We'll be legends in the South Sector!"

"It isn't about being loaded, but it's about our leader reinvesting the profits into the gang rather than taking it for himself. He's so much better than Ulon I nearly forgot he used to be Alvin."

"Alvin? Who's that?"

"Oh newbie, you're in for a tale…"

Despite all their lavish praise, the equipment was not as good as they made it sound. Kyle had gotten Gordon to mass-produce simple arctech equipment that he had designed. None of the items was good or a masterwork by any stretch of the imagination; they had just one simple engraving on each. Kyle walked toward the crate, inspecting the equipment.

Seven Snakes Vambrace (Basic)

An official design by Kyle, leader of the Seven Snakes.

+ 3 STR, + 2 VIT

[Active] Harden (Basic): Increase toughness and durability for a short period of time.

Cost: 1 MP   **Duration:** 1 minute

Cooldown: 5 minutes

Seven Snakes Breastplate (Basic)

An official design by Kyle, leader of the Seven Snakes.

+5 VIT, +2 MAX HP
[**Active**] **Deflect (Basic):** Able to block up to three medium-speed projectiles.
Cost: 3 MP   **Duration:** 30 seconds   **Cooldown:** 1 hour

Seven Snakes Metal Pipe (Basic)

An official design by Kyle, leader of the Seven Snakes.
[**Active**] **Reinforcement:** Increased force when hitting.
Cost: 2 MP   **Duration:** 30 seconds
Cooldown: 2 minutes

The metal pipe was effectively a carbon copy of Riker's metal pipe, the result of his hours spent copying the engraving. Despite his efforts, he had yet to reach the intermediate level for arcia etching, partly due to offloading most of the work to the factory.

Kyle had learned over time that the titles were only granted through repetition, which meant he truly had to grind if he wanted to raise his titles' levels. But for now, it was already good enough.

With the factory producing the equipment necessary to gear up the Seven Snakes, Kyle knew they had more than a winning chance to take down the Ilysian Punks, one district at a time.

Kyle watched the other associates marvel and test out their arctech equipment. Some of them fainted due to arcia exhaustion, unable to maintain the cost required to activate some of the engravings.

"We will train for a month or two to raise everyone's arcia energy to an acceptable level. I will consult Haui for any potions that might help with this endeavor," Kyle explained to the vipers, Damian, and Keith.

"Sir, if we launch an attack on Ilysian Punks, what if they counterattack and raze our businesses? We don't have anything left to defend with," Damian pointed out.

"Don't worry about that; I've already called for backup."

* * *

In an abandoned mine somewhere in the Culdao Peaks, screams and shouts of fighting could be heard echoing down the long, dimly lit corridors, the rocky texture of the walls stained with blood and leaking arcite fuel.

Gulak gulped as he walked down the corridor with trepidation. This used to be his home, where he had fond memories of delivering nearly rotten limbs from humans and other creatures to the joyful mothers who were resting in each small room.

Now, the rooms had long lost their prior splendor, demonized into a harrowing hell of pain and torture. Gulak straightened his back as much as he could, keeping up a false bravado as he continued. *That accursed human! It's all his fault!*

It would have been simple to overthrow his reign as soon as he left, but what he left behind in a human female form was far more sinister and deadly than the goblins could have expected.

They tried to break free many times, but each time the human—no, the monster—stopped them. Even as they pleaded for mercy, not a single word left her lips.

Gulak eventually reached the source of the screams and shouts, an enlarged room originally meant for goblin children to play together. Now, it was instead a makeshift fighting arena where goblins and humans alike were desperately fighting their hardest against what seemed to be feral mindless humans that had engravings all over their skin. *Zombies. A result of Kyle's human experimentation.*

Feldon grunted as he was shoved onto the floor by a feral zombie, the saliva from its mouth dripping onto his face. He quickly shoved a metal pipe in a jab fashion, slamming it right into its neck, with copious amounts of blood spurting out.

The same scene was played out all over the room, making it seem like a horror movie. Regardless, Gulak was not enraged, nor was he compelled to help. Instead, he bowed, clearly speaking out loud. "Master Sasha, the accursed hum—Lord Kyle has requested your assistance in the city of Raktor. The message says to bring those who are ready."

As he finished, a figure leapt down from an alcove in the ceiling, landing onto the floor without a sound. With a flash of her hands, she immediately grappled and restrained each zombie in one swift motion. Some of the zombies tried to lash out at her, but her movement was swift and fluid, as though she was dancing through the horde, targeting each one with precision while aware of her surroundings.

The humans and goblins let out a sigh of relief, knowing that the training session was over.

The zombies were not raised from the dead—instead, they were the failed results of Kyle's arcia engraving experiments, humans who had lost their minds through the intense pain.

"Finally, I get to leave this place!" Feldon relaxed, massaging his accursed muscles. He had signed up to be a company manager, not a grunt, and it's been more than two months since he's been stuck here with his family.

Granted, he was not treated badly, but the training routine every day was mandatory, making him feel like he was in a military boot camp. It was a necessary measure, however, as many gangs and daring adventurers attempted to raid the goblin mine in order to control the source of the Euria Seeds.

However, the goblins and company employees that had been slowly gathered over the course of three months were a sufficient deterrent to many attackers, thanks to the training by Kyle as well as the leadership of Master Sasha.

Sasha clapped her hands, immediately prompting the humans and goblins to line up. There were now more than fifty company employees as well as a hundred goblins, a veritable force to be reckoned with in the Culdao Peaks.

Instead of speaking, Sasha motioned with her hands toward a female clerk standing behind her, who cleared her throat. "It's time to show our strength and to make Lord Kyle proud. However, only seven will join her, as the nature of the mission is small. It is also required to have enough members here to defend the goblin base. Only humans."

Many of the goblins were dejected to hear that, some of them previously holding out hope they'd get to travel in a human city. Imagine all the limbs and torsos they could eat.

Feldon's face faltered but soon held an expression of determination. "I can do this. Let's do this! For my family's sake!"

Gulak's eyes lit up. *The strongest humans leaving means we finally have a chance!*

Just as he began to snicker to himself, he noticed a shadow looming over him. Gulak looked up to see the ferocious gaze of Sasha, intimidating him into instinctively bowing and retreating. *Forget it; if we rebel, she'll only come back and make things worse for us!*

Chapter 36

Kidnapping

Two weeks later, at the Lusty Arcian...

"What? We're expanding the brothel again?" Slavin was shocked, with Keith presenting the numbers to him.

"We have more than enough funds now to purchase a few more floors. We'll do it slowly, but the end goal is the entire building. Any problems?" Keith smiled.

"Of course not; I assume half of the floors are to serve as a front for the brothel?"

"Indeed, your... beauty school has been quite useful in providing ample evidence for the enforcers to ignore this location. However, the brothel is still under-defended." Keith recalled the last time the Red Lions attacked the brothel.

The Ilysian Punks gang was still snooping around the district, and they had already tried to flush out the Seven Snakes from the businesses. However, the increased defense has been able to protect the businesses thus far, so it was not a big issue.

With the war looming on the horizon, Keith also asked Slavin to hire a few mercenaries just in case of an attack. Even though they were in a temporary alliance with the enforcers, that did not mean the enforcers would help them defend their district or come to their aid in a fight. There was no doubt among the Seven Snakes that the enforcers were more than willing to let dogs eat dogs.

Keith pack up his documents into a briefcase, wearing his suit. Slavin examined him, a sense of nostalgia hitting him as he recalled how young Keith and Damian had been when they first joined the Seven Snakes.

"Where are you heading next?"

"Oh, one of the safehouses. I have to calculate how much spare cash we have in case we need to replace any of the new equipment. Why?"

"I'll escort you."

"No need. I already have two associates with me posted by Niko." Keith motioned with his hand toward the window.

"Ah, a big shot now, huh? My little Keith, all grown up. Let me escort you. It's not safe around the district now with the Ilysian Punks attacking every other day."

Keith finally relented, the four of them leaving the Lusty Arcian and walking through the streets. There was a palpable tension in the air as people scurried away or around them. "The probing attacks over the last few weeks have the locals spooked," Slavin noted.

"While our defense has been rock solid so far, the Ilysian Punks are not really mobilizing their entire force. They are trying to grind us down and erode the support we've garnered over the last few months. It was already hard enough to repair our broken reputation from Ulon's legacy, but no one wants to get caught up in the wars," Keith said with an air of clarity, having learned a thing or two from Kyle.

"You know, didn't you used to dream of being a scholar in one of the top universities?" Slavin suddenly changed the subject. "I even remember Damian saying he would be the security guard of that university which you chose."

Keith felt an embarrassing cringe come over his body as he involuntarily shuddered. "Don't remind me of that! Those were dreams of a naïve boy lost in his own world, oblivious to the workings of the city."

"I don't think it is a naïve dream. Maybe with the gang's help, you could still get in," Slavin joked.

Keith chuckled in response. "A Seven Snakes scholarship? That'll be the day! I don't even think I want to waste that kind of money on myself."

"Or maybe even Kyle might open a university just for you. A pretty good place to launder some money by spending it on ridiculous projects, don't you think? I heard he's already funding a professor."

"That's a bit too far-fetched, I think. Kyle wouldn't—" Keith suddenly stopped talking, noticing three foreign individuals standing opposite the street, glancing at them as they smoked their pipes.

Slavin also immediately noticed them. It was hard not to—everyone knew almost everyone here in these parts. As for the Seven Snakes, it was their job to know who was going in and out of the district.

"We need to move quickly," Slavin urged, picking up the pace.

The three foreigners also followed along. Their jackets flapped in the wind as they strutted, with one of them having his hand permanently in the inner pocket of his jacket. They trailed behind Keith, Slavin, and the two Seven Snakes associates down the long street.

Just as they approached one of the main junctions, Keith and Slavin suddenly darted into an alleyway while the two accompanying Seven Snakes associates pulled out their metal pipes and approached the three foreigners, who were equally unafraid.

"New to Raktor?" one of the Seven Snakes associates jeered toward the foreigners. "If you need a map, I know somewhere you can buy it."

The three foreigners did not reply, instead immediately pulling out their arctech pistols and firing bursts of projectiles that shredded the outside suits of the associates, knocking them over. "Hide the bodies in the alleyway," one of the foreigners ordered the other two.

"Yes, captain." The other two foreigners moved forward to hoist the two Seven Snakes associates up. Just as they bent over, the two associates lifted their waists up and used their legs to clamp around the necks of the foreigners, grappling them to the ground.

The suits of the associates were ripped in shreds, revealing a hidden Seven Snakes breastplate that managed to block the projectiles coming in. As the two tumbled and tousled on the ground, the foreign captain did not stop to help his comrades, instead running toward the alleyway which Keith and Slavin had entered.

As he rounded the corner, a fist came hurtling toward his face. His battle instincts kicked in, and he narrowly dodged it. Caught off guard by the fist, he nearly lost his balance as he dodged yet another punch from Slavin, who had been waiting for him around the corner.

The foreign captain rolled onto the ground before regaining his stance and pulling out an engraved knife. Slavin's eyes squinted as he recognized the knife. "So, the Ilysian Punks are finally pulling out the big guns."

"Shut it, Yual scum," the captain spat as he lunged with precision, targeting Slavin's vitals and organs with the discipline of a military soldier. Slavin blocked as much as he could, but he was no match for the captain, his arms and legs being shredded by cuts and stabs. Despite the one-sided fight, Slavin was still grinning.

"Smiling before your death? Happy to meet your fictional divine emperor?" the captain mocked.

"Never believed in that, but I know you're here for Keith. I'm just a small fry, so regardless of how long I hold out here, it'll only make it more of a win for me." Slavin smirked.

"You make it sound like we only brought three of us."

Keith ran as hard as he could, panting as he could feel the cold air of the city searing his lungs with every breath he took. He had not been doing the physical training routine due to his duties with the finances, but he was now regretting not even practicing running. His calves and thighs burned as he ran for more than five minutes at a near sprint speed. *Just a bit more!*

As he turned the corner of the alleyway into the area of one of the known safehouses, he was immediately grabbed by a burly hand, covering his mouth and preventing him from screaming out loud.

Keith's eyes could already see half of the safehouse guards taken out, with the other Ilysian Punks fending off the Seven Snakes' associates. Niko was fighting off as many as he could, but they were outgunned and outmatched in terms of combat ability. Niko noticed Keith being captured at the back, yelling, "KEITH!"

A quick chop to the back of the neck followed by an uppercut into Niko's chin knocked him out for good. "We've got the target. Retreat!"

* * *

Keith gasped for air as a bucket of ice-cold water was splashed onto his face, causing the locks of his blonde hair to droop down, clinging to his cheeks. He tried shifting his arms, but he was bound to a chair with tight ropes and metal handcuffs.

He glanced around the room, only to notice a heavily tattooed man sitting in a chair in front of him, a wild grin plastered on the man's face. The man was flanked by three guards, the one holding the bucket being the same captain that had caught him.

"Makoa," Keith muttered, recognizing the sub-leader of the Ilysian Punks. "I was half-expecting Javel to show up instead."

One of the guards smacked Keith across the face with a hard punch. "That's General Javel to you, bitch. The man is a Versian war hero and our boss!"

"I'm not Versian." Keith spat out a glob of blood. "A Versian war hero merely means a murderer who killed thousands of Yual citizens."

"You!" The guard started winding up a punch, but Makoa stopped him.

"He's riling you up. Calm yourself down and remember your training. And as for you, you don't seem surprised at all," Makoa remarked as he observed the calm expression on Keith's face.

"I always knew this was a possibility."

"I could tell from the ferocity of your guards. Too bad they were lacking."

"Just get this over with."

Makoa chuckled. "What a brave little kid. You can still work for the Ilysian Punks if you want to, even if you're not Versian. Both you and your brother can transfer over—as long as you spill the beans on where the guns are. Don't think I don't know you guys were planning to attack us."

"What guns?" Keith played dumb, wearing a confused look.

"And here I thought we were on the same page. The hard way it is, then." Makoa motioned with his hand, prompting two guards to move forward. They wrapped Keith's head in a rucksack and tilted the chair over a basin of water behind them.

The water surged around the rucksack, clinging to his face and evoking the instinctive fear of drowning. Keith's body convulsed as he fought against the restraint of the chair, but the two guards firmly held him down, watching Keith thrash for a good twenty seconds before pulling him out.

Loud gasps for air filled the room as Keith choked involuntarily. "Are you ready now?" Makoa asked.

Keith coughed out water but still wore a weak smile under the drenched rucksack. "That's all you guys have?"

Makoa laughed out loud. "You've got balls, kid. Let me know when you're ready to talk, hmm? You two, keep going until he's done."

Keith gritted his teeth as he felt the chair tilt back once again, his mind holding onto hope that his older brother and Kyle would come to save him. *Makoa won't kill me. As long as I hold on...*

Makoa and the captain left the room, walking through the Ilysian Punks' hideout. "The kid knows we're not going to kill him, so make sure to bring him to the brink. If he ever goes too far, heal him a bit, then continue. Break his mind," Makoa ordered.

"Just like we did it in Versia." The captain nodded. The two of them walked down a hallway toward the double door. The sounds of cheering and booing could be heard from beyond.

Makoa opened the doors, revealing an underground boxing arena with nearly ten thousand viewers in the audience, screaming at the fighters going toe-to-toe with deadly weapons in the bloodstained ring.

"COME ON, YOU IDIOT! I SPENT MY WEEK'S PAY ON YOU! DON'T LET ME DOWN!"

"JUST DIE ALREADY, CUNT!"

The viewers jeered and roared as the fighters threw swings, jabs, stabs, and kicks at each other, battling it out in a bloody gladiator duel. Makoa ignored the spectacle, instead walking toward the VIP viewing area, where five servants had already prepared a spread of food and drinks for him, laid out on a glass table in front of a velvet sofa adorned with scantily clad ladies.

"What about the Seven Snakes? Most likely, they will try to attack us to free Keith," the captain inquired as Makoa sat down on the sofa.

Makoa grinned as he picked up a glass of whiskey, swirling it. "They have no idea where we are, so how could they ever find us? With our observers watching the moves of all their higher-ups, the moment Kyle makes a move, we'll know in a split second. If they strike, we'll swarm their district in one fell swoop and destroy all their businesses before the Red Lions and the Wretches catch wind of what is happening."

"So Keith is the emotional bait."

"Exactly. He must not die. We must continue to dangle him in front of them. No matter what moves they make, they'll lose in the end."

Chapter 37

Rescue

Gordon inspected the new prototype barrel that came from the factory floor, checking the engravings. "It's a bit rough around the edges, so the efficiency isn't extremely high. Maybe if we modified the engraving to be more spaced out, that would result in less interference between the traces..."

He quickly stepped over the mess of books left open on the carpeted floor of his office, trying to find a related text, but not before passing the barrel over to Kyle, who inspected it as well.

"The rifling is too uneven; the ball projectile would not have the stability I need. You have to redo this barrel," Kyle remarked.

"I can do that, but this barrel design is completely different from all the other guns in Raktor right now. I've never seen anything like it. Did you design it yourself?" Gordon tried to probe.

Kyle didn't reply, instead focusing his attention on the remaining parts laid out on the table. He examined the muzzle brake as well as the stock of the gun, checking their mechanical tolerances.

Kyle still could not get over the fact that the gun did not have any sort of firing mechanism, as it was powered by arcia energy instead of gunpowder. While it acted similarly to a particle rifle, the mismatch in technology still slightly threw him off.

Just as Kyle was about to point out a few more mistakes, the door banged open to reveal a clearly flustered Damian. "Kyle, they got him! They kidnapped Keith!"

"Who?"

"Who else? The Ilysian Punks, those fuckers! We need to form up and strike back immediately, I'm going to call everyone into the main base—" Damian frantically explained, clearly in turmoil.

"No. Don't make a single move. I will call Adrian first to understand the situation. We will not move now," Kyle retorted, shocking Damian into silence.

Soon, the shock on Damian's face was slowly replaced with anger. "What are you saying? Are you telling me to let my younger brother get tortured to hell?!"

Gordon was frightened by the sudden tension in the room, his eyes frantically glancing between Kyle and Damian. "No, we will save him. But now isn't the right time."

"The 'right' time?" Damian's eyes narrowed. "Why do I feel like you were expecting this all along? Were you using Keith as bait?"

"Don't be stupid." Kyle didn't reply any further, taking out an arctech radio and calling Adrian. "Did you track who kidnapped Keith?"

[Yes, but too many of our scouts are being marked by their observers. We can't move around much, but we managed to pinpoint the rough location of their hideout.]

"Then we need to go now! What the fuck are we waiting for?" Damian was about to leave when Kyle suddenly walked up and grabbed him by the shoulder.

"Don't make any rash decisions; they are watching our every move. The moment our forces leave the district, it's game over for us."

[Damian, he's right. The observers are tracking the boundaries of the districts, and they have snitches among the locals. That's how they were able to snatch Keith in the first place!]

Damian was obviously not listening. "Then we just sit here like ducks? I'm going to save my brother, with or without you guys!" Damian scoffed, trying to slap Kyle's arm away. However, Kyle's grip was like iron, crushing Damian's shoulder.

Damian threw a fist at Kyle, who easily caught it with his other hand. With a swift kick from Kyle to the shins, Damian was brought to the ground, dropping onto his knees as Kyle continued to hold him down.

"And what are you going to do when you go over alone? Get yourself kidnapped? I didn't make you the underboss to be emotionally manipulated. Take a deep breath," Kyle ordered.

Damian wanted to retort, but the words were stuck in his throat. *I still can't beat Kyle; what hopes do I have alone against an entire gang?* He inhaled deeply, letting out a long sigh. "You can let go now; I'm fine."

"Good. There will be time for revenge, but for now, we stay put." Kyle returned to the gun parts on the table, assembling them with the barrel into one of the longest rifles Damian and Gordon had seen. A weird-looking telescope was mounted to the top of the gun as well, with Kyle peering through it to check the zeroing.

"But then who is going to save Keith if we can't move?" Damian asked in exasperation. "The Red Lions? The enforcers?"

* * *

[ANNNNNND HE'S KNOCKED DOWN! CAN HE GET UP A SECOND TIME?!]

The crowd roared, the thunderous cheers and boos echoing off the walls of the expansive underground boxing arena. It was another rowdy night as usual, with hundreds of viewers and betters trying to claw back their winnings.

On the side, there were alcoholics in debt, continuing to drink non-stop; hijackers trying to hustle their stolen goods; fencers making connections; and uptight business leaders nervously glancing around with their bodyguards, hoping to get a good word in with the district leader, Makoa, to gain permission to enter the market.

Makoa was at his usual table in the VIP viewing section, bored out of his mind while resting his chin on his hands. He motioned toward the ring, getting the attention of the coach.

The coach nodded in response, conveying the signal to the knocked-down boxer, who got up slowly but painfully, wincing as he could barely see out of his eyes. The boxer stared across the ring at the jubilant rookie, who was already on the verge of celebrating his win.

The round proceeded as normal, with the limping boxer somehow being able to avoid a knockout until the gong rang.

[WHAT A SPECTACULAR FIRST ROUND! COULD WE SEE A COMEBACK? BETS FOR THE NEXT ROUND ARE OPEN NOW!]

The bookies were swarmed in an instant, with the crowd clamoring for tickets as young boys yelled out the odds. Makoa didn't care; his attention was now focused on the bound man kneeling down next to the table, his face swollen from multiple beatings. "Enforcer Staten, this is the third time we've met."

"Fuck off, punk. Kill me and get it over with. Isn't that what you're best at?" Staten sneered through the blood dripping down his face.

A low chuckle rose from Makoa, and the six girls laughed along with him. "Don't devalue yourself. You're much more useful to me alive than dead. For now."

Staten grimaced, knowing what he was implying. From the view of the VIP section, he could already make out more than two dozen local enforcers as part of the crowd, already trapped in the never-ending cycle of gambling and debt.

"Didn't know you punks knew anything about business acumen."

"Staten," Makoa said. "This is the third time you've interfered with our businesses. We're usually nice to our fellow citizens, especially those who keep the public peace here in our beautiful Raktor."

"You're just a gang of thugs. Match-fixing is hardly a proper business."

"A matter of perspective. I'm in a dilemma as to how to… change your view of us. No family, no relatives. You're the perfect enforcer, with no weaknesses. However, I believe I have a solution…" Makoa motioned to a guard, who brought a Euria-infused Stamina Potion stolen from the Red Lions.

"You'll never get anything out of me."

"The human body begs to differ." Makoa grabbed the potion and walked over to Staten, forcibly opening his mouth with his large hands. "Drink up!"

Staten tried to resist but soon involuntarily drank the potion, coughing wildly as Makoa slammed him onto the ground. "Tell me why the enforcers are increasing their raids into Ilysian Punks' territory!" Makoa roared into Staten's ears.

"Fuck you!" The retort from Staten earned him another punch, causing the man's mouth to bleed internally.

"Another tough nut. When does the effect kick in?" Makoa asked the guards.

"Three days later, assuming three potions are drunk in a single day."

"Good. Listen here, Staten. You can leave anytime you want. As long as you follow the rules around here."

"The inquisitors will never let you—"

Makoa delivered a fearsome kick to the enforcer's stomach, causing him to gag. "Your narcissistic emperor and his cronies are not going to help you. Get him the fuck out of here."

The next round had begun, with the previously limping boxer suddenly regaining strength out of nowhere and fighting back hard. It was still a close match, but the boxer managed to knock out the rookie just before the end of the round. As the gong rang thrice, the crowd roared in response, no doubt having won or lost their entire lives' fortunes.

[AND THAT'S IT FOR THE END OF THE FIRST MATCH. THIS SECOND MATCH HAS A NEWCOMER, AND IT'S A LADY AT THAT!]

A loud wave of gasps of shock and wonder went through the crowd as an unknown lady stepped out onto the ring from the sides. Her eyes were dead, showing no signs of emotion as people around her continuously catcalled her.

The lady glanced around the crowd, noticing a few random audience members who nodded back in response. They were spread out among the crowd, somehow inching closer to the Ilysian Punks arena guards that covered the exits of the arena. They all made a discreet sign with their hands, nodding toward the lady.

The lady then looked up, noticing the VIP section and Makoa's visage at the edge of the viewing platform. A small tattoo on her neck glowed red, with a clear voice entering her mind like a wireless connection.

[Sasha, report in. Any signs?]

[Makoa, local leader spotted. Beginning mission.]

Sasha stared at the rabid crowd, who were catcalling and jeering her for showing up. The arena was open to all and every fighter, regardless of experience. People just wanted to see blood; who cared who it came from?

"Did you end up in the wrong place, little girl? Shouldn't you be in the kitchen?"

"Where's your husband? He's looking for you outside, so go home! You don't stand a chance here!"

The jeers barely registered in her mind as she focused on her telepathic communication with Kyle. Kyle had used the Designate Follower skill on her, enabling him to converse with her despite her being mute.

Sasha did not show any outward reaction, acknowledging it internally. On the other side of the ring, the arena organizers were jubilant.

"I knew it; she's driving our view count up! Most of the audience sincerely believes that she won't win, so they are going to bet against her."

A guard quickly reported to Makoa, who grinned widely. "Interesting. Stage a win for her, and send a fighter who can take a few hits. Seems like this girl can deliver a few." He continued to plan his attack on the Seven Snakes, unaware that the Seven Snakes were in the heart of his nest.

The announcer's voice was barely audible in the boxing ring, but a loud cheer went up as Sasha's opponent appeared.

[GIVE IT UP FOR MASON!]

Apparently a popular fighter, Mason was not overtly muscular but had the right weight and body for fleet movements in the ring. Known for his footwork, Mason waved happily to the crowd while the coach gave him a cryptic hand sign.

Losing to this girl? Fuck... Mason internally groaned, but he accepted the job. He wasn't doing this for the fame, though. None of the fighters were. *Let's just make this an easy loss. She doesn't look like she can deliver really strong hits.*

The bookies were overwhelmed with bets riding on Mason, with Makoa ordering the Punks to match bets on the lady, aiming to sweep up the entire round. It was easy to earn money that way, and Makoa was more than happy with the appearance of the lady.

The referee lined the two of them away from each other and promptly began the match. The two fighters circled each other as the crowd incessantly cheered Mason.

"Sorry, lady. I might not know your reason, but I'm here to win." Mason grinned, side-stepping and feigning, throwing a few probing punches.

Sasha simply matched his footwork, like a dance, somehow able to keep up with him. Mason was content with this pace, acting cautious, but soon the coach signaled to attack more.

Mason nodded, beginning to attack more seriously. He threw a few jabs and hooks, while continuously cornering the lady, forcing her near the edge of the ring.

Sasha only dodged, never retaliating with her own attack so far. This meant Mason would not be able to lose the match as planned. "Stop dodging and fight back!" Mason goaded Sasha on, increasing the speed of his punches.

Finally, as a single right hook was about to land on Sasha's face, Mason suddenly felt a cold shiver run through his entire body, forcing him to back off immediately as though he were being eyed by a predator far beyond his means.

However, it was far too late. Sasha's right fist was already in front of his own face, the punch landing right on his nose and bashing his face in with a resounding crunch. The force was completely unexpected, with Mason toppling over onto the floor, his hands grabbing his nose that was profusely bleeding.

The crowd was equally confused by the sudden force shown by Sasha, which did not match her body stature. Before the stunned referee could stop them, Sasha leapt forward and delivered a strong kick to the side of Mason's head, the bones' cracking echoing across the ring. Mason's body immediately went limp as a mush of blood leaked out of the back of his head.

The sudden increase in skill shocked Makoa, alarm bells ringing in his head. He locked eyes with Sasha, fully comprehending what she was here for. "Grab her now!" Makoa ordered, with the Ilysian Punks immediately leaping onto stage and trying to restrain her.

Chapter 38

Boss Fight

The arena devolved into a frenzy, with the audience thinking that the ensuing fight was part of the show. The fence surrounding the ring shook violently, and the crowd cheered on the Ilysian Punk Guards and Sasha. Everyone was here to see blood.

Sasha deftly avoided the first lunge, parrying with her arm and twisting her body to deliver an elbow strike right into the first punk's head. An arctech aura burst out from her right hand, increasing the force of the strike and snapping his neck and instantly killing him.

The other two guards fared no better, being eliminated with precision punches all aimed at their heads. Makoa's eyes squinted before motioning for more guards to attack her. *Who is this girl? Did the Wretches finally send one of their famed assassins?*

However, Makoa noted that the fight was not just happening in the ring but on the exits as well, with random audience members fighting against the Ilysian Punk guards. The audience members were well-equipped—arctech equipment hidden underneath their clothes augmenting their strength and skills.

Makoa quickly grabbed an arctech radio handed over by a servant, barking into it. "Observers, where the fuck are the Seven Snakes now!?"

[Boss, we've spotted Damian at the food market, and Kyle was last seen eight hours ago coming out of the factory, but he headed into one of their dummy bases.]

Then who the hell is attacking us now?! "What are you idiots doing? Swarm them now!" Makoa roared, spurring the remaining Ilysian Guards to move down to apprehend Sasha. He also began to leave the VIP section, heading toward the armory to gear up.

Sasha exhaled slowly, having defeated the three guards. She could already see the rest of her strike team stirring up a fight among the crowd against the other Ilysian Punks. Glancing up again at the VIP section, she noticed that Makoa was now missing. [Sir, target on the move.]

[The priority is to rescue Keith. Most likely, Makoa will personally guard him,] Kyle replied over the wireless communication engraving.

Sasha nodded to herself, noticing two more Ilysian Punks, geared with basic armor and swords, charging toward her. She nimbly avoided the first swing, pushing out with her palm against the lower chin of the first punk, slamming his jaw into his skull and sending him spiraling onto the ground.

A sword swing swiped across her head as she instinctively ducked and spun around in a crouching position, delivering a strong kick to the shin and cracking the bone within. The second Punk screamed out in pain before Sasha recovered to a standing position and elbowed him right in the face, causing him to stagger back and drop his sword.

Sasha picked up the sword and immediately slashed his neck, moving toward the fighters' entrance and entering the hallways. As she turned a corner, an Ilysian Punk ambushed her, throwing a punch aimed straight at her face, but she spun to the side and slashed off the arm in one fell swoop, followed by a forward thrust into the Punk's neck.

"Who the fuck are you?!" one of the Ilysian Punks yelled out from across the hallway, armed with a repeating crossbow aimed at her. He fired off two shots in succession, but Sasha simply used one hand to lift the dead body of the Ilysian Punk she just killed and used it as a pincushion as she charged forward.

Before the crossbow user could retreat, Sasha used all her strength to fling the dead body at him. The corpse slammed into him, forcing him to fall to the floor.

In a blink, Sasha was already on top of him, stabbing her sword in a swift downward thrust into his vitals. She grabbed the repeating crossbow and the pack of bolts, running down the hallway and checking for Keith.

Sasha assumed that the holding cells were located below, so she took the first staircase she found that led down. However, as she stepped off the first flight of steps, a resounding crack echoed through the entire stairwell, causing the concrete below her to collapse.

The fall had her crash into a pile of rubble below as the soot and dust kicked up all over the base floor, obscuring her vision. Sasha quickly recovered, instinctively blocking a metallic fist aimed straight at her torso with her sword, which broke in half from the sheer force it was subjected to.

Another metallic fist came swooping in fast, nailing Sasha right in the exposed ribs and sending her flying into the wall with a loud thud, her bones fracturing internally as her body slumped to the ground.

"For an assassin, you're doing a piss poor job. The Seven Snakes did not pay you enough to afford arctech equipment?" Makoa grinned as he moved toward Sasha. Arcia engravings on the surface of his two metallic gauntlets glowed purple and churned as the arcite fuel pack strapped to his belt gurgled away, feeding the gauntlets through pipes.

Makoa could tell that Sasha had no obvious arctech equipment on her except for the stolen crossbow, which made him let his guard down. However, a sudden green aura surged from the base of her spine, healing her bones and damaged muscles at a visible rate. Makoa quickly lunged to attack, but Sasha was already anticipating it, diving out of the way and performing a recovery roll to get back into her fighting stance in a single motion.

"What the...?" Makoa was confused, but he was not given the time to comprehend what had happened; Sasha immediately fired off the remainder of the crossbow bolts before tossing it away and charging with two knives previously hidden in her clothes. Makoa raised his gauntlets in a defensive posture to block the bolts, one of which lodged itself in his thigh.

Sasha tried to dash in close to stab Makoa, but a single swing of the gauntlets forced Sasha to back away, lest she get slammed into the wall again. While she had a healing engraving on her back, it took arcia energy to activate it—using too much would cause her stamina to plummet.

"Bitch!" Makoa roared as he threw straights and hooks at Sasha, who sidestepped most of them, the two of them dancing in circles on the uneven pile of rubble. As Sasha ducked to avoid yet another swing, she kicked a loose stone in the pile of rubble with all her might, dislodging it.

Makoa stepped forward, only to find himself falling over as the rubble beneath him began to slide down. Sasha quickly dashed forward with her knives, activating their engravings to slash at the now exposed pipes between the arcite fuel pack and gauntlets.

The pipes flailed wildly as they were chopped off, spilling arcite fuel that sprayed all over the area, coating it with a distinct smell and color. Makoa landed on his back as well, crushing the fuel pack under his own weight. "URGH!"

Before Sasha could close in for the final blow, Makoa suddenly aimed the glowing gauntlet at her, which fired off like a rocket toward her. The unexpected projectile caught her off-guard, the gauntlet slamming right into her guts and pushing her back into the pile of rubble.

Makoa grunted as he stood back up, removing his now-dead gauntlets and tossing them off into the puddle of arcia fuel. "Looks like I won't have the chance to interrogate you." Makoa retrieved a match from his belt, lit it, and flung it into the puddle before retreating down into the basement.

The arcia fuel erupted into flames, burning straight toward Sasha, who was still badly hurt. Makoa did not stay around to make sure she died, instead focusing on his own survival. *Shit, I lost my arctech equipment! At least I still have my belt. I have to get out of here, along with Keith!*

Makoa rushed down the basement, passing by countless holding cells where traitors, slaves, and enforcers were held. They were all shocked at the condition of Makoa, a sliver of hope appearing in their hearts.

Makoa ignored them, heading straight for Keith's holding cell, where the captain and the two subordinates that had been posted to guard him were already waiting for him. "Boss, what's the plan now?"

"Give me your arctech radio!" Makoa snatched the radio away from the captain. "This is Makoa Montoga. Get a wagon up to Exit C right now!"

[Yes, Boss!]

"Grab the prisoner. We need him alive as a hostage. You—follow me. You two, head down that way and make sure every attacker is dead! Don't let anyone through the fire!"

The two guards nodded, rushing off while the captain hoisted the unconscious Keith on his shoulder, making a beeline for their secret exit. It was a long underground tunnel that led to an alleyway exit one block away.

As they reached the end of the underground tunnel, a large metallic door awaited them. Makoa quickly rushed to the door, tapping on it with a secret pattern. However, there was no reply from the other side. The captain grimaced as Makoa gave him a knowing look, prompting the captain to retrieve his arctech pistol at the ready.

Makoa retrieved a master key from his belt, unlocking the metallic door from his side. Makoa pushed the door outward in a rapid swing, with the captain immediately clearing the room with the arctech pistol. None of the guards stationed there could be found, the room was completely empty. The sounds of rain could be heard echoing down a short stairwell that led to the street level.

"You, go check if the area is clear. Hand me the prisoner." Makoa motioned to the captain, who complied with the order. The captain stepped up silently with trepidation, wary of his surroundings. He peeked his head out of the entrance, noticing the alleyway to be completely empty and devoid of the two guards that should be nearby.

He waited for a minute before realizing there was truly no one around. A rumbling sound of an arctech wagon could be heard pulling up to the exit of the alleyway, with the captain squinting. He spotted the emblem of the Ilysian Punks on the wagon, signaling to Makoa that it was all clear.

"About damn time." Makoa grunted as he hoisted Keith's limp body up, jogging toward the wagon with the captain. The driver was already waiting for them at the front. They tossed the body into the back and hopped on themselves. "Go now! What are you waiting for?"

"Yes, sir!" The driver anxiously stepped on the pedal, but before he could turn the steering wheel, a loud bang and a subsequent whizzing sound was accompanied by the shattering of glass. "What the fuck?!" Makoa could only say those words as the driver fell over onto the steering wheel, his feet still on the pedal as the wagon veered off the street and slammed into the wall of a building, frightening the residents within. They immediately scrambled to barricade their doors.

The bang frightened the pedestrians on the street as well, causing them to flee in all directions or take cover in one of the nearby buildings.

The crash nearly concussed Makoa, but he was quick to recover. He slapped the unconscious captain awake. "Get up, idiot! We're under attack!"

"Wh-What?! From where?!"

"Get out there and find out!" Makoa ordered him, and the captain immediately complied. The moment the captain stepped out of the wagon, however, another loud bang was heard, this time followed by the squelching sounds of brain and meat as a hole was drilled through the head of the captain, his body crumpling to the ground instantly.

[SYSTEM MESSAGE]
You killed Ilysian Punk Guard Captain, +400 EXP.

Makoa was shocked. *A pistol? No, a rifle. But from where?!*

He patted his belt, checking to make sure it was still working. Subsequently, he grabbed Keith's body to use as a hostage and slowly stepped out of the wagon. "I DON'T KNOW WHERE OR WHO YOU ARE, BUT IF YOU TRY ANYTHING. I'LL SNAP HIS NECK!" Makoa roared out into the open, his eyes frantically darting around, trying to find the shooter.

No one replied, which gave Makoa even more confidence as he started to retreat into the alleyway. *This way, he'll only have one angle to shoot me from.* However, before he could step back, a spiraling metallic ball projectile the size of a marble slammed into Makoa, a resounding bang reverberating through the surroundings.

His belt activated, and a personal energy shield suddenly protected him.

However, the force sent Makoa stumbling backward, causing him to drop Keith onto the floor with a thud. As he staggered back, two more shots were fired at him, depleting the energy shield and knocking him back even further. The belt vibrated violently as the shield flickered. Makoa's eyes widened as he realized his protective barrier was about to dissipate.

Fuck the hostage! I have to survive, myself!

He quickly sprinted down the alleyway and disappeared, leaving Keith on the floor. Soon, the sniper revealed himself to be Kyle, walking up to the unconscious body of Keith and checking his pulse. Kyle noticed the numerous slash marks on Keith's face, hands, and legs. The man had been whipped till the skin was raw.

He glanced down the alleyway, noticing he would not be able to catch up with Makoa. *Yet another heritage from the Galactic Era. It seems Versia is where I should find my answers.*

[Sasha, I have Keith with me.]

Back in the collapsed stairwell, the two Ilysian Punks ordered by Makoa to clear out the base watched the raging fire. "Makoa said not to let anyone through the fire, but how is anyone going to clear this?"

Just as he finished the sentence, a human figure suddenly leapt through the fire, slamming straight into one of the punks. "GAH!" The punk gasped as he was knocked onto the floor. Before the other punk could react, a glowing fist was already in front of his face, pummeling him with a severe concussion.

The first punk struggled to see who attacked him, only to see a lady with her clothes half-burnt, along with burn marks across her face, healing at a visible rate. Her skin was peeled off by the burns, revealing the bloodied, throbbing flesh beneath. "Mon-Mon-Monster!"

Sasha walked up to kick his head with as much force as possible, snapping his neck in a single instant.

[Do we retreat now?] the woman replied on the wireless channel.

[No. Kill everyone. Not a single Ilysian Punk gets out alive.]

Chapter 39

No Holds Barred

All the inquisitors could see in the morning was a smoldering wreck of a wagon that had crashed into a building. No bodies could be found, and if there were, they would have been burnt to a crisp, apparently dying after the wagon's arctech engine caught on fire.

"The Seven Snakes are definitely not playing around..." Mason remarked as he inspected the scene, which was now cordoned off by the enforcers. The fight had taken more than a few hours ago, with the enforcers finally responding to reports of loud explosives and shockwaves in the area.

"Dynamite bombs, sir?" Kitana queried. The wagon's engine was clearly blown out, with the blackened body of the driver still lifeless over the steering wheel.

"Perhaps. Seems that the Seven Snakes know how to make their own chemical explosives. Either way, we're long past worrying about guns—if the Ilysian Punks have the shipment, we're looking at an all-out conflict."

"Sir!" An enforcer ran along the street toward the two inquisitors, saluting. "We've found the crates mentioned. It's definitely the military guns that were stolen from the factory."

"So Kyle is serious about this alliance after all... Cordon off the entire block. I want every enforcer to scour this area to figure out how the hell the Ilysian Punks managed to get their hands on it."

***

Makoa panted as he jogged down the alleyway, having run more than two districts away. He had not been directly injured in the fight, so his mind remained clear, continuing to ponder over what the hell had just happened. It was nearing daybreak, the glimmer of the local star peeping out from just below the horizon.

Shit! I just lost a raid against assassins hired by the Seven Snakes! Makoa grimaced internally. He would very much prefer to keep the loss of his base and hostage a secret from the higher-ups, but he knew it was a futile effort—they always found out in the end.

Thus, Makoa made a beeline for the main base—it was better if he turned himself in. As he approached the lobby of a luxurious hotel owned by the Ilysian Punks, the two guards were taken aback by the soot and grime coating parts of Makoa's body.

"Stop ogling with your mouths open and get me to the boss," Makoa demanded. "NOW!"

The guards quickly escorted him into the lobby and into an arctech elevator, which chugged slowly up to the highest floor. The doors slid open to reveal a solely glass room, providing a panoramic view of the South Sector and beyond. The height of the hotel was a mere ten stories, but it was enough to give a sense of awe.

Makoa shrugged off the two guards who tried to support his arms, walking by himself into the center of the velvet-carpeted room, facing an empty desk and chair. He sat down on one of the sofas, catching his breath as he waited. He locked eyes with a butler who was standing at the side nonchalantly.

"You look terrible," the butler remarked.

"Shut it."

"You'd better have a reason for disturbing my sleep." A low voice wafted in from behind Makoa, and the man immediately stood up and bowed toward the source.

"Good morning, General Javel!" Makoa performed a ninety-degree bow before recovering into a standing posture and saluting.

"Relax. We're not in Versia anymore." General Javel chuckled, the wrinkles on his old face scrunching up as his face took on a gentle smile. "So, I assume you got hit by the Red Lions?"

"No, sir." Makoa shook his head as he watched Javel stroll over to his office chair. "It's the Seven Snakes; they hired assassins to hit our district."

"For what reason?"

"I... I was trying to find the source of the missing gun shipment that we hijacked. It was last seen in the Seven Snakes' district, so I've been performing probing attacks for the last few weeks."

"And let me guess. You follow the doctrine of stealing a valuable hostage to pressure them."

"Sir, I did not expect the Seven Snakes to be able to hire that many assassins! They also had a sort of cannon that could precisely target me from far away."

"How far?"

"I did not see the shooter myself, but I estimate five hundred meters or even more."

Javel's eyes squinted at Makoa as he ran his hands over the velvet chair. "That's a tall claim, Lieutenant Makoa. Five hundred meters is double the range of any known rifle in existence. Are you sure?"

"I'm confident." Makoa nodded vigorously.

Javel scanned Makoa's face before sighing. "I trust your instincts. Alejandro, how soon can we move?"

The butler bowed in response. "Sir, we can spare 150 men to attack the Seven Snakes immediately. However, they are the reserves for our continuing conflict with the Red Lions and the Wretches. Tapping into this resource may weaken our stance against them."

Javel pondered, thinking carefully.

"Makoa, you will be in charge of the counterattack force. Prepare yourself. We launch in a month. Continue the probing attacks," Javel ordered, to which Makoa complied and hastily left the room. *Granting a chance for revenge is a simple method of motivation.*

Javel sighed as he glanced out of the glass windows, overlooking the city. Alejandro walked up next to him, also looking at the view. "Sir, what are you thinking about?" the butler asked.

"I'm thinking there is a ploy afoot. I don't know who the mastermind is yet, but we're about to enter a total state of war. A small gang suddenly appeared with advanced technology mere weeks after the shipment of weapons was intercepted...It's too coincidental."

"Indeed. The recent auction in the Central Sector seems to be part of this same chain of events."

"Who do you think is behind it?"

"Either the Wretches or the Red Lions. We have been in a stalemate for a year now; no doubt they are looking for additional avenues to attack us from. Enlisting the help of smaller gangs is a valid tactic."

"Reasonable. But what if it is the small gang that is instigating all of this? The Seven Snakes—did they not just have a fight with the Red Lions recently? They also had a change of leader."

"That's a bit too far-fetched. They lost the fight against the Red Lions, and a 'change of leadership' is hardly enough to pull that gang out from the gutter that Ulon dropped them in. Even if they did 'win' the fight, it was only against Wrent."

"And yet none of Makoa's probing attacks worked, and they even hired assassins to rescue the hostage."

"I will confirm with Nest on who hired them, if any. However, I am more inclined to believe that the Red Lions are propping them up as a puppet gang of sorts. They are simply scapegoats."

Javel frowned for a moment before nodding in agreement. "Agreed. Set up an in-depth defense plan for our front against the Red Lions. Lure them into our districts and ensnare them while our counterattack force deals with the Seven Snakes."

"Yes, sir."

* * *

Wrent's face was confounded as he stared at the message he had just received. It had been an easy last three months, with his reputation in the Red Lions increasing thanks to his position as the main potion supplier for the entire gang.

Due to the contract with Kyle, Wrent was now purchasing potions in bulk, allowing the Red Lions to have an easier time fighting the Ilysian Punks and the Wretches. He still remained as a sub-leader, though he was now fully in charge of logistic issues instead of fighting on the frontlines.

However, the message he received was shocking.

Order from the Mane of the Red Lion:

Left Paw of the Red Lion is to attack the Ilysian Punks with all available forces in fourteen days' time. There has been verified intel that the Ilysian Punks are planning to raid the Seven Snakes with a large force in three days. Utilize this gap to take control of one more district.

"HAH! FUCK YOU, KYLE! YOU FINALLY GET WHAT YOU DESERVE!" Wrent gleefully shouted out loud in his office, nearly jumping up in joy at the thought of his hated enemy being utterly destroyed.

Sure, the Red Lions had a non-aggression pact with the Seven Snakes, but it was not a defensive one. Wrent would be more than delighted to take advantage of the situation. However, upon taking a closer look at the letter, he noticed it did not have a seal or a mark representing the Mane of the Red Lion. *Weird, but maybe Leo did not have the time to mark this properly.*

Wrent immediately called his top subordinates into the room. "Round up the men; prepare for war against the punks from Versia in fourteen days!"

Elsewhere in the district, the patrolling Red Lions squads received the order via their arctech radios, slowly pulling back toward the base. A lone squatter kid eyed the movements of the Red Lions squads before running off into the alleyways.

The kid turned the corner to meet Adrian, who was already talking to other squatter kids. "Mister, the Red Lions are pulling back to the base!"

"That means the letter worked. Thank Yual that Wrent is a gullible idiot." Adrian let out a sigh of relief and tossed a few rakels to the squatter kid, much to the whining of the others. "Stop whining. If you want it, you gotta work for it!"

Adrian utilized the squatter networks to track the various movements of the gangs, as well as to spoof the Red Lion letter. In truth, it did not matter even if Wrent checked its legitimacy with the main base. It was a verified fact that the Ilysian Punks were attacking the Seven Snakes.

[Adrian, are you done?] Kyle's voice crackled over the arctech radio.

"Yes, sir, everything has been set up."

[Good. Maintain visuals of Ilysian Punks and Red Lions. Both sides should be well aware of what is happening.] Kyle ended the communication, leaning back into his office chair.

"Sir, the Ilysian Punks must be watching the Red Lions' movements intently as well. With such a mobilization, it will send a warning sign to the Ilysian Punks." Monica offered her opinion. The vipers were gathered in front of Kyle.

"Exactly." Kyle nodded. "If they attack us, the Red Lions will take a huge bite out of them. If they don't, that means more time for us. Our objective is to stall any major conflict for as long as possible. Every day helps us close the gap. Don't forget that it's only been six days since our associates received their equipment."

Niko and Monica nodded in agreement. Kyle dismissed them as he readjusted his battle plan for the upcoming conflict, drafting up all possible scenarios. He then took a tour of the various bases, where the associates were divided up into different groups.

He spotted Damian desperately training hard alongside them, struggling to activate the arctech equipment while sparring with other associates. "Grh!" Damian grunted as he felt his body screaming out in fatigue due to the low amount of arcia energy his body could hold.

Damian was the only one attempting to push his limits, while half of the associates were mostly resting, too tired to continue. The original training routine, as stated in the textbook Kyle had, was to expend and use arcia energy to train resilience continuously, but at the rate it was going, it seemed that the Ilysian Punks would attack them before they were ready.

He had already attempted multiple keywords on the associates, trying to see if the holographic interface he had could help him see their MP. However, much to his dismay, the system did not react at all. Kyle had already long suspected that others did not have the same system as he did, but he was not about to assume that he was the only one in the entire world.

Kyle decided to pay Haui a visit at his alchemist store, which had its security and layout much improved. The agreement between the two of them had enriched Haui, making him a very wealthy individual.

As he entered the newly expanded alchemist store, Kyle immediately headed to the basement in silence, where Haui was working on creating new recipes. The alchemist barely turned around to greet Kyle, simply continuing with his work.

"I need a potion to restore arcia energy."

"I don't have a recipe for that."

"You have health potions and stamina potions; why not arcia potions?"

"Would you like to drink arcia fuel directly? The fact is that such a recipe that doesn't involve melting of the stomach is one of the utmost secrets of the Alchemists' Guild, and I myself am not privy to it."

"So there's no way to speed up the training of arcia energy?" Kyle frowned.

"I've heard of mages training in the caves near Tryas, but otherwise, no. If you had enough money, maybe you could buy arcite ore and line the walls with it. I don't think you'll be stupid enough to do that, right? Right?"

Chapter 40

Allocating Points

Two weeks later...

Keith woke up groggily, noticing he still had bandages all over his body as he lay on a white bed. He gingerly touched his face as he struggled to sit upright, feeling the new skin that was most likely the result of a health potion or Kyle's Necklace of Healing.

The door suddenly swung open, revealing Damian carrying a bucket of fresh water and a cloth. However, the sound of splashing water frightened Keith, who immediately curled up into a defensive ball—an instinct developed from the days of torture under Makoa.

"Keith, you're awake!" Damian quickly ran over, placing the bucket on the floor before reaching out in a hug. Keith instinctively recoiled from the motion, the mental trauma still hurting him deep inside.

"Sorry... I just need some time." Keith apologized for the sudden reaction, and Damian nodded in understanding.

"It's all right. I'll be here if you need me, okay? Just call me on the arctech radio if you need anything," Damian said in a gentle tone and left the room. As he closed the door behind him, his face curled up into a furious expression. *Ilysian Punks, you fuckers!*

Damian fumed as he stormed through the base, frightening the associates who walked past him. It was in the early morning before their regular physical training routine, but he was already heading over to the training arena to practice. He had been doing so for the last two weeks, training non-stop for the inevitable conflict. *If I don't do the extra work, how will I be strong enough to protect Keith?*

He noticed two associates simply lounging about in a break room, joking and relaxing. Their carefree attitude pissed Damian off instantly. "What the fuck are you two doing?! Why aren't you training?"

"Huh? It's more than an hour till the training routine—"

"AND YOU THINK THE ILYSIAN PUNKS ARE GOING TO WAIT FOR US?" Damian roared, taking out his pent-up frustration of inability on them. "GET UP AND TRAIN NOW!"

The associates grumpily complied, complaining about how they felt like they were in a military boot camp rather than a criminal gang as their superior stomped.

However, when he entered the training arena with them, instead of the well-arranged training equipment and sparring rings as usual, it was a complete mess, with multiple other associates grabbing arcite ore and placing it around the room.

Dozens of arcite ore sacks were stacked in the corner of the room, with Kyle directing the associates around. There were even a few mini caves of densely packed arcite ore, where a few associates were stuffed inside its cramped interior, apparently practicing their arcia energy. It felt like a mine, albeit with cubicles of arcite ore, making for a bizarre scene out of this world. If Damian did not know better, he would have assumed he had been transported to a mountain of sorts.

"Wh... What's going on?" Damian was surprised, losing his prior anger in confusion. He also noticed a small midget in a cloak next to Kyle, who seemed to be giving Kyle advice on the proper placement.

"I'm improving our training conditions," Kyle replied without turning back.

"Lord Kyle, put more arcite ore here. The flow is not right! Here!" the small midget exclaimed in a growling and broken accent, making Damian curious as to who this newcomer was.

The midget turned around to reveal a goblin's face, shocking Damian. "What?! You brought it from the Culdao Peaks?"

"I had to. Gulak has experience making such a chamber. I'm sure it will do a good job, isn't that right, Gulak?" Kyle smiled.

"Yes, yes, of course!" Gulak nodded vigorously, having already been reminded clearly of both Kyle's and Sasha's strength. If the chamber was ill-designed, Gulak knew there would be immediate punishment not only for it but for the rest of its tribe.

"Damian, we need more arcite ore. Buy some from the workshops or factories nearby."

Damian's mouth was already agape at the amount of ore being layered into the room. "We need more?! This is already close to a few million rakels!"

"Yes. Buy another few million rakels' worth."

"But that will bring our surplus down immensely!"

"Money isn't meant to be hoarded indefinitely. Do you want to get stronger or not?"

Damian was about to retort but decided against it. Kyle was correct; there was no point hoarding when there was an imminent conflict with the Ilysian Punks on the horizon. If he wanted to have a shot at getting proper revenge, they had to pull out all the stops. "Yes, sir."

Kyle observed the rest of the operation as more and more arcite ore was layered in. The training room was starting to look more like a naturally formed cave than anything else. He glanced at Gulak, who currently had its eyes closed, apparently trying to feel the flow of arcia energy.

Damian dutifully brought back the extra arcite ore, completing the chamber. Gulak nodded in satisfaction. "Yes, yes. This is the same as our chamber! It is how we do holy tattoos!"

Kyle's eyes squinted, realizing something he had missed while he was in the Culdao Peaks. He had performed the engraving on the slaves in their respective rooms rather than the dedicated arcia chamber. "So, the success of engraving depends on the environment?"

"Yes, more arcia in air, more power and easier!" Gulak nodded.

"Engraving? Like engraving objects?" Damian queried, still unaware of what Kyle exactly did in the Culdao Peaks.

Kyle used his direct communication channel via the Designate Follower skill. [Sasha, come here.]

Sasha immediately entered the chamber, saluting Kyle. "Spar with Damian. Use all engravings."

[Yes, sir.]

"What? What engravings?" Damian was still utterly confused, not seeing any form of arctech equipment on Sasha. Without warning, Sasha threw a high kick at Damian, who instinctively blocked it with his arm.

In a fluid combo, Sasha delivered three to five hits, with Damian blocking in a defensive posture with his forearms. *Her hits are nothing special. I don't see what Kyle is talking abo—*

Suddenly, Sasha's right fist glowed under its bandage as she threw a straight punch. The resulting force sent Damian stumbling back, knocking him off balance. With a sweeping kick, Damian found himself hitting the ground hard, staring at the ceiling now lined with arcite ore.

"You... You have arctech engravings on your body? But how?!" Damian finally realized what was going on, but his mind could not figure out how it was possible when Sasha wasn't a mage like Theorin was.

He was not an expert on arctech design or use of arcia energy, but he had a sinking feeling that this engraving was the key to his advancement in combat strength. "Again!" Damian jumped up to his feet, preparing to spar with Sasha again.

Kyle did not stay to watch the two of them spar, leaving the chamber with Gulak. He led the goblin to another room, where Monica was handling prototype handguns that were handcrafted by the ten associates and assembled by Kyle. Only the vipers would be allowed to use the handguns, as Kyle did not want them to be too obvious.

However, there was still a surplus of two hundred handguns laid out on a table. More was being produced daily, though Kyle was not planning to get the factory completely involved. While Monica was inspecting each of them, she nodded at Kyle's arrival.

"I need the two of you to work together on this job. For every ten handguns, distribute eight handguns to as many weapon dealers as possible. Don't let them find out that you're Seven Snakes. In fact, it would be even better if Gulak did the sale."

"How much do you want them sold for?"

"Doesn't matter. The objective is to get as many guns out there into the sector. Flood the market. If you have to give them away for free, do it."

"What if they reverse-engineer it?"

"They won't be able to immediately; I have a failsafe built into them. The smarter ones will figure out its underlying principles even if we don't sell them." Kyle knew Baron Cain most likely had already hired men to take a look at the handgun. Technological progress surged like a raging tide whenever a proof of concept appeared, pushing the boundaries.

Monica frowned. "What do we do with the remaining handguns?"

"Stash them deep and put them in a thick metal safe. As deep as you can find. Somewhere no arctech radio signal can reach. When Keith makes a full recovery, get him to find a suitable location. Under no circumstances can the enforcers find that stash."

"You got it. But if all of these get traced back to us, we're dead."

"You let me worry about that part. Gulak, before you go, did you bring the knife?"

Gulak obediently presented a knife wrapped in a cloth to Kyle, the Taboo Knife he used for Sasha's engraving.

Kyle gave them a few more minor orders before returning to his office. On his table lay two other items—the sniper railgun he had used to attack Makoa and the ancient exosuit spines.

Now that Kyle had a method of improving the training rate of the associates, it was time to figure out how he could boost himself even more. He checked his statistics again.

The titles had been extremely useful to him so far, as well as the class skills and the mana points. However, he had yet to check out the Strength or Dexterity stats. With no description of the stats, he was unable to determine what they related to.

The stats seem to be exponential in nature... Kyle surmised, as he had been gaining stats with every level-up, but it did not feel like a linear power-up. He could clearly tell he was significantly stronger than he was when he first arrived, especially with the increase in MP. The Charisma stat seemed to affect his looks as well, but did not increase with levels.

He also noted he had a lot of free points from the level-ups, but he had been holding on to them due to his reluctance to rely too much on the system. *If the class selection was any indication, if I dumped all my free points into a specific stat, it would most likely be extremely painful.*

There was no doubt that for the upcoming fight, he would need everything he could get his hands on. Kyle decided to put all his free points into strength, dexterity, and vitality.

Information: Free points allocated.
+15 STR, +15 DEX, +20 VIT

Kyle felt a slight surge trickle through his muscles, a rejuvenating effect coming over him. It wasn't much at all, which was underwhelming to him. He clenched his fist, testing his new strength, but he felt only a little stronger than he had been before.

Welcome to Raktor!

Kyle Hawthorn: Level 15
Max HP: 52(+0)(+0)(+0) | Max MP: 23(+0)(+5)(+0) | Max STA:
52(+0)(+0)(+0)

Status Effects
None

Stats

Race: Human | **Class:** Crime Lord | **Subclass:** Unassigned
STR: 102(+29)(+0)(+0) | **DEX:** 94(+41)(+0)(+0) | **INT:** 91(+50)(+3)(+0)
VIT: 67(+2)(+3)(+0) | **CHA:** 21(+10)(+1)(+0) | **Free Points:** 0

The stats in the system are far too unreliable. Kyle shook his head in disappointment, thinking about what had just happened. He had tested them before, right after killing Ulon.

My class upgrade was painful and lasted almost ten hours, yet seventy points of stats did not do much of anything. What is the difference?

Before Kyle could contemplate any further, a Seven Snakes associate knocked on the door. "Sir, I think you should head to the new arcite training chamber. You need to stop them!"

"Stop them?" Kyle was confused, quickly leaving the office and heading over.

In the training ring, Damian was desperately throwing jabs and hooks at Sasha, who nimbly dodged and twisted her body, avoiding the slow punches. The spar looked more like a mockery, where Sasha barely seemed to make any effort to move around.

On the other side, Damian was fighting hard to even keep up, sweat and blood covering his face with bruises on his body. The associates could only stand at the side and watch as their underboss gritted through the pain, pushing through with sheer determination. Despite him clearly being on the losing end, his undying perseverance ignited a burning sense of pride and respect among those under him.

Even Sasha was amazed at the vitality of Damian and the number of punches that Damian was able to endure, her own knuckles beginning to throb from the non-stop hits. *Is this the power of siblings?* Sasha wouldn't know; she had been torn away from her family for so many years.

While Sasha was in an introspective mood, Damian's eyes glinted as he spotted an opening. He let out a loud roar before throwing a straight punch at her face. In a blink, Sasha grappled the arm and flung him overhead by using her body as a pivot, slamming him back first into the ground.

"Fu... FUCK! AGAIN!" Damian bellowed as he got straight up, unfazed by the sudden defeat and getting into a fighting stance again. Sasha nodded and continued the spar, respecting Damian's tenacity.

The same result was repeated over and over again, but Damian gritted his teeth and kept trying. However, no matter what strategy he tried to use, he could not beat the lady or land a single punch on her. *Is this all my training has amounted to over the last three months?!*

The engraving on Sasha's right hand glowed again, prompting Damian to avoid the hit. However, Sasha followed it up again with rapid activations, showing her prowess in using the engravings to augment her combat style. The fist landed on his forearm, nearly cracking his arm and sending him sprawling onto the ground again for the umpteenth time.

Damian cursed to himself as he winced and doubled over. *How the fuck am I to protect Keith when I am this weak?!*

"Enough," Kyle's voice wafted over the rocky chamber as he entered. "You're far too driven by anger to train properly. You keep repeating the same mistakes over and over. How long do you want Sasha to keep beating you up? Days?"

Damian gritted his teeth and clenched his fist. "I need to be stronger. I will do anything to be stronger! Kyle, give me the engravings too!" He had seen over the course of his sparring with Sasha just how effective they could be.

Kyle frowned. "The process is extremely dangerous. The chamber we have now may increase the success rate, but you might die or lose your mind."

"It doesn't matter. I might as well be dead at my current strength!"

"Are you sure?"

Damian nodded with determination, his eyes feisty and driven.

Kyle did not try to convince Damian otherwise anymore. It would be a good thing if Damian became stronger as well. "Sasha, clear out the room and prepare for the procedure."

[Yes, sir.]

The chamber was cleared of associates, leaving only Damian on a surgery table of sorts while Kyle and Sasha prepared the necessary equipment. Sasha strapped all of Damian's limbs to the table, preventing him from any movement. Kyle unveiled the Taboo Knife, polishing its edge with a grinding stone.

"Do you want the same force engraving?"

"No, give me a defensive one." Damian shook his head. He knew his body was not fast enough to perform counterattacks, so it was better to play a more defensive role. "One that can block bullets."

* * *

In a food market on the far side of the South Sector...

An armored man weaved through the dense crowds, packed like sardines in an underground bazaar, a sleazy atmosphere thick with Euria smoke assaulting his nose.

The sound of metal armor clinking was drowned out by the din of the crowd as dealers sold all sorts of exotic goods and illegal weapons. He shoved his way through, with the crowd actively avoiding his gaze as though he were a god.

"Kaya butter, straight from Proco! Exotic taste unlike anything you have tried here before in your life guaranteed!"

"Nest is recruiting mercenaries—sign up today and get a sign-on bonus. Multiple slots available in Versia!"

"Behold! Fifteen handguns of the highest quality here. Don't think they are anything like your usual arctech pistols—these babies can shoot up to three times in a row, even if you're a normal human!"

That callout attracted the attention of everyone. The crowd gathered around the stall was amazed, whispering frantically among one another. Small-time bandits, criminals, and other thugs all jostled with one another to get a better look at the weapons.

"Limited availability, yours for only sixty thousand rakels!"

"Sixty thousand rakels?! That's a rip-off! Might as well buy an arcite fuel pack with that cost!" one of the thugs yelled from the side.

"I'll buy it!" A smuggler grinned and grabbed a handful of rakels out of his hands, handing them over to the dealer.

"Deal! Pleasure doing busine—" Before the dealer could hand over the gun, the crowd was physically shoved apart by the armored man.

"This stall is now closed. Move along," The armored man said with clear authority, a monotone voice rumbling from the metal.

Immediately, the crowd began to disperse, many not willing to contest him except for the smuggler who had just paid. "HEY! I PAID HIM; IT'S MY GUN! WHO ARE YOU TO—"

Before the smuggler could finish his words, the armored man grabbed the smuggler by the head and slammed him onto the ground, finishing the man off with a swift step to the neck, which easily cracked it open.

The dealer was frightened, his heart palpitating as he tried to make a run for it. *Fuck, fuck, fuck! I can't get caught by the guards of this black market!*

However, the armored man grabbed his shoulder in an instant, delivering a punch to the face that knocked him out immediately. Retrieving the arctech radio slung by his side, he tuned the channel before speaking into it.

"Report. I've spotted handguns entering the black market. Put me through to Baron Cain."

Chapter 41

First Volley

"So, you're the Seven Snakes' dedicated brewer?"

"And you're the new arctech designer. How did Kyle enslave you?"

Gordon had a confused expression on his face. "Enslave? He helped install me as the factory manager." Gordon was now working on a large arctech radio, a modification ordered by Kyle.

He wondered as to why he would need a radio that large. *Is he planning to run his own radio station or something? With this throughput, the radio can reach the entire city. Or is he trying to make sure he can reach something?*

Eric Dicar scoffed, "Idiot, you know that you're not truly free. If you ran right now, Kyle would chase you to hell himself. Mark my words."

"But why would I run? I already feel like I'm at the top of the world here! I don't see you running either."

"I... I have recipes to learn."

"And I have engravings to learn too!"

Gordon and Eric exchanged a knowing look, having met for the first time. They were now in Gordon's factory office, waiting for a supposed meeting with Kyle.

"So... you too?" Eric queried.

"It seems we both have our suspicions. Why don't you start first?" Gordon motioned with his hand.

"I postulate that Kyle is a time traveler."

"Impossible, I've asked around. He used to be known as Alvin before his current personality took over."

"Fine. Time traveled and took over a body. Soul possession or something."

"Wait, you believe in souls?"

"I sometimes feel my soul leaving my body after a bad drink."

Gordon groaned. "Look, that's a bit too far-fetched. I have a better theory—Alvin was the original amnesiac, and Kyle was his original personality! He is probably from a foreign land, perhaps beyond the Great Waves, that has much better technology than us."

"Okay, now that's ridiculous. Everyone knows there's nothing beyond the Great Waves."

"You don't know that for sure! Just because no one made it back does not mean that there is nothing out there."

"Pssh, and you dare diss my soul theory?!"

The doors to the office swung open to reveal Kyle striding in. Without skipping a beat, he headed over to the only remaining military crate in the Seven Snakes' district, pulling out a mortar and a cannonball. Kyle got straight to the point. "We need to create an improved version of this."

Eric and Gordon immediately snapped out of their previous conversation, paying Kyle their undivided attention. "Improve?! Using this is basically waging a full-scale war!"

"Exactly, which is why I called the two of you."

Gordon nodded but soon glanced at Eric. "Wait, I understand why you would need me, but why Eric?"

* * *

Two weeks later...

Makoa stood on a balcony, overlooking a large square where 150 Ilysian Punks were gathered to assault the Seven Snakes' district. He watched as they loaded up their pistols and armor, some even stocking up on potions.

This was the staging area, not far from the Seven Snakes district. *Never before did I have to use this many punks to crush a single district...* It had been a month since the loss of his base, with Makoa preparing everything in advance for this assault.

"Sir, your gauntlets and recharged shield are ready. General Javel reminds you that the shield is extremely precious. In the event that you lose, you must destroy the shield to prevent it from falling into enemy hands." One of the Ilysian Punks' messengers reported to him.

"I understand. Send my thanks to Javel." *This is my last chance at redemption, so I'm not going to let it slip away. It's all or nothing!* "Get all the squad leaders into this room. It is time for the briefing."

With the squad leaders gathered in front of the map of the Seven Snakes' district, Makoa began his explanation. The entire operation was designed in a military fashion, as many of the squad leaders were former Versia military soldiers.

"We will strike from three points—north, northwest, and south. The main bulk force will be through the north, with a hundred allocated to them. Each squad will have ten members and focus on rooting out the Seven Snakes and forcing them to surrender."

"What about civilians? We won't know who's supporting them or not."

"No indiscriminate killing—we don't want to turn the local populace against us. We're targeting the Seven Snakes themselves. Collateral damage is fine, but under no circumstances—"

Before Makoa could continue, a sudden whizzing sound could be heard in the air, sparking an instinct long drilled into him from past Versian wars. "MORTAR ATTACK!"

The Ilysian Punks immediately vacated the open areas, heading into the buildings around the staging area as Makoa spotted a projectile hurtling through the air toward them from the balcony. The projectile slammed into the cobblestone floor of the staging area, completely missing everybody.

"Hah! They miss—"

A billowing sphere of fire and flames burst out from the projectile, exploding in a dazzling explosion that rocked the entire area. The glass rumbled with ferocity as the shockwave rippled through the area.

Thousands of small fragments were flung in all directions from each projectile, slamming into the walls and windows, shattering them. A few unfortunate Ilysian Punks who were looking through the windows were immediately impaled by the ensuing onslaught of glass shards, crying out in pain.

The characteristic tubing sound of the mortars could be heard as they slowly sailed over the buildings, raining even more fragments down onto the area. A few of the projectiles even exploded in mid-air, coating the ground with fragments.

What kind of mortar explosive is that?! What the hell is going on?

"SQUAD LEADERS, GET YOUR MEN OUT OF HERE AND LAUNCH A FULL ASSAULT! STICK TO THE PLAN!" Makoa roared under the booming explosions. The squad leaders were all trained, immediately following the orders and bellowing commands on their respective arctech radios.

The conflict had begun.

The sounds of explosions and gunfire frightened the local residents caught in an all-out conflict between the Seven Snakes and the Ilysian Punks.

"Can the Seven Snakes win this? What is going to happen to us when the Ilysian Punks take over?"

"I don't even think Kyle can beat the Ilysian Punks. Their entire attack force is here!"

The streets were rife with chaos as the Ilysian Punks pushed their way into the Seven Snakes district. The squads worked in a disciplined fashion, clearing the urban blocks, building by building.

In a residential building, a family of four was cowering in the room, barricading their door. The dull thuds of mortar fire and screams could be heard echoing down the rows of apartment buildings and bouncing off the cracked walls. The father quickly grabbed his two daughters, keeping their heads down while he flipped tables, using them as cover against any potential entry from the front door.

"Stay quiet!" the father warned the daughters.

"Daddy, what's happening?"

Before the father could respond, the door was slammed violently, causing the two daughters to shriek. The father and mother desperately tried to cover their mouths, but the youngest was already on the verge of tears.

Muffled voices from beyond the barricaded doors could be heard, the foreign accent of Versia clear as day. "Sir, there seem to be people in this room. Should we breach?"

"Smash down the door or set it on fire. Our job is to clear each marked building of Seven Snakes and those in them. We don't have time to vet the residents. Clear the safehouse, then burn everything else!"

"Yes, sir."

The Ilysian Punks were not out to wantonly kill residents but to flush out the hideouts or safehouses of the Seven Snakes. Unfortunately for the family of four, there was a regular safehouse of the Seven Snakes located in this building, forcing the Ilysian Punks to clear it out.

The father's eyes darted around the family's house, the living room now a mess from the chaos. *I need a weapon, fast!* He grabbed a knife from the kitchen counter, holding it closely as he kept his ears peeled, listening for any additional footsteps.

Instead of hearing an attempt to break down the door, a matchstick striking sound could be heard before the distinctive roar of fire crackling from beyond could be heard. The father's heart plummeted, but he kept his face stern. *I have to stay strong, at least for my daughters.*

Before long, a thick cloud of smoke began to waft through the seams of the barricaded door. "Daddy, the door is on fire!" the youngest cried out in a shrill voice, finally beginning to panic.

"It's okay, it's okay. Just stay calm." The father calmed them down, handing them wet cloth as a temporary stopgap measure. It wouldn't be of much use, but right now it was better than nothing as he tried to look for a way out.

The mother was also beginning to panic, worried about the impending asphyxiation. "We need to open the windows to let the smoke out, quickly!"

"No! Don't open the windows, they'll—" The father tried to stop his wife, but as soon as the mother swung the windows open, a single rifle shot nailed her right in the chest, piercing her heart instantly. Her body felt back on the floor, convulsing from the pain.

"FUCK!" the father yelled, quickly scrambling over to the wife. "I told you not to open the windows; they'll think you're trying to shoot at them!"

The wife tried to reply but could not utter a word as the bullet was lodged deep in her heart, the blood filling her innards and lungs. "Don't worry; I'll save you. Damian will be here in no time with a health potion. Just stay awake, stay awake. Stay with me." The father desperately gripped the hand of his wife as he tried to find something to stem the bleeding.

Time seemed to drag on as the continued crying of his daughters and the pained breaths of his wife lasted for an eternity. The echoes of gunfire, explosions, and mortars whizzing through the air were the only music he heard.

Soon, the wife's hand lost its grip, her eyes gazing into the far beyond. The father could not say anything, only doubling over in shock.

Just as he began to sob, the sounds of the Ilysian Punks reentering the building could be heard. "Where did they shoot at?! Which room? Blow it up!"

The father immediately racked his brains, trying to figure out an escape plan, but was at a complete loss. Even if he tried to escape via the now-open windows with his daughters, he would simply be shot down in a similar fashion. Rappelling down to the lower floor was tantamount to suicide.

He could try to extinguish the fire, but it would be a clear sign to the Ilysian Punks that someone was still alive in the room. *Where the fuck are the Seven Snakes?! Aren't they supposed to protect the district?!* The father put his ears to the room's wall, trying to hear beyond the fire.

However, sounds of fighting suddenly could be heard beyond the crackling of flames. "It's the Seven Snakes! Kill them all!"

Gunfire and metal clashes echoed through the walls of the buildings, the cries of men falling. "Why aren't my bullets hurting hi—ARGHHH"

A squelching sound could be heard, along with the snapping of bones. Soon, loud footsteps could be heard over the fire approaching the room. The father quickly moved from the wall, grabbing a knife from the kitchen and preparing to defend himself. "Get behind me, quickly!" he urged the daughters.

The barricaded door was suddenly wrenched apart, the fire hardly affecting the man who began to clear the barricade. "Anyone alive!?" the man roared in.

"Damian, I'm here! I'm here!"

"Alex, fuck! I'm coming in!" Damian shoved away the burnt wooden debris, running in. His eyes landed on the wife's body, stunned. Damian tried to find the words to console him, but Alex just shook his head, tears streaming down his face.

"You need to move. We have shelters nearby. We'll give Martha a proper burial. Think of your daughters!" Damian urged, the sounds of fighting still echoing down the streets.

Alex finally nodded in agreement, quickly hoisting up his wife's body while Damian carried the two daughters. As Damian passed the other Seven Snakes associates in his crew who were also in the building, he ordered them to check every other room and save whoever they could.

"Grab whatever equipment you can from the dead bodies! We need everything we can to fight them off!"

The two of them ran down the open street, hugging close to the building walls. With the local enforcers keeping a wide berth of the conflict as per their agreement, nothing was preventing both sides from devolving into a brutal conflict.

They soon reached a barricaded street, with countless sandbags and makeshift wooden palisades serving as cover. It protected a chunk of the street, where many of the local residents were already evacuated.

Alex's scenario was not unique, with many losing their loved ones or being forced to abandon them in the heat of the conflict. Damian grimaced as he watched the forlorn faces of those he personally knew. He had grown up in the district with Keith, after all, and many of those here were like kin to him.

"Alex, stay here with your daughters. Take shelter in the basement over there." Damian pointed out a stairwell at the side of a building that led deeper. "We have food and water to last a few days if needed."

However, Alex did not move, instead grabbing Damian by the shoulder, his eyes burning with revenge. "No, Damian, I don't need food and water. I need a weapon."

Chapter 42

Close Quarters

Eric Dicar winced as he plugged his ears with his finger, the screeching sound of the mortar tubes and the deafening thuds nearly blasting his eardrums apart. "I didn't sign up to be an artillery crew!"

Gordon wiped the sweat off his brow as he and two other associates lugged a custom-made metal spherical ball and loaded it into the base of the mortar before closing the hatch. "CLEAR!" Gordon yelled and pressed the trigger.

The ten arcite fuel packs, stacked haphazardly next to the mortar, chugged furiously. They powered the acceleration engravings along the side of the tubes that were currently glowing red hot. With a bang, the metal ball was lobbed up high and far away, sailing toward a building far away.

Adrian's voice crackled over the arctech radio. [You're off target. You need to hit it fifty meters to the right!]

"Fuck!" Gordon cursed, motioning to Eric to prepare the next batch of explosive. It'd already been three hours since the battle had begun, with their mortar performing the first strike.

There was not enough time to mass-produce the explosives, requiring Eric to mix them on the spot. The formula was far too dangerous for others to handle—a simple rounding error in the percentages may very well cause the projectile to blow up in the associates' hands.

The fighting with the Ilysian Punks had yet to spread through the whole district, with only the northern blocks embroiled in conflict.

Damian, Monica, and Niko were in charge of the defense, helping save the local residents as well as stem the incoming assault of the Ilysian Punks.

However, they were clearly far outnumbered—it was a nearly three-to-one disadvantage. What helped the Seven Snakes hold their ground was the armor and handguns provided to them, allowing them to survive for longer than expected.

Damian gritted his teeth as he activated the "Harden" engraving on his body, protecting himself from a gunshot as he fought in the ruined Golden Snake casino. The engraving had boosted his internal arcia energy, along with the nonstop training in the arcite chamber.

Grabbing a half-broken metal chair, he swung it around as a weapon, knocking out two punks onto the ground as the rest of his crew clashed in an all-out melee brawl. Countless casino chips and cards were scattered on the ground as the Ilysian Punks continued their objective of wrecking every Seven Snakes hideout and business.

Damian continued undeterred, focusing on making sure none of the associates under him died by blocking for them. The enemy squad leader cursed as he checked his arcite fuel pack's level, being the only one with an arctech pistol.

With a loud roar, Damian immediately targeted him and charged, slamming into his waist and tackling him onto the ground. The arctech pistol was knocked out of his hand, disconnecting from the arcite fuel pack and clattering against the floor amid the sounds of yelling and punches. The two enemy gang members grappled each other in a desperate life-or-death match, trying to suffocate each other.

Damian's eyes landed on the arctech pistol lying on the corner, reaching out with one hand to try and grab it. They tussled and tumbled on the ground, throwing punches at each other while both of them scrambled for the arctech pistol.

The enemy squad leader managed to grab the pistol again, desperately trying to reconnect it with his fuel pack, when he realized his fuel pack had already been crushed by Damian. The momentary shock left him open, allowing Damian to deliver a rapid combo of three punches and knock him down again. "Stay down, cunt."

The enemy squad leader tried to get up but was suddenly hit on the head by a metal pipe that nearly caved his skull in and caused blood to spurt through his hair. "THIS IS FOR MARTHA, YOU FUCK!" Alex slammed the pipe down repeatedly, bellowing out his rage.

Damian did not stop him. He was also angered at the Ilysian Punks for what they had done to Keith. He checked in with the rest of his crew, of which five were seriously injured. "Head back to the shelter and get more health potions."

While the rest of the associates complied and carried the wounded, Alex did not listen, continuing to hit the Ilysian Punks squad leader in the face, mashing it into a mess of meat. "Alex. Alex. HEY, ALEX, STOP!" Damian shouted and grabbed Alex. "You're injured too! Think of your daughters; they still want you alive back at the shelter!"

Alex was about to shrug him off until he yelled out in pain as Damian poked a finger in Alex's gaping wound on his waist. "There's plenty more of these fuckers to take revenge on. You need to stay alive!"

"Huff... Huff... You're right. Sorry." Alex took a deep breath and staggered toward the exit of the casino, nearly fumbling onto the floor before Damian quickly supported him.

The crew headed back to the shelter, rotating with another squad, which headed out to defend them. Already, the exhaustion was visible on the Seven Snakes associates, barely propped up by the Stamina Potions. However, the potions did not alleviate the mental fatigue from the close-quarters combat in the city.

At the Lusty Arcian, Niko and Slavin were involved in a desperate, protracted battle, both sides firing at each other in the large, expansive lobby of the beauty school, with broken pots and mirrors strewn on the floor. Makeshift barricades and tables were used as cover that Niko crouched behind. In his right hand was a handgun crafted by Kyle.

"How long more till the Red Lions attack the Ilysian Punks?! They must know we're in shit by now!" Niko roared into his arctech radio as yet another shot whizzed past his cover.

[I don't know, but the Red Lions don't seem to be making a single move!]

"WHAT?! Then what the hell are we buying time for?!" Niko cursed. "We're going to lose the Lusty Arcian and maybe even the Seductive Serpent at this rate!"

[There are even bigger issues—there's a fifty-man-strong squad from the Ilysian Punks moving to the south of us!]

Niko's face balked. He was under the impression that the force attacking them right now was the main force. *There's more?!*

[Sasha and I will handle it,] Kyle suddenly said.

On the roof of a building, Kyle laid down flat and mounted his arctech railgun, aiming down an open street. He peered through the scope, zooming in on the approaching Ilysian Punks.

Five squads marched down the open streets, all far more armored and equipped than the punks attacking in the north. Kyle noticed a wagon being escorted in the middle of their formation filled with arcite fuel packs, supposedly serving as their mobile supply station.

Kyle marked the five squad leaders but focused on one, who he fired the first bullet at. With a significant recoil, the metal ball nearly broke the speed of sound, hurtling toward the Ilysian Punks formation.

In an instant, the metal ball tore a hole through the squad leader's head, killing him before he could even react.

[SYSTEM MESSAGE]
You killed Ilysian Punks Squad Leader, +200 EXP.

"Fuck! The long-range cannon is here! Get to cover!"

Kyle fired two more times, killing yet another squad leader while missing another as the Ilysian Punks broke formation, sprinting all over the place.

[SYSTEM MESSAGE]
You killed Ilysian Punks Squad Leader, +200 EXP.

The Ilysian Punks began to break into the nearby buildings and shops, using them as cover as they moved from door to door or through the alleyways to stay out of Kyle's line of sight.

Kyle immediately unmounted the arctech railgun and headed down to the ground floor. "Sasha, hunt them one by one before they spread too far into the district!"

[Yes, sir.] Sasha was already on the way there. This time, she wore a full coat, with the interior layered with arctech armor. The armor barely slowed her down as she sprinted down the streets toward the closest squad, who were disorganized as their leader had just collapsed.

The shop owners cowered in fear behind the cashier as half of an Ilysian Punks squad barged into the bakery. They quickly closed the door behind them, barricading themselves in as they hauled the shelves. "Shit, what do we do now? Our leader is dead. The arctech radio is on his body!"

Before anyone could offer their opinion or suggestion, Sasha kicked her way through the store glass, shattering the window. With a handgun in her hand, she fired three rounds in rapid succession at the closest Ilysian Punk—two in the body, one in the head.

She then ducked as another punk swung his crowbar at her head. Taking advantage of her position, she smashed her leg into his groin and deflected a punch coming from the side. In a flurry of jabs, punches, and kicks, she quickly knocked out four members.

The last surviving member ran out into the streets, yelling at the other Ilysian Punks. "The assassin is here! The assassin is here!"

Instead of chasing him down the streets, Sasha instead chose to exit the bakery through the back alleyways, trying to flank around and target another squad. However, the moment she turned the corner, a familiar metal gauntlet knocked right into her left shoulder, sending her soaring into the air as she twisted her body into recovery, the armor mitigating some of the damage.

"So we meet again, *assassin*. How much did the Seven Snakes pay you? Was it worth your life?" Makoa grinned, nine punks standing behind him in the alleyway with their arctech pistols at the ready. "Shoot her."

Sasha gritted her teeth and activated her breastplate's ability, sending out three dark-green projectiles that countered the volley of shots. However, six shots made it through, with three missing her and the remaining three nailing her in the thighs and waist, causing her to stagger onto the ground on one knee.

Makoa motioned with a single hand, the Ilysian Punks moving forward to finish her off. Sasha's eyes burn with determination, unwilling to go down without a fight.

As the first knife was thrust at her, she deftly dodged and twisted the wrist holding the knife, forcing the attacking punk to drop it. She moved fluidly as she avoided and weaved through the attacks, parrying and slamming them into the walls. The healing engraving on her back worked overtime, but with the bullets lodged deep in her body, the wounds couldn't be fully healed, causing her movement to slow down over time.

The pain surging from the embedded bullets caused her to falter, a hit from a metal crowbar landing right on her back and slamming against the armor with a dull thud. Before she could recover her posture and counterattack, Makoa suddenly lunged toward her, delivering a flurry of punches that caved in her armor, shredding her full coat apart to reveal the dents underneath.

However, before Makoa could follow up, a loud, familiar bang slammed into his energy shield from behind, staggering him. *The long-range cannon—what?!* He turned around and saw who it was. "The Seven Snakes leader? GET HIM!"

The squad members turned and rushed the shooter, but the handgun in his left shot with precision, firing three times in quick succession.

[SYSTEM MESSAGE]
You killed Ilysian Punks Thug, +50 EXP.

The remaining squad members were undeterred and rushed at him, swinging wildly from all angles. Kyle dropped his handgun onto the floor and wielded his arctech railgun with both hands, using it like a blunt staff.

Penchant for Violence.

His body surged with strength as his muscles enlarged, and his perception was also mildly improved. With the additional free points added to the stats, the boost was becoming more apparent to Kyle. Even his brain seemed to run at a faster speed, allowing him to react faster. *This is like a Galactic Era combat stimulant.*

The first attacker gritted his teeth and swung a crowbar from the right, but the reach failed to hit Kyle as he took a step back.

He jabbed the barrel of the railgun into the stomach of the first attacker like a spear before swinging it down on another attacker, coming at him from another side in a downward hit. He immediately swiveled to use his railgun's body to block a bullet fired by a punk who had managed to reload during the fight.

Kyle charged forward with the railgun, slamming its body into the nearest attackers and crushing their bones with a single hit. A solid jab was enough to cause a punk to be knocked out of the fight, whimpering on the ground from the pain.

Makoa was astonished by the sheer strength Kyle possessed despite his lean stature. *Where is he getting this power from? He doesn't even have an arcite fuel pack! Is he a mage?*

Kyle slammed the butt of his railgun down on an incapacitated punk's neck, killing him instantly.

[SYSTEM MESSAGE]
You killed Ilysian Punks Thug, +50 EXP.

"So, is this all you've got?"

Chapter 43

Demise

Makoa gasped for air as he crawled on the floor, the broken pieces of his metal gauntlet stabbing into his arms. A hand grabbed his head and lifted him up, causing him to grunt in pain.

Kyle bent over and touched Makoa's belt.

[SYSTEM MESSAGE]
Ancient Personal Defense Shield
Lost technology created in the Galactic Era. Limited to humans less than three meters tall. Usage depends on battery level.
Modified by Harrison.

Harrison? That's the Versian man at the auction house. Interesting. "Where did you get the energy shield from?" Kyle asked, lifting Makoa up by the neck with one hand alone and hoisting him over the bodies of twenty other Ilysian Punks thugs.

At the side, Sasha spat out a mouthful of blood while she moved her own hands within her bullet wounds, prying out the embedded metal pieces that fragmented within her flesh. Without a sound, she ripped the last metal piece from her thigh, finally activating the healing engraving on her back and sealing up the wound.

"Like I'm fucking going to tell you any—" Makoa yelled out in pain as Kyle twisted a knife into his waist. "Just kill me and get it over with."

"You're a precious hostage, and I have someone here who would love to have a chat with you."

Makoa grinned with his bloodied teeth, half of them missing from the fight. "Are you sure this is over? I'm not the only one in the Ilysian Punks, you know."

Kyle squinted his eyes while his arctech radio coincidentally crackled into life, with Adrian's voice frantically shouting on the other side. [Kyle, they got another force coming to attack us!]

"Haven't the Red Lions begun their assault on the Ilysian Punks?" Kyle dropped Makoa to the floor.

[I don't know what Wrent is planning, but the Red Lions are not making a move at all!]

"Hah, fools!" Makoa laughed with a hoarse throat. "You thought the Red Lions were your allies and that you could use them to outplay us? They, too, want to see you in ruins! They won't make a move until you've been wiped clean—only then will they enter this district and steal your potion production methods. General Javel will clean you up and then use this district as a trap for the Red Lions!"

In the northern district, Damian and Niko fought desperately against the new wave of Ilysian Punks who were now attacking the shelter. "Weren't they supposed to have less than two hundred members? Where did these fuckers come from?!" Damian roared as he swung wildly with a makeshift club, his former weapon already broken in half.

Niko couldn't reply; he was already slumped against the ground, breathing heavily as he tried to put pressure on his waist, which was bleeding profusely. "I... I think we're fucked..."

"NO! Don't give up on me, Niko! Stay awake!" Damian roared as he grabbed the arm of an Ilysian Punks thug and twisted it, using his body as a pivot. "Kyle will come to save us! I believe in him!"

What Damian did not know was that for all the enhancements Kyle had from the system, it was not possible for Kyle to reach them in an instant. It would take more than five minutes for Kyle to even make it over if he sprinted.

All around him, fellow Seven Snakes associates were falling down, the exhaustion from the hours of combat having finally taken its toll on them. Compared to the fresh Ilysian Punks, they were no match.

Even Damian was beginning to lose hope, wondering if this was how the Seven Snakes gang would come to its end. He grunted as he forced himself to keep fighting, trying to stem the tide of Punks. Behind him were thousands of local residents hiding in the basements. It was down to him to defend!

"ARGHHHH!" Damian bellowed as he fought with all his might, throwing punches and kicks. Soon, however, he was grappled to the ground by three punks, restraining him while he thrashed.

"Shut him up!" the enemy squad leader ordered, with Damian glancing at the blue sky as a metal pipe swung down onto him. Just as he flinched instinctively, he heard a cry of pain as the punks holding him down were knocked aside like bowling pins.

Damian opened his eyes to see a fluttering pearlish white coat stained with grime and blood as the wearer swung a warhammer around, smashing the skulls of the punks apart with the glowing yellow tip infused with engravings. *What?! An inquisitor?*

The inquisitor rampaged through the street, swinging the warhammer with a single hand while her other hand wielded an arctech pistol, firing blatantly at the Ilysian Punks. "COME ON!" the inquisitor yelled, a wide grin on her face as she began to clobber everyone who got close to her.

"Shit, stop her! It's the Mad Dog!"

Kitana laughed as she kicked a fallen punk's chin and slammed the head of her warhammer on his head, crushing it into a paste. Her eyes glinted like a predator, marking each of the Ilysian Punks as she moved on like a one-man army, slaughtering her way through the new Ilysian Punks force.

Look at all this EXP bundled up together for me!

The Ilysian Punks were no match for her strength, some of them horrified and trying to flee. Even shooting her was of no use, as the inquisitor coat was layered with projectile defense engravings as well.

Kitana sneered at the fleeing Ilysian Punks members, slamming her feet into the ground. A rush of yellow arcia trails snaked out across the ground with her foot as the source, causing the cobblestone to surge forward and wrap around the legs of twenty Ilysian Punks, making them unable to move.

"Wha... What the fuck is this!" one of the Ilysian Punks managed to exclaim before the warhammer's head smashed his jaw into smithereens, along with a follow-up strike hitting his knees and snapping them off.

The restrained Ilysian Punks were horrified while their allies fled back to their district, carrying the wounded. Kitana smiled as she slowly walked up to the remaining nineteen Ilysian Punks. "By order of the Sanctum, you shall now be purged."

* * *

General Javel's face was grim as he watched the smoke plumes spiraling out toward the sky from the Seven Snakes district while Alejandro desperately tried to make sense of what was happening on the ground. "Sir, it seems our forces have been routed by the Seven Snakes. Half are either dead or captured, with the rest fleeing back into our districts."

"And I assume the Red Lions are gearing up for an all-out attack at this very moment."

"Yes... sir. The Wretches are also preparing for war, while the enforcers are aiming to raid us. It seems like the gamble has failed."

"Not yet. There's still one more card we can play." General Javel picked up his arctech radio, tuning the frequency to a separate channel. "Sebastian, I know you're listening on this channel."

[Always astute as ever, Javel, but it seems that you have been exposed.] Sebastian chuckled.

"Are you willing to help us?"

[And why would I do that?]

"Don't play dumb with me. I know that while you've been helping us fight against the Red Lions and Wretches, you've also been supplying them at the same time. You want this protracted war. With the Seven Snakes tipping the battlefield, your three-way war may be gone."

[Hmm... An interesting proposition. I will send you an elite squad, one of our very best. They will arrive at the headquarters within an hour.]

"Thank you." General Javel ended the conversation, smirking to himself. "Alejandro, relay defensive orders to all units. Distribute all remaining military equipment to whoever is left. We'll plunge this area into chaos and make them regret attacking us. With the support of the Ardent Cretins, we may be able to negotiate a ceasefire after a week of fighting."

"Yes, sir."

The Ilysian Punks quickly reformed their defenses, preparing for the inevitable counterattack from all sides. The repeater carbines, military armor, and mortars were given out like candy, arming the entire force.

Soon, the elite squad of the Ardent Cretins arrived, decked from head to toe in engraved knight armor and wielding heavy polearms. Each of them had three arcite fuel packs embedded within the armor, fueling its exorbitant energy consumption. While their overall speed was extremely slow, they could take an enormous amount of punishment and still come out on top.

"Good! Very good!" General Javel nodded happily. "We will have you fight against the Red Lions directly, as they pose the largest threat now. Alejandro, you will—"

Before General Javel could complete the sentence, the closest Ardent Cretins thug reached out and grabbed Javel by the neck while the rest surrounded him and quickly restrained him. "WHAT? What is the meaning of this? Alejandro, stop them!"

Javel's eyes landed on Alejandro, who did not react at all and stood quietly at the side. Realization dawned on him, a scowling expression forming on his face. "ALEJANDRO, HOW DARE YOU!"

"Under the authority of Baron Cain, I hereby arrest you for treason and espionage against the Yual Dominion; illegal smuggling of guns to foreign powers and the formation of secret societies; and consistent flouting of the prohibition bans. How do you plead?"

"FUCK YOU, ALEJANDRO!"

"General Javel, you're too fixated on your Versian heritage. Why help a homeland that has no gratitude for you? I will not die for a home I have not stepped foot in for twenty years."

"TRAITOR! Mark my words, once I get out, you and your descendants will suffer! Not even the Grand Waves will save you!" General Javel yelled as he thrashed on the floor before one of the Ardent Cretins delivered a strong punch to his face, knocking him out cold.

"That's if they even let you go. Take him away and hand him over to the Magda. Bishop Vernette will be pleased." Alejandro smirked as two Ardent Cretins hauled him away.

Sebastian's voice wafted over the arctech radio. [Good work, Alejandro.]

"Don't forget your promise," Alejandro warned.

[Of course. You will get your position among the Ardent Cretins. However, there is still one more part to the deal.]

Alejandro nodded, walking across the room toward an inconspicuous bookshelf. He ran his hands over the bookshelf, feeling the grooves between the books and ultimately stopping at a yellow-painted leather cover.

With a single twist, the bookshelf rumbled as it swung open to reveal a hidden elevator leading to a basement deep beneath the ground. Alejandro and two Ardent Cretins members entered the elevator, which rumbled as it descended more than five floors underground.

The elevator door swung open to reveal a large storage cavern with countless crates stacked up along its walls. "This is everything the Ilysian Punks have hoarded over the last three years. Guns, potions, gold. This is the main stash. The main entrance is in the West Sector, while the exit is beyond the city walls."

The two knights inspected the crates, noticing there was far more military technology here than just the shipment that had gone missing. It seemed that the Ilysian Punks had actually been doing this for years rather than just recently.

[Ah, so that's why the shipment of guns went past the Seven Snakes district.]

"It is easier to throw the enforcers off our trails by planting the entrance far away from our area."

[And the exit?]

Alejandro led the two Ardent Cretins thugs to the far end of the cavern, where the rushing sound of water could be heard.

"An underground river that leads to a cave in a nearby forest, from which couriers can easily pick it up and smuggle them into Versia. The transport route works both ways."

[Brilliant, Alejandro. You will be rewarded.]

As soon as Sebastian said that, the two Ardent Cretins members grabbed Alejandro, restraining him from behind. Shocked, Alejandro struggled against the metallic armored arms that locked his limbs. "I followed your orders to the letter and even gave you the stash! What the fuck more do you want?"

[The Ardent Cretins have no place for traitors like you, Alejandro. Cut him up and dump the body in the river. I'll be there shortly]

Chapter 44

Aftermath

Kyle grabbed the head of yet another Ilysian Punks and punched it hard, his fist cratering the punk's face in. While he had managed to clear out the Ilysian Punks from the Seven Snakes district, he was surprised as to how easy the counterattack was the following day after the initial assault.

Damian, too, was wary, afraid of an imminent counterattack. However, the Ilysian Punks' entire top hierarchy seemed to have crumbled in an instant. "Do you think it was the inquisitors that helped us?"

Kyle did not see Kitana in action but had already heard from Damian about how she killed the second wave of Ilysian Punks, effectively saving the Seven Snakes. The description of how Kitana restrained the punks threw alarm bells into Kyle's mind. *Unique arctech equipment? Or another system user?*

He was not that arrogant to believe he was the only system user in the world—there was a good chance that Kitana was one too, but he did not have evidence, especially since he had yet to meet another system user.

Whatever the reason for the inquisitors' help was, he was now able to preserve most of his forces and get them back into fighting condition the very next day, enabling them to fight for control over the adjacent districts owned by the Ilysian Punks.

The Ilysian Punks tried to reorganize and fight back, but with their command hierarchy in shambles, they fell like dominoes.

It was now a mad race against time, with the Seven Snakes, Red Lions, and the Wretches trying to cut up the districts owned by the Ilysian Punks.

"Clear out this pub and move onto the next block. We need to reach the other district before the Red Lions get there."

Kyle had the Seven Snakes split up into different squads, conquering and staking their claim on each urban block in sequence. The residents were alarmed by the fighting, but the rival gangs only targeted each other as long as they stayed out of the way.

The enforcers were also going in at full force, raiding the main base of the Ilysian Punks. By the time night fell for a second time, the conflict was over as abruptly as it had begun.

* * *

Kyle walked through the new district the next day, with the place springing back into life. No longer did the residents cower in fear, heading back to work as though nothing had changed. For those who had lived in Raktor long enough, such gang conflicts were as common as the change in seasons. It did not matter to them who was in charge of them, as long as they could carry on with their ordinary lives.

"Keith, set up the same events we did for our previous district. We have to build some goodwill in the new district to properly assimilate it into us," Kyle ordered Keith, who was walking behind him and taking notes of the damage to some of the businesses.

They inspected one of the Ilysian Punks' former pubs. The bar and tables had been smashed to smithereens by the brawl. A few Seven Snakes associates were already inside, cleaning up and hauling the dead bodies outside. Keith noted that a few of the employees were dead, sighing as he saw two associates haul a dead bartender out. "It's going to take two hundred thousand rakels to fix up this mess, and then we need to hire more people to replace them."

"How much cash do we have left?"

"After repaying the Crimson Swords, producing the arctech equipment, funding your pet railgun, and building custom explosive liquid for a mortar? About four hundred thousand left. Do you have another exotic handgun to auction, by any chance?" Keith sighed.

"You know the value will be deprecated."

"Then you'd better hope the Violet Demons don't try to attack the goblin den anytime soon. With both you and Sasha gone, our defenses there are sorely lacking."

"We'll gather more recruits to defend that area," Kyle replied, stepping out of the damaged pub and back onto the street.

In the distance, he could see plenty of freshly recruited Seven Snakes associates cleaning up the streets of debris and broken weapons. Wagons of dead Ilysian Punks members were carted off, to be dumped unceremoniously in the mass graves far beyond the city's walls.

Alex was one of the newly recruited Seven Snakes associates, staring at some of the tied-up punks who had surrendered. If it were him from two days ago, he would have personally taken a knife and cut all of their heads off one by one. However, he had long lost the burning desire for revenge, now only torn with despair at what had happened to his wife.

While he was lost in his depression, staring blankly at the ground, a hand tapped his shoulder frantically. "Alex, Alex. ALEX! Stand up straight. The boss is here!"

Alex jolted back to reality, straightening his back as the new recruits lined up straight. Kyle walked past them, inspecting each of them from head to toe.

Many of them were residents of the Seven Snakes district, caught up in the war. Some joined for fame and money, others joined for protection, but the vast majority were driven by hatred and a desire for revenge. Alex was one of them.

"Under the laws imposed by the Sanctum of Yual, murder is unacceptable. In normal circumstances, you would have immediately been arrested by the enforcers and hauled away to prison, potentially enslaved to mine arcite ore in Tryas. However, as long as you listen to me and follow my orders, this fate shall never befall you," Kyle said as he walked slowly, his voice as clear as day.

"Know this: once you join the Seven Snakes, there is no turning back. If you wish to retract your membership, do so now. Walk away and live a normal life."

However, no one budged. Everyone stood straight and firm. Alex, too, did not budge, despite having lost the original reason why he had fought back against the Ilysian Punks in the first place. His two daughters were counting on him to survive, and with his house in ruins, he needed all the extra money he could get.

Many of the other fresh recruits were of the same mindset. With their homes and lifestyles now in ruins, it was unimaginable how long they would have to toil away as a construction worker, a chef, or a factory worker to make back what they originally had. Being under the Seven Snakes was a different story altogether—fame and fortune came easily as long as you were a part of it.

None of them were frightened by pain any longer, having fought side by side against the Ilysian Punks to defend their families.

"Good, then you are now all associates of the Seven Snakes. Work hard, and you will receive your due reward in equal amounts. Carry on." Kyle dismissed them, letting them resume their work.

Kyle continued through the two districts that they captured, repeating the same speech to different groups of fresh recruits. What the recruits did not know was that he had deliberately delayed the response time of the Seven Snakes to the attacks of the Ilysian Punks in order to create more chaos and drive up the desperation of the people. He needed more tragedies to happen to break the normal lifestyle of the citizens, making them flock toward him for security. *Just like a protection racket.*

And unsurprisingly, it worked like a charm. The Seven Snakes now had more than fifty fresh recruits, doubling their numbers in just a short three days. More work would have to be done over the next few days to integrate them into the gang properly, but for now, Kyle was happy with how the gang was growing. *We will need to make the gang more hierarchical to prevent leaks and betrayals. I must add another intermediate rank, perhaps "cobra"?*

He soon came across Damian, who was helping give out food to those affected by the conflict and setting up a soup kitchen similar to the one they had established before.

More than a hundred residents were gathered, covered in a haphazard mess of clothing to protect them from the environment, as their hands shakily accepted the bowls of soup. Damian smiled as he gave out each bowl, trying to make small talk with the residents.

From behind Damian, a young man eyed him and the Seven Snakes emblem on his shoulder angrily, retrieving a knife from his pocket and slowly closing the gap from behind, planning to stab him in the back.

As the young man lunged without a word, the knife stabbed into the flesh and caused Damian to scream. However, the blade did not push as far as the young man would have hoped. Immediately, two of the Seven Snakes associates grabbed the young man, pinning him down on the ground.

"FUCK YOU SEVEN SNAKES! YOU KILLED MY FATHER!" the young man roared in anger as he thrashed on the ground, fighting against the associates. He used his mouth to bite deep into the arm of an associate, forcing the arm to let go of him as he tried to scamper away.

Instead, he ran headfirst into Kyle, knocking into his leg and bouncing backward. "YOU! I'LL KILL YOU!" The young man recognized Kyle as the leader of the Seven Snakes, throwing a punch. Kyle dodged the attack, causing the young man to stumble forward and trip onto the floor.

"This weakling! And you want to avenge your father? Pathetic." Kyle motioned for the two associates to grab him. "Drag him out."

The young man was dragged out to the front of the soup kitchen stall, kicking and screaming while Damian pulled the knife out of his back.

"Fellow residents. We are working hard to clean up and provide you with new housing as well as food," Kyle said to the crowd of residents as he walked behind the young man.

"But you all seem to not be too cooperative, so let me make this clear."

Kyle grabbed the arctech handgun out of his suit's inner holster and aimed it at the back of the young man's head, pulling the trigger. The brains and flesh were splattered in a spray onto the floor, coating the ground with blood and gore. A few of the residents shrieked in panic, but many were simply frightened and rooted to the ground.

"Anyone—ANYONE!—who tries to go against me and hurt my people, you now know what's coming. THE SEVEN SNAKES RULES THIS PLACE NOW!"

The young man's body was dropped onto the ground, limp, as his head lolled to the side. "Clean this up," Kyle ordered the two associates as he adjusted his suit, putting the handgun back in its holster.

Damian nodded, unfazed by how Kyle had reacted. He had long known that Kyle would fully retaliate against anyone who tried to go against him or hurt the Seven Snakes. He felt a bit of sympathy for the young man, but he also felt an increase in loyalty, knowing that Kyle was willing to go that far to get revenge for him.

Kyle continued walking down the street, meeting up with Keith again. "Did you see the enforcers?" Kyle asked.

"No, why? Are we not in a temporary alliance?"

As soon as he asked, three arctech wagons turned the corner and drove toward them, bearing the insignia of the enforcers and the Sanctum of Yual. The wagons came to a halt right in front of Kyle, with fifteen armored enforcers jumping out and surrounding him, aiming their rifles at him.

Mason stepped out of the first wagon, smoking a pipe as he grinned at Kyle. "Alvin Tersa. Under the powers vested in me by the Inquisition of the Sanctum of Yual, you're under arrest."

Chapter 45

Trump Card

Bishop Vernette frowned as she read through the reports over the last few days.

While the raid on the Ilysian Punks had been going on, someone had been disseminating cheap repeater handguns much like the one sold in the auction, prompting countless small-time criminals to buy them.

Baron Cain could not control the flow of handguns, leading to an increased crime rate across the South Sector, with thugs now using the handguns to threaten and raid shops and businesses. The gun situation was completely getting out of hand. More and more enforcers were being injured in the line of duty.

At this rate, Bishop Vernette could tell that the baron was losing his patience. One wrong misstep, and the bishop could say goodbye to her current well-paid position.

The doors to her office burst open as Mason escorted Kyle in.

"Sorry for the rough handling," Bishop Vernette apologized as Mason uncuffed Kyle in the bishop's office. "We had to show we were doing something."

Kyle didn't seem fazed by the handcuffs, nor did his skin show any sign of pain or soreness. Kitana stood by the side, eyeing Kyle carefully.

"I assume you have something you need me to do." Kyle did not beat around the bush, getting straight to the point.

"Where are the remaining guns?" Mason asked.

"Remaining guns? I handed over every single crate I've found in the Ilysian Punks territory."

"Don't fuck with us. We know exactly how many crates have gone missing. And all of a sudden, your members appear with handguns that look exactly like the one sold in the Central Sector's auction house. The exact same ones are showing up all over the black market. Every fucking second-rate thug will have one by the next year."

"And just like those second-hand thugs, I needed everything I could get my hands on to win. The black market sells a lot of things—I'm sure you know that better than I do."

"I'm assuming it's the same for the mortars, then."

"How observant."

"Alvin." Mason straightened his coat. "I'm not going to ask again. Where. Are. The. Remaining. Guns?"

Kyle looked Mason in the eye, unflinching. "I don't know. They are most certainly not in my territory."

"And you expect me to believe that? It seems you got the biggest haul out of this entire fiasco. I'm even inclined to believe that you instigated the Ilysian Punks to steal from the factory in the first place!"

"An unfounded accusation."

"We'll see about that. Maybe a few weeks in prison will help you talk."

Kyle did not reply, showing no expression on his face whatsoever, causing Mason to get even more visibly frustrated.

Mason ordered two enforcers to come in and drag him out to a holding cell. Kyle shrugged their hands off, walking by himself.

As the doors closed behind Kyle, Mason sighed, looking at Kitana and Bishop Vernette. "Well? What do the two of you think?"

Kitana shrugged her shoulders. Her skill, Eyes of Truth, could see through optical illusions and such but could not make out if someone was lying or not. *Maybe when I hit my next class upgrade, I'll get Ears of Truth or something of the sort.*

Bishop Vernette was equally hesitant. "I don't think he is the one holding on to the remaining crates. We're still missing ten crates, and even if he's lying, he will only have one crate at most. Holding that many is a veritable death sentence for such a small gang as his."

"I'll wait for our enforcers to report back before making a final call." Mason crossed his arms, plopping down onto the sofa. Two minutes passed in silence while the bishop continued to read reports of increasing gun violence.

Soon, an enforcer entered the office, bowing to the inquisitors and the bishop. "Sir, we've checked the entire Seven Snakes district and found no traces of any guns."

Mason stood up in shock. "Not even a single crate? Gun barrels? Bullet tests? Firing ranges?"

"Nothing, sir. All we found was some evidence of a factory manufacturing a few arctech armor pieces, but nothing related to guns."

"He's hiding them; I know he is!" Mason slammed his fist on the holster of the sofa.

"Uhh, sir? There's one more thing."

"What?"

"There's a protest going out now right outside the Magda. It seems to be composed of the local residents, calling for Kyle's release."

"Who the fuck is riling them up?!" Mason gritted his teeth in anger, but he already knew the answer deep down. *Of course, it's the Seven Snakes members!*

The bishop walked up to the window of her office, overlooking the protesting crowd who held signs and arctech loudhailers shouting out.

"JUSTICE FOR KYLE!"

"RELEASE OUR PROTECTOR!"

"You!" Mason pointed at the enforcer. "Gather ten of your men and clear them out!"

"Belay that order," Bishop Vernette interrupted. "Release Alvin now."

"But if he's hiding the guns…"

"Then we will catch him in the act there and then. It is not worth going against public opinion right now. They see the Seven Snakes as their protectors and defenders."

"You know it's the Seven Snakes members that are fueling the crowd. No doubt they bribed or hired a few civilians and squatters to form a protest. I don't believe—"

Bishop Vernette rubbed the bridge of her nose, her face fatigued. "Understand this, Mason. You may have a job to do, but I have a position to protect. I will not let you jeopardize my authority over this South Sector."

"You giving up Kyle to them shows a lack of authority instead!" Mason countered.

"It is only a matter of time before public opinion begins to swing against Kyle once again. Soon, they will see the Seven Snakes for what they are—what every gang is—an organization dedicated to fleecing as much cash from them as possible. It is at that time that we strike. Furthermore, the longer we hold Kyle, the more public opinion will turn against us. Would you like for reporters to publish our faces in newspapers in Tryas?"

Mason finally understood the angle the bishop was aiming for. "I understand. But I still think—"

The arctech phone line on the bishop's desk rang, prompting the woman to pick it up. A moment of hesitation reigned in the air, the bishop listening intently as relief washed over her face. "Yes, sir. I understand. I will have him released right away."

* * *

Kyle was hauled out of the holding cell, uncuffed for the second time today, by Mason, who had a sour expression. "It looks like things are not turning out the way you expected them too," Kyle said.

"Don't think you're scot-free. I'm always watching you. The moment you slip up, you can forget about life outside the arcite mines," Mason threatened.

"A word of advice from me then—perhaps you should consider if the other gangs had a part to play? I heard rumors that the Ilysian Punks were uncharacteristically poor or lacking in wealth when their main base was cracked open. But what do I know? I never made it that far in—I'm sure you can verify that with your observers." Kyle smirked.

Mason didn't reply, merely cursing under his breath as he dragged Kyle out toward the entrance of the Magda Chapel.

As he stepped out into the daylight, the crowd cheered and roared as they saw him emerge. For some unknown reason, a red carpet was laid out right through the middle of the crowd at the base of the marble steps, along with a smiling noble standing right in front of him.

"Ah, the man of the hour! Savior of the South Sector! I am truly sorry for the mistake I made. How could we ever arrest a model citizen of the Yual Dominion?" Baron Cain grinned widely as he patted Kyle's back, waving at the crowd and smiling at all the reporters who turned up to cover the protests.

Another showman. Kyle decided to play along, bowing to Baron Cain. "Thank you for your kind words, Baron Cain."

"Please allow me to reward you. I would like to invite you to my dwelling."

"Of course, I am grateful for the invitation."

They entered the baron's personal arctech wagon with the luxury turned up to eleven. Kyle, however, was obviously not impressed, having experienced far more in the Galactic Era. His expression remained calm, not flustered nor tempted by the wealth on display around him.

Baron Cain smiled and gave a final wave to the crowd as the wagon departed, before sitting down opposite Kyle. Without a word, Cain slowly pulled out the "Oriental Bloom" handgun from his suit, resting it on his lap.

"You don't seem surprised by this sequence of events."

"I've been told that I need to work on my expressions."

"And you don't seem flustered at all by this handgun."

"Should I be?"

"Who sold you the other prototype handguns?"

"The black market has everything, Baron. If you would like, I could recommend a dealer to you, though I'm sure you know every dealer there is in the South Sector already."

"You're the one who sold this handgun in the auction house, didn't you?"

"What auction?"

"Don't play dumb with me, Mr. Tersa. I have my own information network. Do not take me for a fool. If I wanted to, I could have you locked away in a slammer or slave-mining for the rest of your life."

"If you're willing to take a hit to your reputation, that is. Does the lord of the city, Count Leon, know that the guns are proliferating in the South Sector? I recently heard gun violence is on the rise. Not a very good look for a baron barely five years into the role."

"Are you threatening me?"

"I'm only laying out a scenario. I'm not a criminal, Baron Cain. I simply run an organization aimed at generating the most profit through various means." Kyle leaned back into the chair. "Now you have a problem, and I offer a solution."

Baron Cain didn't reply, prompting Kyle to continue. "Guns of a certain nature have begun to proliferate on the black market, allowing normal thugs to purchase and use them. In fact, almost any normal human can use them, not requiring an arcite fuel pack. Sure, they can only get off a few shots, but that's enough to perform a mass shooting if they wanted to."

"Get to the point."

Kyle smiled, knowing he had hooked the baron. "I have a way to disable all existing handguns on the black market. But in the event I am imprisoned or killed for any reason, existing orders with my subordinates both inside the city and outside will distribute even more guns into the city. And I'm sure that wouldn't put you in a very good light with Count Leon."

Baron Cain stiffened up, thinking about the repercussions. He was indeed planning to imprison Kyle, which was why he had performed the entire publicity stunt in the first place.

With that, he could make an excuse that Kyle was staying at his place as an honored guest, preventing his subordinates from throwing a fit. He stared at Kyle's face, noticing that Kyle seemed to have been expecting this.

Baron Cain quickly thought through all the possible scenarios. Killing him would set off a chain of events he did not want to deal with. With handguns in full proliferation now, it would be impossible for him to mobilize the enforcers to crack down on every single thug who had one. He had no idea how many handguns Kyle had distributed onto the black market.

"If I accept your solution, you must cease all gun distribution immediately."

"Of course. Peace in our time. However, the orders I gave my subordinate still stand."

"How does your solution work?"

"You will see it in action tonight, but time is ticking. If I don't return to the Seven Snakes district by the next three hours, I'm afraid that even *I* won't be able to stop it."

"So if you don't stop it within a day..."

"Then feel free to imprison or kill me. It wouldn't matter at that point after all."

"Fine." Baron Cain ordered the driver to turn around and drive the wagon back to the Seven Snakes' district.

The wagon soon reached the district, and Kyle stepped off onto the street. "A final piece of advice. Keep your handgun in a thick metal safe if possible."

Baron Cain was stunned by the sudden advice, but Kyle was already walking off, while a reporter nearby began to observe the baron. "Get us back to the mansion right now!" Baron Cain urged.

Kyle entered the former Seven Snakes base, where the vipers—Sasha, Damian, and Keith—were waiting for him. "Sasha, set up the large arctech radio with Gordon in the room."

[Yes, sir. Already on it.]

"Good. Whoever still has their handguns, place them here on the table."

Niko was confused but still complied with the order. "Why? What's going to happen? Is this a ceremony?"

"A show of force."

As soon as the large arctech radio was set up, Kyle activated it and tweaked the interior engravings into a different position. Instead of speaking into it, Kyle took an engraved metal plate and slotted it in, modifying the arctech radio.

No one felt anything, but the handguns began to glow red hot from the inside, a sizzling cracking sound instead emitting from the interior.

Damian was the first one to comprehend what was happening immediately, his face breaking out into a wide grin. "Holy shit! You're self-destructing all the handguns in the city! HAHA! Imagine the baron's face right now!"

Niko nodded but was still a bit confused. "Wait, but does this mean we lose our handguns as well?" He pointed at the melting handguns.

Kyle chuckled for the first time. "This is simply to show the baron and the enforcers that we destroyed our handguns as well. But this isn't the only set of handguns we have, remember? Time to expand."

Chapter 46

Innovation

A month after the fall of the Ilysian Punks...

"So I just have to stand here?" A little girl with pigtails glanced around the room, while a large arctech device was aimed right at her, four black lenses staring her down.

If she did not know any better, she would have assumed it was a monster of sorts, but she had complete faith in the man behind the machine, who was currently modifying its innards with a hot pointed iron serving as an etcher, changing some of the arctech engravings on the fly.

"Yes, dear, just stay right there. Papa's going to show you a miraculous invention!"

"Like the dragonfly you showed me?"

The father stuck his head out and grinned at the girl. "Even better. Just give me a minute."

He focused back on the interior again, mumbling to himself as he carefully rerouted some of the arctech engravings. "Just have to add a few more traces here to reduce the high-speed load of the incoming light... FUCK!" He yelped as the hot iron accidentally touched one of his fingertips, making him almost drop it and wreck the rest of the machine. The hot iron, however, scratched the surface of an engraving, rendering it completely useless.

"No, no, no!" The father groaned as he noticed the error, trying to take subsequent deep breaths to calm down. *Stay calm, Reese. This is your big breakout moment; stay calm. We still got a few days to sort this out.*

"Daddy, how long do I have to stand? I'm tired…" The little girl whined as she shuffled uncomfortably, her eyes already locked onto the sofa nearby.

"Sorry, dear, it's going to be a while more. Let's take a break." Reese smiled weakly, turning off the arctech etcher and stepping back. The room was a mess of metal and engravings, save for the sofa, where the little girl rolled around happily.

Reese shambled over to a workbench filled with broken engraving plates and tools scattered in an unruly fashion. "Need to find a replacement… It's better if I did the modifications here…"

He pulled a wooden stool up to the table to sit, rubbing his deep black eyebags that had never gone away since he had begun this project. It had been nearly a month and had been nothing short of a miraculous run.

His arm instinctively reached out to the right, attempting to grab something as he stared at the engraving in front of him. The observant little girl quickly jumped to her feet and ran out of the room, but soon returned with a shocked face. "Papa, we're out of potions!"

"What?! We're out of Stamina Potions?!" Reese's face balked, but he took yet another deep breath. "It's okay, darling. I don't need the potions to get this done. Only one more final stretch to go."

That final stretch turned into hours, with the little girl having gone to sleep in her own room while Reese toiled through the night. His body felt lethargic, his arms weak, and his thighs aching from the numerous nights he had spent trying to make this thing perfect.

Just as soon as he was about to give up and turn in for the night, the doorbell rang softly, ringing like a charm. Reese's face immediately lit up, and he scampered to the door, frantically opening it to reveal a well-dressed gentleman in a black coat.

"Hello, Reese. I've come to check up on the progress of your project."

"Sir Kyle, thank goodness you're here! I'm currently trying to fix a few issues here, and I may require your help once again."

"Of course." Kyle smiled genially before motioning to an associate behind him carrying a crate of Stamina Potions. "You, put it in the kitchen and wait for me outside."

The associate nodded, with Reese making way for the two of them to enter the house. The man quickly led Kyle into the workshop, explaining the issue with the engraving. "The main problem I'm facing right now is that there seems to be residual energy being emitted from the machine toward the lens. From my understanding, the entire device should be completely passive."

"Let me have a look." Kyle sat on another wooden stool and examined the engraving in question. "Bring over the schematic diagrams."

Reese pulled out an entire stack of papers, each detailing a specific part of the machine and its connections. Kyle flipped through each page, tracing the error through its various supposed connections. "I found the error. You have the engraving connected to these wrong four ports, causing the engraving to be connected and form a radiative effect."

"Radiative...?"

"Never mind. The point is, you'll have to redo a few parts in the machine. Can you make it for the demonstration debut?"

"I..." Reese was about to say yes, but he checked the number of modifications he would have to make, which would be more than he could do in the next two days. He could barely keep himself awake, even in front of his biggest investor in the project yet.

"Okay. I'll get the factory to manufacture the parts for you right away. I will be back in the morning. You should get some good rest. Don't want you messing up the demonstration."

"Th-Thank you, sir!" Reese stood up and bowed deeply, his face filled with gratitude. He would never forget how hard and long he had fought at the University of Raktor to get this project done, only to find Kyle as an investor the moment he went out drinking and crying in a pub. He also owed him his life for saving him from a pub brawl in which he was nearly killed.

This project would truly be his big breakthrough. Kyle had already signed a contract to co-found a company that could commercialize the product if the demonstration was successful. He could already imagine his face and name plastered across the billboards of the city, along with the company logo. *I'll be rich and successful!*

However, he was still suspicious of Kyle. It was natural. They were going to be co-owners of the new company, after all. *I don't know if Kyle has something unique planned.*

* * *

The university's theater was not particularly crowded for the demonstration debut, with only a few other faculty professors and merchants yawning in the front row seats. However, the turnout was still more than anything Reese could have expected. He peeked his head out from the backstage area through the stage curtains, spotting the dean of the university sitting there as well.

Hah, you old fucker. You did not even give me the time of day when I started! Reese gripped his fist tightly as he recalled that humiliating moment, the lowest point of his career as a university professor. He knew the dean would most likely be the first to pounce on the successful demonstration.

On a viewing box near the top, Kyle looked expectantly down on the stage, supporting Reese.

The lights of the theater began to dim slowly, all eyes now focused on the brightly lit wooden stage. Reese rolled the arctech machine out, which looked like a rectangular box-shaped device half the size of a human with four black lenses jutting out conspicuously.

Reese cleared his throat and faced the audience, his white hair now slickly combed down and his clothes cleaned—though his deep eyebags remained a testament to the work he had put in. "Fellow professors, potential investors, and other viewers such as my students, today I am proud to reveal an invention that will revolutionize the way media is used to enrich our lives."

"For generations, we have relied on paintings and scribbling on parchment to convey images, memories, and meanings through the generations. This machine here represents a complete overhaul of this limitation, allowing us to store our most precious moments in the form of paper."

A theater employee suddenly ran up to the dean in the front row, whispering urgently into his ears. Within seconds, the dean stood right up, quickly following the employee out of the theater. It did not matter to Reese, who was more than happy to see the old geezer gone.

"I present to you—the light-capturer!"

Kyle internally winced at the name but did not show any outburst of emotion or groan. It was a different world that he was in now—he could hardly expect the name to be the same. Also, if he did use or convinced Reese to use the name "camera," "holo-recorder," or the countless Galactic Era–branded names, it might give him away to those in the know.

With the existence of the Ancient Exosuit Spine as well as the energy shield wielded by Makoa, which was now in his possession, he was acutely aware that there was more to the world than a simple "reincarnation."

"The light-capturer does what its namesake does. Capture light. The prevailing theory of our world is that we see things through reflected rays of light, and as such, the device is a reimagining of current optical magnification engravings, instead routing the information captured and putting them onto paper. An example is now being distributed by the assistants."

A few pieces of paper were distributed around, with a photo of Reese's daughter on it. Many of the audience members gasped at the detail, though Kyle was hardly impressed. In his view, it was the most pixelated holo-image he had ever seen.

"That's right; this is not a painting, nor was it mass-produced by a printing press. This is a light print of a scene! And today—"

The doors to the theater suddenly banged wide open, with ten thugs entering the theater. Reese was taken aback by the sudden entrance, while the audience members were all confused. Squinting his eyes and looking at the leader of the thugs, an expression of recognition began to dawn on his face. "Yo... You! You were at the pub!"

"So were you, pretty boy. Big day for you, huh? Think you can get into a fight with me at the pub and get away scot-free?!" The leader of the thugs grinned as he twirled a crowbar, strutting down the aisles while his fellow thug members spread out among the audience, watching them closely.

"I was drunk then! I already apologized!" Reese exclaimed. "Please don't do this, I swear I'll repay you next time for any grievances I may have caused you."

The leader hopped up onto the wooden stage, eyeing the light-capturer. "Nice toy you've got here. Would be a shame if it was smashed into pieces!" The leader brandished the crowbar, smashing the very future and dream that Reese had been focused on for every waking hour of his life in the past month.

As the metal parts were dented and the lens was shattered into tiny, brilliant black pieces, Reese instinctively roared and lunged forward in a desperate bid to protect the machine. However, the leader immediately swung the crowbar at him, hitting Reese right in the head and knocking him out.

"GUARDS!" an audience member shrieked before she too was hit over the head by a metal pipe by one of the thugs.

The leader kicked the unconscious Reese, flipping his body over. "Oh, don't think passing out is the worst I can do to you. BOYS! Grab the body and machine out of here!"

"Ya, bosmang." The thugs complied, with two hoisting the body up and two picking up the valuable parts of the machine. As soon as the door closed behind the leaving thug group, the entire audience broke into a frenzy, running all over the place.

"Professor Reese got kidnapped! Call the dean and the enforcers, quick!"

"Where did the dean go? Where are the university guards?!"

* * *

Reese woke up groggily, noticing his head was still pounding with liquid dripping down his forehead. No... It was blood—*his* blood.

Jolting awake, the sudden movement had him fall over backward in the chair that he was tied to, crashing onto the bare, concrete floor with a resounding crash. The glass windows that pockmarked the ceiling shone brightly into his eyes, causing him to wince.

"Look, the cunt is awake." The leader smirked as he stood up from the barrel he was sitting on, striding over with his crowbar.

"Wh-Why are you doing this?" Reese asked weakly, the blood loss and the impact still making him dizzy and unable to get a good grasp on where he was.

The leader squatted next to Reese and grabbed his face. "The same reason why everyone in Raktor does something—money. And you look like a hundred thousand rakels to me now."

"What?!"

"That's right. Someone put a contract on you! Do you really think that I, the great Tyler fucking Won, would barge into a university and risk getting caught by the enforcers just so I could fuck you up for a pub brawl a month ago? HAH!"

If the thumping in Reese's head was not already bad enough, it got even worse with this realization. *Who paid the thug gang to kidnap me? Was it my jealous colleagues? The dean?!*

Soon, a man dressed in inconspicuous attire entered the warehouse, clearly of a different class than the leader of the thugs. "Good job catching him."

"So you're the client. Fuck that, where's the money? I don't want to mess with Kyle any longer if necessary."

"Not until I ask the hostage some questions." The client adjusted his collar, walking up to Reese, who looked petrified. He did not recognize the person at all, but he began to put two and two together quickly. *Shit, he's here to steal the technology from me!*

The leader groaned loudly. "Fuck, are you serious? Fine, have it your way. But fifteen minutes more, and we're out of here."

Before the client could retort, a series of screams and cries echoed through the empty warehouse, prompting the remaining thugs to stand up, their faces wary.

"Who the fuck is that?" The leader dropped Reese back onto the floor, walking up to the main warehouse entrance, where the sounds of fighting could be heard.

An injured thug staggered to the door, limping toward the leader. "Who is attacking us?!"

"It's him! The Seven Snak—" Before the thug could finish, his head was crushed in by a neon red arctech hammer, breaking through the skull in a smooth downward motion.

[SYSTEM MESSAGE]
You killed Thug, +50 EXP.

Reese gaped in shock, having never seen an actual fight break out before. It looked like an entire movie scene to him as the wielder of the hammer charged forward, smacking each of the thugs with a single hit and killing them. Even the leader of the thugs stood no chance against Kyle's strength.

"Wh-What!? Kyle!?" the client exclaimed, running over to Reese and grabbing him to use as a hostage shield. Within a minute, Kyle had killed all the thug members in sequence, as though it were a choreographed fight scene. Reese was naturally happy. *He came to save me!*

"Stay back! Otherwise, I'll kill him!" The client began to sweat profusely, his eyes glancing back and forth, looking for a way out. The tip of the crowbar pierced Reese's skin, drawing blood.

Kyle stopped moving.

"Good. Now we can make a deal. You don't want your precious Reese here getting hurt, do you? Don't try anything funny." The client tried to understand what was happening. *How did Kyle get here so fast? Was he tracking the thugs? I should have shifted the hostage immediately.*

"Oh, I won't. But I can't say the same for her," Kyle replied.

"Her?"

The glass windows in the ceilings were shattered, with a female figure landing right behind the client as they were showered in glass shards. In one swift motion, the lady grabbed the neck of the client and pinned him to the ground. His limp body slumped to the floor, releasing Reese onto the ground with a thud.

"Thank Yual, you're here!" Reese nearly cried tears of joy. However, instead of helping Reese up, Kyle quickly moved over to the client, grabbing his mouth and preventing him from clenching down. He used his hands to pry the client's mouth open, reaching inside and checking for any suicide pills or killchips—a habit from the Galactic Era.

Kyle continued checking, stripping the client's clothes and patting him down for any other equipment, while Sasha held him down. As he removed the shirt from the struggling client, he noticed a unique chest engraving with five interlocking lines that were all connected as part of a whole.

"First question: Who hired you? Seeing as you attacked us, you know exactly what we're capable of," Kyle inquired in a threatening tone and lifted the man up.

"I... I swear, I didn't want to do this! I'm just a front for Harri—" Before he could complete his sentence, the interlocking engravings on his chest suddenly lit up, causing the client to double over and spasm violently.

Kyle and Sasha immediately backed off, expecting an attack, but instead, the client screamed as the engraving's light grew stronger. Shortly after, smoke began rising from his chest, and his body began to smolder. The engraving suddenly ballooned into a small but brilliant ball of flame, engulfing the client in an instant and cutting his painful shrieks short.

The flame was unnatural, burning nearly instantly and turning the client's body into a charred, blackened figure.

[What was that, sir?] Sasha was shocked, having never seen anything like it.

Reese, too, was in utter shock as Kyle turned his attention to setting him free. *What kind of human would be willing to set himself on fire to prevent divulging information to the enemy?* "That's a crazy sense of loyalty! Madness!"

"No." Kyle shook his head, clearly remembering the facial expression of the client before the activation. "He didn't set himself on fire. It seems like our new enemy is smarter than expected."

Chapter 47

Light Thrower

Two weeks later...

Gulak raised its staff, a vicious expression written all over its face as it flashed its sharp, yellow teeth. "There is nowhere left to run now, human! You die here!"

"Kyaaaa! Somebody, save me!" a scantily clad girl screamed and cowered, clasping her ears.

"No one is here to hear your screams or save you, girl!"

Gulak stepped forward, its eyes piercing at the girl with clear desire. The girl shivered even more as she watched the goblin slowly approach her.

"Don't worry, my fair maiden! I'm coming to save you!" a loud masculine voice boomed into the cavern that the two were in, prompting the both of them to turn their heads toward the source.

Gulak could barely see the entrance of the cavern, the brilliant light shining brightly and nearly blinding its eyes. All it could see was the figure of a human man, along with a fluttering cape from behind. However, it caused him to instantly bare its teeth at the figure in hatred. "Curses! It is you again! How did you find us?!"

"Nothing can ever escape me, the mighty... err... enforcer man?"

"CUT! CUT! CUT!" Merissa screamed with all her might, throwing a book on the ground in sheer frustration. "You dense little fucker! How many times are we going to go through this fucking scene, you little shitbag!"

The vulgarities spewing out from the former slave-turned-clerk captured by Kyle and Sasha were of no surprise to the rest of the crew in the cavern. The light-capturer operator simply yawned, while a goblin nearby, who was carrying a heavy metal pole with some kind of weird-looking arctech device at the end, wobbled.

"Stupid Feldon, always ruining my chances at being a star!" Gulak joined in the berating of the "enforcer man."

"ARGH!" Merissa grabbed her hair, nearly ripping it out of clumps. "Everyone, take five! Feldon, in my office—NOW!"

The supporting crew was used to this sequence of events, immediately exiting the cavern and heading for the mess hall. The goblin nearly dropped the metal pole onto Gulak's head before the latter grabbed the head and supported it, scowling at the goblin. "Idiot! If you break this device that Kyle crafted, it is over for us!"

Back in the newly expanded office, Merissa was clearly exasperated, storming into the room and slamming a book on the desk. The assistant clerks nearby were not flustered or worried at all, knowing that Merissa was on a rampage. And for a good reason too.

Merissa sat down in her chair, glaring at the meek Feldon, who was still wearing the cape. "Feldon. Can you please explain what the schedule is for today?"

Feldon gulped instinctively, nearly stuttering as he said, "W-We are to do the final action scene for the movie, with Kyle personally coming in to watch the new version."

"That's right—the DEBUT MOVIE!" Merissa yelled at the top of her lungs. "You think Kyle will be happy with your performance so far? This is the fifteenth take we've done this morning! Do you want to return to Raktor or not?!"

"Yes, of course I do!" Feldon nodded vigorously, knowing that this was one of his options to return to the city of Raktor.

"Then this is your fucking chance to reinvent yourself as a new person so you can live happily with your family in Raktor! Why the fuck do you keep fucking up a different line every single fucking take! You're lucky you were handsome when you took on the role at the start—because right about now you look like a fucking pile of steaming hot SHIT!" Merissa cursed louder.

"I'm sorry! Please give me another chance! I promise I'll do it right this time!"

"Oh yeah? Recite your lines for the scenes one more time."

"Uhhh... 'I am an enforcer of Yual! Nothing can ever escape my sight!'"

"Good. Fuck up one more time, and I'll personally stuff the sound recorder pole up your ass."

* * *

Bishop Vernette sat gingerly in a standalone velvet chair, with Mason flanking her. "That's all we need? An empty room?" Mason asked warily. *Why do I feel like I'm about to get assassinated here?*

Kyle groaned as he watched Reese set up the light-thrower machine, projecting a blank white image onto the opposing wall.

"This machine doesn't look too special—it seems like it is simply a spotlight shining white. We have plenty of that in our arsenal," Bishop Vernette remarked.

Soon, the image on the wall changed to reveal a title scene, shocking the bishop and Mason. What frightened them even more was how there were suddenly the sounds of goblin laughter echoing around the room.

Mason retrieved his arctech pistol from his belt, scanning the room and noticing the source was coming from a separate arctech radio. "What the fuck is going on?"

The bishop did not respond as violently as Mason, enthralled by the opening scene of the Culdao Peaks forest. "This... this is real? Not an optical illusion engraving?"

"Optical illusion engravings cannot change on the fly, ma'am," Kyle patiently explained. "In order to achieve this, it is required to update the image multiple times a second. Preferably thirty times a second."

"Yes, this is the invention of the century! Mark my words!" Reese nodded his head vigorously. It had been two weeks since they set up the company. Reese had completely quit his job as a professor, serving as the co-founder, full time under Kyle. He didn't dare stay away from Kyle any longer, especially after the kidnapping.

Mason too stopped and watched the movie, but his main interest was in the technology. *So it seems that the arctech radio is synchronized with the images shown on the wall...*

The movie was only a short five minutes, with a blazing-fast story. Mason nearly choked at the end when he saw how gaudy the "enforcer" acted. "That's not one of ours, right?"

"No. This is simply a demonstration movie of what these machines can do." The light-thrower machine began to wind down and eventually powered off.

The bishop remained silent, pondering while Mason was examining the light-thrower machine carefully. "You... You made this yourself?" Mason asked Kyle.

Reese cleared his throat. "*We* made it together, just to be clear. I had the idea for years!"

The bishop motioned to the inquisitor, beckoning him to come closer while she looked at Kyle. "Alvin and Reese, please give us a moment to discuss further before we talk business."

"Of course." Kyle left the room, leaving the two of them alone.

"Ma'am, it is fairly clear that Alvin has an ulterior motive for all of this. Need I remind you of what happened a few weeks ago with the handguns?"

"It does not matter. The handguns were destroyed—end of story. But what he and Reese have invented here has immense value."

"Sorry, Vernette, but I don't see—"

"Mason, this machine could be the turning point. It could even elevate me to a cardinal," the bishop said, cutting him off before he could finish. "If we play our cards right, the reputation of the enforcers will be improved by miles."

"What do you mean? I don't understand."

"With the ability to record these um... movies, we can steer public opinion toward a better perspective. Have them understand what the enforcers are exactly doing and so on."

"But what is the best way to do that? Surely it is not using a gaudy, childish movie like that, right? Right?"

* * *

Damian grunted as he lifted up a sack of concrete with one hand, hauling it over to the mixer while another associate poured water. The building was an entire mess, completely hollowed out. It was an abandoned residential apartment, but now the associates and a hired construction crew were hollowing out and breaking down most of the walls to form a vacant space.

It had been a month and a half since the fall of the Ilysian Punks. In that time, the Seven Snakes had reconsolidated their control in their home district while slowly stabilizing the new districts they had captured from the Ilysian Punks.

The Crimson Swords debt had been fully paid off as well, a burden completely lifted off their shoulders. Damian chuckled to himself as he recalled how frantic they were when confronted with the million-rakel debt. *A million rakels? That's nothing compared to the New Year party we just had.*

With the new year heralded in with a victorious celebration, the morale of the Seven Snakes was higher than ever before. Now, their gang had progressed so fast over the last four months to achieve even greater heights than he could ever imagine. Loans of a million rakels seemed puny in hindsight, especially when he stood in front of the abandoned residential apartment, the land deed completely in the Seven Snakes' name.

"I don't understand. Why are we building grand steps like those in front of the Magda inside this building?" Niko scratched his head, looking again at the blueprint for this room. A few associates gathered around to check the layout as well, their heads confused by the completely different architecture and room design than they were used to. *Putting velvet chairs on large stairs facing a blank wall? What is going on?*

"Is he trying to build a theater or something? Doesn't look like any of the ones I've been too," another associate replied.

"Who knows, maybe Alvin finally went full loony," Niko murmured.

"Alvin? Who's Alvin?" One of the newer recruits cocked his head in confusion.

"Oh boy, I remember the good ol' days when I was just like you..."

The layout of the building was weird and novel to the associates—a theater at the very top with multiple restaurants and shops along the way. Kyle mentioned to Damian that this was called a "hypermall," but Damian had no idea what the fuck that meant, or even what "hyper" meant.

Regardless, most of the current income of the Seven Snakes was thrown into this, plus every available associate that was not working in other businesses. However, even that was not enough, prompting the Seven Snakes to issue daily jobs to those in the district who wanted it.

Plenty of homeless squatters and poor folks took up the work immediately. For those who were on the weaker side, Keith hired them to handle the logistics and negotiations with potential tenants who would set up a restaurant or shop in the "hypermall." The new clerks formed the basis for administrative capacity within their business. The transition to legal businesses had begun.

Keith frowned as he calculated the potential legal earnings from the theater, working out the total footfall. *It doesn't seem viable at all. Why did Kyle choose this location of all places?*

Kyle, too, dropped by from time to time, bringing along Gordon and Eric Dicar to see the construction. "What?! Who would use a heat engraving system in a shop?" Gordon exclaimed, knowing that such luxury was only reserved for the nobility.

Eric was not too concerned about that. He was more concerned with the hidden pubs that would be embedded into the area. "You're planning to sell alcohol in your new 'theater' too?!"

Kyle pointed at a map, showing them the nearby buildings. "The location of this theater is out of the way of the center, but there are more than enough roads leading here. We'll charter regular wagons from each of the districts we control to this hypermall, boosting people's collective recognition of the place. The light shows that will be held in the new theater will give us an initial boost. The objective of the entire hypermall is to elevate the local residents to a higher standard of living."

Gordon caught on to what was happening. "You want to make our district the envy of everyone else in the South Sector."

"Exactly. Once we complete this project, it will demonstrate our willingness and the 'need' for our inclusion in the local society. Running pubs and brothels doesn't exactly fulfill that goal." Kyle nodded.

This had always been the plan since he caught wind of the development of the camera, reported to him by one of his associates who had seen the pub fight.

This allowed him to establish a privately owned movie company headed by him and Reese, making his position much more legitimate. The money used to build the new hypermall was less legitimate, but the locals would not care about it if it improved their standard of living.

If everything played out correctly, Kyle could create a chance for himself to garner a reputation on a more legal and genuine basis. He understood that positions obtained solely through violence were untenable. *A crime lord is always actively balancing the scales between reputation and illegal deeds, never going too far on either side.*

Furthermore, such an economic project would give him the necessary resources to fight toe-to-toe with the Ardent Cretins in the near future. Despite having defeated the Ilysian Punks, Kyle was well aware that he did not do it on his own. Any direct physical conflict with the Ardent Cretins would result in complete failure. *Only an economic war within the sector or external benefits can give me the edge necessary to compete.*

"This will put us into the spotlight, potentially endangering all our other operations!" Eric frantically pointed out. "Everyone knows that you are the leader of the Seven Snakes as well—would the enforcers not simply investigate and dig up the evidence?"

"Ah, I have already reached a mutually beneficial deal with the enforcers under the name of our new private movie company. That reminds me, Gordon. I need you to handle filming tomorrow."

"Filming? In the city? If you're planning on filming the production lines, I can assure you it is absolutely boring."

"Don't be ridiculous. We would never film anything that boring. Instead, we're filming a protest."

Chapter 48

Protests

"It is Nona, our goddess, who has shaped the earth as it is; who has laid out every food, animal, monster, and plant for our needs. And the Word of the Goddess states—'I have created everything on this planet for the enjoyment of the human race. Who dares claim that humans shall not consume what I have created?.'"

"YEAH, YEAH!" The throng of people gathered on the streets, cheering at a person standing on top of an arctech wagon that slowly chugged forward, forming a parade.

"Yet the Sanctum of Yual claims that consumption of such *sacred* goods is a sin and beyond what we, the common folk, can handle." The person donned a blinding red robe, his head adorned with what seemed to be an ornamental oriental piece. He held an upright posture, his speech passionate through the arctech loudhailer as the crowd roared back in response.

"YEAH!"

"The audacity, folks! The audacity of the religion to demean you. To put you lower than those who serve the 'living god,' the Emperor of the Yual Dominion. Are you not sapient? Are you not capable of self-control? Are you not HUMAN!?"

"WE ARE HUMAN!" The crowd was riled up, with a loud wave of fanfare exploding across the street.

"Then let us show them our displeasure! Show our anger, our wrath! Only by marching out in solidarity can the rulers of this city truly understand what they have created—injustice among the common folk. Rise, brothers. Rise!"

"YEAAAAAAAH!"

A few cries from the front of the parade were heard as people began to spot a blockade at the front. Fifty armed enforcers had their wagons parked sideways to block the streets.

The enthusiasm of the crowd noticeably fell, with the cheering and shouting being toned down a good amount. "Brothers, we are here simply to show our presence. We are not violent—for our Goddess Nona has proclaimed the divine worth of every human soul. Despite their misguided views, it is our duty to peacefully convert them."

A wave of murmurs spread through the crowd, with many agreeing. No one wanted to get into a conflict with the enforcers—as much as they hated the idea of the prohibition bans on alcohol, they did not want to be imprisoned or lose their jobs.

"We are peaceful protesters! We shall show our stance here and now by camping in the stre—"

Suddenly, a loud shattering of glass was heard as a shop's window was smashed into by a few protesters, with many scrambling in to grab the goods and rakels from the shop. The shop owner did not dare fight against the mob, immediately running away.

The red-robed person's face balked immediately. "Brothers, we are not here to raid or pillage, but to change the laws! Why are we—"

"HEY, YOU STUPID CUNTS! GET OFF THE STREETS!"

He turned to face the source of the voice, noticing it was a group of masked thugs. "YOU'RE FUCKING UP OUR TERRITORY HERE! BREAK IT UP!"

The thugs shoved their way through the crowd, trying to forcibly disperse it. The enforcers did not make a single move and simply watched the spectacle.

"Hey, we're just doing a peaceful protest here!" One of the protesters tried to square up against the thugs.

"Oh yeah? Protest against this!" The thug immediately swung the metal pipe in his hand on the protestor's head, knocking him out cold.

Immediately, the protesters began to scream and panic. "You fucking bitches!" another protestor yelled as he charged with a group toward the thugs, forming a massive melee brawl that soon spread throughout the entire crowd.

The red-robed person was shocked and confused. "Stop fighting! Stop fighting!"

However, the protesters were not listening any longer, fully caught up in the heat of the battle. They were not about to just let the thugs hit them and get away with it. They had to exact revenge and defend themselves.

The protesters began to spread out over the street, the chaos and conflict spreading even further. Many of the protesters were not there because they believed in Nona, the goddess, but rather to take part in the movement.

Some used the chaos to raid and pillage some of the shops, and when the fighting spilled out into the residential blocks as protesters and thugs chased each other, the local residents too got caught up in the fighting.

[PROTESTERS, THIS IS YOUR FINAL WARNING. VIOLENCE AGAINST RESIDENTS WILL NOT BE TOLERATED. STAND DOWN IN THREE MINUTES OR WE WILL BE FORCED TO TAKE ACTION,] a loudhailer echoed across the streets.

The warning was not heeded by anyone in the protesting crowd, with each person fighting for a multitude of reasons. Those that tried to run from the fight were chased down by the thugs, forcing them to fight back to defend themselves.

[TIME'S UP. MOVE IN!]

The enforcers marched forward in a row, with protesters lashing out at them in the heat of the battle. They were immediately pinned down and arrested by the better-equipped enforcers before being hauled off to a detention center.

At the top of a building, Gordon peered through the lens of the light-capturer machine. "Magnification lenses seem to be doing pretty well. We're getting a lot of good images here."

"Why are we filming the protest?" Reese asked Kyle, who was staring intently at the leader of the protest.

"The enforcers are our very first customer. This is not the first time this protest has happened," Kyle explained slowly, turning to face Reese to observe his reaction. *He was originally a university professor, so he may have some issues...*

Reese wasn't dumb, immediately getting the gist of it. "We're selling them a movie showing how violent the protesters are."

"Yes, the revenue and the recognition of our movie company will spread even faster with the support of the enforcers. This will help us offset the cost of the building."

"Monetizing influence, I understand." Reese nodded his head.

"I would have expected you to be more displeased."

"Before I was kidnapped, I would have thrown a tantrum at this. But after... I can clearly tell some corners have to be cut if I want to live and see my invention through," Reese explained, though a hint of wariness could be seen in his eyes. *Kyle may very well try to kill me or have me removed if I ever go against his plans...*

"That's good, then." Kyle smiled as though nothing was wrong, patting Reese on the back. "Gordon, I think that should be enough footage for now."

Gordon nodded. "Right. But what do we do about the audio recordings?"

"The thugs will bring them back to our base. Let's wrap it up."

* * *

The red-robed person was tossed into the holding cell along with a group of protesters. He had been badly beaten by the enforcers during an interrogation, his skin raw and his robe nearly ripped to shreds. "Brother Long Hua, are you okay?" One of the protesters quickly moved over to check his wounds.

"Thank you for your concern, brother. This is part of the tribulations the Goddess has given us, so I will bear the pain." Long Hua struggled to get up.

"Damn these enforcers!" Another protestor chimed in as he slammed the wall.

"Fret not, my brothers. I have been to many other countries—it takes time, effort, and most importantly, persistence."

The other protesters' eyes lit up, quickly clamoring around Long Hua. "So it is true! You have visited other countries!"

"Indeed I have, and the number of our brothers has stretched far and wide across countless sovereignties."

"Even in Versia?"

"Oh, far more than Versia and the Yual Dominion. Hwayul, Irimeo, and Kharaku—those are the major countries that I have visited thus far, not to mention the innumerable towns and cities that fall in between jurisdictions."

"That's strange," a protestor interrupted. "My mom is from Hwayul and I never heard anything about this religion before."

"Of course—our brotherhood is repressed across the entire continent, so it is no wonder that the news regarding us is heavily controlled! The governments do not want such a religion to become dominant."

"Ah, that makes sense," the protesters all murmured in agreement.

"But this also means that the movement is suffering heavily. We need money for the cause, to further support our fight against unilateral oppression."

"How will the money be used?"

"As our missionaries are ostracized and shunned widely, the money will be used on smuggling us into various cities, as well as daily necessities."

The protesters and Long Hua talked for another hour or two, with Long Hua continuously preaching to them, increasing their zealousness.

Soon, an enforcer opened the holding cell's gate, releasing them. "Don't you idiots think about trying to raise another riot anytime soon. Especially you, Long Hua. This is the second time—go against the Sanctum of Yual one more time, and you'll be sentenced to slavery in the mines."

"The laws of your countries do not bind me as much as the Word of the Goddess."

"Whatever, fuck off." The enforcer shooed them off. The protesters walked off together toward their previous gathering point, where some of the more persistent protesters were already waiting.

"Brother Long Hua, I will donate a few hundred rakels to the cause," one of the protesters quickly offered, clearly enticed by the prospect of social change.

"Me too, anything to change the prohibition!"

The protesters all stood in solidarity, handing over rakels to Long Hua. "My brothers, your stay in heaven next to our Goddess will be glorious. Your graciousness will be remembered for centuries, unlike those who rest on their laurels, lording over us!"

"Yeah!"

"Our compassion far surpasses theirs. However, it is not the right time to push for the cause immediately now. We must bid our time, slowly building our strength. I will contact all of you soon. For now, focus your eyes on the final goal, and persist!"

"Yes, Brother Long Hua!"

Long Hua left the area, holding on tightly to the bag of rakels he had just collected from the protesters. He glanced behind him a couple of times, and as soon as he was a few urban blocks away, he quickly made a sharp turn into an alleyway.

Reaching into a hidden bag lodged behind a trash pile, he patted the grime off of it before pulling out a new set of clothes. He stuffed the red robe and headset into the bag and placed it back. A grin appeared on his face as he double-checked the number of rakels he had managed to get. *Looks like I've exhausted this sector—perhaps it's time to move onto the next one.*

As he strolled out of the alleyway, he was suddenly approached by a well-dressed gentleman, who was clearly muscular under the impeccable formal suit. "Brother Long Hua, I have finally found you! But why are you not dressed in your red robe?"

Long Hua was caught off-guard, quickly coughing and clearing his throat. "Ahem, I need to lie low for a while in order to avoid being arrested by the enforcers once more." He quickly hid the bag of rakels behind his back, smiling genially at the gentleman. "Are you one of the followers of Nona as well?"

"Yes, I was very inspired by your passionate speech during the protest yesterday!" The gentleman nodded his head.

"Good, but this is not a good time for us to discuss such things out in the open. I'm sure you understand how the enforcers are."

"But of course! I have a wagon ready nearby if you need me to ferry you anywhere. Perhaps I can offer a tithe of my own as well at my very own restaurant..."

Long Hua's eyes glinted with greed as he stood further upright, enhancing his "holy posture." "The Goddess will bless you for your offering, my brother. Lead the way."

They entered a simple arctech wagon, though Long Hua noticed a lingering smell that he could not quite put his finger on. *Potions? A bit suspicious for a restaurant owner... but it is good to have a wealthy supporter.* Long Hua wouldn't say no to being treated like a king.

The gentleman motioned for the driver to carry on while smiling widely at Long Hua. "I am thoroughly impressed with how well you riled up the crowd. You have an elegant way with words."

"All thanks to the Goddess Nona, who has blessed me to be her mouthpiece. To be able to have my words heard by the masses is my only goal."

"Hmm, but your skills seem to be underutilized. Such a shame. Also, judging from the bag of rakels, that doesn't seem to be your only goal."

Long Hua immediately squinted, his expression souring. "You're not a follower. Let me out immediately."

"Long Hua—or should I call you by your real name, Selas? Born in the Hwa Dynasty and raised in Versia, joined the military at the age of 13. Dishonorably discharged under General Javel for selling and trading contraband goods, as well as selling classified information to other countries. Also publicly charged for leading an insurrection against the ruling Versian government."

Long Hua brandished a knife from his clothes, aiming it at the gentleman. "I don't know how you got that information, but know that you are now dead to me."

Before Long Hua could do anything even more, the gentleman lunged forward, with the knife striking against a hidden vambrace under the formal suit, clanging against the armor. In a rapid combo, the gentleman grappled Long Hua and twisted his wrist, forcing him to drop the knife as he screamed in agony.

"ARGGHHH! W-who…WHO THE FUCK ARE YOU?!"

"Your new owner. Your skills will be put to a far better use than scamming the locals."

Chapter 49

Hypermall

One month later...

Baron Cain shifted his gaze uneasily as he adjusted his necktie and collar, glancing around the ballroom nervously. It was packed, with many noble families laughing and eating happily, mingling with each other.

"Ah, Cain Detrius. It's been a while since we met." A lesser noble walked up to him.

"Indeed. I believe the previous gathering two months ago, the New Year celebration, was the last time we met." Baron Cain focused his attention on the short, stocky man, who clearly had an ulterior motive instead of just small talk.

"Yes, you don't usually come to any other gatherings apart from these quarterly ones, don't you? I do have a few acquaintances that would be more than happy to have your company. There is room for tangible benefits here."

"I will consider it; however, right now I have my hands full."

"Ah, that ugly building in the South Sector that has just been built? What an eyesore that is, and to think it was built by the common folk. How repulsive. I assume you're going to take it down?"

"I am working on it," Baron Cain curtly replied. *Mind your own business, you fucking twat.* If the lesser noble next to him was just a common folk or an inquisitor, he would have him caned or whipped immediately.

However, even though the lesser noble did not hold a land or title, he and everyone else here had some form of ties with each other due to inter-familial marriages. Baron Cain eked out a fake smile as the lesser noble continued to talk his ears off, obviously intending to pry out what the baron's next steps were.

"I've heard the construction union is extremely unhappy about how the building was done. Rumor has it that it was a brand new construction company that seems to be building at near cost rather than matching union prices."

Baron Cain simply nodded in response, unwilling to divulge any further. Indeed, he knew that Kyle was the one who had set up the new construction company. The building was fairly innovative in some aspects, with the construction company filing for intellectual property protection from him.

He had yet to approve the process, but he was naturally afraid of antagonizing Kyle—it was only through the compromise they made that the spread of repeater handguns was stopped indefinitely. Kyle had kept true to their word, with no more handguns hitting the black market.

However, he did not underestimate Kyle, knowing that the man could retaliate against any perceived aggression from his side by releasing a hidden stash of handguns. It was what he would have done in his position as well, after all. In short, he could not do anything to Kyle on the outside. The gang leader seemed to have him in a stranglehold for now.

Kyle did not push the baron too much, falling in line with the other gangs and also providing him with a tithe of their profits on the same percentage as the Ardent Cretins. This assuaged the baron's ego, knowing that whatever profits the Seven Snakes made, he would have a cut of it. Otherwise, he would have blocked all land deed sales to the Seven Snakes.

He swirled the wine in his glass with his left hand, the hilt of his handgun tapping against the interior of his suit. He had followed Kyle's advice and left it in a thick metal safe, saving it from whatever methods of arctech deactivation Kyle had. A team under his payroll was already trying to reverse-engineer the handgun as well as come up with a replica. *Maybe I can sell such an invention to the military myself.*

"Announcing the entrance of Count Leon!" a servant called out loudly, with the grand double doors of the ballroom revealing a blonde-haired man dressed in a fully decorated blue uniform, walking in with a big smile.

The lesser nobles and barons clapped as Count Leon walked in, his features dazzlingly handsome. He walked up briskly to the front of the ballroom, swiveling around on his heel before facing the audience.

"Fellow members, thank you all again for attending this quarterly gathering of Raktor. I understand that many of you have pressing issues to petition me, and today is exactly the day to do so. However, before I start, I would like to say a word to honor one of our own, who has done a tremendous job. Baron Cain, please." Count Leon motioned to the baron, who was slightly shocked.

As Cain walked up, his brain was running through all the reasons why he was called up. In fact, the very reason why he was so nervous at the start was that he thought that Count Leon would admonish him for losing the guns in the first place.

"Baron Cain is an exemplary ruler—he was able to quell and root out a foreign power's attempt at stealing our technology. With such extensive evidence of Versia's interference in our affairs, we now have justification for retribution and to seek reparations from Versia. Not only that, he did it all in a span of three months, stabilizing the South Sector!"

Cain smiled as he gently bowed to the clapping audience, though his eyes were still glancing at the count's ecstatic expression. *So Count Leon made some money off threatening Versia, thanks to my initial failure, while I got nothing but an irritating gang leader on my side. How convenient.*

* * *

"Quickly, quickly! Ollie, we're going to be late!" A kid slapped another kid right on the face, causing him to jolt awake.

"Late? Late for what?"

"The opening of the new... erm... arcade? Shopping arcade. Something like that?"

"Shopping? We have no money even to buy groceries, let alone go shopping! Are you sleepwalking? Shut up and let me sleep."

"I heard that there would be free candy given out!"

"We're going immediately!" Ollie shot up from his makeshift bed on the hard warehouse, changing into his clothes quickly without missing a beat. The abandoned building they lived in was terribly rundown, the paint on the walls clearly peeling off, while the double-decker beds creaked loudly as other kids also scrambled to get ready.

Ollie cupped his hands under a water tap, wincing from the near ice-cold water, before splashing his face and rubbing with an obviously used towel. "Come on, Ollie, quick!"

"I'm coming, I'm coming!" Ollie scampered out of the room, running down the hallway with the rest of the kids. However, the boy suddenly came to a halt, stopping right outside a makeshift tent barricaded by rusty barrels and dirty clothes. "Mister, do you want candy? I can bring some back for you!"

"Thank you kindly, but there's no need to. You go enjoy yourself now." The old squatter smiled weakly, obvious beads of sweat trickling down his wrinkles and chaffed skin.

Ollie nodded, sprinting off to catch up with the group of kids. They laughed and shouted as they ran out onto the streets, avoiding the scowling pedestrians and raging wagon drivers. "Where's the new shopping arcade? Which street is it?"

"I heard it's a single building with thousands of shops inside!"

"Thousands? How is that possible? Don't joke around; I work at the factory part-time! Even *I* know you can't fit in that many."

"It's true! I heard Guang Hwa say it himself! He even told me directly that we get a free hot bath when we get there!"

"Okay, now that's too farfetched!" OIlie panted as he sprinted, slowing down to a walk. "They'll never let us into that place now—even the public baths don't accept us!"

"I'm serious, Ollie, come on!"

The kids ran down a series of blocks and finally reached an extremely crowded cross junction. They could barely see above the heads of the adults that were all standing there, but they knew the crowd was ogling *something*. "Let's squeeze to the front!"

They used their small bodies to push through the legs of the crowd, weaving through as they managed to get near the front. As they got closer, they began to hear a voice speaking passionately as it was propagated over multiple arctech radios spread across the street. "That's the guy! That's Guang Hwa!"

[Today marks the beginning of a new era in this district. The building behind me offers the best services, food, and entertainment, at a level unheard of in this district, not to mention the very first light-thrower theater!]

The crowd murmured between each other, all of them gradually becoming more excited. Word of the invention of the light-thrower had been spread quite thoroughly, especially with the enforcers using it to improve their reputations. Many of them had already seen movies of the protesters attacking the enforcers, only to end up arrested.

[Fret not—the first meal, item, and theater ticket you buy in this shopping mall is free today!]

"FREE?!" One of the crowd members was shocked, his excitement organically spreading to the people around.

[That is right. The Golden Snake Construction Company is proud to sponsor the opening day of this building. As its spokesperson, I shall now declare the building—OPEN!]

Guang Hwa turned around and cut a symbolic ribbon, much to the fanfare of the people. The floodgates literally opened, with the crowd rushing forward to enter the building. However, the members at the front of the crowd immediately slowed down upon seeing the fifty or so Seven Snakes associates, all armed and armored, serving as the private guards for the shopping arcade.

There were even enforcers stationed at the entrance, glaring down at the approaching crowd members. The mob immediately calmed down, word traveling rapidly from the front to the back.

"Shit, the enforcers are here! Don't push!"

"Why the fuck do you care about the enforcers—the stuff in that shopping arcade is free! We have to move before it's gone!"

"Idiot! Have you not seen how badly the protesters fared when they attacked the enforcers?"

"You're the idiot! I was there at the protest myself; it was the thugs who attacked first!"

"Don't lie to me! I saw the light-thrower pictures; it was clearly the protesters who attacked first!"

Just like that, the effect of the edited movie Kyle and the enforcers had distributed began to take root in the people, instilling them with more fear and less inclination to fight against the enforcers.

The crowd began to queue up in an orderly fashion, guided by the enforcers and the Seven Snakes guards. Ollie and the other kids quickly ran up to Guang Hwa, swarming him. "You promised us candy, Guang Hwa!"

"My name is Long H—oh, hi kids!" Guang Hwa caught himself before he leaked his old name. Revealing it will be far too dangerous, the name Guang Hwa only being a moniker. He squatted and rubbed the nearest kid's hair playfully. "Yes, of course, there's candy! There's a candy shop right inside. Just queue up, and you'll get it in an instant! First taste is free!"

Ollie immediately queued up. The Seven Snakes guards vetted each individual, checking them for hidden weapons and so on and ultimately allowing them to enter. Ollie peeked through the queue, already seeing people browsing the candy shop and clothing stores beyond the glass doors.

As Ollie walked up to the guard, the guard blocked his path and pointed him to another entrance at the side. Ollie noticed that the guards were redirecting all the unkept and shabbily dressed folks there, causing him to get mad. "HEY! YOU'RE DISCRIMINATING!"

"Go to that entrance, or you won't be able to get in."

Ollie was about to grumble before Guang Hwa suddenly bent over next to him, smiling at him. "Don't worry, we just have to get you cleaned up!"

"The last person to say that to me robbed me of everything! You think I'll believe a cunt like you?" Ollie retorted, about to storm off when his friends quickly stopped him.

"Fine. How about this? All of you kids can follow me in. Surely I can't rob all of you at the same time, right?"

"YAY, GUANG HWA!" The kids screamed his name, running forward quickly into the side entrance. Ollie followed along warily, still keeping an eye out for anything suspicious. However, as soon as he entered the side entrance, his jaw dropped immediately. "This... This is madness!"

In front of him was the interior of a wide indoor bath house, with more than thirty separate pools and a thousand showering cubicles, and it seemed that there was still more construction going on in the upper levels from the thumping sounds above as well as the Seven Snakes associates lugging material up.

Naturally, the kids did not care, immediately stripping their clothes off and placing them on   a shelf before trying to sprint into the pools. However, Guang Hwa quickly stepped in front of them, blocking them. "HEY! YOU PROMISED US A HOT BATH!"

"I did, but you have to shower first!"

The water coming out of the shower was heated, much to the surprise of Ollie, who had lived his entire life with nearly cold water, save for the heated barrels in his squatter tent. He closed his eyes and let the hot water wash the sludge and stains that had been on his body for months, his mind in pure bliss.

"Scrub! Scrub hard!" A few of the workers in the bathhouse came to pass the kids a simple bristle scrub, with Ollie recognizing one of the workers. "Bola? How did you get here? I thought you were working at a construction site!"

"Ollie! You made it! I got a job from the Golden Snake people; they pay real good money, and you get to almost live like a king on your off days. You know there's a dorm for workers here, too? It's amazing!"

Ollie was even more shocked, his mind in turmoil as he continued to listen to his friend gush about how the work life was here and his time hanging out with the Seven Snakes. *This... This is it! This is my ticket out of the slums!*

Chapter 50

Collusion

The opening day of the shopping arcade was in full swing, with hundreds of visitors flocking toward the shopping malls.

Kyle watched the entire affair from the top-floor office's balcony, overlooking the front lobby of the shopping arcade, a mere five stories above. Keith was already giddy with excitement, watching the visitors browse the various stalls. "This is it! I can smell the money!" Keith laughed, the grin on his face nearly permanent.

"Don't get ahead of yourself—we need to make sure the first light-thrower show is perfect," Kyle warned. "Have the associates patrol the floors regularly, especially the bathhouse."

Keith quickly calmed down, nodding in agreement. "Got it. I'll keep an eye out."

"Good." Kyle exited the office, intending to make a tour around and ensure everything was going according to his plan.

The shopping arcade layout was simple—he decided not to innovate too much lest unknown organizations be watching him. It was clear to him that he was not the only one aware of Galactic Era technology, which meant he had to keep a low profile.

As such, each of the companies he established had a figurehead in place to serve as the public face. If Kyle wanted to grow his influence legally, he needed frontmen to absorb the shock and hate where necessary. Of course, the locals knew that he was the main guy in charge, but that was not the case for foreigners and other districts' residents who would come over to patronize the "shopping arcade."

Even if the enforcers and lesser nobility knew who he was and how much he controlled, it was still better to stay out of the public spotlight as much as possible—no reason to pose front and center just to jeopardize his position.

Kyle reached the bottom of the lobby through an arctech elevator, feeling the cool wind that blew through the corridor of the shopping arcade. He limited the innovations within the shopping arcade to three main points: temperature control, light-thrower cinema, cleaning inventions

These three innovations are hardly revolutionary—they should not freak out anyone working with Galactic Era tech... Kyle was acutely aware of his animosity with Versia now, especially Harrison, who seemed to have targeted his technology. He had no doubt that the Ilysian Punks and those who were backing them from beyond the border would return to harass him or to take revenge. *I may need to go to Versia eventually to settle this. Perhaps I can gain something there to use as leverage against the Ardent Cretins.*

Kyle didn't know what to expect in Versia yet, but as long as there were benefits to be had, Kyle would grasp the opportunity as hard as he could.

As he walked out to the front lobby, he noticed Guang Hwa smiling at a group of reporters, his face covered in makeup to make him look like a completely different individual, lest he be recognized as Brother Long Hua or worse, his real identity as Selas.

"President Hwa, can you tell me what inspired you to start such a large project?"

"Of course. The Golden Snake Construction Company is, first and foremost, dedicated to the betterment of the common folk. We want to improve the standard of living for everyone in our district. However, it is not limited to just this district alone—we would like to extend our hand to everyone in the city of Raktor to come and visit at least once!"

"Offering free entry to the bathhouse for everyone seems to be a completely unprofitable venture; how is the company funding any of this? The cost to clean such a large bathhouse meant to serve thousands will be astronomical!" A reporter jabbed an arctech radio in front of his face, obviously trying to dig out some dirt.

"Indeed it would be... if we were relying on current technology. However, we have partnered with our sister company, Cobra Cleaning Solutions, in order to alleviate such a cost. I cannot divulge further as the innovations are a secret. However! Today, on this glorious opening day, we will be showcasing the first public screening of a light-thrower show!"

"A light-thrower show? Is it the same machine that the enforcers have been using to campaign recently?"

"Indeed, it is. The enforcers have worked very closely with our new theater company—Silver Snakes Productions. And speaking of the devil, here he is!"

The reporters turned to see the Seven Snakes guards clearing a path as a luxurious arctech wagon pulled up, with Reese stepping out in a slick tuxedo, his hair clearly well-done and his skin glistening in the daylight.

Kyle glanced over to a Seven Snakes associate who was filming the entire thing with a light-capturer. He walked up to the associate and lightly tapped him on the shoulder. "Don't aim at the reporters, aim at Reese."

"U-Uh, yes sir right away!" The associate was nearly shocked to death by Kyle's sudden approach, hastily repositioning to get the correct viewing angle.

The reporters immediately swarmed Reese as he got out of the wagon, clamoring and asking him questions. "One at a time, people, one at a time!"

"Reese, you have been credited with the invention of the light-capturer and light-thrower—how do you feel right now?"

"I feel vindicated. I am proud and happy that there were so many people who came out in support of my work. It has been a long hard journey with many obstacles, but I am glad to say that today is a new era in theater and the entertainment industry!"

Reese continued to answer questions with a steadfast expression, his eyes winking at Kyle, who hung back. Kyle nodded his head, satisfied with the performance so far.

The crime lord walked around the perimeter of the shopping arcade, heading toward what was set up to be a transportation hub of sorts. Dozens of arctech wagons were here, with many local residents disembarking and entering the shopping arcade.

He watched as a packed arctech wagon entered one of the berths, unloading a dozen families who looked as though they were coming to a theme park. He spotted Monica in the front passenger seat of the wagon, who waved to him.

"How's the transportation so far?" Kyle asked as he approached.

"Working fine. As you can see, I managed to negotiate a fair working wage for all the drivers here; they won't have any qualms about what we're doing," Monica replied as she glanced around suspiciously, her eyes locked on an enforcer who was helping to guard the perimeter of the shopping arcade as well. "We working with them now?"

"It's complicated. They won't arrest us outright, but if they see it right in front of their faces, they'll act."

"Got it." Monica nodded before beckoning for Kyle to get on as well.

"Hey, you. Drive into the basement," Monica ordered the driver.

"Basement? How can you drive into a basement?" The driver was confused, glancing around.

"Idiot, it's at the end of the hub. I taught you during your induction. You need servicing; go there."

"Who says I need servicing?"

"Says me. You're working for me now, remember?"

The driver grumbled to himself as he restarted the arctech wagon, driving into a downward slope that led to an underground warehouse below the shopping arcade, where the unused wagons were stored.

"I'll take over from here; go wait in the break room." Monica urged the driver out, who quickly scampered away.

Monica drove the arctech wagon into a service workshop, where two Seven Snakes associates were already waiting. Kyle hopped out of the back of the wagon, motioning for the two associates to begin.

They began to remove the floorboard, revealing barrels of alcohol layered into the base of the wagon. Grunting as they lifted it and placed it onto a trolley, they followed Kyle from behind as he led into a double door at the back of the workshop, which opened to reveal a full-fledged pub, packed to the brim with customers.

The Seductive Serpent's branch had been open here, with Eric Dicar personally stationed at the mall. He was laughing as he served customers non-stop at the bar, happily explaining all of the different types of alcohol here. Kyle recognized nearly all the customers as regulars at the other Seven Snakes' businesses, noticing Karl and the factory workers partying at the back.

Eric noticed Kyle, his joyful expression quickly diminishing as he quickly sauntered over, bowing to Kyle.

"How's the bar going?"

"First day, and it's already a riot. Sales are through the roof. Honestly, you should've placed the brewery here." Alas, the new branch did not have space for the brewery.

"Better to keep things separate for now. Harder to track."

"Right. I heard Reese is already at the theater. You should head over."

Kyle nodded, heading to the projector room of the theater on the top floor of the shopping arcade. A group of associates were still running around in the room, setting up everything for the upcoming show.

"Ah, ah, ah. One two three, radio check." Gordon's voice boomed across the theater, blasting out from the various arctech radios placed around.

"Gordon, any issues?"

"Everything is working perfectly; we're good to go in a few minutes," Gordon replied without looking back as he double-checked the audio playback, making sure it was properly synchronized. "Sound is okay. So is the light-thrower. However, I've been monitoring the arcite fuel consumption of the entire building. Do we even have enough money to pay?"

"Only for the next three months."

"We need to find a more stable source of arcite ore; maybe we can set up our own energy company as well. Have you considered expanding to Versia?"

"Versia? Is it good for arcite ore?"

"Not as good as Tryas, but at least you don't run the risk of angering the nobility here."

Versia... I do have plans to head over eventually, but it is not the right time... Kyle could hardly leave the Seven Snakes as they were right now. With multiple legal companies in the spotlight, he knew enemies could come from anywhere.

"Anywhere that's closer to Raktor?"

"Hmm... we had an operation in the Culdao Peaks, and I recall it used to be an arcite mine. Perhaps you could find undiscovered veins there? I know the nobles gave up fighting the goblins, so there's a chance they missed something."

"I'll think about it."

The theater was already packed to the brim, with the seating capacity being five thousand and many more standing in the aisle. Reese was just about finished with his opening speech on the main stage.

"And without further ado, I present to you the first commercial movie by the Silver Snake Productions: Princess Rescue!"

Gordon flicked the light-thrower on while activating the audio playback device at the same time. The opening scene began to show on the grand white wall that was as smooth as marble, reflecting the images perfectly.

The audience gasped in awe as they saw the largest moving "painting" they had ever seen, complete with audio as well as a tribal drum beat echoing through the theater.

In the depths of the mountain, a lone princess captured by a goblin tribe cries for help... Who can save her?

"Kyaaaa! Somebody, save me!"

The princess's voice resounded, drawing the audience more and more into the scene.

An evil goblin grins widely as he steps closer to the princess. "No one's here to hear your screams nor save yo—"

Without warning, the light-thrower machine suddenly cut off, losing power completely. The arctech radio faltered too, the audio warbling and distorting as the theater was plunged into complete darkness.

"What? What's going on? Is this part of the show?"

"I can't see anything; what happened to the painting?!"

Kyle quickly grabbed an arctech radio off a nearby table, barking into it. "What's going on? Why isn't the backup kicking in?"

[Sir, someone sabotaged both the main and the backup arcite fuel generator. It's a complete mess in here!]

"Fuck! Get the associates in here now to handle the crowd. Guang Hwa, grab a loudhailer and calm down the crowd!" Kyle stormed out of the projector room and into the office. The entire shopping arcade had somehow lost power, with the arctech engravings originally powered by a single grid no longer working as expected.

Even the backup was not working, fueling Kyle's worst fears. Keith was already in the office, desperately trying to call an arcite fuel company. "We need an arcite fuel generator here as soon as... What do you mean no? I'm willing to pay five hundred thousand rakels—no, a million rakels for you to come down right now!"

Keith's face balked as the radio went silent, causing him to grip the table in anger. "Kyle, no company wants to help us at all! What's going on?! It feels like they are ganging up on us!"

"Even the ones we have a contract with?"

Keith nodded, with Kyle gritting his teeth. *It's too much of a coincidence.* Whoever sabotaged the opening day knew exactly what was going to happen, and there were a few people who would have the incentive to do so. *Could it be Harrison again? No. A Versian industrialist wouldn't have that much power in Raktor. Only a few other individuals would have such power...*

"Looks like it's time to have a chat."

Chapter 51

Sustainability

Three days later...

Sebastian sipped on a cup of tea at a luxurious restaurant in the Central Sector. As he placed the cup down, he could already hear agitated footsteps approaching him from behind.

"The great leader of the Seven Snakes, this agitated. You should be happier—your opening day for the shopping arcade went extremely well, save for the slight delay," Sebastian said without turning around.

"A delay you engineered."

"An unfounded accusation."

"I know the Ardent Cretins have a tight grip on the unions here. You've been pressuring them to increase the price of arcite fuel for us," Kyle said as he sat opposite Sebastian, his face clearly incensed.

"Mr. Kyle, I am a proponent of the free market. You cannot sincerely believe I am to blame for the increase in price. Perhaps the market has shifted significantly since you built the shopping arcade?"

"I doubt the market can shift enough for a company to be willing to renege on a prior contract."

"Perhaps the company may be facing certain personal issues of their own." Sebastian smiled.

"Personal issues created by you?" Kyle scoffed.

Sebastian sighed. "I do not control the decisions of business owners. You must understand that some of these businesses are also owned by foreigners like—and I certainly do not claim to influence all business decisions. If they decide to increase the price, I too am at their mercy. And I'd prefer not to retaliate, lest the Mad Dog get sent on us again."

"Let's cut to the chase. How much would it take for you to stand down?"

"Not everything is about money, Mr. Kyle. Isn't that why you provided an entire free bathhouse service to the entire district?"

"You want me to shut down the shopping arcade."

"Again, not my wishes. I do not speak for others. But right now, they are feeling very, very threatened by you. Who am I to restrain them? I am but one man."

"Seems that I have been talking to the wrong person then. My apologies." Kyle got up to leave, not bothering to talk any longer. It was clear that he and Sebastian would not be able to come to a compromise.

Kyle knew why Sebastian had launched an attack: the new shopping arcade was pulling in too many customers and causing the other businesses in the city to suffer. Coupled with the addition of a new transportation hub as well as a free bathhouse, the footfall was tremendous.

Landlords across the South Sector were losing their tenants as they were lured by the Golden Snake Construction with competitive rental rates and promises of increased traffic. Even local small gangs who ran a protection racket were also threatened by their food market stall owners escaping their grasp, all fleeing toward the shopping mall, selling affordable food to the poor who were already there for the free bathhouse.

Kyle already had plans to establish a cheap food market area next to the shopping mall to centralize the traffic further, increasing his power and influence. However, while he expected local business owners to be angry, he did not expect Sebastian to get involved, especially considering that the shopping arcade was nearly five districts away from where the Ardent Cretins ruled.

He's threatened by the growing influence I have over the local population. Kyle had been doing public projects ever since he joined—free soup kitchens, public cleanup events, and so on. He knew from centuries of crime in the Galactic Era that being in a gang meant finding a balance between the amount of good and evil done to society.

The addition of the shopping arcade was meant to make Kyle and the Seven Snakes nearly indispensable in the society of Raktor, where any attacks against them would suffer severe public backlash from the residents, who now had a taste of a higher standard of living thanks to the improved utilities and jobs provided by the gang.

However, this would not come to fruition as long as they did not have a stable supply of arcite ore. Even the black market was somehow afraid of selling directly to Kyle, forcing him to spend far more than the market price in order to get it.

It's an economic war.

Kyle headed back to the shopping arcade, where the footfall had significantly reduced compared to the opening day. The first light-thrower show was a complete dud, causing many to lose confidence in the shopping arcade.

In the office, the rest of the Seven Snakes' higher-ups were already discussing the situation. Keith noticed Kyle's entry, addressing the leader immediately. "It's not looking good, sir. Even our construction company is unable to get new building projects due to the perceived failure of the shopping arcade. Many of the lesser nobles are unwilling to give us the tender either, favoring other companies."

Damian nodded. "It's the same with food and water as well. The large suppliers of flour and fish are somehow refusing to supply any restaurant or stall owners under us. If we don't solve this issue by this month, most of them are not going to renew their tenancy contract, regardless of how much footfall we have."

"We need arcite fuel to keep up the transportation network. Forget about refueling the shopping arcade—they don't even want to refuel our wagons regardless of where we drive to." Monica grumbled.

Reese was clearly dejected, slumping into a chair. The first public showing of his invention had failed tremendously, causing his mood and motivation to plummet.

"The fucking Ardent Cretins need to be taken down a peg. Why can't we do the same thing we did with the Ilysian Punks and just bloody their nose for a bit?" Niko suggested.

"Are you crazy? We might have gotten larger over the past month, but we're nowhere close to matching the numbers the Ardent Cretins have. Hell, we might not even come out unscathed if we fought the Red Lions right now!" Damian retorted.

"Has Wrent replied to our request for commercial contracts?" Kyle asked.

"No, sir. It seems the Ardent Cretins have already gotten to them."

"So we are truly alone in this war..." Kyle sat down at his desk, clasping his hands together as he racked his brain, formulating a quick plan.

"Let's summarize the situation: We *can* buy what we need; however, the prices are daylight extortion. We are being isolated by everyone under the Ardent Cretins' thumb."

"Yes, sir. Assuming we continue to buy at the current black market price we've been paying, we'll run dry in less than a month."

Keith nodded his head. "The main issue we need to tackle right now is how to get more arcite fuel. Any ideas?"

Damian raised his hand. "We could try strong-arming the companies into submission."

"Not feasible. The Ardent Cretins would be guarding them, and I do not want to come into a physical war with them."

"I did mention we could either look to Versia or the Culdao Peaks for sources of arcite ore; however, it would be a tough ordeal to set up a transportation route that would not be hijacked or harassed by other gangs."

"So we're isolated, unable to expand, and unable to trade outside the city," Kyle summarized.

Keith squinted his eyes. "You don't seem particularly flustered. Do you already have a plan?"

* * *

Gordon's office was now littered with countless pieces of paper as he and Reese argued, continuously modifying a single engraving and jotting down the changes.

In the middle of the office was a dismantled light-capturer, as well as a pile of depleted arcite ore devoid of any energy.

Kyle was there too, his right hand holding a normal arcite ore while the other held a depleted one.

Arcite Ore
A condensed form of arcia energy, stored in a solid state.
Can be converted into a fuel form to power engravings.

Depleted Arcite Ore
Solid arcite ore but lacking in energy.
Cannot be used any longer.

The system says that it can't be used, but is that truly the case? Kyle knew that arcite fuel generators effectively extracted the energy from such ore into a liquid form, forming arcite fuel that would then provide power in a similar fashion.

Kyle posited that it was possible to refill the ore again with arcia energy, seeing as arcia energy could be converted into other forms of energy. He just had to find the right engraving.

"Okay, let's go over this again. The light-capturer can capture images by essentially capturing the rays reflected by them, which then exists as energy for a short period of time before the images are stored onto our reel," Gordon explained.

"Exactly, so what we need to do is modify the engraving such that the collected light energy will be pumped into the arcite ore!" Reese nodded his head in agreement.

"So why the hell are you making the engraving bigger before we even made any modifications?!"

"Right now, the engraving is far too small to see tangible results. The amount of light energy collected is miniscule—we need a larger one to prove it works!"

While the two of them chased down a path of solar energy hinted to them, Kyle was focused on finding a way to convert mechanical energy and pumping it back into the arcite ore. *The efficiency would be much lower, but it would be a form of regenerative fuel as well. Perhaps this would allow me to harvest wind energy as well.*

If Kyle had his way, he would have built a partial Dyson sphere around a star or spread out a net of dark energy harvesters in deep space and be done with it, but he had to start small here.

He grabbed a copy of an arctech wagon's mechanical shaft engraving.

Arctech Wagon's Shaft Engraving
The workhorse of the industrial era.

Converts arcite energy into mechanical motion with 50% efficiency.

He created a simple prototype setup where the mechanical shaft engraving could be turned continuously with a rotating handle while the engraving was trailed off to form a connection to a metal plate on which the depleted arcite ore rested.

Turning the shaft as fast as he could, the metal joints of the test setup creaked as the rotation nearly shook the frame apart. However, he could see a trickle of arcia energy being deposited back into the arcite ore. *It seems that the engraving is tailored in one direction. I will have to reverse-engineer it.*

Kyle had experience with the engravings, working together with Reese and Gordon to break down the base parts. Reese brought his entire book collection of arctech design, with Kyle spending two days just reading through the books, learning how to break down the engravings into modular parts.

It wasn't as easy as him simply duplicating the engraving like he had done in the past. All of the engravings he had done before were simple copycats of the textbook he had or a copy of what the goblin shaman had recorded in its den. He had never delved deep enough into the inner workings of an engraving.

His proficiency in arctech engraving began to grow over the days as he continuously iterated his prototype setup, trying new modifications. Every try seemed to result in failure, with the efficiency of conversion being less than one percent. *It's not enough; I need a higher percentage if we are to survive this economic war!*

A week passed, and even Gordon and Reese were starting to lose hope. Kyle had lost count after five hundred tries, simply going through the motions and continuing to tweak the engraving. As he engraved the next design iteration onto yet another metal shaft, a new system message popped up.

Title Obtained: Arcia Engraver (Intermediate)
Carving away like a madman is a good way to move up in the world.
+10 INT, +6 DEX, +20% chance at improving quality of final arctech equipment.

His brain was immediately loaded with information on how to improve the quality of the arctech engraving, his hands working quickly as he threw away the half-engraved metal pipe and started anew. His fingers were rock-steady as he slowly etched into the surface of the metal, even and distributed. Kyle even began to feel a slight sense of disgust when he recalled the now relatively shoddy work he had done in the past.

Completing the engraving, he placed the completed metal shaft into the test setup, the mental exhaustion of working over a week already taking its toll on his brain despite the consumption of Stamina Potions. He spun the handle again, with the shaft's engraving clearly working better and smoother.

The depleted arcite ore seemed to recover at a visible rate, though it was still not as efficient as the conversion from arcite to mechanical energy.

Mechanical Arcia Regenerator

Put your muscles to work.

Converts mechanical energy to arcia fuel with a 10% efficiency.

"Better than nothing."

Welcome to Raktor!

Kyle Hawthorn: Level 15

Max HP: 52(+0)(+0)(+0) | **Max MP:** 23(+0)(+5)(+0) | **Max STA:** 52(+0)(+0)(+0)

Status Effects

None

Stats

Race: Human | **Class:** Crime Lord | **Subclass:** Unassigned

STR: 102(+29)(+0)(+0) | **DEX:** 97(+44)(+0)(+0) | **INT:** 96(+55)(+3)(+0)

VIT: 67(+2)(+3)(+0) | **CHA:** 21(+10)(+1)(+0) | **Free Points:** 0

Equipment
Necklace of Healing (Basic)
For the timid of heart.
+3 INT, +3 VIT, +1 CHA
[Active] Heal (Basic): Restore a tiny amount of health.
Cooldown: 10 seconds

Magus Ring of Theorin (Intermediate)
A ring from a former wielder of arcia.
+5 MAX MP, +25% MP regeneration

Projectile Defense Vambrace (Basic)
Blocks a certain number of projectiles when activated.
+3 DEX, +2 VIT
[Active] Point Defense: Fires energy bolts to block up to ten projectiles.
Cost: 3 MP   Duration: 1 minute or 10 successfully blocked projectiles
Cooldown: 15 minutes

Skills
Intimidation Aura (Basic)
Control those who oppose you with fear.
+50% intimidation success chance.
Duration: 5 minutes   Cooldown: 1 day

Penchant for Violence (Basic)
A good crime lord must be fluent in the language of the underworld.
All combat stats temporarily increase by 100% for a short duration.
Duration: 15 seconds   Cooldown: 10 minutes

This is My Turf (Basic)
No one gets close to you without your word.

Creates a selective domain that enemies can't approach.

Duration: 30 seconds   **Cooldown:** 3 hours

Designate Follower (Basic)

Can't be a crime lord without underlings.

Marks any sapient being as a follower, enabling telepathic communication.

Current Limit: 1 Follower   **Range:** Limited

Titles

Former Crime Lord

A bigshot in your previous life. So much for that, huh?

+10 INT, +10 CHA

Martial Arts Expert

The best things between you and death are your fists.

+10 STR, +10 DEX

Murderer

Everyone has to start somewhere.

+2 STR, +10% increased damage to humans.

Potion Inspector (Intermediate)

It seems that you are somewhat of a scientist yourself.

+10 INT, increased accuracy of the examined potion's description.

Potion Crafter (Intermediate)

This title was supposed to be given on successful potions, but the failures are pretty hard to watch.

+10 INT, increased accuracy of examined potion's description, +10% chance to craft an intermediate potion when using basic materials. +5% chance of discovering basic potion recipes per attempt. This effect can be stacked and is reset on discovery.

Healer (Basic)

This doesn't seem like the right way to use healing...
+5 INT, +10% healing effectiveness

Martial Arts Instructor (Basic)

With great power comes great muscular bodies—apart from yours.
+5 STR, +3 DEX, +10% ability to break down moves.

Arcia Engraver (Intermediate)

Carving away like a madman is a good way to move up in the world.
+10 INT, +6 DEX, +20% chance at improving quality of final arctech equipment.

Torturer

Pain is sometimes the best language.
+5 INT, +2 STR, +2 DEX, + 10% torture effectiveness.

Tracker (Basic)

Helps when those keys are always misplaced.
+5 DEX, +25% increased vision and hearing range.

Goblin Observer (Intermediate)

Entering the den of a goblin tribe alone is quite a feat.
+10 DEX, +50% success at learning goblin language.

Goblin Killer (Basic)

Greenskin bad, humanskin better.
+10 STR, +5 DEX, +2 VIT, +10% damage to goblin-type enemies.

Arctech Gunsmith (Basic)

Death handcrafted and delivered at high speeds.
+5 INT, +3 DEX, +10% chance to craft an intermediate pistol when assembling.

Chapter 52

Hierarchy

"My God. You actually did it!" Reese celebrated as he and Gordon watched Kyle demonstrate the Mechanical Arcia Regenerator. It was quite a sight to watch the Seven Snakes' boss sweat while turning a prototype shaft.

"But the efficiency is extremely low—how are we going to find such a large source of mechanical energy in the city?" Gordon pondered.

"Perhaps we could build a waterwheel on the main river that runs through the city?"

"No way—the Ardent Cretins will never allow us to move that blatantly if they could. Also, we would have to submit a petition to Count Leon. We might have to either place it on our own buildings that we already own or look further."

Kyle raised his hand and stopped the conversation. "Let me worry about that part. How's the progress on the modification of the light-capturer engraving?"

"It's not working, sadly. I believe the concept has been implemented correctly, but there's simply not enough light available to be concentrated on the engraving to make it even remotely possible. Based on our calculations, we would need to cover an entire district in such engravings to even power one floor of our new bathhouse."

Kyle looked at the dismantled light-capturer, bending over to sort through the separated parts. "Focus your efforts on concentrating the light onto the engraving itself. We can use the lens to redirect light to the engraving."

Reese was initially perplexed before his face lit up in understanding, nodding vigorously. Gordon was still trying to figure out what Kyle was saying. "Wait, doesn't that mean we still have to place that many concentrating mirrors around either way?"

"Yes, but making the mirrors is easier and cheaper than placing engravings that could be easily damaged by the weather all over the city."

"Exactly! We can funnel a large area of light onto a single engraving, reducing our material cost!" Reese excitedly explained, working out a plan immediately.

The three of them got into action, planning exactly how much would be needed. Kyle picked up the prototype light-converting engraving that the two of them had been working on for the past week.

Light Arcia Convertor

Harness the power of daylight in the palm of your hand.
Converts visible light waves to arcia energy with 5% efficiency.

"The efficiency of this engraving is far too low... only a few percent," Kyle pointed out, stunning Reese.

"How do you know the efficiency of the engraving without testing it?" Reese was slightly suspicious. Even he did not know the exact percentage, and he was the one who made it in the first place.

"I can tell from the differences between my mechanical engraving and this one. Here, have a look. This specific trace is shorter and wider, reducing the amount of arcia current loss and making it more resistant to interference from other traces..."

Kyle explained the understanding that he had gleaned from the activation of his Arcia Engraver title, enlightening Reese further and distracting him from his slip-up. "You're right, I never thought about that! And to think that I used to call myself a professor!"

"Also, you can consider modifying this part to be more lenient. Right now, it is limited to a specific band of frequency for visible light."

"Fre... What?!" Reese's eyes squinted once again.

"Right. Let me handle the modification of this engraving—you two work on the plan of materials needed. I will try to get the efficiency of this engraving as high as possible."

Kyle brought the prototype to another workshop, making sure the other two could not see him. Through his practice over the course of a week of modifying the mechanical engraving, he could now pinpoint the exact parts of the engraving that could be reworked.

Specifically, he intended to rework the frequency limitations of the light converter, enabling it to catch other forms of radiation as well. *As long as the rest still believe that it is only converting light, I should not be throwing too many danger signs.*

He reworked the frequency portion of the engraving before making four more copies in a bid to enhance it. The Arcia Engraver title gave him a twenty percent chance of gleaming new inspiration and raising the quality of the engraving, which then allowed him to learn more about what could be improved.

He had tried to do it multiple times with the mechanical engraving, but it seemed like there was a cap to the quality level of the engraving, so the amount of inspiration he could get was limited. It was as though the system interface had a hard limit on what improvements it could make to the engraving that Kyle worked on.

After repeating the same process on the light-converting engraving, Kyle began to get frustrated as he made his hundredth one over three days. He grumbled to himself as he made the next one. *Wasn't the chance supposed to be twenty percent? One in five? How is it possible?*

Just as he said that in his head, the title's effect triggered, giving a familiar surge of information to his brain and nervous system, his hands moving automatically to improve the engraving in front of him. *About damn time.*

Kyle picked up the completed engraving.

Electromagnetic Arcia Convertor
Harness the power of stars in the palm of your hand.

Converts electromagnetic radiation to arcia energy with a maximum of 67% efficiency, depending on frequency efficiency of 22% for visible light waves.

Not too shabby. If I could find a radioactive source... Kyle began to think about the Culdao Peaks. Perhaps he could begin mining there again. He had already sent Sasha back there a month ago to handle the goblin den as she saw fit.

Niko entered the workshop, bowing to Kyle. "Sir, you called for me before?"

"I need you to bring these mechanical engravings over to the goblin den at Culdao Peaks. Make sure the wagon is protected well—the Ardent Cretins will try their hardest to cut us off as much as possible. Hand them this document as well."

* * *

A week later...

Gulak let out a relaxed sigh as it soaked into a pool of hot water. Already, the vast improvements in the quality of life had made the goblin shaman forgo any thought of leaving the den or even attempting to rebel against Kyle. *Would be even better if the goblin envoys from the goblin kingdom never came at all—after all, we're at the edge of the Culdao Peaks.* For now, it decided to enjoy what it had.

"This... This is life," it remarked in a soothing, relaxed voice before a sudden splash of water went right into its large nostrils, causing it to gag and sneeze.

The goblin kids laughed as they played in the common pool, splashing around in hot water powered by the new arctech engravings layered into the stone walls.

"Stop disturbing me! I'm relaxing! You're ruining my moment!" Gulak raged and flung a handful of water back at the kids.

It expected the kids to fight back, but instead, the kids were horrified and began doggy-paddling and scrambling to the other end of the pool. "Hah! That's right! Me shaman! You bette—"

"Gulak, what are you doing here?" A familiar female voice caused it to tense up, one that has haunted every waking moment of Gulak's life since Kyle left.

Gulak gingerly turned around, smiling meekly as it slowly got up out of the pool. "Lady Merissa, I—"

"No excuses. Have you completed the installation of the wind converters and light converters? Have you completed the tunnel to Raktor?!"

"Yes... mostly."

"What do you mean, mostly?! Do you think we gave you the engravings for free? Is this bathhouse for free? You got a day to fix everything up, or else I'll tell Sasha."

"Tunnel cannot be finished that fast! Will take at least three more months!"

"Better than you wasting your fucking time here. MOVE!"

Gulak tensed up even more, nodding its head vigorously. "Yes ma'am!" It quickly scampered off, completely naked.

Merissa did not care at all when she saw the wrinkled genitals on full display, having lived with the goblins for close to four months now. She sighed as she continued her rounds through the goblin den, which had been reinvented to include various modernized features.

The lights were improved, as were utilities and the sewage system. The goblins were cleaner than ever before, and none of them complained about it. However, she still had to continuously scold the goblin workers who attempted to skive at every minute, forcing her and those under her to always be on the lookout.

On top of that, she had to make sure they continued to expand the tunnels toward Raktor. Kyle did not want to have a supply chain continuously running overground, which was prone to ambush and hijacking. Right now, they had already dug a few kilometers over the past four months, though it was getting harder to ventilate the tunnels. *Three more months till we reach the outskirts of Raktor. We need more workers!*

Merissa stormed back toward her office, where Feldon was already waiting for her. "When will I be able to return to Raktor? Am I not a movie star now?"

"You won't be a movie star until we establish a proper supply route of replenished arcite ore to the city! And besides, if you entered Raktor right now without a disguise, the Violet Demons would lynch you on entry."

Feldon was about to retort that he could act as a squatter in order to enter the city, but he knew Kyle would also find out about his departure. He could also hardly smuggle his entire family out of the goblin den, though life here had been relatively peaceful so far, save for the constant raid attempts from other gangs who were still trying to encroach on the Euria Seeds.

Before Merissa could continue scolding him, a burst of static erupted on the arctech radio mounted in the office. The bursts came in a specific pattern, causing Merissa's eyes to light up. "Call Gringer, Gobalt, and

Gulak immediately! Have them gather all the goblin warriors immediately!"

"What? I thought we were working on the supply of arcite ore?"

"Exactly! MOVE!"

The goblin den kicked into action, with the warriors forming up into groups. A few humans were embedded into their ranks, the humans being the squad leaders of the goblins.

They stood at attention at the entrance of the mine, with Gulak, Gringer and Gobalt standing at the front. The gates of the fort soon opened to reveal Sasha, who entered with bloody hands gripping a struggling goblin.

The goblin was noticeably different, with a tattoo marking his affiliation with another tribe. "Ahah!" Gulak exclaimed with joy upon seeing the predicament of the goblin.

Every goblin warrior shuddered with excitement, while Feldon was still at a complete loss. "Wait, what's happening?"

Merissa smacked the back of his head. "I covered this four days ago, you idiot! We're annexing another goblin tribe!"

Sasha made a few hand motions, and the warriors immediately followed her out of the mine to assault the neighboring goblin den. Trained like a paramilitary organization, the human squad leaders converted the sign motions into verbal orders for the goblins that did not understand.

Over the past week, Sasha had been implementing the same strategy that Kyle used to subjugate the first goblin den by stalking and hunting the members, which left the den to forage for food. Now with a significant force backing her, she did not need to stalk as long as Kyle did, enabling her to launch an assault immediately.

It was a nearly overwhelming victory, with the new battle tactics that Kyle and Sasha had drilled into the goblins, plus the ubiquitous use of crossbows and bows, giving them an immense advantage over the enemy, who still relied on brute force tactics.

Gulak gloated as it stepped into the enemy's den with its warriors, watching the enemy try to flee through the mining tunnels. The fighting was harsh and brutal, but the enemy goblin tribe stood no chance, even with all the traps and ambushes they set up.

Soon, the enemy goblin tribe's warriors were diminished, resulting in the complete surrender of the tribe. Gulak stood at the top of a rock formation, speaking to the enemy goblins. "Be happy! For I am Gulak, your new shaman! Your old shaman, weak and powerless! I, Gulak, will give you happiness!"

"No!" An elderly goblin stood up in defiance, pointing its wrinkly green finger with long yellow nails toward Gulak. "You work with humans! You are no longer goblin! We see your machines! Betrayal of ancestors!"

Gulak snapped his fingers, prompting Gringer to move forward with two warriors to grab the elderly goblin, dragging it out to the front as its children and relatives screamed and tried to pull him back. The warriors smacked and beat up those who resisted, while the elderly goblin was hoisted above, next to Gulak.

Gulak grinned as he pulled out from his belt a prototype handgun, planting the tip of the barrel right into the neck of the elderly goblin, blasting the brains of the goblins out in a spectacular splatter that showered onto the screaming goblins.

"Who else? WHO ELSE?!" Gulak roared, aiming the handgun toward the crowd. They all cowered in fear, and no one dared speak out. Gulak did not see them as goblins any longer; he only saw them as new slaves. He was already celebrating at all the slave labor he could now delegate. *My tribe shall no longer be slaves!*

"Good. First, it is time to work!"

Chapter 53

Ambush

Leyton breathed slowly as he lay flat under a shrub, the dense foliage masking his presence, save for a small little opening through which his eyes peered out, overlooking a sandy road long weathered by wagon wheels.

He gripped the arctech radio tightly, checking the volume dial on it. Setting it too loud might spook anyone nearby, and he couldn't talk loudly either. His left hand remained on a military-grade repeater carbine next to him as he continued observing any movements.

Suddenly, a loud roaring sound was heard next to him, causing him to tense up immediately. He soon realized it was the snoring of his partner, who was dozing off while both hands were still holding onto the rifle.

"Idiot, wake up!" Leyton hissed softly. "The fucking Seven Snakes will be coming anytime soon!"

The partner did not wake up until Leyton smacked the back of his head, jolting him awake. "What, where?! Are they here?!" he asked frantically, his eyes darting around.

"Shut up! If Gray finds out you've been sleeping on the job, you can forget about getting promoted next year."

The partner rubbed the back of his head gingerly, wincing as he relaxed. "Pah, you really believe the spiel Sebastian gives every year? They won't promote us—they need foot soldiers like us to do the dirty work. Ain't complaining; the pay's pretty good, and look at the slick weapons they gave us!"

Leyton didn't retort, knowing that there was truth to what his partner was saying. It's been a while since they left the slums three years ago to join the Ardent Cretins. Back then, their naïve eyes and attitude made them feel like they were kings of the world. Until they met the higher-ups and realized they never even made a dent in the social ladder, barely even moving up a rung.

Still, Leyton would not return to the slums willingly. He was far too addicted to the standard of living of a gang associate. That was exactly why they were here.

Suddenly, the distinctive sound of an arctech wagon began to loom from the path coming down from Culdao Peaks Town. The partner grinned as he clenched his rifle tighter, aiming down the iron sights, but Leyton didn't move yet, observing with his keen eyes.

The wagon soon came into clear view, chugging along slowly as it rattled down the sandy gravel path, bouncing with each pebble the wheels rolled over. The partner took aim but was blocked by Leyton quickly. "Stop, don't shoot yet!"

"What? Why? I thought we were supposed to shoot!"

"Not at every wagon that comes by, you idiot! We only want the Seven Snakes one—you want to be the reason we start a war with the Violet Demons?!" Leyton pointed to the edge of the wagon, which had a cryptic rune indicating that the merchant operating the wagon was under the protection of the Violet Demons.

"Right... Sorry." The partner sheepishly smiled.

Leyton turned on his arctech radio, speaking quietly into the receiver, "One sinner heading to Raktor."

[Copy that. Any signs of snakes?]

"No sir, nothing south."

[Roger. Keep looking.]

Leyton heaved a sigh of relief as he watched the wagon go past before scowling at his partner. "Next time, wait for me to make the call first, all right?!"

"All right, all right! I'm sor—"

Leyton quickly covered his partner's mouth, shutting him up. "Shut up and listen. You hear that?"

The partner's eyes widened with confusion, trying to hear as well. After a brief moment, he shook his head. He grabbed Leyton's hand and got it off his mouth, spitting out a glob of saliva. "What are you hearing?"

Leyton glanced around his surroundings, looking up at the tree branches. "It sounded like footsteps of humans…"

"Really?" The partner immediately tensed up, looking all around them too. He trusted Leyton's instincts, which was why they were paired as a spotter and a gunner duo in the first place.

However, the sound of an arctech wagon began to distract them and dominate the environment, following the same sandy road. This time, Leyton noticed no markings on the exterior of the wagon at all.

"Are we clear to shoot?" the partner asked hastily.

"Wait…" Leyton waited for the wagon to go past them before he checked the back. The familiar glow of arcite ore glinted blue through the seams of the cloth at the back. "Shoot! Shoot the wheels!"

The partner fired a round, cocking his gun and firing another. The two shots were spot on, hitting the spoke of the wheel and causing it to dent. The wobbling of the wheel caused the wagon to falter and skid off the road, slamming right into a tree trunk far away from the duo.

"Sir, snakes with blue spotted. Wagon down. Requesting hit."

[Good work. Moving in. Pincer from the back.]

"Yes, sir. Come on; we need to make sure no one makes it out alive." Leyton and his partner rose to their feet, helping each other up.

However, before they could even stand up straight, five shots of a handgun were fired toward the partner. The man's armor flared to life, firing point defense projectiles to block the shots, but two made it through and nailed him in the chest and neck, causing him to scream in a gurgle of blood as he fell over.

Leyton's training kicked in, and he immediately dived for cover behind a tree trunk as he readied his own rifle, cocking it. He peeked out from the side, trying to spot who was shooting at him, but the forest was suddenly quiet, as though nothing had happened.

Shit, I have to warn the others! Before Leyton could turn on the arctech radio again, a female figure dropped down from the tree branches above him, landing right in front of him. Leyton yelped as his vision was overwhelmed by an armored knee that smashed his nose right and slammed his head against the tree trunk.

His world spun as he slumped to the floor, dizzy from the concussive impact, while the female figure whistled with her free hand as the other held a prototype handgun. Leyton's eyes widened as he recognized the handguns. *The ones circulating in the black market a month ago? Weren't all of them destroyed?*

At the command of the whistle, three goblins sprinted over, quickly grabbing Leyton and the dying Ardent Cretins member. The duo was hauled off deeper into the forest.

Back at the road, the front of the wagon was smashed in as though the metal itself had wrapped around the tree trunk. Smoke rose from the machine while five armed soldiers appeared from the woods, each wielding military-grade guns and armor.

"Clear the area. Where's the driver?" the leader asked as one of the soldiers moved up and broke the door to the driver's seat open.

"Sir, there's no one inside! They must have rigged it to drive straight!"

The five soldiers immediately tensed up, holding their repeaters at the ready. "Retreat. We've been compromised."

"Sir, what about Leyton?"

"He's probably been captured already. Move!"

The five soldiers quickly moved through the forest away from the main road, continuously checking behind their backs. The leader began to spot signs of goblins stalking them from their left, leaping through the trees from branch to branch. "Fire a few shots in their direction! Scare them back!"

As they raised their repeaters to aim to the left, Sasha and the other goblins struck from the right, firing at them. Sasha emptied the entire clip of the handgun into one soldier, overwhelming his point defense engraving and killing him on the spot.

The sheer number of arrows also caused the point defense engravings to be powered down, enabling the goblins to attack with crossbows and bows.

Grunting as he hefted his repeater, the leader aimed with pinpoint precision, sniping the heads of the goblins, which resulted in five confirmed kills. After he had fired his twentieth shot, he pulled the trigger again to no effect, prompting him to reach for his belt for the next magazine.

In that split moment, Sasha sprinted toward him, forcing him to use both hands on his rifle to block a punch from Sasha's glowing right hand. The engraving on her hand boosted the force imparted, smashing the wooden cover of the repeater and bending the metal barrel hidden within.

The leader dropped the repeater immediately and threw a punch at Sasha, who blocked it with her left arm as she took a step back to avoid tripping on the dropped repeater, before lunging again with a kick from the right, nailing the leader right in the waist.

Sasha winced from the pain erupting from her shin that had smashed into the military armor, allowing the leader to recover and retrieve a small knife out, stabbing and slicing toward the woman.

"Men! Split up!" the leader roared, still intending to retreat. However, he could see from his peripheral vision that all his soldiers had already been knocked out by the sheer number of goblins. He could see from the branches that there were nearly fifty of those little green monsters.

"Shit!" the leader cursed as he tried to sprint away, only for a barrage of arrows to be fired toward him, piercing his flesh from behind and eliciting a scream of pain.

Sasha slowly walked up to the injured leader, bent over to grab him by the collar, and lifted him up. She inspected the military armor, noticing that it was similar to the ones the Seven Snakes had hijacked from the Ilysian Punks. *This... could be a problem.*

* * *

Haui smiled as he looked around his new store, right smack in the middle of the shopping center facing the front lobby. The workers were busy setting up the shelves to display all sorts of potions, while he pointed out where some of the equipment should be placed in the back room.

"Liking your new store?" Kyle asked as he entered, shaking hands with Haui.

"I am, indeed. Sometimes, I wonder why I have been hiding in that dodgy old little hut for such a long time."

"But you're not giving it up yet."

"Of course. A man of my intellect can surely handle two stores, can't he? I do have a few apprentices under me that can handle the more mediocre potions and their production."

"I was under the impression you were against selling potions at a cheaper rate to the... common folk."

"Let's just say you now have enough economic power to 'slightly' resist the Alchemists' Guild. There is merit to sheer quantity after all," Haui replied. "I've put in an official proposal for this store. It is still currently undergoing vetting. With your recent accomplishments, I'm sure this store will be licensed, though do be prepared to pay certain taxes to the guild. Through me, of course."

Kyle nodded in agreement. He had specifically invited Haui to set up a potion store here, with the potions aimed at being sold at a more affordable price than his previous store. The reason why Kyle could not outright sell the potions was that he did not have a license from the Alchemists' Guild.

Thus, Haui was the simple solution. With this, Kyle would have yet another reason for people to come to the shopping center, boosting the footfall yet again. By creating as many amenities in one place as possible, he could reinvent the entire nearby area as an economic hub under his control.

"I noticed you had a few issues with arcite fuel recently. Will I have to deal with intermittent outages?"

"The arcite fuel issues are sorted right now. However, there is still the issue of traders not willing to sell basic goods such as food and ingredients to us."

"I can solve that easily." Haui smiled. "There may be black market traders who are afraid of earning the ire of the Ardent Cretins, but there will also be enemies who are more than willing to see the Ardent Cretins fall. And also those who just want money regardless."

"Then I thank you in advance." Kyle was aware of Haui's deep network and ties to the underground. After all, Haui brewed all sorts of poison for assassinations and hitjobs—such ingredients would not be easy to get legally.

"Perhaps you can thank me with a bigger tithe of your profits from the potion business. I am handling the taxes for the Alchemists' Guild, after all."

"Your tenancy here is already free."

"Well, it was still worth a try."

Kyle bid farewell to Haui, walking around the shopping arcade. The roof of the building was now plastered with concentrating mirrors, while a consistent flow of arcite ore from the Culdao Peaks was guarded by Monica and other associates. Depleted ore was then funneled to the goblin den and to a few light converters placed around the districts they owned, with Gordon providing the leftovers from the factory production lines.

The supply chain was coming together, and with Haui now helping him to solve the other issues, the shopping arcade was now back in full swing. Now that they were in the clear, able to survive without relying too much on external help, his eyes were set on the companies that had previously refused to sell to him.

You wanted an economic war? You're going to get one.

Chapter 54

Retribution

"Berth 9, wagon arrived ten in the morning. Attacked by small-time thugs, with light damage to its exterior. The driver says that a restaurant was doing roadworks that blocked half of the road. They are really pulling out all the stops this time," Monica reported as she walked with Kyle and Keith through the basement, where the main logistics for the shopping arcade were handled.

The basement was filled with wagons unloading food and ingredients, as well as arcite ore from the Culdao Peaks operation. Kyle noticed some of the wagons had severe dents on the side, as well as one whose wheel had been completely torn off, having to be towed in.

"So first they raised the prices to extravagant amounts, and now they are trying to obstruct our deliveries." Keith shook his head as he entered the administrative office, checking on the books while the clerks frantically jotted down the delivery times. Each of them reported the times and events to a manager, who was marking the points in the city where the deliveries were attacked.

"We've already lost two wagons today just from hijacking. Niko has been working hard putting guards on each of the wagons, but the manpower is getting intensive." Monica grumbled as she looked at the map. The majority of deliveries were routed through Ardent Cretins' territory, being the shortest and quickest way out of the city. The Seven Snakes' three districts were like an island in a sea of enemies.

"I understand," Kyle replied as he observed the patterns of delivery hits. "The hits seem to be occurring in the same areas all the time. They have formed a net." It was a bit of an issue—the arcite ore that was replenished by the new renewable energy setups at the Culdao Peaks was theoretically illegal.

Kyle could hardly call in the enforcers to cover it, seeing as his arcite ore would be taxed. Furthermore, word would spread among the nobility that a new arcite ore mine would be found, which would jeopardize his entire goblin operation. Gulak certainly would not be happy.

"Any hits done by the Ardent Cretins?"

"No. Every hit seems to be done by hired thugs. It seems the Ardent Cretins are being especially careful." Keith shook his head.

"Or it is really the group of companies opposing us that are really having a beef," Monica pointed out. "The patterns seem more like a loosely organized attempt at disruption than a centralized force. I suspect the companies are working alone for various reasons."

"Who are the companies so far?"

Keith shrugged. "Well, just about every food supplier in the South Sector has refused to do business with us. Thanks to Haui's connection, we're buying them from the North Sector now, but they still have a chance of getting intercepted in the Ardent Cretins' territory."

"Okay. Call Damian and Guang Hwa in. It's time for some payback."

* * *

"Goddammit! Not again!" Solomon crushed the slip of paper in his hand into a small ball as he tossed it into a basket at the corner of his office. The arctech radio on his table seemed to gloat at him as it continued to rattle off, the announcer's voice filling the room.

[And it looks like it's lights out for Team Rising Stars, who unfortunately have just suffered a severe arctech malfunction. This might very well be the end of their championship run!]

Fuck! I put half my savings on this bet! Solomon cursed under his breath. He quickly took out his accounting book, flipping through quickly and checking the profits. His pudgy finger traced down the column of expenses, his face scowling.

"Secretary!" he roared as he stormed out of his office, frightening the administrative clerks right outside. He marched up to a scrawny man's table, his bulky build intimidating the latter into a quivering mess.

"Boss, I didn't do anything wrong! It wasn't my fault!"

"Huh? What are you talking about?"

"You're angry about the failed hijacking yesterday, right?"

"What on earth are you saying? I'm angry about the expenses on amenities for the workers! Why is there a three hundred thousand rakel cost for the fucking renovations!"

"But Boss, last week you said to the workers that you wanted to improve the living standards of their dormitory—"

"I want you to reverse it. Immediately!"

"The backlas—"

"I don't care about the backlash from the workers. Cancel it immediately!" Solomon grumbled as he walked out of the office onto a catwalk overlooking a factory where potatoes were being manually processed by thousands of workers.

There were not many big specialized machines on the factory floor for mass-stripping or cleaning. Instead, the workers washed and peeled the potatoes to prepare them for packing before storing them away in arctech cooler boxes to keep them fresh longer. The largest machine that Solomon had purchased was a conveyor belt, as the cost of labor in Raktor was extremely low due to the extreme poverty many of the slum dwellers faced.

Solomon walked along the catwalk to another office, where a frustrated subordinate was arguing on the phone. "If you don't accept the new contract, you can forget about getting your food ever again in the South Sector!"

[I'll take my chances with the Seven Snakes—they seem to be doing pretty well with the shopping arcade. Goodbye, cocksucker.] The restaurant owner on the other end hung up, causing the subordinate to be frustrated and the veins on his forehead nearly popping.

"What's going on? Why did he cancel the contract?" Solomon interrupted the subordinate's solo tantrum show, prompting the man to regain his senses and bow to his superior, Solomon, quickly.

"Uhh, sir, remember how we talked about sanctioning any businesses related to the Seven Snakes?"

"Yeah? What about it? What's wrong?"

"Well, it's already been two weeks since we started, but the shopping arcade hasn't collapsed."

"I know. That's why we've been targeting their deliveries, haven't we?"

"Yes, but the footfall there is immense—it's drawing away customers that would have normally gone to the restaurants we supply!"

Solomon's face twitched. "That's exactly why we imposed the sanctions: to prevent that exact scenario from happening!"

"Sir, it's already happening. Today alone, we just lost five restaurants. They are all relocating to the Seven Snakes district area."

"Fucking twats, get some hired thugs to beat them up!"

"That's what I tried to do yesterday, but our hired thugs got beaten up instead by the Seven Snakes! The restaurants are being treated like VIPs!"

Solomon did not reply just yet, pondering as he paced the room, looking at the piles of canceled supply contracts. *First, I lose half of my savings, then I lose my customers. The sanctions were supposed to bring money, not make us crash like this!*

"So what do you suggest?" Solomon asked. "You must have a plan in mind."

"I believe the only way out of this is to work with the Seven Snakes."

"ARE YOU OUT OF YOUR FUCKING MIND?! Imagine the humiliation I will have to face for being a traitor to the other companies!"

"Yes, but think about it! Based on our current rate, we're operating at a loss. We won't be able to survive the month!" the subordinate retorted.

"Especially considering you just blew half of our cash. Don't think I don't know you used the factory funds to bet on the races."

Solomon wanted to retort but calmed down. He had to think rationally. *He's right. At the rate at which we're going, the sanctions are unsustainable. But being a turncoat is even worse... or is it?*

"Send a letter to the Seven Snakes asking for parley. If we are the first to turn over, the Seven Snakes must be more than willing to sign a beneficial contract with us."

The subordinate immediately got to work, quickly drafting up a letter. Solomon was about to head back to his personal office when he suddenly heard a commotion from the factory floor—a loud clamor. *What the fuck is going on?*

"Comrades! How long will you toil under an ungrateful master? How long will you suffer and work aimlessly, only to be thrown to the side once your limbs have dried out? How long?"

An agitator dressed just like them was speaking out. The workers were still confused by the new guy, who had just been hired the day before. *Wasn't he a newbie? Why is he standing on three crates?*

However, the words he spoke resonated deeply with many of the workers' hearts, and a sense of disenchantment surrounded them. "High above you, the owner of this factory grins down at you, thinking of all of you as simple sheep, mindless and obedient!"

"But the boss said last week he was going to renovate the dormito—"

"Is that true? Are you sure? Do not believe the lies of the owners unless you see and hear them for yourself! Behold, the secretary of the boss himself!" The agitator motioned with his hand, prompting a burly partner to drag forward the secretary, captured during his toilet break.

"What the fuck?! SECURITY!" Solomon yelled at the top of his lungs, sprinting as fast as his obese body would allow him to, heading down to the factory floor.

The panicking secretary immediately nodded his head as he was lifted up high by one hand, screaming out in fear, "It's true! The boss just canceled the renovation!"

"What?!"

"Why? He just promised us last week?"

"What the fuck is this? I promised my family we would have a nicer room to move into!"

The workers began to get more agitated, while the factory guards began to charge toward the agitator. "Don't let those two fuckers get away!" Solomon roared.

"Damian, run!" Guang Hwa screamed, quickly sprinting away. Damian was astounded at the speed with which Guang Hwa fled. He had pegged him for a man with minimal physical capabilities. *When it comes to saving his own skin, he sure can put in the work.*

Damian was not as fast as Guang Hwa, getting tangled up in a fight with the factory guards, who swung batons at him. Activating his Harden engraving, he shrugged off all the attacks, delivering a basic one-two punch to each of them, knocking them out cold.

Ever since Keith had been kidnapped, Damian had been tirelessly working his ass off, improving his arcia energy flow as well as synchronizing his attack with his new engraving skills. He built himself into a much more muscular build, going above and beyond in his training routine. As it stood right now, he could flip an arctech wagon if he wanted to.

With the guards knocked out, Damian easily made his escape, running in a separate direction from Guang Hwa.

Solomon was enraged, shouting and screaming at the workers, "What are you numbskulls doing!? Go and chase them!"

Instead of listening, the workers all began to converge on Solomon, their eyes filled with rage.

"Where's the dormitory renovation you promised us?!"

"What did you do with the money?"

"It's none of your business! Back off now! Otherwise, you won't have a job!" Solomon threatened, but it fell on deaf ears as the workers started to physically grab him.

"Stop dodging the question!" One of the workers grabbed Solomon by the collar before being quickly slapped away onto the ground by him.

"You dare touch me?! ME?! I AM YOU—" Before Solomon could enter his final form, the workers all began to attack him, throwing punches, kicks, and potatoes from afar.

Solomon cowered and rolled on the floor, scampering away from the angry horde of workers as he tried to escape the factory. *Fuck, I can't die here!*

The workers began to trash the factory, stealing whatever valuable parts there were from the nearby machinery. Some of the more desperate workers began hauling sacks of arcite ore out of the factory, hoping to make a quick buck.

My assets! How am I going to repay my debts now? Solomon nearly cried to himself as he limped out of the factory, hearing the loud bangs and explosions behind. The tears he shed were not for the administrative clerks and subordinates being beaten up by the workers, but for the amount of loans he had taken out to build the factory in the first place.

It's no problem. I'm sure the Ardent Cretins will lend me more money! I just have to talk to Sebastian, and everything will be right as—

As soon as he stepped out onto the street, Solomon was grabbed by the collar for the second time that day. He found himself surrounded by five Seven Snakes associates who stared daggers at him.

Kyle smiled as he lifted Solomon up with one hand despite the man's weight, causing his stubby legs to dangle. "You!?" Solomon was shocked.

"Hello, dear factory owner. You seem to be in trouble. Perhaps the Seven Snakes can be of assistance?"

Chapter 55

Undercurrents

A week later...

"Why hasn't the shopping arcade been taken over yet?! They should be bankrupt by now!" The chairman tapped the table as his fingernails rasped against the hardwood.

A wave of murmurs spread around the table, where more than two dozen business owners sat. "I say it's due to us letting incompetent twats into the prestigious South Sector Business Owner Union of Raktor. Unable to even enforce a simple sanction against an uppity upstart, pah!" An older gentleman grumbled as he chewed vigorously. Before long, he hacked out a large glob of spit tainted with crushed leaves into a spit bowl.

"Indeed! Back in my time, we would just hit every store and shop they owned, no questions asked. Why, we used to burn down entire villages just to kill the supply chains!" another elder chimed in, nodding vigorously.

"Shut up, old fart! The enforcers might be looking the other way right now, but if we go that far, who knows if the Mad Dog will be unleashed on us."

A visible shudder spread through the business owners. The tale of the Mad Dog had spread far and wide through the South Sector, her undying thirst for violence insatiable. Many saw her brutality as a much-needed reprieve from the stranglehold that the gangs held over the city.

But for the owners, they knew that if they were caught and exposed, there would be no mercy from her. "I heard she had been posted to the West Sector."

"Ah, no doubt to keep the two major gangs under control. Knowing that she's far away brings me relief."

"Still, the Seven Snakes are on very good terms with the enforcers. Let's not give them any ammunition with which to charge us."

The chairman gritted his teeth. "All this useless bickering won't do us any good! I want to know how to take down the Seven Snakes, and fast!"

The owners all nodded, grim expressions plastered on their faces. It had been three long weeks of continuous refusal to supply any business of the Seven Snakes, harassing other smaller companies into siding with the union instead, and even hiring thugs to disrupt the deliveries.

"We need to put more effort into forming a blockade. We must be united in this aspect; otherwise, just hijacking a few deliveries here and there is not going to make a dent in their finances!"

Someone scoffed from across the table. "United? How dare you say 'united' when I've personally seen thugs hired by Solomon hijacking my delivery wagon?"

Solomon was startled, glancing around rapidly in confusion. "Me? I haven't hired any thugs in a week!"

"Don't bullshit me! If anything, I think that you are working as a double agent!" The rival owner continued to accuse Solomon.

The eyebrow on Solomon's face twitched. "You dare accuse me?! I think it's you who incited my workers to revolt against me just last week!"

As the two bickered on the table, a sense of discord began to spread through the other owners. "Speaking of that, Deliah, I've noticed you've begun to poach my farmers," a sturdy man accused a well-dressed lady in a blue, Victorian-style dress.

The lady smirked, unfolding a quaint blue oriental fan and hiding her face. "Whatever do you mean? I simply offered them a better price."

"How dare you? The situation is already as bad as it is, with many businesses moving over to the Seven Snakes' district! Why are you contesting me?!"

"Just because we're in a union does not mean that it's a fixed market, darling. Supply and demand. Haven't you learned that when you failed in Tryas?"

"You...!"

"ENOUGH!" The chairman slammed the table, interrupting the bickering occurring between the owners. "There is no reason to compete with each other! If we can take down the Seven Snakes, there'll be a bigger pie for all of us to share!"

The owners grumbled among themselves, nodding non committedly. The cracks between the owners were starting to show, fueled by the accusations lobbied at each other.

Solomon gave a slight wink to his rival, who winked back in return. They had planned this from the start, planning to draw out the hidden actions that each company had actually been doing to each other. Both of them were already working for Kyle.

The union was made up of a loose gathering of companies, but they were primarily competitors with each other. The chairman tried to convince them to ride it out for a while longer before they finally dispersed. He sighed to himself, watching the owners leave the meeting hall, with only one person remaining on the other end of the long table.

The person nodded his head at the chairman, permitting him to approach. "I hope you have labeled those who were clearly incompetent. Many of their businesses are about to falter from such a simple economic sanction of just three weeks. What a rubbish business model," the person remarked.

The chairman wiped his forehead, his hand clearly trembling. "Sebastian, I don't think we can hold the sanctions for another month. My businesses may be stable for now, but eventually, the Seven Snakes will come to dominate."

"I know." Sebastian smiled gently as he leaned back into his chair. "I never expected Kyle to give up that easily."

"What?!" The chairman was stunned. "Then what was the point of all of this?!"

"To weed out the incompetent among us. To strengthen the South Sector as a whole. To buy time. To prepare. There are plenty of reasons, chairman." Sebastian took out three rolls of blueprints, laying them out on the table.

The chairman walked over to take a look, gasping. "This... This is the construction blueprints from the Seven Snakes for the shopping arcade! How did you get your hands on it?"

"Kyle would like to believe his gang is watertight. Everyone has a price, do they not? Your sanction has bought enough time for me to build my own rival shopping arcade, with a few improvements. Naturally, you will have a share and first dibs on any property development next to it."

Sebastian had never planned to implement a long-term economic sanction—it was simply to put enough pressure on the Seven Snakes and stall their growth while the Ardent Cretins reverse-engineered the design of the shopping arcade. Though, he would not mind if he held it longer, just so he made sure he was on top.

The chairman's previously confused face slowly turned into the expression of a man who had nailed a deal. "I understand, Sebastian. The longer the sanction..."

"The higher chance you have to knock out your competitors within the union itself. Absorb those who fall to the wayside or are unable to handle the economic pressure. Those that survive will have proven their business model; the rest will be subservient to you. Consolidation at its finest."

* * *

Reese whistled as he slid his hand over the varnished table, glistening with a smooth, glossy surface. He grinned, looking around the posh office, complete with an overview of the streets outside through transparent glass walls.

Ever since he established the Silver Snake Productions company with Kyle, his lifestyle has only been on the up and up. His invention of the light-capturer and the light-thrower was the turning point for all of this to happen.

His little daughter laughed happily as she played around with her assigned Seven Snakes bodyguard, the two of them running around the room. Reese smiled as he recalled how close he had been to losing it all due to the kidnapping. It was only thanks to Kyle that he had managed to survive.

Though he had suspicions that Kyle had been the one who put out the kidnapping contract in the first place... *Maybe it was all a ploy to simply foster a sense of respect and loyalty in me.*

That didn't matter to him as much anymore, having gotten used to the way the Seven Snakes were running things, both legally and illegally. He was only human, after all—he would do anything to see his little girl well-fed and treated. *Oh, and a bit of luxury for myself doesn't hurt.*

An employee of the company entered meekly, bowing to Reese as her eyes were a bit confused by the burly bodyguard chasing the little daughter slowly around the room. "Sir, the payment for the rental has come in, but they say they will require an extension in the contract. They have provided the additional payment for the extension as well."

"Which one?"

"The anonymous buyer from three days ago."

Reese nodded his head in understanding. "Hmm, as long as they paid. Any ideas what the buyer was using it for?"

Part of the idea behind renting out the equipment was to spy on the buyers and figure out what they were using the devices for. Sometimes it was to film an extravagant wedding at the bequest of a rich baroness from another city; other times, it was an inspired movie-maker wanting to make an independent show.

This allowed Kyle and Reese to monitor the growing interest and spread of the light-thrower industry, or, as Kyle called it, the "media" industry. This would help them stay ahead of the competition.

"No, sir. The buyer was prepared and shook off the observers almost immediately."

Suspicious... Reese pondered a while before dismissing the subordinate. This was the first anonymous buyer they had, making him wonder what they were using it for. *Reverse-engineering? It won't be possible with the failsafe that Kyle and I have implemented.*

The laughter of his daughter shook him out of deep thought, making him smile. *Money is money.*

Just as he was about to head over to play with his daughter as well, Kyle entered the office, immediately motioning to the bodyguard to leave the room.

"We need to work together to make a degraded version of the engravings."

Reese had learned a lot of new terms and concepts over his time with the Seven Snakes, but Kyle's words nearly threw him for a loop.

"What?! You want to make the engravings worse?" Reese was appalled by the very notion Kyle had put forth. He had spent his entire life improving engravings—was he just supposed to sabotage them now?

"Relax. I never said we were degrading our own products—rather, we will be creating a less efficient version of it."

"But why?! Are you intentionally going to create bad products to sell to our customers? That would hurt our reputation."

Kyle fumed, prompting Reese to stop arguing and let his superior explain. Regardless of Reese's current financial status, Kyle still intimidated him. Reese was well aware that Kyle could easily kill him if he truly wanted to.

"You understand that right now, the light-capturer and light-thrower engravings are company secrets, held only by the two of us, correct?"

"Yes. That is why we vet every buyer and their background to trace if the technology is being reverse-engineered. I also engrave every single one of them manually myself."

It was the only way to control the spread of technology—Kyle did not trust Gordon's factory workers to be immune to bribery or extortion, potentially leaking details of a mass production process. It was better to keep the supply low and subsequently raise the rental prices.

Reese thought quickly about why Kyle wanted a degraded version of the engraving, his face lighting up in understanding. "I get it now! This is ingenious! When's the deadline?"

"Tonight."

* * *

A Seven Snakes associate gingerly adjusted his sleeves, pulling his right sleeve back to check the time. He leaned against an arctech wagon parked in an inconspicuous alleyway, far away from the prying eyes of the pedestrians who filled the streets.

He tapped his foot impatiently, constantly checking the time on his watch as he glanced down the decrepit path. A loud clang was heard, causing him to jump in fright as a rat scampered across the alleyway, dashing between piles of trash and depleted arcite ore.

"Seriously, why am I always the one taking all this risk!" the associate complained, scratching his bald head furiously and trying to soothe an itch on the back of his neck.

He waited a few more minutes before finally getting impatient and grumbling to himself. "Fucking thugs. Can't even keep to a time." He opened the driver's door, only to hear the distinctive click of an arctech pistol whirring. The associate gulped instinctively, raising his arms in surrender as he turned around slowly, coming face-to-face with a three-man group.

Two bodyguards carrying thick briefcases flanked a lanky businessman, the most distinctive part of his snazzy suit being the pink feather in his cap and the purple handkerchief in his breast pocket, fine embroidery lining its edges.

"Took you long enough, eh?" The associate smiled, having already expected them, while the two bodyguards moved forward around him, checking if there was anyone else in the wagon.

"All clear, sir," one of the bodyguards said to the lanky businessman, who grinned widely, clearing his throat.

"Guang Hwa, president of the Golden Snake Constructions. Or should I say, Brother Long Hua? The instigator of the most recent religious protest, if I recall."

"It wasn't a religious protest, but a call to freedom," Guang Hwa scoffed.

"Feisty. Now, where are the goods?"

"All right here, in the wagon. Where's the money?"

"Hahaha! Who knew that the great Kyle would be so easily taken down by a greedy subordinate? I feel sorry for him recruiting you to be the spokesperson."

Guang Hwa scowled, reaching his left hand down to undo a button near his neck, revealing a metal choker that ran right around his neck. The bodyguards immediately stepped forward to check the engravings on the neck, ensuring that it was not a tracker engraving.

The lanky businessman was amused and clearly intrigued. "You two, search the interior of the wagon and make sure our friend here was not followed."

He took a step toward Guang Hwa, examining him. "Interesting. It is quite funny to see the head of a prominent Golden Snake Construction wearing such a thing. However, the design is indeed unique. Perhaps you might be interested in selling it to me as well?"

"Fuck you, if this thing goes off, my head goes with it."

"It is a tough choice, but it is one that I am willing to make."

"Shut up. Where's the money?"

"Relax. You will get it once you are clear."

The bodyguards checked every nook and cranny of the arctech wagon, examining even the spokes of the wheels for any hidden devices or engravings.

"So, who's the buyer on the other end?" Guang Hwa asked.

"Keep asking questions like that, and I may be inclined to think you are an enforcer mole."

"Except I already sold you the blueprints for the construction before. Went rather well, in my opinion."

"A fine deal indeed." The lanky businessman scratched his chin.

"This deal would be even better for you, would it not? I can't imagine any other information dealer on the black market getting such a catch as this. You'll be the talk of the town for a while."

"Surprisingly cognizant for a slave." The information dealer neither denied nor confirmed Guang Hwa's comment.

An arctech radio on the belt of the dealer crackled to life. [Sir, no signs of the Seven Snakes or any enforcers nearby.] The bodyguards soon exited the wagon, nodding their heads to indicate that it was clear of booby traps.

The dealer walked to the back of the wagon, lifting the cloth that covered them. Arranged in a haphazard fashion was one copy of nearly everything that the Seven Snakes had innovated for the construction of the shopping arcade, including a complete light-capturer and light-thrower at the back.

"Jackpot. This will fetch an extremely high price." The dealer couldn't help grinning as he stepped into the back of the wagon, looking around intently before turning to snarl at Guang Hwa. "I don't see any manuals or notes here—you promised to bring whatever documentation they had as well."

"I'm just a spokesperson—you think I would know which exact piece of paper to bring? It was already hard enough for me to get my hands on these devices," Guang Hwa complained.

The dealer bent over to activate the light-thrower, which churned and projected a still image of the Silver Snakes Productions' logo. "Seems to be in working order. You two, drive this wagon off and do a switch in the next district. Split it up into three separate wagons before converging, got it? Safehouses B and D."

The bodyguards nodded, entering the driver's seat, much to the confusion of Guang Hwa. "Hey, why are you driving off my wagon? How the hell am I supposed to get back? The Seven Snakes will find out and—"

"Don't you worry about that. I brought more friends to take care of that."

Two more men walked into the alleyway, obviously hired thugs under the dealer's command. Guang Hwa's eyes narrowed, knowing what was happening immediately. "You! You promised me five million rakels!"

"And? Don't you know the rules of Raktor? A contract can only be enforced by the strength of both parties. No one is on your side; no one even knows we signed the contract. Even if I break it, no one is going to intervene for you, not even the Seven Snakes. After all, you betrayed them, didn't you?"

"Bitch, if I survive, I'll tell the entire world of your—"

"That's if you survive. Enjoy the rest of your life." The dealer smirked, leaving the alleyway as another ten thugs entered the alleyway, surrounding Guang Hwa with a bored expression.

"All right, say your last words and make your peace." The leader of the hired thugs yawned, the job being just another one in his books.

Guang Hwa was clearly panicking, his eyes darting all over the roofs. "Come on, Boss! Whatever the fuck you're planning, do it now!" he screamed in fear.

"Huh?" The leader was confused, hearing the sound of something hurtling toward him from above. His instincts kicked in, causing him to jump out of the way and assume a fighting stance.

"Get all of our men in here NOW!" He did not underestimate the enemy, immediately recognizing that it was a trap by the Seven Snakes.

Out of the dust cloud caused by the crash came Kyle, cracking and stretching his limbs, as if to warm his body up. "Been a while. Damian, Niko, Adrian. Do you have eyes on the dealer?"

[Intercepting now.]

"Good. Let's have some fun."

Chapter 56

Sabotage

Kyle deftly sidestepped the incoming punch and ducked as a sword swung horizontally over his head. With a quick counterswing of his hammer, he fractured the ribs of the first thug before swiveling around him and kicking him in the back. The thug crashed into one of his allies.

Three swings and an arrow came in straight at him, forcing Kyle to hop backward, his speed faster than that of the average fighter, thanks to his increased Dexterity. The leader did not look surprised, simply ordering the thugs to corner Kyle even tighter. "Killing the Seven Snakes leader would be the biggest haul of our lives!"

Penchant for Violence!

A familiar surge of power rushed through Kyle's body, strengthening his muscles and sharpening his vision. The world around him seemed to slow down even more, with his combat stats all doubled and improved. The stats reported to him via the statistic screen were not linear in effect, but a 100% increase was always welcome.

The movements of the thugs were in slow motion to him, making it easy for Kyle to parry the incoming strikes. To the cowering Guang Hwa, who was cowering at a safe distance, Kyle looked as though he was moving extremely fast, with ungodly reaction speeds. The sight burned Kyle's strength into Guang Hwa's heart even more. *Fuck! I just had to be enslaved by such a monster!*

The increase in combat strength and speed caught the leader off-guard. Before he could even reorganize the thugs, half of his dozen-strong squad was already dead, each killed in one hammer blow from Kyle.

[SYSTEM MESSAGE]
You killed Hired Mercenary, +100 EXP.

What? They give 100 EXP? Kyle had expected a low amount of EXP—when he had first killed a Red Lion Thug, he had gotten a mere 10 EXP.

A sinister grin began to spread on his face as he twirled the hammer by its handle in his right hand, staring right at the leader. "Shit! Hold him off! I'll finish the job!"

"Yes, si—" Just as the thugs steeled themselves for their eventual demise, it came faster than expected in the form of Kyle's lunging strike, dancing through the remaining five thugs and killing all of them in a swift motion even before the leader could move three steps.

"Damn you!" The leader pulled out a blunderbuss from his back, blasting it right at Kyle. The Projectile Defense Vambrace Kyle had activated was not enough to block the multiple pellets, the engraving fizzling out and pierced by them, irreversibly damaging it. The leader shot another round, with half of the pellets making it through to hit Kyle right in the chest.

"I got you now!" the leader roared, drawing his sword and thrusting it at Kyle.

However, Kyle was not hurt at all, the breastplate underneath having blocked the rest of the shots as he dodged the stab. After recovering his posture, he delivered a lightning-fast front kick to the leader's head, knocking the man down onto the ground.

"Wait, I'm just a hired—" Words no longer came out of the gurgling mouth of the leader; his throat had been snapped in half by a single stomp of Kyle's foot.

[SYSTEM MESSAGE]
You killed Hired Mercenary Leader, +250 EXP.

Your level has increased from level 15 to level 16!
All stats increased.
Bonus free points granted.

Guang Hwa meekly stepped over the dead bodies of the thugs, afraid to approach Kyle but also equally afraid to try and run away now. Kyle barely gave him a glance as he grabbed his arctech radio while walking to a parked arctech wagon nearby. "Where's the dealer?"

Damian's voice came through the radio. [Sorry, sir. We did not manage to catch him, but Adrian is still on his tail.]

"No matter. Give me his current location, I'll handle the rest."

In another building in an adjacent district, in a room filled with a cluster of radios and old newspapers, as well as multiple copies of the map of Raktor and its surrounding areas. Two clerks scrambled around as they listened in to all the public radio stations and checked up on the latest news. Each of the maps was marked with a note denoting recent happenings.

The door was suddenly flung wide open, with a flustered dealer storming through the room.

"Sir, I have news that the military is increasing their purchase of arcite ore and recalling their reservists. I believe—" the clerk said urgently before the dealer cut him off, waving his hands frantically.

"NOW IS NOT THE FUCKING TIME!" The dealer grabbed the clerk by the collar and roared, "There are enemies coming for us!"

"Wh-What? Why?"

"The fucking Seven Snakes! You two go and defend with the rest of the guards! What are you giving me that blank look for? I OWN YOU! Now go!"

The clerks scrambled out of the office, each grabbing a repeater handgun. The handgun was not of the same design as Kyle's, but a far worse and less efficient design—a result of reverse-engineering. With all the original copies of Kyle's handgun destroyed, the reverse-engineering was an attempt at duplicating the concept rather than the actual mechanism.

The dealer panicked as he scrambled around the room, grabbing a sack and stuffing everything valuable he had hidden around the safehouse. Just as he was about to finish up, the sounds of screaming and fighting were already echoing through the building that he was in, causing him to tense up even more.

Fuck, fuck, fuck! The dealer cursed inwardly, quickly lifting the sack over his shoulder and heading toward the exit. *It's fine; my thirty guards can stall him long enough for me to make my escape. I just have to make it to—*

The dealer opened the door only to see a smiling Kyle, barely panting as countless guards lay scattered along the ornate hallway behind him, rolling on the ground incapacitated. "Wha—"

Kyle grabbed him by the mouth, causing him to drop the sack with countless precious jewels and ornamental figures. "I've heard that you've been stealing certain secrets from me."

"I only purchase what is put in front of me. It is your own men who betrayed you."

"I have already dealt with him. It doesn't change the fact that you are in possession of the goods."

The dealer noticed Kyle was up to something. If the gang leader had been truly angry, he would have already been dead. The dealer knew as much. "How much do you want?"

"Ah, signs of intelligence. You sold the construction blueprints to the Ardent Cretins for a nice five million rakels, did you not?"

So the first deal was a trap too! The dealer was astonished that Kyle was using his own blueprints as a money-making scheme. He already knew what Kyle was going to ask for next. "So you want me to hand over the blueprints, the goods, AND pay you back five million rakels?"

"Oh, I think you are misunderstanding something. I want ninety million rakels now. You can keep the blueprints."

"What?!" The dealer was completely confused now. Ninety million rakels was more than his entire fortune three times over, but the dealer took a second glance at the whimpering guards outside; burly men turned into crying babies. "How the fuck am I supposed to give you that amount of money?"

"You're an information dealer, are you not? Do what you do best."

* * *

Two weeks later...

The shopping arcade built by the Ardent Cretins was having its grand opening day, with a much larger turnout and fanfare thanks to the immense marketing budget the union and Sebastian had thrown in. The shopping arcade was significantly larger, spanning an entire urban block, unlike the single-building size of the Seven Snakes', adding even more to the grandeur and the "wow" factor.

Hundreds of businessmen, wealthy middle-class and lesser nobles turned up, with the shopping arcade this time dedicated to only the upper class. The Ardent Cretins actively blocked the slum dwellers and poorer folks from approaching the area, making it a limited area.

This is the way to make a shopping arcade profitable—why pander to those with no money? Sebastian smirked as he stood by the side, watching the chairman take the stand with an opening speech.

"This may not be the first shopping arcade established in Raktor, but it is most certainly the biggest. We promise the best in entertainment and satisfaction to all our patrons here—a dedicated zone!"

The crowd nodded in agreement; many of the attendees had previously shunned the Seven Snakes shopping arcade due to the influx of lowborn workers and poor individuals. Many of them detested the idea of giving out free amenities to the public, though they internally admitted that it had a dramatic increase in footfall.

As such, upper society was split on which model to follow. With Sebastian's new shopping arcade, the ardent supporters of the class hierarchy finally had something to back. Sebastian had no shortage of investors who wanted to establish a limited shopping arcade tailored to the wealthy. The notion was not unique at all.

"And without further ado, we shall now open the new shopping arcade! Enjoy the luxuries we have to your heart's content!"

Unlike the surging crowd that tried to force their way in during the Seven Snakes' shopping arcade's opening day, the crowd here was a lot more mannered, entering in an orderly fashion. Sebastian spotted a familiar face in the throng of people, causing him to smile as he made his way over.

"I did not expect you to actually accept the invitation."

"A senior must always support his junior. Is that not the case?"

"You don't seem particularly surprised at the construction of this shopping arcade."

"Of course, the innovations I have implemented are hardly cutting-edge. Even a layman could make his own, given the right understanding. It was only a matter of time."

"Well then, as thanks for your warning, I would like to inform you that your innovations are out on the black market for everyone to see. I could give you the name of the dealer who has been leaking them," Sebastian said with a tinge of glee in his voice as he watched Kyle's face twist in anger. "Perhaps even now, other businesses in other sectors are buying the information right now."

Kyle looked furious. "Thank you for the tip. I wish you only the best for the rest of your opening day." He stormed off, not bothering to enter the shopping arcade.

Most likely, he is going to perform a purge of the Seven Snakes. Sebastian did not know who had been the one who leaked the information, only that he had bought it from the dealer as the middleman. He gloated to himself, walking into the shopping arcade guarded by two Ardent Cretin bodyguards, watching the attendees visit the countless shops.

The first hour was truly a success, with the temperature control engravings cooling the air within the corridors and shops while extravagant lighting awed the customers. Sebastian had only invited the very best that the South Sector had to offer—beauty products, fashion, and jewelry were all on display here.

"Sir? Sir... You are needed at the main control office," an Ardent Cretins thug whispered to Sebastian. The man promptly followed the man, entering an office on the top floor with a dozen engineers all arguing with each other.

"What's the matter? What's going on?"

"Sir, it's hard to explain, but our estimates of the arcite fuel consumption are off by a slight margin."

Sebastian narrowed his eyes. "What do you mean?"

"The temperature control engravings—the efficiency is much lower than expected."

"How much are we talking about?"

"It's not much, but..."

"Tell me the numbers."

"The efficiency is only about seventy percent at best."

"Did we not estimate at least eighty percent efficiency?"

"Yes, but..."

At that moment, another engineer burst in through the office door. "Sebastian, sir! The lights are flickering! I think the lighting engravings are overheating!"

"Turn off a few of them to alleviate the strain. All of you, keep working on improving the design. Surely the twelve of you can beat an old university professor from a small gang, can't you?"

"Uh... yes, sir."

Sebastian wasted no time, heading up to the duplicated light-thrower theater's projector room, which had more than five employees scrambling inside preparing for the debut show. "Are you sure you've tested the light-thrower?"

"Yes, sir, we did a test run yesterday with a sample movie. It ran smoothly for a good fifteen minutes."

"Try it now."

"Sir?"

"Try it now!"

The employee hastily activated the light-thrower, projecting the sample movie on the theater screen. Not even after a minute had gone by, the image began to flicker, and sounds of hissing sparks could be heard inside the light-thrower machine.

Sebastian immediately assumed it was a failsafe implemented by Silver Snakes Productions, quickly opening up a side panel of the light thrower and inspecting it. Already he could see the traces on the engraving warping as it fizzled out, resulting in the weird behavior.

"Cancel the light-thrower show."

"But sir, that's the main attraction of the—"

"CANCEL IT—NOW!" Sebastian yelled, prompting the employees to quickly scamper out of the room, relaying the order to the others. *That fucking slimy dealer—charging me for more than twenty million rakels for this sham?! I will find him and kill him!*

Chapter 57

Arms Industry

Despite the sanctions against the Seven Snakes' shopping arcade, it had been holding up well for more than a month since its inception. Already, it had become a mainstay for local residents, both from within the district and beyond, to visit.

The light-thrower shows brought countless visitors from other sectors to watch the movies, while the free bathhouse accommodated the poorer people, improving their livelihood.

With the growing business of the shopping arcade, more and more employment opportunities began to open up as businesses and shop owners began to snap up the neighboring units, trying to entice customers who flocked to the shopping arcade.

Squatters even began to shift residences nearby, with Golden Snake Construction beginning to renovate nearby buildings into mass accommodations. While the facilities were lacking in that there were only mass toilets and a barebones room, it was more than enough for the perennially homeless people.

Of course, the catch was that the squatters had to be employed in a Seven Snakes–related business, legal or not. Wages were still paid via the construction company, but in reality, it was a no-show job, where the squatters would then work in pubs, casinos, or brothels.

The stronger ones were whisked away secretly to the Culdao Peaks goblin dens, assisting in the modernization of the caves into a burgeoning industrialized society. Kyle had never been the one to place all his eggs in one basket—there was always the off chance that Raktor might suffer in the future. It was always good to have a backup plan.

As the bathhouse and shopping arcade became a hotspot for gatherings, it was easier to influence the local population into believing that the gang was a force for good. Many began to idolize the gang lifestyle, once again increasing the number of associates to nearly double what they had before. Now, the number of members neared two hundred of them, with expectations that it could swell to five hundred in another few months.

Kyle smiled as he read a few newspapers reporting on the recent string of events that led to the Ardent Cretins canceling their light-thrower debut show. Many other impatient companies who had bought from the black market information dealer without checking also suffered heavily, having to scale back their expansion plans.

These reported events led to an increase in the reputation of the light-thrower theater in the Seven Snakes' shopping arcade, making it the go-to destination for high-quality movies. More importantly, the movies being shown were much better than the amateur movies that other sectors were showing.

Short story arcs lifted right from the Galactic Era were modified for the local audience, such as the blockbuster hit *The Ring of the Lords*. However, Kyle had to heavily modify the story in the event that another person with knowledge of the franchise would pick up on it. He garbled the storyline, but the audience still lapped it up, with already a few well-known citizens being avid theater-goers.

Also, the companies that tried to barge in on the rental market for light-throwers and light-capturers were stunted by the "bad" engravings Kyle had designed and leaked on purpose, further boosting the brand name of the Silver Snakes as one of quality and assurance.

"Everyone, I am proud to announce that, as of today, we have finally turned a profit on the shopping arcade!" Keith announced to the office filled with administrative clerks, who all cheered.

"So when are we getting our bonuses?" A clerk raised his hands.

"Nice try. If we can keep this up for a month, I'll think about it." Keith chuckled before walking up to Kyle's desk, who seized him up.

"Keith, status report on all companies and businesses. Keep it brief."

"Yes, sir. Our pubs and brothels have increased footfall thanks to our truce with the enforcers. Everyone knows the Seven Snakes districts are well-protected, so the mental barrier that most people had is starting to crumble."

"Moving on. The Silver Snakes Productions have reported a monthly profit, mainly due to the rental equipment. As of now, we have been making a loss on the theater tickets."

Kyle sighed, rubbing his forehead. "We don't have much choice here. If we priced it appropriately, only the middle and upper classes would be able to attend. Continue."

"Yes, sir. Golden Snake completed the construction of the mass apartments and dormitories a week ago. No faults or issues have been reported as of now. The cost of utilities such as arcia power lines to each room is still being calculated."

"That's fine; we don't have enough arcite ore to power it... yet."

"We had three prospective clients, one of which is Baron Cain."

"Baron Cain?" Kyle was astonished to hear that the noble in charge of the South Sector was directly requesting the construction company's services. "What's the contract for?"

"Yes, sir, quoting directly from the letter sent: 'A request for a quote regarding the construction of a metallurgy factory in Raktor that will mainly produce processed metal ingots. Specifically, high-grade steel ingots.' It also stressed that the factory be completed swiftly, should the contract be accepted."

Kyle raised his eyebrows even higher, surprised. "Give the letter to me. I'll handle it." *Something isn't right. Why would that greedy baron want a metallurgy factory when most current construction projects do not rely on it? Unless...*

Damian entered the office, walking right up to Kyle's desk and saluting. "Sir, the black market dealer has skipped out of town. The safehouses seemed to have been burned down. I've heard rumors of multiple gangs and thugs after his life."

"Of course; he sold the degraded engravings that break apart after a certain period of time. I'm sure they will find the right people to fix it, but it is still going to take time and effort." Kyle nodded. "Did you find anything else?"

"Yes, sir. I found scribblings on an undamaged desk. It seems to be the notes of a clerk working right under the information dealer." Damian handed over a leatherbound notebook filled with scribbles that were barely legible.

Kyle quickly read the contents. *Hmm, seems like he was keeping track of all the information so he could make it out on his own when he wanted to. Commendable.* The journal was surprisingly detailed and clear in terms of the date and timing of occurrences, stringing a pattern together.

Kyle flipped to the pages that covered the last two weeks, immediately noticing what the pattern was leading to. "Keith, what has the military been doing?"

"Hmm? I recently heard they increased their bulk orders of arcite ore. Apart from that, I don't know. Oh! There are military exercises that are going to be held nearby, but it's an annual event, so it's not too surprising."

"When is that?"

"Hmm... It's planned to be half a year from now. Why? What did you find in the journal?"

Kyle didn't reply, instead asking Keith and Damian to bring all the old newspapers collected over the past two weeks, corroborating the journal with the events reported in the newspaper. *Stockpiling of energy sources, the concentration of military personnel, activation of reservist forces... and now the baron wants to build a factory?* "Did the baron state when he wanted it done?"

"No, but he did say he needed it swiftly..."

Kyle now knew exactly what was happening. How could a crime lord of the Melsura Star Sector not infer from the events right in front of his eyes?

"Keith, gather everyone of importance here. Our previous plan of expansion has to be changed dramatically."

* * *

Baron Cain stepped out of his wagon, escorted by five bodyguards, as he marveled at the shopping arcade. He had not attended the opening day itself and was seeing it for the first time. *Impressive.* He could now see why all the lesser nobles and landowners were so riled up by this new trend.

"Ah, Baron Cain. Pleased to be of service! I am Guang Hwa, President of the Golden Snake Constru—"

"Shut up and bring me to someone who actually matters."

Guang Hwa was noticeably irritated by the condescending look, but he still put on a fake smile and led the baron to a specialized, well-decorated VIP room for meetings, with enough posh and luxury to make the baron feel as though he were in another noble's dwelling.

Kyle was already waiting for him, getting up from his velvet chair and bowing. "Thank you for coming, Baron Cain. The Golden Snake Construction company is honored to have you as a potential customer."

"Hmph. As you should." Cain sat down opposite him in a regal chair. "Let's get to the point. I want a quote on how much the steel factory would cost."

"Of course. I can easily provide the numbers, but I believe we can offer something of additional benefit that may interest you."

"What benefits can you give? A steel factory is a steel factory."

"I am referring to other events that should not fall on certain prying ears. Rumors of war." Kyle glanced at the five bodyguards surrounding them and Guang Hwa.

"Leave us." Baron Cain motioned to his bodyguards, with the five and Guang Hwa complying. As soon as they left the room, Cain's face turned extremely sour. "How the hell do you know? Espionage against nobility can be considered a crime."

Kyle whipped out the journal he had. "Taken from a black market dealer's clerk. Make of that what you will. I only inferred the gist of things; I am not clear on the details."

"So what? You're just a gang. I doubt you have anyt—" Baron Cain caught himself before continuing, his eyes narrowing as he realized what Kyle was hinting at. "You're insane."

Kyle smiled. "How about you hear me out before you dismiss it? If you have heard everything I had to say and still want the base quote, I won't press the matter."

Baron Cain hesitated for a moment but ultimately nodded, prompting Kyle to continue.

"I can roughly gather from your countenance that your attempt to sell a new technology regarding firearms to the military has failed spectacularly." Kyle stood up and began to slowly pace the room.

Only because you placed your failsafe inside. "That's a groundless assertion—you don't know if I tried."

"That's true, but I also understand that the nobility has a large burden when attempting any military maneuvers. Your contribution to the military is directly tied to prestige. Anyone who shirks this obligation may and has been stripped of their titles, if any. But if your contribution remains among the top, the emperor will recognize you and award you a higher title or more concessions. That was how Count Leon made his initial rise fifteen years ago."

"For an amnesiac, you seem to know history too well."

"Will having a simple steel factory be enough? I'm sure other nobles out there have much better resources and opportunities to contribute. Are you satisfied with your current standing?"

"Speak directly and stop beating around the bush! What exactly are you proposing?"

"You already know what I am proposing. Give me half of the funds and the license to expand the steel factory into a weapons factory as well. I'll cover the rest. But I must retain overall control of the factory."

Baron Cain had already expected this. "You are asking me to certify a criminal organization to have the legal license to produce guns? After all you've done? Are you mad?"

"Why not? Extraordinary times call for extraordinary measures. Also, the company created to run it will be clean. At least to the outside world. As long as you just give your word, you will shoot through the ranks, not even needing to lift a single finger."

Cain was a greedy person, so Kyle's speech already appealed to him directly. He could already envision the countless heaps of merits and concessions he would receive once the war was won. He was also confident that Kyle had the technology and methods to elevate his contributions. After all, the war with the Ilysian Punks had clearly shown Kyle's capabilities.

"What's in it for you? You won't receive any awards or prestige from doing this."

"Baron Cain, I've said this before. I am a businessman, first and foremost, who had the unfortunate luck of dealing in certain ventures of high profit. Of course, I will do everything I can to come out swinging at such an exciting time, will I not? I simply want to improve my position in society, as you do. Shall we work together?"

Baron Cain was irked by the comparison, but he internally agreed with Kyle. Both of them sought to climb the social ladder—everyone wanted to move to the next rung. Even Count Leon was no different. After all, was that not why the war was about to be started?

Originally, the baron felt that the war would be a burden on him. However, with the possibility of a new venture with Kyle, he was starting to see the war as a boon instead. "Let me consider it and get back to you."

"I understand. However, please understand we may not be able to meet the deadline the longer it is delayed. Our entire construction company will work on it." Kyle bowed as Baron Cain stood up.

"Not a word of this is to spread to anyone else, especially of the war. Do you understand?"

"Yes, Baron Cain."

As Cain left the premises with his five bodyguards, Kyle could not help smiling to himself back in his office. "Keith, did you find any more information on when the diplomatic mission from Versia is coming in?"

"Yes, sir, but only fragments. They are arriving in Raktor to negotiate compensation with Count Leon in approximately a week or so. The exact day of arrival is hard to pinpoint."

"Does not matter. Keep an eye out for their arrival."

"Yes, sir, but why are you looking for the Versia diplomats? Are you afraid that they might take revenge for what we did to the Ilysian Punks?"

"No, Keith. I have a business proposal for them. One that will definitely pique their interest."

Chapter 58

Double Agent

The procession was public, as the Versia diplomatic team arrived via a wagon convoy protected by more than three dozen guards. The diplomats stared in curiosity as a dozen light-capturers had their beady black lenses aimed at them.

The news of the light-capturer invention was not particularly new in Versia, where a few entrepreneurial companies had already tried to create their own knockoffs. However, it was still a sight to see it spread through society so quickly. News companies were capitalizing on the new medium of information rapidly, its changes echoing through the city of Raktor.

"Ah, Minister Dekar. It is good to finally meet you in person." Count Leon was already in position, ready to receive them at the grand steps to the central office that handled all affairs in the county. He bowed to a man wearing a sharp, tight uniform adorned with tens of medals, signifying his rank and position in the government of Versia.

"It is good to see you as well, Count Leon." Minister Dekar smiled as he stretched out his hand, shaking Count Leon's hand in a sign of goodwill. Both of them had wide smiles on their faces, as did the rest of the accompanying diplomatic group and the four barons who stood behind Count Leon.

The reporters quickly recorded the entire event, speaking rapidly into their arctech recording devices, their voices to be released alongside the recorded light-capturer movies.

The dignitaries wasted no time, immediately following Count Leon into the meeting room, where two long tables were laid out facing each other, with chairs already pre-designated for each member of the diplomatic team.

The opposing parties chatted with each other, exchanging small talk as they waited for the meeting to begin. Many of them knew each other from both sides, having met before in their former jobs or through diplomatic missions both before and after the previous war.

"Everyone, we shall begin." Count Leon announced, taking his seat right in the center of the Yual Dominion's table.

As soon as the meeting began proper, however, the air immediately became tense, with the two teams clearly knowing what this was all about.

"So, to clarify the purpose of this meeting: your citizens have been caught red-handed smuggling weapons into Versia from Raktor, and—"

"Ex-citizens, need I remind you," Minister Dekar interjected. "General Javel had been previously stripped of his citizenship. And so have all of the... Ilysian Punks' members."

"And the Versia military has been directly complicit in this entire affair."

"How strange. This sounds like a simple case: Your nation can't keep its criminal organizations under control. I would also like to officially state that the Versia military has not received any of these aforementioned weapons, none whatsoever."

"Criminals that stem from your nation are directly sabotaging Raktor to empower Versia. I have direct evidence that your military personnel, former or not, are actively assisting in the transfer of these smuggled goods." Count Leon motioned with his hand, prompting a servant to bring forward a stack of papers, placing them in front of the diplomatic delegation.

"Each of these papers represents a formal license to transport weapons around the country of Versia, signed off directly by an official of the government."

"We have already dealt with the corrupted official, but the fact remains that the guns have never made their way into the formal military. It is purely a criminal transaction, from one black market to another. We did not actively plan for nor support such activities—our own Versian enforcers are performing an investigation right no—"

"I don't care about what your enforcers are doing!" Count Leon snarled, raising the tension even higher. "The simple fact as I see it is this: It is Versians who have been smuggling guns out of our military facilities INTO your country, and you must pay!"

"I find that accusation ungrounded and misleading—the government of Versia does not claim to have jurisdiction or control over every single citizen that has been excommunicated and stripped of citizenship! Such a statement would lead me to also accuse your ex-countrymen of establishing human trafficking rings in my own country as well!" Minister Dekar shot back. "On top of that, your military shows clear signs of mobilization, something that is clearly aimed at Versia!"

"Is my military not allowed to perform military exercises within our sovereign territory? We have been performing the same exercise every two years."

The barons and the Versian delegation remained silent as the argument was solely waged between the minister and the count. Both sides were unwilling to back down, but the minister knew that he had already lost the moral ground. It was an undeniable fact that the guns had indeed been smuggled into Versia. He tried his hardest to deflect or counter with other examples, but Count Leon stayed on task.

"Here is my ultimatum: Your country will catch all criminals involved in the smuggling and distribution of Yual Dominion's technology, as well as pay back reparations of an equivalent sum. The hijacking of our military facilities has negatively impacted our economy, resulting in losses of nearly 500 million rakels in total."

"Ridiculous! You want us to be your hunting dogs and compensate you as well?! I would like to remind you that the original reason for the smuggling to occur was because you, too, have potential corruption brewing in your own military. How is it possible for a small gang to smuggle that many guns? Surely not without inside information?"

The negotiations went back and forth before the meeting concluded indecisively, adjourning for a lunch break. Count Leon signaled toward Minister Dekar, prompting the man to follow him into a side room, which was a simple resting area with amenities.

Closing the door behind him, Count Leon gave a smile, his countenance far different from the aggressive mannerism he portrayed in the meeting. He shook hands with Dekar again, slightly confusing the minister.

"Ah, I guess your predecessor did not inform you of what is going to happen." Count Leon smirked as he poured himself a glass of wine, sipping on it carefully. "Did you ever wonder how your predecessor was able to buy such a grand mansion despite the paltry government salary your 'democratic' system pays you?"

Dekar squinted his eyes in comprehension. "You're saying he accepted bribes. From you."

"Minister Dekar, I'm sure you are a proud citizen of Versia who believes in the democratic system, but be honest with yourself. How hard have you been working to support the people of Versia, with nothing but a pittance of a salary to show for it? Despite being a representative of an entire nation! The business owners are all earning far more than you! I hear Harrison is making more than ever. Do you not think it is unfair?"

"I will not be so easily sway—"

"Ah, listen to my offer first. I will give you fifty million rakels as well as show clear signs of demobilization across the country. The military exercise will be postponed as per usual. You get to go back home and claim that you are a herald of peace, solving the crisis. I will also give you custody of General Javel and every other Ilysian Punks member that is rotting in jail in due time, letting you show off to the people that you have worked hard to ensure that your people remain free. What a good story, is it not?

Your political career will be legendary! Or perhaps you would prefer the alternative of war?"

The meeting soon resumed after the lunch break, with the diplomatic delegation taking their seats once again. Many of them expected the same argument to be continued between Count Leon and Minister Dekar, but surprisingly, there was little opposition raised by the minister anymore.

"Fine, we shall pay the compensation of 500 million rakels. But in return, you must cease the mobilization of Yual Dominion forces at our border! Also, you must release all Versian citizens currently in custody back to us." Minister Dekar put on a strong façade.

"A fine compromise. Under the authority bestowed upon me by the emperor, I accept the deal on behalf of the Yual Dominion. Let us hash out the finer details of transfers now."

The meeting took another three days as the members of the diplomatic team scrambled to hash out the clauses in the deal, covering every possible legal loophole in the agreement. The Yual Dominion tried to sneak a few terms into the agreement, which were immediately caught by the delegation, prompting a few arguments and accusations of unfair treatment.

As the procedure was going on, Minister Dekar was resting in his room when a diplomat knocked on his door. "Come in."

"Sir, apologies for disturbing you."

"It is of no matter. What is it? Has the count tried to sneak in a separate clause yet again?"

"No, sir, the Yual Dominion has stopped trying to do so for now. I received word that a certain individual would like to meet you, though he is only willing to meet you outside Raktor."

"Outside Raktor? Preposterous! Sounds like a trap to simply assassinate me!"

"He says we can bring as many people as we want. Also, he sent us this. We have checked it to ensure it's neither a bomb nor an assassination device." The diplomat handed over a metallic case embellished with an ornamental design that seemed oriental.

This... This is! Minister Dekar's eyes widened in shock. Everyone had heard about the first civilian repeater handgun sold in an auction at the Central Sector of Raktor. Even his agents had reported on the design of the handgun, touted as being better than most current military guns.

Dekar opened the case to reveal a replica of the Oriental Bloom that Baron Cain owned, though it was not exactly the same. "He's the creator?!"

"In the note provided with this case, he claims he is not the creator but someone who has managed to decipher the inner workings behind the handguns. He wants to discuss a potential agreement for Versia."

Minister Dekar was more than happy to hear this. The reason why Versia was always on the back foot was due to its perceived weaker military strength and a smaller economy. After all, their gross product did not even match a third of Raktor's economic output. He would never admit it publicly, but the government was definitely complicit in the smuggling of guns from Raktor in order to alleviate the imbalance in military strength.

Now that he had a chance to meet with an arctech designer able to level the playing field, he was not going to let up that easily.

"Where is the meeting point?"

"Around the Culdao Peaks area. I suggest we use a body double to make the Yual Dominion believe that we are returning to Versia while another wagon takes you to the secret meeting point."

* * *

The plan was put into place immediately, with Minister Dekar and a team of a dozen Versian guards disguised as a merchant escort moving out from Raktor toward the Culdao Peaks.

They blended in easily into the hordes of merchants in the now-expanded Culdao Peaks Town, with the marketplace increasing in size and the wealth of the town increasing. More and more people were migrating into the town in search of fame and fortune, while other merchants began to invest in supporting industries to facilitate the travelers and other traders who bought and sold the Euria Seeds.

A lone hooded man was waiting for them in an alleyway, immediately turning and walking into the forest while Dekar and the guards followed. *Where is he taking us? I've heard rumors of domesticated goblins, but surely he does not intend to use the hostility of the goblins against us?*

The Versian guards were all well armored under their normal clothes, complete with an armor set as well as an arctech pistol. Dekar gingerly stepped through the dense foliage, though there was a clear, rough path created by the continuous movement of workers carrying Euria Seeds.

Suddenly, five goblins appeared on the treeline, leaping past the guards overhead, who all reacted instantly and held their pistols at the ready.

"Hold your fire. They're making sure you weren't followed." The lone hooded man turned around, with fifteen goblins lining up behind him.

"Wha—How did you domesticate the goblins?" Dekar couldn't help asking. Even in his homeland, there were many failed attempts at restraining the goblins, causing losses and continuous rebellions.

One of the goblins clearly took offense at the insult at being treated like cattle and was about to retort when the hooded man raised his hand. "You do not need to know how I did it, only if I can deliver. The playing field between both militaries is hilariously skewed, and both you and I know Versia needs a helping hand."

"So you want us to buy weapons from your operation here in the Culdao Peaks...?"

"Of course. I would like to aid in the upgrading of the Versian military to counter Raktor aggression."

Dekar grew wary. *He must have an ulterior motive.* "Why have you not done this for the Yual Dominion? Surely they would pay you a higher price."

"Their motivations are not aligned with mine. I am a firm believer in Versia sovereignty. The governing principles of the Yual Dominion are far too backward for my liking. Although, I am open to have a further meeting when you are ready to negotiate further."

What rubbish. He is obviously in it for the money, but he is right. This is something the Versian military needs dearly. Instead of revealing his cynicism, Dekar had a wide grin on his face.

"Ahah, a fellow supporter of democracy! Of course, we welcome your help! However, these... negotiations must be held in Versia, though I would prefer that these goblins do not follow you."

Dekar glanced again at the fifteen goblins, many of whom snarled back at him. *If he comes and stays in Versia, I will be able to deploy better spies than the ones we have in Raktor to steal the design. It seems that these goblins are not easy to bribe. Maybe that's even better—I can capture him myself. I have to hook him in first.*

"That is only possible if your government gives me the assurance that I will not be attacked or enslaved within Versia itself." The hooded man countered. "My technology and learnings are a prize in itself. Any attempts to steal them will be met with... unnecessary complications for you and your men trailing you."

"Of course, of course, we would never hurt you" Dekar grinned widely, hiding his shock at the hooded man's awareness of his hidden bodyguards scattered around the forest in case a fight broke out. "In fact, as a representative of the state, I myself will issue you a letter of approval for your direct entry into Versia!"

"Then I look forward to future negotiations. Send me a messenger when you are ready."

"Indeed. I look forward to a fruitful relationship, Mister...?"

"Greyborn. Kris Greyborn."

Chapter 59

Refocus

A week later...

The Seven Snakes were in a complete frenzy as Kyle began to ramp up the production.

Keith was over the moon with the baron's acceptance of the steel and weapons factory, but was confused by his leader's next request.

"Wait, you want me to find people who look exactly like you?"

"It is normal for every person to have a doppelganger somewhere in the world. As long as they look about sixty to seventy percent alike, we can make up for the rest using makeup and disguises."

"What are you planning this time?"

"There is a chance that I will go to Versia after a few months; once this factory project is completed and our control of the districts have stabilized."

"What?!" Keith exclaimed.

Kyle had already made up his mind the moment he met Minister Dekar. Hedging his bets on his new venture was far safer than relying entirely on the purchase of his weapons by Count Leon's military. There would be a clear cartel and barrier to entry.

Always have an escape route planned. Versia was that escape route if it really came down to the wire. He had no clear loyalty to Raktor nor Versia, only the place that would give him the most profit. If Raktor did not provide that, then Versia would have to do.

To reduce suspicion from the local nobility and other gangs about his potential months-long disappearance in the future, he needed to find a doppelganger that could potentially act as him and throw off any potential observers watching him. He had already risked a lot heading over to the Culdao Peaks to negotiate with the minister.

"So you just want me to go to the streets and grab those who look the most similar?"

"Yes, try to find six if possible." Kyle nodded his head, causing Keith to sigh and shake his head, wondering what Kyle was up to now.

"There's no reason to go to Versia—we have no connections there and almost no stake. You'll be pretty much going in blind," Keith pointed out, trying to dissuade Kyle. "Versia is also too far away from us, so you won't be able to access our current assets as well!"

"I will prepare well in advance, do not worry. We have half a year ahead of us." Kyle waved his hand dismissively. "Look at what I started with in the Seven Snakes as well, and look where we are now."

Keith was about to retort but held his tongue. He wanted to argue that Kyle did have certain connections, but he realized that he was thinking about "Alvin." With Kyle's prowess, he would succeed nearly everywhere—why would Versia be any different?

"The Seven Snakes would have to expand eventually. Moving to another city or country is always a given with time. We as a whole have to think further, especially once we have secured our position here. I know you feel that, as we are right now, our progress will always be hampered by the Ardent Cretins incessantly. They are still restricting us economically. The way we overcame the original debt to the Crimson Swords was by expanding to the Culdao Peaks. Versia will be no different."

"You won't be going alone, right? If you die in Versia..." Keith couldn't bear to think of what would happen if Kyle died. He recalled how, just a few months ago, they had been a small gang of twenty to thirty members.

Today, they numbered close to three hundred, thanks to the recruiting efforts of the free soup kitchen, public cleanup events, and bathhouse.

Keith would not dare to claim that the Seven Snakes were completely united as a capable force, but it was a far cry from the paltry command of Ulon. If Kyle were to die, this entire pyramid would most likely fall apart. Keith wasn't as strong as Kyle to be able to hold the entire gang through charisma and strength. No one else in the Seven Snakes was, all putting their respect on Kyle rather than each other.

"Of course not. We will see over the course of our preparation. But I do have a few guides in mind." Nearly all of his underlings were critical, and those that were not were ill-suited to serve as Versia guides or even bodyguards.

"Okay, I will immediately try to find the body doubles as soon as possible." Keith saluted. Just as he was about to leave Kyle's office, Niko barged in, panting wildly as he held a folder of documents in his right arm.

"Sir..." Niko panted, an exhausted grin on his face. "We got it! We got the license for the weapons factory!"

Kyle, too, had a wide smile on his face, immediately standing up and grabbing the licenses from Niko's hand, checking them. "Call everyone into the office for a celebration. Now," Kyle ordered Keith, who nodded immediately.

It took half an hour for all the vipers, the company heads, Gordon, Eric, and Damian to pause their current tasks and return, wondering what was so urgent for Kyle to call all of them back in. Only Keith and Niko had excited expressions on their faces, while the rest were utterly confused.

"You all have followed me for months, and some have followed me for nearly half a year now." Kyle began his speech. "Since I took leadership in the Seven Snakes, we have grown exponentially, with our reputation and name soaring and reverberating throughout the South Sector. Even the gangs in the other sectors talk about us and our exploits on a regular basis with wonder and amazement in their tones."

"Today, I would like to announce that as of this day, for the first time in Seven Snakes' history, we have an official license to manufacture weapons for the military, just like every other major gang!" Kyle proudly showed off the license to them, causing Damian to nearly exclaim in shock.

Such a license represented one of the top positions in society—not any ragtag group could obtain it unless they had a master's approval from the Society of Friendly Weaponsmiths. Even for the bigger players, it was a feat unachievable just by asking. Every holder of the license had to prove their ability to deliver and would make an obscene amount of money from every military contract. Only the Ardent Cretins held a similar license within the South Sector.

Even Monica, Adrian, and Eric were at a loss for words. Just four months ago, they were simply a ragtag crew smuggling moonshine to businesses that continuously tried to undercut them. In fact, they had been planning to leave the Seven Snakes at the start. Yet now, they stood as one of the top members of the South Sector, respected by everyone. Their aspirations for freedom had already been assuaged by the sheer respect they received.

Eric nearly shed a tear when he recalled how far he had come. A disgraced university professor affected by the prohibition by the Sanctum of Yual was now a mogul in alcohol distribution and production. His recipes were the backbone of the entire operation, ensuring a consistent stream of dirty money into the Seven Snakes and his own pockets.

Gordon, too, was grinning to himself as he patted Reese on the back. He had just been a lowly arctech designer with no future—it would have taken him ten years alone even to have a shot at being the factory manager, but he now held authority as well as prestige.

Sasha was not too concerned with the license, but her own journey under the direct tutelage of Kyle had made her into a force to be reckoned with. No longer was she known as a weak, mute slave that could be easily bullied, even by other slaves. Instead, she reigned at the top next to Kyle, being the second strongest in the Seven Snakes.

Damian was the most sentimental of them all. He had been there from the very beginning, having seen the second personality of Kyle take over Alvin. Previously, he had an issue with the new personality taking over Alvin's body, but as he watched the meteoric rise of the Seven Snakes over the months, he was not sure if he even wanted Alvin back at all. Hell, if Alvin's main personality ever resurfaced, Damian would be the first one to beat it out of him and try to get Kyle back.

Seniors, mentors, First Leader Theorin. The Seven Snakes have returned to their rightful position. Damian sniffled as he rubbed his nose, getting emotional.

Guang Hwa, on the other hand, was unfazed by all the obvious emotional signs that everyone else was showing. *I got fucking enslaved by Kyle. Why would I be happy he's getting stronger?! Fuck!*

"We have suffered setbacks and obstacles, but each day, it is us that have prevailed, that have overcome every enemy that stood in our way. I could not have done it without you, and I truly cherish all of you as partners in this endeavor to rise beyond our station in life." Kyle's tone was gentle and tinged with sincerity.

Suddenly, his face grew grim. "However, what comes next will be the toughest period of our growth. If we make it past the next year, we will be unrivaled in the South Sector for years to come. The information I am about to share with you is of the highest confidentiality—and I trust each and every one of you here."

"The war between Versia and Count Leon is inevitable—the resolution signed between the two of them is but a farce. The reasons are unclear to me, but it is a fact that in half a year or more, Count Leon's military will be assembled for an exercise on the outskirts of Raktor. This could be a potential spark that ignites the conflict, and thus a new phase in the economy of the South Sector. As such, I will ensure that the Seven Snakes gang is in the right position to capitalize on this situation."

"This means that there will come a point in time where we must expand to Versia to win on both sides. For now, we will focus on strengthening our position in the South Sector, while I prepare for future plans. There will come a time where I and others will leave the Seven Snakes in all of your capable hands. Hence, you all will have to step up and ensure the Seven Snakes are on track. And don't you even think about running away." Kyle shot a sharp glare at Guang Hwa, whose cheerful smile was immediately cut short.

"Damian, you will speed up recruiting. Establish a second layer below the vipers, known as cobras, to reward associates who have stuck with us since the beginning. Have the best of them become crew leaders, and let them operate independently in a squad hierarchy to reduce overhead administration. We need all the manpower we can get to control the districts."

"Keith, prepare the logistics needed to build the weapons factory requested by the baron. This is the first external project that the Golden Snake Construction Company is undertaking—everything needs to go perfectly. We need workers, skilled ones who can drive the weapons factory forward in order to win the supply contract."

"Eric, ramp up the production of alcohol and begin storing it. Once the war kicks in, alcohol is going to be highly valued in both Raktor and Versia. Every excess should be accounted for and stored in separate warehouses for future use."

"Monica, continue to ensure that our transportation network is working as intended. Feel free to use the funds available to you to expand the fleet and our reach. Start providing regular transportation route services to underserved districts to increase our influence."

"Adrian, start contacting black market dealers and keep up to date on any information they might have. We need to know about any event that happens as soon as it happens, no questions asked. Continue to observe the movements of the Wretches, the Red Lions and especially the Ardent Cretins. Track all their high-profile members and make sure we know exactly where they are every time."

"Niko, you're still in charge of security. We need our current districts to be the hallmark of safety. Ensure all our deliveries are on time. If a hijacking of our wagon occurs, make sure to report it to me immediately. Continue to protect our pubs, casinos, and brothels—no-name thug gangs may begin to eye us as easy targets as soon as we announce our project and shift manpower to build the weapons factory."

"Gordon, your experience as the factory manager will come in handy, and you will be the overall lead for its production. The current factory will now be converted into the weapons factory. Check the documents that I will give to you later for details on what I intend for the factory to do. The larger the scale that we achieve, the more our influence and reputation will increase."

"Speaking of reputation—Reese, you will be in charge of marketing. We want to promote a positive brand image, so work with Guang Hwa on building a public reputation for our companies and district, including the factory. All light-capture films should work toward our districts being known for stability unlike the other violent areas. This way we can pull more people over."

Kyle continued to give a few more minor orders before concluding the meeting. "When I took over leadership, I only had one goal in mind—to grow the Seven Snakes into a power that cannot be contested."

"Yes, not even the Ardent Cretins will be able to pin us down any longer!" Damian nodded.

"Forget about the Ardent Cretins—they are insignificant to the bigger plan in the long run. Are you truly satisfied with having just less than a quarter of a small city under your control? Do you not want to grow larger than just a few districts?"

The rest were shocked at what Kyle had just mentioned. They could barely envision themselves reigning at the top of Raktor. Sure, Damian might have daydreamed about it at some point in his life, but to actually fix it as a goal?

The word "impossible" appeared in their minds, but yet, for some reason, the very presence of Kyle seemed to defy that impossibility. He seems to be larger than life, an indomitable leader who has led them all this far beyond their wildest dreams. Who among them could imagine having gone toe-to-toe with the Ardent Cretins in an economic war and stayed standing?

"Not even the entirety of Raktor will be enough for me!" Kyle declared. "Kregol, Perial, the entire Yual Dominion shall fall under my whims alone with due time. And when I'm done with them, not even Versia, Proco, or those hiding beyond the Great Waves can escape my grip!"

The ambition of Kyle sparked a fire in their hearts, daring them to aim as high as they could. Every notion of obstacles or setbacks was thrown out of their minds, replaced by a zealous belief in Kyle and his leadership. Each of the vipers had their own mindset, but all had aligned to follow Kyle as far as the road would take them.

"And if you think that is enough for us—that we should be content with having the entire planet respect us—you are wrong. For even the stars themselves will bow before us in due time!"

Chapter 60

Inkling

Deep underground in an unknown location of Versia...

The sound of panting and grunting filled the wide cavern, with the flashes of metal striking metal glinting through the darkness, illuminating the shadows thrown by the arctech lamps situated all over the ceiling.

A dozen rock spiders circled and scaled the walls, their red, beady gem-like eyes glinting at the man who was currently being assaulted by three of their brethren. The man heaved as he brandished a sword in each hand, duel-wielding and spinning while he parried each of their strikes.

The man did not have enough hands to parry, with one spider breaking through and launching a stabbing attack with two of its pointed legs.

His eyes glowed lightning-blue, with a surge of lightning arcing like a power line down his skin, accelerating his motions to levels impossible. Within a split second, he had accurately stabbed his sword into the red, beady eyes of each of the three spiders.

[SYSTEM MESSAGE]
You killed Rock Spider, +500 EXP.

The rock spiders collapsed with a shriek, their bodies going limp as the man kicked them to the side, his legs bloodied and stained with slimy, dried dirt hardened between his joints. He wiped the sweat off his grimy forehead, grinning to himself as he watched three of the other dozen spiders begin to saunter down toward him, taking the place of their fallen brethren.

[SYSTEM MESSAGE]
Trial failed.
You did not manage to kill a dozen spiders within the aforementioned time limit of three minutes.

The trial has been reset.

The man did not pay any attention to the holographic message in front of him, simply swiping it away as he prepared for the new round of enemies. The level of skill that he displayed was more than enough to clear the trial with ease, yet for some reason, the man was still stuck here, slowing himself down on purpose.

A voice called out from the edge of the cavern, showing a servant dressed like an explorer. "Sir Soren, your breakfast is ready." In front of him were two metal tins filled with what looked like baked beans and a slab of kaya butter on white bread.

"Almost finished!" the man said through his gritted teeth as he blocked a stab from the spider, parrying it with his lightning-infused sword. Although he had cut the spider's leg off, he did not finish it. "I forfeit the trial!"

[SYSTEM MESSAGE]
Trial forfeited.
Failure is the mother of success.

You may enter the trial again after three hours.

He let out a sigh as the spiders began to back off, retreating back into their holes in the cavern walls. One of them even scampered past the servant, completely avoiding him as it burrowed deep into the wall. "That was a good exercise. If I stay here for three months, I'll catch up to my siblings in no time!"

"Sir Soren, need I remind you that the amount of EXP that you are receiving from these spiders will exponentially decay over time? This is not an efficient long-term leveling method. You need to—"

"Yes, yes, I know. Why are you nagging exactly in the same way as Mother? I've been changing dungeons, haven't I?" Soren scratched his chin as he strutted over, plopping down onto the ground in a crude manner and grabbing the metal tin off the floor along with the kaya bread. "Mmm... Tastes like home. I'm sure glad you came along with me."

"I did not have a choice, sir. You used your points to—"

"To request your assistance instead of asking for a weapon or a specific posting. Yes, Rayner. I've heard the story before; I was there, remember?"

"And you will do well to remember that I will not help you with the next phase too."

"But that can change as well, can it not?" Soren grinned, causing Rayner to sigh in exasperation.

They soon finished their breakfast, with Soren licking the leftover kaya off his thumb as he picked up his dual swords again. "Well then, round three it is! Statistics!" he declared, checking his stats once more. "Only a bit more to go to the next level."

"Sir, the trial will not reset for another two hours. We should find another place first."

"You're right; we can easily clear up some of the mobs nearby."

Soren and Rayner packed up their equipment, with Rayner hefting the backpack over while Soren whistled as they trekked down through a derelict hallway.

The walls were made of brick, covered in moss and algae, which thrived in the damp, moist areas illuminated by the arctech lanterns eternally turned on along the hallways. Countless skeletons lay along the floor, which they gingerly stepped over. A good majority of them were monster skeletons, but a few were distinctively human.

"Remnants from the Heavenly War, it seems."

"Pah, useless old farts. If it weren't for their incompetence, we would be masters of this world already," Soren scoffed. "If I had been alive back then, I would have easily turned the tide with just a single blade."

"It is good to have such confidence, but perhaps you should work on your foundation first?" Rayner insinuated.

Soren scowled at Rayner, ignoring him and continuing to walk down the hallway toward a location they had previously marked. The number of skeletons left behind began to decrease sharply as they approached the hallway, causing Rayner to stop Soren for a moment.

"Be careful. Even the elders of the clan are wary of entering such a place."

"Then all the more for the great Soren to show them who's better! I did not choose you to act like Mother, you know!" Soren berated Rayner, shrugging off the woman's hand and storming off farther into the hallway.

They soon reached a large, throne-like room, except it was filled to the brim with rubble, except for the center pathway that was adorned with a stained red carpet, nearly blackened from the soot and dust accumulating over who knows how long.

On the throne sat a rock golem nearly the size of a small hill. It had four arms along with three crystal eyes embedded into each of its three heads.

The room shuddered as the rock golem began to shift, the crystal eyes filling up with life as they shone emerald. The rubble around Soren began to form into humanoid shapes, albeit some with additional limbs and many featuring a tail. All of them were made of rocks, consolidating around a single core well protected by various layers of metal.

"Well then. Good luck, sir. I will see you for lunch."

"Thanks, Rayner." Soren grinned as he brandished his two swords. "All right, bring it on then!"

[SYSTEM MESSAGE]
Trial of the Emperor
A fallen race seeks to take revenge on those who trespass.

Clear Conditions: Defeat the Emperor.

Afterword

War is coming and Kyle will have new enemies, new technologies, and an all-new locale to further his criminal empire in preparation for the coming storm.

Can't wait for book two? You can read advanced, unedited chapters on Patreon and join the conversation on Discord.

If that isn't enough, check out another MoonQuill publication, ***Apocalypse: Reborn as a Monster.*** It's a fantastic book with a weak-to-strong MC, written from a unique perspective in a system apocalypse. With over 3.5 million views on Royal Road, it's sure to keep you entertained. Watch as Thorian Steelblade, a former human general, comes to terms with his new monster form, and struggles to survive to reclaim his former glory. Pre-order or read it on Kindle Unlimited.

Thank you for reading a MoonQuill original novel. More exciting stories can be found at www.moonquill.com and on our platform, www.moonquillnovels.com.

We would greatly appreciate it if you would take a moment to leave a review. Every review helps the author and supports their ability to continue writing fantastic books for everyone to enjoy!

Additionally, we're looking for dedicated ARC reviewers and experienced readers to join our beta reader team. To learn more, drop us an email at info@moonquill.com or stop by our Discord.